THE FOREST OF TIME
AND OTHER STORIES

The Forest of Time

AND

OTHER

STORIES

Michael Flynn

A TOM DOHERTY ASSOCIATES BOOK
NEW YORK

THE FOREST OF TIME AND OTHER STORIES

This book is printed on acid-free paper.

Edited by David G. Hartwell

A Tor Book
Published by Tom Doherty Associates, Inc.
175 Fifth Avenue
New York, NY 10010

Tor Books on the World Wide Web:
http://www.tor.com

Tor® is a registered trademark of Tom Doherty Associates, Inc.

Design by Fritz Metsch

Library of Congress Cataloging-in-Publication Data

Flynn, Michael F.
    The forest of time and other stories / Michael Flynn.—1st ed.
        p.   cm.
    "A Tom Doherty Associates book."
    Contents: Introduction—The forest of time—Great sweet mother
—On the high frontier—The common goal of nature—Grave
reservations—Mammy Morgan—Spark of genius—On the wings of a
butterfly—The feeders—Melodies of the heart.
        ISBN 0-312-85526-5 (hardcover : acid-free paper)
        1. Science fiction, American.   I. Title.
PS3556.L89F67   1997
813'.54—dc20   96-31890
                                                                      CIP

First Edition: April 1997

Printed in the United States of America

0 9 8 7 6 5 4 3 2 1

Rita Marie Singley Flynn
"The Mut"

CONTENTS

———◆●✕●◆———

THE FOREST OF TIME
AND OTHER STORIES

Introduction

Why do I write science fiction? First, because I like reading it. Our father used to tell us really strange bedtime stories. About aliens and trips to Mars and strange inventions. After lights out, my brother Dennis and I would tell stories to each other. (Which often became so noisy with sound effects that our parents had to visit several times to get us to Be Quiet and Go to Sleep.) I recall inventing a world of intelligent dinosaurs, complete with maps and a history and a card index for each country. Dennis invented a language. It took a long time before we realized that other kids didn't *do* things like that. Well, that was their loss. They probably sat around all day complaining that they were "bored."

Dennis and I decided to write our own tales—in pencil, in spiral notebooks—when we were nine and ten. We based them on Pere's recitals. One day, we found Pere's stash of *Worlds of IF* and discovered that those stories had been cribbed from Ray Bradbury, Damon Knight, et al. Our notebook now contained a very loose, *ad lib* reconstruction of Damon Knight's "To Serve Man." What disillusionment! We thought Pere had made those yarns up himself. Even years later, I would be hit by déjà vu (all over again, as the great Yogi used to say) while reading an old story. Where have I heard this before? Oh, yeah . . . Bedtime story.

The first book I ever checked out of the public library was *Space Captives of the Golden Men*. (You always remember your first time.) Before long, Dennis and I had read through the entire children's section, including all the wonderful Heinlein and Norton juveniles. When we ran out of books, we marched over to the librarian and asked to check out SF from the adult section. The librarian made us read from a novel by Leigh Brackett and explain the passage before she would permit us that boon.

Later, with two other friends, Red Scannell and Dan Hommer, we laid out a vast history of the future called *Ad Astra,* and divvied the writing up among the four of us. Thus we created the Shared Worlds concept back in the 1950s—and I even have the newspaper clipping to prove it. Parts of *Ad Astra* survive to this day, thanks to my mother, The Mut, who saved them.

Somewhere along the line—maybe when I was twelve or so—I started sending stories to *Galaxy* and *The Magazine of Fantasy and Science Fiction.* I knew enough to type double space and use carbons (Remember carbon paper and yellow copy sheets?) I did not know enough to write a good story, however; and so collected an impressive assortment of rejection notes. My finest hour came in high school, with a three-page rejection letter from John W. Campbell, Jr. at *Analog.* He ripped my poor story to shreds. Being unsophisticated, I did not realize that the letter meant "put the shreds back together in a more interesting way and let me see it again." Consequently, my fictional debut was delayed by about twenty years.

My parents never put down these early efforts; nor did they treat them with oh-isn't-that-cute condescension. Pere did offer the occasional literary suggestion, but he was a grown-up, so what did he know? The Mut even wangled Dennis and me an interview in the hometown paper.

As this collection was being compiled, and after I had sent David Hartwell the first version of this introduction, the Mut died. It was not a long illness, and it was a peaceful death. There are worse ways to go than surrounded by a loving family. Yet, she left us all too soon, and we will all miss her dreadfully.

The Mut was my biggest fan. She read all my stories when they came out and hyped them to all her friends. About "The Forest of Time," she always wanted to know what happened afterward and was I ever going to write a sequel. She did not live to see this collection; but I had told her earlier that it would be dedicated to her. And, by some odd coincidence, my brother Kevin's latest book came out dedicated to her. He gave her a copy when she was home, before she went into the hospital for the last time, hoping to surprise her. (He hadn't told her of the dedication.) In true Mut fashion, she read the title page, the copyright page, and even the ISBN number, then *skipped* the dedication page and went on to the text. She had the most wonderful deadpan wit.

I suppose if I had come from a dysfunctional family, I would have more material to use in my stories; but I didn't, and I guess I'll just have to learn to live with that.

The Importance of Being Sciffy

Why do I write science fiction? Second, because I think it is important. Science is not so much a collection of facts as it is a method for converting ideas into facts. Its "rules" are so fundamental to our culture that they are as invisible as water to a fish. The first rule is that Anyone Can Play; that is, anyone gets to challenge any idea (indeed, that all ideas must be challenged—even, in some cases, tested to destruction). The second rule is that a statement is not true because Someone Authoritative says it is true, but because the method used to test it gives the same results regardless of who does the checking or who made the statement.

Truth is independent of Authority. This is heady stuff. It is the source not only of particle physics and organic chemistry, but of most Western political and social institutions—indeed, of liberalism itself, in both its left- and right-wing versions. Can you imagine investigative journalism without those two axioms? Progressive education? Experimental fiction? (Notice how the metaphors of science inform the arts: we investigate, we progress, we experiment.)

Science is democratic, but not in the sense that knowledge is decided by popular vote. Every scientist in the world can vote that global warming is a fact—or that it is not—and in neither case would it make it so. Science is democratic because Anyone Can Play. You need no Special Talent or Magic Power; you need not be descended from the Ancient Blood or be blessed by the Elder Gods. All you need is patience, careful study, and a basic objectivity. (This is the spiritual fault line separating SF from its more aristocratic cousin, fantasy. It is why a story can be science fiction or fantasy fiction, but not both.) Your ideas (and challenges) are just as good as anyone else's. Not that they are TRUE, mind you; but they are subject to the same ruthless winnowing, equally entitled to be tested and attacked. You throw your beautiful idea into the ring and watch it get hammered by ugly facts. Only the survivors will be accepted—tentatively—as knowledge.

Tentative Acceptance is not as emotionally satisfying as Absolute Faith. That patient demand—"How do you know? What are the facts?"—can be irritating to folks who Already Know the Truth Because It Has Been Revealed (or Because, by Damn, It *Should* Be True). Stephen Schneider, an advocate of the ideas of global warming and of ozone depletion has said that *"[W]e have to offer up scary scenarios, make simplified, dramatic state-ments, and make little mention of any doubts we may have. Each of us has to decide what the right balance is between being effective and being hon-est."** Buy this argument and you kiss the Age of Reason good-bye. And be-fore you pucker up, some of you out there, be really, really sure you know what you are throwing away.

The scientific outlook creates a constant turnover of ideas, great and small. The phlogiston theory of heat. State socialism. The Taylor system of labor. The Bohr model of the atom. The Edsel. Slavery. "It seemed like a good idea at the time." But . . . *How do you know? What are the facts?* Slavery flourished for millennia in every part of the globe, but it could not survive in a world of liberal, scientific inquiry. There were too many ob-servable facts that argued against it, no matter how diehard the True Be-lievers. Within a century of the Age of Reason, slavery was dead—at least, in the West. Many of the most deeply held ideals of those who profess to disdain "materialist science" are themselves the consequence of vigorous, rational argument against long-held, but hurtful customs and beliefs.

This scientific outlook is at the core of the best science fiction. Some people call SF the "Literature of Change." I prefer to call it the "Litera-ture of Challenge and Change," since the challenge to the old ideas is an inherent part of the process. Archetypal SF involves speculative *techno-logical* change: wormholes or time travel or what it means to be human; but SF shades off into other sorts of change, as well. The challenge may stem from speculative ideas in anthropology, psychology, or any other field—provided the rules of science are followed. At one extreme of the genre, we find space operas, in which the science provides only the stage props. At another extreme, the science is very nearly absent and we call the story SF only by courtesy. Here, SF fades off into fantasy, its polar op-posite. Over there, into "technothrillers." And over there and there, into "mainstream" or into "magical realism." (There are more than two ex-tremes, friends, when you have more than one dimension.) Science fic-tion can be written into virtually any genre. You could conceivably write

---

*quoted in "Our Fragile Earth," *Discover*, Oct., 1987.

a romantic Western science-fiction mystery—and the chain bookstore owners would go nuts trying to figure where to shelve it. It would wind up in the SF section. Depend on it.

David Hartwell, editor at Tor Books, who selected and arranged the stories in this collection, has asked me to write a few words about each, maybe *shmooze* a little in between about the writing or about SF. A fair warning: since in some cases I will discuss particular points of the story, you may want to read the tale before you read the afterword. If you find the conversation distracting, by all means, skip it and enjoy the stories.

The Forest of Time

It was the autumn of the year and the trees were already showing their death-colors. Splashes of orange and red and gold rustled in the canopy overhead. Oberleutnant Rudolf Knecht, Chief Scout of the Army of the Kittatinny, wore the same hues mottled for his uniform as he rode through the forest. A scout's badge, carefully rusted to dullness, was pinned to his battered campaign cap.

Knecht swayed easily to the rhythm of his horse's gait as he picked his way up the trail toward Fox Gap Fortress. He kept a wary eye on the surrounding forest. Periodically, he twisted in the saddle and gazed thoughtfully at the trail where it switchbacked below. There had been no sign of pursuit so far. Knecht believed his presence had gone undetected; but even this close to home, it paid to be careful. The list of those who wanted Knecht dead was a long one; and here, north of the Mountain, it was open season on Pennsylvanians.

There were few leaves on the forest floor, but the wind gathered them up and hurled them in mad dances. The brown, dry, crisp leaves of death. Forerunners of what was to be. Knecht bowed his head and pulled the jacket collar tighter about his neck.

Knecht felt the autumn. It was in his heart and in his bones. It was in the news he carried homeward. Bad news even in the best of times, which these were not. Two knick regiments had moved out of the Hudson Valley into the Poconos. They were camped with the yankees. Brothers-in-arms, as if last spring's fighting had never happened. General Schneider's fear: New York and the Wyoming had settled their quarrel and made common cause.

Common cause. Knecht chewed on a drooping moustache, now more grey than brown. No need to ask the cause. There was little enough that yanks and knicks could agree on, but killing Pennsylvanians was one.

He remembered that General Schneider was inspecting the fortress line and would probably be waiting for him at Fox Gap. He did not feel the pleasure he usually felt on such occasions. *Na, Konrad, meiner Alt,* he thought. What will you do now? What a burden I must lay upon your shoulders. God help the Commonwealth of Pennsylvania.

He pulled in on the reins. There was a break in the trees here, and through it he could see the flank of Kittatinny Mountain. A giant's wall, the ridge ran away, straight and true, becoming bluer and hazier as its forested slopes faded into the distance. Spots of color decorated the sheer face of the Mountain. Fox Gap, directly above him, was hidden by the forest canopy; but Knecht thought he could just make out the fortresses at Wind Gap and Tott Gap.

As always, the view comforted him. There was no way across the Kittatinny, save through the Gaps. And there was no way through the Gaps.

Twenty years since anyone has tried, he thought. He kicked at the horse, and they resumed their slow progress up the trail. Twenty years ago; and we blew the knick riverboats off the water.

That had been at Delaware Gap, during the Piney War. Knecht sighed. The Piney War seemed such a long time ago. A different world—more innocent, somehow. Or perhaps he had only been younger. He remembered how he had marched away, his uniform new and sharply creased. Adventure was ahead of him, and his father's anger behind. *I am too old for such games,* he told himself. *I should be sitting by the fire, smoking my pipe, telling stories to my grandchildren.*

He chewed again on his moustache hairs and spit them out. There had never been any children; and now, there never would be. He felt suddenly alone.

Just as well, he thought. The stories I have to tell are not for the ears of youngsters. What were the stories, really? A crowd of men charged from the trench. Later, some of them came back. What more was there to say? Once, a long time ago, war had been glamorous, with pageantry and uniforms to shame a peacock. Now it was only necessary, and the uniforms were the color of mud.

·   ·   ·

There was a sudden noise in the forest to his right. Snapping limbs and a muffled grunt. Knecht started, and chastised himself. A surprised scout is often a dead scout as well. He pulled a large bore pistol from his holster and dismounted. The horse, well trained, held still. Knecht stepped into the forest and crouched behind a tall birch tree. He listened.

The noise continued. Too much noise, he decided. Perhaps an animal? Then he saw the silhouette of a man thrashing through the underbrush, making no attempt at silence. Knecht watched over his gunsight as the man blundered into a stickerbush. Cursing, the other stopped and pulled the burrs from his trousers.

The complete lack of caution puzzled Knecht. The no-man's-land between Pennsylvania and the Wyoming was no place for carelessness. The other was either very foolish or very confident.

The fear ran through him like the rush of an icy mountain stream. Perhaps the bait in a trap, something to hold his attention? He jerked round suddenly, looking behind him, straining for the slightest sign.

But there was nothing save the startled birds and the evening wind.

Knecht blew his breath out in a gust. His heart was pounding. *I am getting too old for this.* He felt foolish, and his cheeks burned, even though there was no one to see.

The stranger had reached the trail and stood there brushing himself off. He was short and dark-complexioned. On his back he wore a rucksack, connected by wires to a device on his belt. Knecht estimated his age at thirty, but the unkempt hair and beard made him look older.

He watched the man pull a paper from his baggy canvas jacket. Even from where he crouched, Knecht could see it was a map, handsomely done in many colors. A stranger with a map on the trail below Fox Gap. Knecht made a decision and stepped forth, cocking his pistol.

The stranger spun and saw Knecht. Closer up, Knecht could see the eyes bloodshot with fatigue. After a nervous glance at the scout's pistol, the stranger smiled and pointed to the map. "Would you believe it?" he asked in English. "I think I'm lost."

Knecht snorted. "I would not believe it," he answered in the same language. "Put in the air your hands up."

The stranger complied without hesitation. Knecht reached out and snatched the map from his hand.

"That's a Pennsylvania Dutch accent, isn't it?" asked his prisoner. "It sure is good to hear English again."

Knecht looked at him. He did not understand why that should be good. His own policy when north of the Mountain was to shoot at English-speaking voices. He gave quick glances to the map while considering what to do.

"Are you hunting? I didn't know it was hunting season."

The scout saw no reason to answer that, either. In a way, he *was* hunting, but he doubted that the prisoner had meant it that way.

"At least you can tell me where in the damn world I am!"

Knecht was surprised at the angry outburst. Considering who held the pistol on whom, it seemed a rash act at best. He grinned and held up the map. "Naturally, you know where in the damn world you are. While you have this map, it gives only one possibility. You are the spy, *nicht wahr?* But, to humor you . . ." He pointed northward with his chin. "Downtrail is the Wyoming, where your Wilkes-Barre masters your report in vain will await. Uptrail is *Festung* Fox Gap . . . and your cell."

The prisoner's shoulders slumped. Knecht looked at the sun. With the prisoner afoot, they should still reach the fort before nightfall. He decided to take the man in for questioning. That would be safer than interrogating him on the spot. Knecht glanced at the map once more. Then he frowned and looked more closely. "United States Geological Survey?" he asked the prisoner. "What are the United States?"

He did not understand why the prisoner wept.

There was a storm brewing in the northwest and the wind whipped through Fox Gap, tearing at the uniform blouses of the sentries, making them grab for their caps. In the dark, amid the rain and lightning, at least one man's grab was too late and his fellows laughed coarsely as he trotted red-faced to retrieve it. It was a small diversion in an otherwise cheerless duty.

What annoyed Festungskommandant Vonderberge was not that Scout Knecht chose to watch the chase also, but that he chose to do so while halfway through the act of entering Vonderberge's office. The wind blew a blizzard of paper around the room and Vonderberge's curses brought Knecht fully into the office, closing the door behind him.

Vonderberge shook his head. He looked at Knecht. "These bits of paper," he said. "These orders and memoranda and requisitions, they are the nerve messages of the army. A thousand messages a day cross my desk, Rudi, and not a one of them but deals with matters of the greatest military import." He clucked sadly. "Our enemies need not defeat us in the field. They need only sabotage our filing system." He rose from his desk and knelt, gathering up papers. "Come, Rudi, quickly. Let us set things aright, else the Commonwealth is lost!"

Knecht snorted. Vonderberge was mocking him with this elaborate ridicule. In his short time at Fox Gap, Knecht had encountered the Kommandant's strange humor several times. Someone had once told him that Vonderberge had always dreamed of becoming a scientist, but that his father had pressured him into following the family's military tradition. As a result, his command style was somewhat unorthodox.

Na, *we all arrive by different paths*, Knecht thought. *I joined to spite my father.* It startled him to recall that his father had been dead for many years, and that they had never become reconciled.

Knecht stooped and helped collect the scattered documents. Because he was a scout, however, he glanced at their contents as he did so; and as he absorbed their meaning, he read more and collected less.

One sheet in particular held his attention. When he looked up from it, he saw Vonderberge waiting patiently behind his desk. He was leaning back in a swivel chair, his arms crossed over his chest. There was a knowing smile on the Kommandant's thin aristocratic face.

"Is this all . . ." Knecht began.

"Ach, nein," the Kommandant answered. "There is much, much more. However," he added pointedly, "it is no longer in order."

"But, this is from the prisoner, Nando Kelly?"

"Hernando is the name; not Herr Nando. It is Spanish, I believe." Vonderberge clucked sadly over the documents and began setting them in order.

Knecht stood over the desk. "But this is crazy stuff!" He waved the sheet in his hand and Vonderberge snatched at it vainly. Knecht did not notice. "The man must be crazy!" he said.

Vonderberge paused and cocked an eyebrow at him. "Crazy?" he repeated. "So says the Hexmajor. He can support his opinion with many fine words and a degree from Franklin University. I am but a simple soldier, a servant of the Commonwealth, and cannot state my own diagnosis in so impressive a manner. On what basis, Rudi, do *you* say he is crazy?"

Knecht sputtered. "If it is not crazy to believe in countries that do not exist, I do not know what is. I have looked on all our world maps and have found no United States, not even in deepest Asia."

Vonderberge smiled broadly. He leaned back again, clasping his hands behind his neck. "Oh, I know where the United States are," he announced smugly.

Knecht made a face. "Tell me then, O Servant of the Commonwealth. Where are they?"

Vonderberge chuckled. "If you can possibly remember so far back as your childhood history lessons, you may recall something of the Fourth Pennamite War."

Knecht groaned. The Pennamite Wars. He could never remember which was which. Both Connecticut and Pennsylvania had claimed the Wyoming Valley and had fought over it several times, a consequence of the English king's cavalier attitude toward land titles. The fourth one? Let's see . . . 1769, 1771, 1775 . . .

"No," he said finally. "I know nothing at all of the time between 1784 and 1792. I never heard of Brigadier Wadsworth and the Siege of Forty-Fort, or how General Washington and his Virginia militia were mowed down in the crossfire."

"Then you must also be ignorant," continued the Kommandant, "of the fact that the same Congress that sent the General to stop the fighting was also working on a plan to unify the thirteen independent states. Now what do you suppose the name of that union was to be?"

Knecht snorted. "I would be a great fool if I did not say 'The United States.'"

Vonderberge clapped. "Right, indeed, Rudi. Right, indeed. Dickinson was president of the Congress, you know."

Knecht was surprised. "Dickinson? John Dickinson, our first Chancellor?"

"The very same. Being a Pennsylvanian, I suppose the yankee settlers thought he was plotting something by dispatching the supposedly neutral Virginians. . . . Well, of course, with Washington dead, and old Franklin incapacitated by a stroke at the news, the whole thing fell apart. Maryland never did sign the Articles of Confederation; and as the fighting among the states grew worse—over the Wyoming, over Vermont, over Chesapeake fishing rights, over the western lands—the others seceded also. All that Adams and the radicals salvaged was their New England Confederation; and even that was almost lost during Shay's Rebellion and General Lincoln's coup. . . ."

Knecht interrupted. "So this almost-was United States was nothing more than a wartime alliance to throw the English out. It was stillborn in the 1780s. Yet Kelly's map is dated this year."

"Ja, the map," mused Vonderberge, as if to himself. "It is finely drawn, is it not? And the physical details—the mountains and streams—are astonishingly accurate. Only the man-made details are bizarre. Roads and dams that are not there. A great open space called an 'airport.' Towns that are three times their actual size. Did you see how large Easton is shown to be?"

Knecht shrugged. "A hoax."

"Such an elaborate hoax? To what purpose?"

"To fool us. He is a spy. If messages can be coded, why not maps?"

"Ah. You say he is a spy and the map, a code. The Hexmajor says he is mad and the map is the complex working out of a system of delusions. I say . . ." He picked up a sheaf of papers from his desk and handed them to Knecht. "I say you should read Kelly's notebook."

The scout glanced at the typewritten pages. "These are transcripts," he pointed out. "They were done on the machine in your office. I recognize the broken stem on the r's." He made it a statement.

Vonderberge threw his head back and laughed, slapping the arm of the chair. "Subtlety does not become you, Rudi," he said looking at him. "Yes, they are transcripts. General Schneider has the originals. When I showed the journal to him, he wanted to read it himself. I made copies of the more interesting entries."

Knecht kept his face neutral. "You, and the General, and the Hexmajor. Ach! Kelly is my prisoner. I have yet to interview him. I gave you his possessions for safekeeping, not for distribution."

"Oh, don't be so official, Rudi. What are we, Prussians? You were resting, I was bored, and the journal was here. Go ahead. Read it now." Vonderberge waved an inviting hand.

Knecht frowned and picked up the stack. The first few pages were filled with equations. Strange formulae full of inverted A's and backward E's.

Knecht formed the words under his breath. ". . . twelve-dimensional open manifold . . . Janatpour hypospace . . . oscillatory time . . ." He shook his head. "Nonsense," he muttered.

He turned the page and came to a text:

"I am embarking on a great adventure. Does that sound grandiose? Very well, let it. Grandiose ideas deserve grandiose expression. Tomorrow, I make my first long-range Jump. Sharon claims that it is too soon for such a field test, but she is too cautious. I've engineered the equipment. I know what it can do. Triple redundancy on critical circuits. Molecular foam memory. I *am* a certified reliability engineer, after all. The short Jumps were all successful. So what could go wrong?

"Rosa could answer that. Sweet Rosa. She is not an engineer. She only sees that it is dangerous. And what can I say? It is dangerous. But when has anything perfectly safe been worth doing? The equipment is as safe as I can make it. I tried to explain about probabilities and hazard analysis to Rosa last night, but she only cried and held me tighter.

"She promised to be in the lab a week from tomorrow when I make my return Jump. A week away from Rosa. A week to study a whole new universe. *Madre de Dios!* A week can be both a moment and an eternity."

Knecht chewed his moustache. The next page was titled "Jump #1" followed by a string of twelve "coordinate settings." Then there were many pages which Knecht skimmed, detailing a world that never was. In it, the prehistoric Indians had not exterminated the Ice Age big game. Instead, they had tamed the horse, the elephant, and the camel and used the animal power to keep pace technologically with the Old World. Great civilizations arose in the river valleys of the Colorado and Rio Grande, and mighty empires spread across the Caribbean. Vikings were in Vinland at the same time the Iroquois were discovering Ireland. By the present day there were colonies on Mars.

Knecht shook his head. "Not only do we have a United States," he muttered.

The next entry was briefer and contained the first hint of trouble. It was headed "Jump #2." Except for the reversal of plus and minus signs, the co-ordinate settings were identical with the first set.

"A slight miscalculation. I should be back in the lab with Rosa, but I'm in somebody's apartment, instead. It's still Philly out the window—though a shabbier, more run-down Philly than I remember. I must be close to my home time line because I can recognize most of the University buildings. There's a flag that looks like the stars and stripes on the flagpole in front of College Hall; and something or other black hanging from the lamppost, but I can't make it out. Well, work first; tourism later. I bet I'll need a vernier control. There must be a slight asymmetry in the coordinates.

Knecht skipped several lines of equations and picked up the narrative once more.

"Jump #3. Coordinates . . .

"Wrong again. I was too hasty in leaving, but that black shape on the lamppost kept nagging at the back of my mind. So I got out my binoculars and studied it. It was a nun in a black habit, hanging in a noose. Hanging a long time, too, by the looks of it. Farther along the avenue, I could see bodies on all the lampposts. Then the wind caught the flag by College Hall and I understood. In place of the stars there was a swastika. . . .

"The settings were not quite right, but I think I know what went wrong now. The very act of my Jumping has created new branches in time and changed the oscillatory time-distance between them. On the shorter Jumps it didn't matter much, but on the longer ones . . .

"I think I finally have the calculations right. This is a pleasant world where I am, and—thanks to Goodman deVeres and his wife—I've had the time to think the problem through. It seems the Angevin kings still rule in this world, and my host has described what seems like sci-entific magic. Superstition? Mass delusion? I'd like to stay and study this world, but I'm already a week overdue. Darling Rosa must be fran-tic with worry. I think of her often."

The next page was headed "Jump #4" with settings but no narrative entry. This was followed by . . .

"Jump #5. Coordinates unknown.

"Damn! It didn't work out right and I was almost killed. This isn't an experiment anymore. Armored samurai in a medieval Philadelphia? Am I getting closer to or farther from Home? I barely escaped them. I rode north on a stolen horse and Jumped as soon as my charge built up. Just in time, too—my heart is still pounding. No time for calculations. I don't even know what the settings were.

"Note: the horse Jumped with me. The field must be wider than I thought. A clue to my dilemma? I need peace and quiet to think this out. I could find it with Goodman deVeres. I have the coordinates for his world. But his world isn't where I left it. When I jumped, I moved it. Archimedes had nothing on me. Haha. That's a joke. Why am I bothering with this stupid journal?

"I dreamed of Rosa last night. She was looking for me. I was right beside her but she couldn't see me. When I awoke, it was still dark. Off to the north there was a glow behind the crest of the hills. City lights? If that is South Mountain, it would be Allentown or Bethlehem on the other side—or their analogues in this world. I should know by tomorrow night. So far I haven't seen anyone; but I must be cautious.

"I've plenty of solitude here and now. That slag heap I saw from the mountain must have been Bethlehem, wiped out by a single bomb. The epicenter looked to be about where the steelworks once stood. It happened a long time ago, by the looks of things. Nothing living in the valley but a few scrub plants, insects, and birds.

"I rode out as fast as I could to put that awful sight behind me. I didn't dare eat anything. My horse did and is dead for it. Who knows what sort of mutations have fit the grass for a radioactive environment? I may already have stayed too long. I must Jump, but I daren't materialize inside a big city. I'll hike up into the northern hills before I Jump again."

Knecht turned to the last page. Jump #6. Settings, but no notes. There was a long silence while Knecht digested what he had read. Vonderberge was watching him. Outside, the wind rattled the windows. A nearby lightning strike caused the lights to flicker.

"Herr Festungskommandant . . ."

"His last Jump landed him right in your lap out on the Wyoming Trail."

"Herr Festungskommandant . . ."

"And instead of the solitude he sought, he's gotten solitude of another sort."

"You don't believe . . ."

"Believe?" Vonderberge slammed his palm down on the desk with unexpected violence. He stood abruptly and walked three quick paces to the window, where he gazed out at the storm. His fingers locked tightly behind his back. "Why not believe?" he whispered, his back to the room. "Somewhere there is a world where Heinrich Vonderberge is not trapped in a border fort on the edge of a war with the lives of others heavy on his back. He is in a laboratory, experimenting with electrical science, and he is happy."

He turned and faced Knecht, self-possessed once more.

"What if," he said. "What if the Pennamite Wars had not turned so vicious? If compromise had been possible? Had they lived, might not Washington and Franklin have forged a strong union, with the General as king and the Doctor as prime minister? Might not such a union have spread west, crushing Sequoyah and Tecumseh and their new Indian states before the British had gotten them properly started? Can you imagine a single government ruling the entire continent?"

Knecht said, "No," but Vonderberge continued without hearing him.

"Suppose," he said, pacing the room, "every time an event happens, several worlds are created. One for each outcome." He paused and smiled at Knecht. "Suppose Pennsylvania had not intervened in the Partition of New Jersey? No Piney War. New York and Virginia cut us off from the sea. Konrad Schneider does not become a great general, nor Rudi Knecht a famous spy. Somewhere there is such a world. Somewhere . . . close.

"Now suppose further that on one of these . . . these *moeglichwelten* a man discovers how to cross from one to another. He tests his equipment, makes many notes, then tries to return. But he fails."

A crash of thunder punctuated the Kommandant's words. Knecht jumped.

"He fails," Vonderberge continued, "because in the act of jumping he has somehow changed the 'distance.' So, on his return, he undershoots. At first, he is not worried. He makes a minor adjustment and tries again. And misses again. And again, and again, and again."

Vonderberge perched on the corner of his desk, his face serious. "Even if there is only one event each year, and each event had but two outcomes, why then in ten years do you know how many worlds there would have to be?"

Knecht shook his head dumbly.

"A thousand, Rudi, and more. And in another ten years, a thousand for each of those. Time is like a tree, a forest of trees. Always branching. One event a year? Two possible outcomes? *Ach!* I am a piker! In all of time, how many, many worlds there must be. How to find a single twig in such a forest?"

Knecht could think of nothing to say. In the quiet of the office, the storm without seemed louder and more menacing.

In the morning, of course, with the dark storm only muddy puddles, Knecht could dismiss the Kommandant's remarks as a bad joke. "What if?" was a game for children, a way of regretting the past. Knecht's alert eye had not missed the row of technofiction books in Vonderberge's office. "What if?" was a common theme in that genre, Knecht understood.

When he came to Kelly's cell to interrogate the prisoner, he found that others had preceded him. The guard at the cell door came to attention, but favored Knecht with a conspiratorial wink. From within the cell came the sound of angry voices. Knecht listened closely, his ear to the thick, iron door, but he could make out none of the words. He straightened and looked a question at the guard. The latter rolled his eyes heavenward with a look of resigned suffering. Knecht grinned.

"So, Johann," he said. "How long has this been going on?"

"Since sunup," was the reply. "The Kommandant came in early to talk to the prisoner. He'd been in there an hour when the Hexmajor arrived. Then there was thunder-weather, believe me, sir." Johann smiled at the thought of two officers bickering.

Knecht pulled two cigars from his pocket humidor and offered one to

the guard. "Do you suppose it is safe to leave them both locked in together?" He laughed. "We may as well relax while we wait. That is, if you
are permitted . . ."

The guard took the cigar. "The Kommandant is more concerned that
we are experts in how to shoot our rifles than in how to sneak a smoke."
There was a pause while Knecht lit his cigar. He puffed a moment, then
remarked, "This is good leaf. Kingdom of Carolina?"

Knecht nodded. He blew out a great cloud of acrid smoke. "You know
you should not have allowed either of them in to see the prisoner before
me."

"Well, sir. You know that, and I know that; but the Hexmajor and the
Kommandant, they make their own rules." The argument in the cell
reached a crescendo. Johann flinched. "Unfortunately, they do not make
the *same* rules."

"Hmph. Is your Kommandant always so . . . impetuous?" He wanted to
know Heinrich Vonderberge better; and one way to do that was to question the men who followed him.

The guard frowned. "Sir, things may be different in the Scout Corps,
but the Kommandant is no fool, in spite of his ways. He always has a
reason for what he does. Why, no more than two months ago—this
was before you were assigned here—he had us counting the number of
pigeons flying north. He plotted it on a daily chart." Johann laughed at
the memory. "Then he sent us out to intercept a raiding party from the
Nations. You see, you know how the sachems still allow private war par-
ties? Well . . ."

There was a banging at the cell door and Johann broke off whatever yarn
he had been about to spin and opened it. Vonderberge stalked out.

"We will see about that!" he snapped over his shoulder, and pushed past
Knecht without seeing him. Knecht took his cigar from his mouth and
looked from the Kommandant to the doorway. Hexmajor Ochsenfuss stood
there, glaring at the Kommandant's retreating form. "Fool," the doctor muttered through clenched teeth. Then he noticed Knecht.

"And what do *you* want? My patient is highly agitated. He cannot un-
dergo another grilling."

Knecht smiled pleasantly. "Why, Herr Doctor. He is not your patient
until I say so. Until then, he is my prisoner. I found him north of the Mountain. It is my function to interview him."

"He is a sick man, not one of your spies."

"The men I interview are never *my* spies. I will decide if he is . . . sick."

"That is a medical decision, not a military one. Have you read his journal? It is the product of a deluded mind."

"If it is what it appears to be. It could also be the product of a clever mind. Madness as a cover for espionage? Kelly would not be the first spy with an outrageous cover."

He walked past the doctor into the cell. Ochsenfuss followed him. Kelly looked up from his cot. He sat on the edge, hands clasped tightly, leaning on his knees. A night's sleep had not refreshed him. He pointed at Knecht.

"I remember you," he said. "You're the guy that caught me."

The Hexmajor forestalled Knecht's reply. "*Bitte*, Herr Leutnant," he said in Pennsylvaanish. "You must speak in our own tongue."

"*Warum?*" Knecht answered, with a glance at Kelly. "The prisoner speaks English, *nicht wahr?*"

"Ah, but he must understand German, at least a little. Either our own dialect or the European. Look at him. He is not from the West, despite his Spanish forename. Their skin color is much darker. Nor is he from Columbia, Cumberland, or the Carolina Kingdom. Their accents are most distinctive. And no white man from Virginia on north could be ignorant of the national tongue of Pennsylvania."

"Nor could any European," finished Knecht. "Not since 1917, at any rate. I cannot fault your logic, Herr Doctor; but then, why . . ."

"Because for some reason he has suppressed his knowledge of German. He has retreated from reality, built himself fantasy worlds. If we communicate only in Pennsylvaanish as we are doing now, his own desire to communicate will eventually overcome his 'block' (as we call it); and the process of drawing him back to the real world will have begun."

Knecht glanced again at the prisoner. "On the other hand, it is my duty to obtain information. If the prisoner will speak in English, then so will I."

"But . . ."

"And I must be alone." Knecht tapped his lapel insignia meaningfully. The double-X of the Scout Corps.

Ochsenfuss pursed his lips. Knecht thought he would argue further, but instead, he shrugged. "Have it your way, then; but remember to treat him carefully. If I am right, he could easily fall into complete withdrawal." He nodded curtly to Knecht and left.

Knecht stared at the closed door. He disliked people who "communicated." Nor did he think Vonderberge was a fool like Ochsenfuss had said. Still, he reminded himself, the Hexmajor had an impressive list of cures to his credit. Especially of battle fatigue and torture cases. Ochsenfuss was no fool, either.

He stuck his cigar back between his teeth. Let's get this over with, he thought. But he knew it would not be that easy.

Within an hour Knecht knew why the others had quarreled. Kelly could describe his fantasy world and the branching time lines very convincingly. But he had convinced Vonderberge that he was telling the truth and Ochsenfuss that he was mad. The conclusions were incompatible, the mixture, explosive.

Kelly spoke freely in response to Knecht's questions. He held nothing back. At least, the scout reminded himself, he *appeared* to hold nothing back. But who knew better than Knecht how deceptive such appearances could be?

Knecht tried all the tricks of the interrogator's trade. He came at the same question time after time, from different directions. He hopscotched from question to question. He piled detail on detail. No lie could be perfectly consistent. Contradictions would soon reveal themselves. He was friendly. He was harsh. He put his own words in the prisoner's mouth to see their effect.

None of it worked.

If Kelly's answers were contradictory, Knecht could not say. When the entire story is fantasy, who can find the errors? It was of a piece with the nature of Kelly's cover. If two facts contradict each other, which is true? Answer: both, but in two different worlds.

Frustrated, Knecht decided to let the prisoner simply talk. Silence, too, was an effective tactic. Many a prisoner had said too much simply to fill an awkward silence. He removed fresh cigars from his pocket humidor and offered one to the prisoner, who accepted it gratefully. Knecht clipped the ends and lit them. When they were both burning evenly, he leaned back in the chair. Nothing like a friendly smoke to set the mind at ease. And off-guard.

"So, tell me in your own words, then, how you on the Wyoming Trail were found."

Kelly grunted. "I wouldn't expect the military mind to understand, or even be interested."

Knecht flushed, but he kept his temper under control. "But I am interested, Herr Kelly. You have a strange story to tell. You come from another world. It is not a story I have often encountered."

Kelly looked at him, startled, and unexpectedly laughed. "No, not very often, I would imagine."

"*Ach*, that is my very problem. Just what *would* you imagine? Your story is true, or it is false; and if it is false, it is either deliberately so or not. I must know which, so I can take the proper action."

Kelly ran a hand through his hair. "Look. All I want is to get out of here, away from you . . . military men. Back to Rosa."

"That does not tell me anything. Spy, traveler, or madman, you would say the same."

The prisoner scowled. Knecht waited.

"All right," said Kelly at last. "I got lost. It's that simple. Sharon tried to tell me that a field trip was premature, but I was so much smarter then. Who would think that the distance from B to A was different than the distance from A to B?"

Who indeed? Knecht thought, but he kept the thought to himself. Another contradiction. Except, grant the premise, and it wasn't a contradiction at all.

"Sure." The prisoner's voice was bitter. "Action requires a force; and action causes reaction. It's not nice to forget Uncle Isaac." He looked Knecht square in the eye. "You see, when I Jumped, my world moved, too. Action, reaction. I created multiple versions of it. In one, my equipment worked and I left. In others, it malfunctioned in various ways and I'm still there. Each time line was slightly displaced from the original location." He laughed again. "How many people can say they've misplaced an entire world?"

"I don't understand," said Knecht. "Why not two versions of *all* worlds? When you, ah, Jumped, you could for many different destinations have gone; and in each one, you either arrived, or you did not."

His prisoner looked puzzled. "But that's not topologically relevant. The Jump occurs in the metacontinuum of the polyverse, so . . . Ah, hell! Why should I try to convince you?"

Knecht sat back and puffed his cigar. Offhand, he could think of several reasons why Kelly should try to convince him.

"You see," the prisoner continued, "there is not an infinity of possible worlds."

Knecht had never thought there was more than one, so he said nothing. Even the idea that there were two would be staggering.

"And they are not all different in the same way. Each moment grows out of the past. Oh, say . . ." He looked at his cigar and smiled. He held it out at arm's length. "Take this cigar, for instance. If I drop it, it'll fall to the floor. That is deterministic. So are the rate, the falling time, and the energy of impact. But, I may or may not choose to drop it. That is probabilistic. It is the choice that creates worlds. We are now at a cusp, a bifurcation point on the Thom manifold." He paused and looked at the cigar. Knecht waited patiently. Then Kelly clamped it firmly between his teeth. "It is far too good a smoke to waste. I chose not to drop it; but there was a small probability that I would have."

Knecht pulled on his moustache, thinking of Vonderberge's speculations of the previous night. Before he had spoken with Kelly. "So you say that . . . somewhere . . . there is a world in which you did?"

"Right. It's a small world, because the probability was small. Temporal cross section is proportional to *a priori* probability. But it's there, close by. It's a convergent world."

"Convergent."

"Yes. Except for our two memories and some ash on the floor, it is indistinguishable from this world. The differences damp out. Convergent worlds form a 'rope' of intertwined time lines. We can Jump back and forth among them easily, inadvertently. The energy needed is low. We could change places with our alternate selves and never notice. The only difference may be the number of grains of sand on Mars. Tomorrow you may find that I remember dropping the cigar; or I might find that you do. We may even argue the point."

"Unconvincingly," said Knecht sardonically.

Kelly chuckled. "True. How could you *know* what I remember? Still, it happens all the time. The courts are full of people who sincerely remember different versions of reality."

"Or perhaps it is the mind that plays tricks, not the reality."

Kelly flushed and looked away. "That happens, too."

After a moment, Knecht asked, "What has this to do with your becoming lost?"

"What? Oh. Simple, really. The number of possible worlds is large, but it's not infinite. That's important to remember," he continued to himself. "Finite. I haven't checked into Hotel Infinity. I can still find my own room, or at least the right floor." He stood abruptly and paced the room. Knecht followed him with his eyes.

"I don't have to worry about worlds where Washington and Jefferson instituted a pharaonic monarchy with a divine god-king. Every moment grows out of the previous moment, remember? For that to happen, so much previous history would have had to be different that Washington and Jefferson would never have been born." He stopped pacing and faced Knecht.

"And I don't have to worry about convergent worlds. If I find the right 'rope,' I'll be all right. Even a parallel world would be fine, as long as it would have Rosa in it." He frowned. "But it mightn't. And if it did, she mightn't know me."

"Parallel?" asked Knecht.

Kelly walked to the window and gazed through the bars. "Sure. Change can be convergent, parallel, or divergent. Suppose, oh suppose Isabella hadn't funded Columbus, but the other Genoese, Giovanni Caboto, who was also pushing for a voyage west. Or Juan de la Cosa. Or the two brothers who captained the *Niña* and the *Pinta*. There was no shortage of bold navigators. What practical difference would it have made? A few names are changed in the history books, is all. The script is the same, but different actors play the parts. The differences stay constant."

He turned around. "You or I may have no counterpart in those worlds. They are different 'ropes.' Even so, we could spontaneously Jump to one nearby. Benjamin Bathurst, the man who walked behind a horse in plain sight and was never seen again. No one took his place. Judge Crater. Ambrose Bierce. Amelia Earhart. Jimmy Hoffa. The Legion II Augusta. Who knows? Some of them may have Jumped."

Kelly inspected his cigar. "Then there are the cascades. For want of a nail, the shoe was lost. The differences accumulate. The worlds diverge. That was my mistake. Jumping to a cascade world." His voice was bitter, self-mocking. "Oh, it'll be simple to find my way back. All I have to do is find the nail."

"The nail?"

"Sure. The snowflake that started the avalanche. What could be simpler?" He took three quick steps along the wall, turned, stepped back, and jammed his cigar out in the ashtray. He sat backward, landing on his cot. He put his face in his hands.

Knecht listened to his harsh breathing. He remembered what Ochsenfuss had said. *If I push him too hard, he could crack.* A spy cracks one way; a madman, another.

After a while, Kelly looked up again. He smiled. "It's not that hard, really," he said more calmly. "I can approximate it closely enough with history texts and logical calculus. That should be good enough to get me back to my own rope. Or at least a nearby one. As long as Rosa is there, it doesn't matter." He hesitated and glanced at Knecht. "You've confiscated my personal effects," he said, "but I would like to have her photograph. It was in my wallet. Along with my identification papers," he added pointedly.

Knecht smiled. "I have seen your papers, Herr 'Professor Doctor' Kelly. They are very good."

"But . . ."

"But I have drawn others myself just as good."

Kelly shrugged and grinned. "It was worth a try," he said.

Knecht chuckled. He was beginning to like this man. "I suppose it can do no harm," he said, thinking out loud, "to give you a history text. Surely there gives one here in the fortress. If nothing else, it can keep you amused during the long days. And perhaps it can reacquaint you with reality."

"That's what the shrink said before."

"The shrink? What . . . ? Oh, I see. The Hexmajor." He laughed. Then he remembered how Ochsenfuss and Vonderberge had quarreled over this man, and he looked at him more soberly. "You understand that you must here stay. Until we know who or what you are. There are three possibilities, and only one is to your benefit." He hesitated a moment, then added, "It gives some here who your story believe, and some not."

Kelly nodded. "I know. Do you believe me?"

"Me? I am a scout. I look. I listen. I try to fit pieces together so they make a picture. I take no direct action. No, Herr Kelly. I do not believe you; but neither do I disbelieve you."

Kelly nodded. "Fair enough."

"Do not thank me yet, Herr Kelly. In our first five minutes of talking it is clear to me you know nothing of value of the Wyoming, or the Nations, or anything. In such a case, my official interest in you comes to an end."

"But unofficially . . ." prompted the other.

"*Ja.*" Knecht rose and walked to the door. "Others begin to have strong opinions about you, for whatever reasons of their own I do not know. Such are the seeds, and I do not like what may sprout. Perhaps this . . ." He jabbed his cigar at Kelly, suddenly accusing. "You know more than you show. You playact the hinkle-dreck *Quatschkopf.* And this, the sowing of discord, may be the very reason for your coming."

He stepped back and considered the prisoner. He gestured broadly, his cigar leaving curlicues of smoke. "I see grave philosophical problems with you, Herr Kelly. We Germans, even we Pennsylvaanish Germans, are a very philosophical people. From what you say there are many worlds, some only trivially different. I do not know why we with infinitely many Kellys are not deluged, each coming from a world *almost* like your own!"

Kelly gasped in surprise. He stood abruptly and turned to the wall, his back to Knecht. "Of course," he said. "Stupid, stupid, stupid! The transformation isn't homeomorphic. The topology of the inverse sheaf must not be Hausdorff after all. It may only be a Harris proximity." He turned to Knecht. "Please, may I have my calculator, the small box with the numbered buttons . . . No, damn!" He smacked a fist into his left hand. "I ran the batteries down when I was with Goodman deVeres. Some pencils and paper, then?" He looked eager and excited.

Knecht grunted in satisfaction. Something he had said had set Kelly thinking. It remained to be seen along which lines those thoughts would run.

Rumors flew over the next few days. A small border fort is their natural breeding ground, and Fox Gap was no exception. Knecht heard through the grapevine that Vonderberge had had the Hexmajor barred from Kelly's cell; that Ochsenfuss had telegraphed his superiors in Medical Corps and had Vonderberge overruled. Now there was talk that General Schneider himself had entered the dispute, on which side no one knew; but the general had already postponed his scheduled departure for Wind Gap Fortress and a packet bearing his seal had gone by special courier to Oberkommando Pennsylvaanish in Philadelphia City. A serious matter if the general did not trust the security of the military telegraph.

The general himself was not talking, not even to Knecht. That saddened the scout more than he had realized it could. Since his talk with the prisoner, Knecht had thought more than once how slender was the chain of chance that had brought Schneider and himself together, the team of scout and strategist that had shepherded the Commonwealth through two major wars and countless border skirmishes.

He dined with the general shortly after submitting his report on Kelly. Dinner was a hearty fare of *shnitz un' knepp*, with *deutch*-baked corn, followed by shoofly pie. Afterward, cigars and brandy wine. Talk turned, as it often did, to the Piney War. Schneider deprecated his own role.

"What could I do, Rudi?" he asked. "A stray cannon shot and both Kutz and Rittenhouse were dead. I felt the ball go by me, felt the wind on my face. A foot the other way would have deprived this very brandy of being so thoroughly enjoyed today. Suddenly, I was Commander of the Army of the Delaware, with my forces scattered among the Wachtungs. Rittenhouse had always been the tight-lipped sort. I had no idea what his plans had been. So I studied his dispositions and our intelligence on Enemy's dispositions, and . . ." A shrug. "I improvised."

Knecht lifted his glass in salute. "Brilliantly, as always."

Schneider grinned through his bushy white muttonchop whiskers. "We mustn't forget who secured that intelligence for me. Brilliance cannot improvise on faulty data. You have never failed me."

Knecht flushed. "Once I did."

"Tcha!" The General waved his hand in dismissal. "The nine hundred ninety-nine other times make me forget the once. Only you constantly remember."

Knecht remembered how he had misplaced an entire regiment of Virginia Foot. It was not where he had left it, but somewhere else entirely. General Schneider (except that he had been Brigadier Schneider) had salvaged the situation and had protected him from Alois Kutz's anger. He had learned something about Konrad Schneider then: The general never let the short-term interfere with the long-term. He would not sacrifice the future on the whim of the moment.

It had been such a simple error. He had improperly identified the terrain. The Appalachian Mountains of western Virginia looked much the same from ridge to ridge.

Or was it so simple? He recalled his discussion with the prisoner, Kelly. *Ich biete Ihre Entschuldigung, Herr Brigadier,* he imagined himself saying, but I must have slipped over into a parallel universe. In my time line, the Rappahannock Guards were on the north side of the river, not the south.

No, it wouldn't work. To believe it meant chaos: A world without facts. A world where lies hid among multiple truths. And what did the general think? What did Konrad Schneider make of Kelly's tale?

Knecht swirled the brandy in his snifter. He watched his reflection dance on the bloodred liquid. "Tell me, Konrad, have you read my report on the prisoner?"

"*Ja*, I have."

"And what did you think?"

"It was a fine report, Rudi. As always."

"No. I meant what did you think of the prisoner's story?"

The general lifted his glass to his lips and sipped his brandy. Knecht had seen many men try to avoid answers and recognized all the tactics. Knecht frowned and waited for an answer he knew he could not trust. For as long as Knecht could remember Schneider had been his leader. From the day he had left his father's house, he had followed Colonel, then Brigadier, then General Schneider, and never before had he been led astray. There was an emptiness in him now. He bit the inside of his cheek so that he could feel something, even pain.

Schneider finished his slow, careful sip and set his glass down. He shrugged broadly, palms up. "How could I know? Vonderberge tells me one thing; Ochsenfuss, another. You, in your report, tell me nothing."

Knecht bristled. "There is not enough data to reach a conclusion," he protested.

Schneider shook his head. "No, no. I meant no criticism. You are correct, as always. Yet, our friends *have* reached conclusions. Different conclusions, to be sure, but we don't know which is correct." He paused. "Of course, he *might* be a spy."

"If he is, he is either a very bad one, or a very, very good one."

"And all we know is . . . What? He loves Rosa and does not love the military. He has some peculiar documents and artifacts and he believes he comes from another world, full of marvelous gadgets. . . ."

"Correction, Herr General. He *says* he believes he came from another world. There is a difference."

"Hmph. *Ja*, you are right again. What is it you always say? The map is not the territory. The testimony is not the fact. Sometimes I envy our friends their ability to reach such strong convictions on so little reflection. You and I, Rudi, we are always beset by doubts, eh?"

Knecht made a face. "If so, Konrad, your doubts have never kept you from acting."

The general stared at him a moment. Then he roared with laughter, slapping his thigh. "Oh, yes, you are right, Rudi. What should I do without you? You know me better than I know myself. There are two kinds of doubts, *nicht wahr?* One says: What is the right thing to do? The other says: Have I done the right thing? But, to command means to decide. I have never fought a battle but that a better strategy has not come to mind a day or two later. But where would we be had I waited? Eh, Rudi? The second sort of doubt. That is the sort of doubt a commander must have. Never the first sort. And never certainty. Both are disasters."

"And what of Kelly?"

The general reached for his brandy once more. "I will have both the Hexmajor and the Kommandant interview him. Naturally, each will be biased, but in different ways. Between them, we may learn the truth of it." He paused thoughtfully, pursing his lips. "Sooner or later, one will concede the matter. We need not be hasty. No, not hasty at all." He drank the last of his brandy.

"And myself?"

Schneider looked at him. He smiled. "You cannot spend so much time on only one man, one who is almost surely not an enemy agent. You have your spies, scouts, and rangers to supervise. Intelligence to collate. Tell me, Rudi, what those fat knick patroons are planning up in Albany. Have the Iroquois joined them, too? Are they dickering with the Lee brothers to make it a two-front war? I must know these things if I am to . . . improvise. Our situation is grave. Forget Kelly. He is not important."

After he left the general, Knecht took a stroll around the parapet, exchanging greetings with the sentries. Schneider could not have announced more clearly that Kelly was important. But why? And why keep him out of it?

Fox Gap was a star-fort and Knecht's wanderings had taken him to one of the points of the star. From there, defensive fire could enfilade any attacking force. He leaned his elbows on a gun port and gazed out at the nighttime forest farther down the slope of the mountain. The sky was crisp and clear as only autumn skies could be, and the stars were brilliantly close.

The forest was a dark mass, a deeper black against the black of night. The wind soughed through the maple and elm and birch. The sound reached him, a dry whisper, like crumpling paper. Soon it would be the fall. The leaves were dead; all the life had been sucked out of them.

He sighed. General Schneider had just as clearly ordered him away from Kelly. He had never disobeyed an order. Angrily, he threw a shard of masonry from the parapet wall. It crashed among the treetops below and a sentry turned sharply and shouted a challenge. Embarrassed, Knecht turned and left the parapet.

Once back in his own quarters, Knecht pondered the dilemma of Kelly. His room was spartan. Not much more comfortable, he thought, than Kelly's cell. A simple bed, a desk and chair, a trunk. Woodcuts on the wall: heroic details of long-forgotten battles. An anonymous room, suitable for a roving scout. Next month, maybe, a different room at a different fort.

So what was Kelly? Knecht couldn't see but three possibilities. A clever spy, a madman, or the most pitiful refugee ever. But, as a spy he was not credible; his story was unbelievable; and he simply did not talk like a madman.

And where does that leave us, Rudi? Nowhere. Was there a fourth possibility? It didn't seem so.

Knecht decided it was time for a pipe. Cigars were for talk; pipes for reflection. He stepped to the window of his room as he lit it. The pipe was very old. It had belonged to his grandfather, and a century of tobacco had burned its flavor into the bowl. His grandfather had given it to him the night before he had left home forever, when he had confided his plans to the old man, confident of his approval. He had been, Knecht remembered, about Kelly's age at the time. An age steeped in certainties.

Spy, madman, or refugee? *If the first, good for me; because I caught him. If the second, good for him; because he will be cared for.* He puffed. For two of the three possibilities, custody was the best answer; the only remaining question being what sort of custody. And those two choices were like the two sides of a coin: they used up all probability between them. *Heads I win, Herr Kelly, and tails you lose. It is a cell for you either way. That is obvious.*

So then, why am I pacing this room in the middle of the night, burning my best leaf and tasting nothing?

Because, Rudi, there is just the chance that the coin could land on its edge. If Kelly's outrageous tale were true, custody would not be the best answer. It would be no answer at all.

Ridiculous. It could not be true. He took the pipe from his mouth. The warmth of the bowl in his hand comforted him. Knecht had concluded tentatively that Kelly was no spy. That meant Ochsenfuss was right. Knecht could see that. It had been his own first reaction on reading the notebook. But he could also see why Vonderberge believed otherwise. The man's outlook and Kelly's amiable and sincere demeanor had combined to produce belief.

It was Schneider that bothered him. Schneider had *not* decided. Knecht was certain of that. And that meant . . . What? With madness so obvious, Schneider saw something else. Knecht had decided nothing because he was interested only in spies. Beyond that, what Kelly was or was not meant nothing.

Even if his tale is true, he thought, *it is none of my concern. My task is done. I have taken in a suspicious stranger under suspicious circumstances. It is for higher authorities to puzzle it out. Why should I care what the answer is?*

Because, Rudi, it was you who brought him here.

Knecht learned from Johann the guard that Vonderberge spent the mornings with Kelly; and Ochsenfuss, the afternoons. So when Knecht brought the history book to the cell a few days later, he did so at noon, when no one else was about. He had made it a habit to stop by for a few minutes each day.

He nodded to Johann as he walked down the cell-block corridor. "I was never here, soldier," he said. Johann's face took on a look of amiable unawareness.

Kelly was eating lunch, a bowl of thick rivel soup. He had been provided with a table, which was now littered with scribbled pages. Knecht recognized the odd equations of Kelly's "logical calculus." He handed the prisoner the text: *The History of North America.* Kelly seized it eagerly and leafed through it.

"Thanks, Lieutenant," he said. "The shrink brought me one, too; but it's in German, and I couldn't make sense of it."

"Pennsylvaanish," Knecht corrected him absently. He was looking at the other book. It was thick and scholarly. A good part of each page consisted of footnotes. He shuddered and put it down.

"What?"

"Pennsylvaanish," he repeated. "It is a German dialect, but it is not *Hochdeutsch*. It is Swabian with some English mixed in. The spelling makes different sometimes. A visitor from the Second Reich would find it nearly unintelligible, but . . ." An elaborate shrug. "What can one expect from a Prussian?"

Kelly laughed. He put his soup bowl aside, finished. "How did that happen?" he asked. "I mean, you folks speaking, ah, Pennsylvaanish?"

Knecht raised an eyebrow. "Because we are Pennsylvanians."

"So were Franklin, Dickinson, and Tom Penn."

"Ah, I see what you are asking. It is simple. Even so far back as the War Against the English the majority of Pennsylvanians were *Deutsch*, German-speakers. So high was the feeling against the English—outside of Philadelphia City, that is—that the Assembly German the official language made. Later, after the Revolution in Europe, many more from Germany came. They were fleeing the Prussians and Austrians."

"And from nowhere else? No Irish? No Poles, Italians, Russian Jews? 'I lift my lamp beside the golden door.' What happened to all of that?"

"I don't understand. *Ja*, some came from other countries. There were Welsh and Scots-Irish here even before the War. Others came later. A few, not many. Ranger Oswoski's grandparents were Polish. But, when they come here, then Pennsylvaanish they must learn."

"I suppose with America so balkanized, it never seemed such a land of opportunity."

"I don't understand that, either. What is 'balkanized'?"

Kelly tapped with his pencil on the table. "No," he said slowly, "I suppose you wouldn't." He aimed the pencil at the history book. "Let me read this. Maybe I'll be able to explain things better."

"I hope you find in it what you need."

Kelly grinned, all teeth. "An appropriately ambiguous wish, Lieutenant. 'What I need.' That could mean anything. But, thank you. I think I will." He hesitated a moment. "And, uh, thanks for the book, too. You've been a big help. You're the only one who comes here and listens to me. I mean, *really* listens."

Knecht smiled. He opened the door, but turned before leaving. "But, Herr Kelly," he said, "it is my job to listen."

Knecht's work absorbed him for several days. Scraps of information filtered in from several quarters. He spent long hours in his office going over them, separating rumor from fact from possible fact. Sometimes, he sent a man out to see for himself and waited in nervous uncertainty until the pigeons flew back. Each night, he threw himself into his rack exhausted. Each morning, there was a new stack of messages.

He moved pins about in his wall map. Formations whose bivouac had been verified. Twice he telegraphed the Southern Command using his personal code to discover what the scouts down along the Monongahela had learned. Slowly, the spaces filled in. The pins told a story. Encirclement.

Schneider came in late one evening. He stood before the map and studied it for long minutes in silence. Knecht sipped his coffee, watching. The general drew his forefinger along the northwestern frontier. There were no pins located in Long House territory. "Curious," he said aloud, as if to himself. Knecht smiled. Five rangers were already out trying to fill in that gap. Schneider would have his answer soon enough.

Knecht had almost forgotten Kelly. There had been no more time for his noontime visits. Then, one morning he heard that Vonderberge and Ochsenfuss had fought in the officers' club. Words had been exchanged, then blows. Not many, because the chief engineer had stopped them. It wasn't clear who had started it, or even how it had started. It had gotten as far as it had only because the other officers present had been taken by surprise. Neither man had been known to brawl before.

Knecht was not surprised by the fight. He knew the tension between the two over Kelly. What did surprise him was that Schneider took no official notice of the fight.

Something was happening. Knecht did not know what it was, but he was determined to find out. He decided to do a little intramural spy work of his own.

Knecht found the Hexmajor later that evening. He was sitting alone at a table in the officers' club, sipping an after-dinner liqueur from a thin glass, something Knecht found vaguely effeminate. He realized he was taking a strong personal dislike to the man. Compared to Vonderberge, Ochsenfuss was haughty and cold. Elegant, Knecht thought, watching the man drink. That was the word: elegant. Knecht himself liked plain, blunt-spoken men. But scouts, he told himself firmly, must observe what is, not what they wish to see. The bar orderly handed him a beer stein and he strolled casually to Ochsenfuss's table.

"Ah, Herr Doctor," he said smiling. "How goes it with the prisoner?"

"It goes," said Ochsenfuss, "but slowly."

Knecht sat without awaiting an invitation. He thought he saw a brief glimmer of surprise in the other's face, but the Hexmajor quickly recovered his wooden expression. Knecht was aware that Vonderberge, at a corner table, had paused in his conversation with the chief engineer and was watching them narrowly.

"A shame the treatment cannot go speedier," he told Ochsenfuss.

A shrug. "Under such circumstances, the mind must heal itself."

"I remember your work with Ranger Harrison after we rescued him from the Senecas."

Ochsenfuss sipped his drink. He nodded. "Yes, I recall the case. His condition was grave. Torture does things to a man's mind; worse in many ways than what it does to his body."

"May I ask how you are treating Kelly?"

"You may."

There was a long silence. Then Knecht said, "How are you treating him?" He could not detect the slightest hint of a smile on the doctor's face. He was surprised. Ochsenfuss had not seemed inclined to humor of any sort.

"I am mesmerizing him," the Hexmajor said. "Then I allow him to talk about his fantasies. In English," he admitted grudgingly. "I ply him for details. Then, when he is in this highly suggestible state, I point out the contradictions in his thinking."

"Contradictions . . ." Knecht let the word hang in the air.

"Oh, many things. Heavier-than-air flying machines: a mathematical impossibility. Radio, communication without connecting wires: That is action at a distance, also impossible. Then there is his notion that a single government rules the continent, from Columbia to New England and from Pontiac to Texas. Why, the distances and geographical barriers make the idea laughable.

"I tell him these things while he is mesmerized. My suggestions lodge in what we call the subconscious and gradually make his fantasies less credible to his waking mind. Eventually he will again make contact with reality."

"Tell me something, Herr Doctor."

They both turned at the sound of the new voice. It was Vonderberge. He stood belligerently, his thumbs hooked in his belt. He swayed slightly and Knecht could smell alcohol on his breath. Knecht frowned unhappily.

Ochsenfuss blinked. "Yes, Kommandant," he said blandly. "What is it?"

"I have read that by mesmerization one can also implant false ideas."

Ochsenfuss smiled. "I have heard that at carnival sideshows, the mesmerist may cause members of the audience to believe that they are ducks or some such thing."

"I was thinking of something more subtle than that."

The Hexmajor's smile did not fade, but it seemed to freeze. "Could you be more specific."

Vonderberge leaned towards them. "I mean," he said in a low voice, "the obliteration of true memories and their replacement with false ones."

Ochsenfuss tensed. "No reputable hexdoctor would do such a thing."

Vonderberge raised a palm. "I never suggested such a thing, either. I only asked if it were possible."

Ochsenfuss paused before answering. "It is. But the false memories would inevitably conflict with a thousand others and, most importantly, with the evidence of the patient's own senses. The end would be psychosis. The obliteration of *false* memories, however . . ."

Vonderberge nodded several times, as if the Hexmajor had confirmed a long-standing belief. "I see. Thank you, Doctor." He turned and looked at Knecht. He touched the bill of his cap. "Rudi," he said in salutation, then turned and left.

Ochsenfuss watched him go. "There is a man who can benefit from therapy. He would reject reality if he could."

Knecht remembered Vonderberge's outburst in his office during the storm. He remembered, too, the map in his own office. "So might we all," he said. "Reality is none too pleasant these days. General Schneider believes . . ."

"General Schneider," interrupted Ochsenfuss, "believes what he wants to believe. But truth is not always what we want, is it?" He looked away, his eyes focused on the far wall. "Nor always what we need." He took another sip of his liqueur and set the glass down. "I am not such a fool as he seems to think. For all that he primes me with questions to put to Kelly, and the interest he shows in my reports, he still has not decided what to do with my patient. He should be in hospital, in Philadelphia."

For the briefest moment, Knecht thought he meant Schneider should be in hospital. When he realized the confusion, he laughed. Ochsenfuss looked at him oddly, and Knecht took a pull on his mug to hide his embarrassment.

"If I could use mescal or peyote to heighten his suggestibility," Ochsenfuss continued to no one in particular. "Or if I could keep our friend the Kommandant away from my patient. . . ." He studied his drink in silence, then abruptly tossed it off. He looked at his watch and waved off a hovering orderly. "Well, things cannot go on as they are. Something must break." He laughed and rose from the table. "At least there are a few of us who take a hard-headed and practical view of the world, eh, Leutnant?" He patted Knecht on the arm and left.

Knecht watched him go. He took another drink of beer and wiped the foam from his lips with his sleeve, thinking about what the Hexmajor had said.

A few days later, a carrier pigeon arrived and Knecht rode out to meet its sender at a secret rendezvous deep inside Wyoming. Such meetings were always risky, but his agent had spent many years working her way into a position of trust. It was a mask that would be dropped if she tried to leave the country. Knecht wondered what the information was. Obviously more than could be entrusted to a pigeon.

But she never came to the rendezvous. Knecht waited, then left a sign on a certain tree that he had been there and gone. He wondered what had happened. Perhaps she had not been able to get away after all. Or perhaps she had been unmasked and quietly executed. Like many of the Old-style Quakers, Abigail Fox had learned English at her mother's knee and spoke without an accent; but one never knew what trivial detail would prove fatal.

Knecht chewed on his moustache as he rode homeward. He had not seen Abby for a long time. Now he didn't know if he would ever see her again. The worst part would be never knowing what had happened. Knecht hated not knowing things. That's why he was a good scout. Even bad news was better than no news.

Well, perhaps another pigeon would arrive, explaining everything, arranging another rendezvous. *But how could you be sure, Rudi, that it really came from her?* Spies have been broken before, and codes with them. One day, he knew, he would ride out to a meeting and not come back. He felt cold and empty. He slapped his horse on the rump and she broke into a trot. He was afraid of death, but he would not send others to do what he would not.

It had been two weeks to rendezvous and back, and Schneider was still at Fox Gap when Knecht returned. The rumors had grown up thick for harvesting. Between the front gate and the stables five soldiers and two officers asked him if a command shake-up were coming. His friendship with the general was well-known, and why else would Schneider stay on?

Why else, indeed. Kelly. Knecht was certain of it, but the why still eluded him.

Catching up on his paperwork kept Knecht at his desk until well after dark. When he had finished, he made his way to Vonderberge's quarters. Knecht's thought was to pay a "social call" and guide the conversation around to the subject of Kelly. Once he arrived, however, he found himself with some other officers, drinking dark beer and singing badly to the accompaniment of the chief engineer's equally bad piano playing. It was, he discovered, a weekly ritual among the permanent fortress staff.

Ochsenfuss was not present, but that did not surprise him.

He was reluctant to bring up the business of the prisoner in front of the other officers, so he planned to be the last to leave. But Vonderberge and the fortress staff proved to have a respectable capacity for drinking and singing, and Knecht outlasted them only by cleverly passing out in the corner, where he was overlooked when Vonderberge ushered the others out.

"Good morning, Rudi."

Knecht opened his eyes. The light seared his eyes and the top of his head fell off and shattered on the floor. "Ow," he said.

"Very eloquent, Rudi." Vonderberge leaned over him, looking impossibly cheerful. "That must be some hangover."

Knecht winced. "You can't get hangovers from beer."

Vonderberge shrugged. "Have it your way." He held out a tall glass. "Here, drink this."

Knecht sniffed the drink warily. It was dark and red and pungent. "What is it?" he asked suspiciously.

"Grandmother Vonderberge's Perfect Cure for Everything. It never fails."

"But what's in it?"

"If I told you, you wouldn't drink it. Go ahead. Grandmother was a wise old bird. She outlasted three husbands."

Knecht drank. He shuddered and sweat broke out on his forehead. "Small wonder," he gasped. "She probably fed them this."

Vonderberge chuckled and took the glass back. "You were in fine form last night. Fine form. Who is Abby?"

Knecht looked at him. "Why?"

"You kept drinking toasts to her."

He looked away, into the distance. "She was . . . someone I knew."

"Like that, eh?" Vonderberge grinned. Knecht did not bother to correct him.

"You should socialize more often, Rudi," continued the Kommandant. "You'll find we're not such bad sorts. You have a good baritone. It gave the staff a fuller sound." Vonderberge gestured broadly to show how full the sound had been. "We need the higher registers, though. I've thought of having Heinz and Zuckerman gelded. What do you think?"

Knecht considered the question. "Where do they stand on the promotion list?"

Vonderberge looked at him sharply. He grinned. "You are beginning to show a sense of humor, Rudi. A sense of humor."

Knecht snorted. He was easily twenty years the Kommandant's senior. He knew jokes that had been old and wrinkled before Vonderberge had been born. He recalled suddenly that Abigail Fox had been an alto. There were other memories, too; and some empty places where there could have been memories, but weren't. *Ach,* for what might have been! It wasn't right for spymaster and spy to be too close. He wondered if Kelly had a world somewhere where everything was different.

·   ·   ·

Vonderberge had his batman serve breakfast in rather than go to the mess. He invited Knecht to stay and they talked over eggs, scrapple, and coffee. Knecht did not have to lead into the subject of Kelly because Vonderberge raised it himself. He unrolled a sheet of paper onto the table after the batman had cleared it, using the salt and pepper mills to hold down the curled ends.

"Let me show you," he said, "what bothers me about Kelly's world."

A great many things about Kelly's world bothered Knecht, not the least of which was the fact that there was no evidence it even existed; but he put on a polite face and listened attentively. Was Vonderberge beginning to have doubts?

The Kommandant pointed to the sheet. Knecht saw that it was a table of inventions, with dates and inventors. Some of the inventions had two dates and two inventors, in parallel columns.

"Next to each invention," said Vonderberge, "I've written when and by whom it was invented. The first column is our world; the second, Kelly's, as nearly as he can remember. Do you notice anything?"

Knecht glanced at the list. "Several things," he replied casually. "There are more entries in the second column, most of the dates are earlier, and a few names appear in both columns."

Vonderberge blinked and looked at him. Knecht kept his face composed.

"You're showing off, aren't you, Rudi?"

"I've spent a lifetime noticing details on documents."

"But do you see the significance? The inventions came earlier and faster in Kelly's world. Look how they *gush* forth after 1870! Why? How could they have been so much more creative? In the early part of the list, many of the same men are mentioned in both columns, so it is not individual genius. Look . . ." His forefinger searched the first column. "The electrical telegraph was invented, when? In 1875, by Edison. In Kelly's world, it was invented in the 1830s, by a man named Morse."

"The painter?"

"Apparently the same man. Why didn't he invent it here? And see what Edison did in Kelly's world: The electrical light, the moving picture projector, dozens of things we never saw until the 1930s."

Knecht pointed to an entry. "Plastics," he said. "We discovered them first." He wondered what "first" meant in this context.

"That is the exception that proves the rule. There are others. Daguerre's photographic camera, Foucault's gyroscope. They are the same in both worlds. But overall there is a pattern. Not an occasional marvel, every now and then; but a multitude, every year! By 1920, in Kelly's world, steamships, *heavier*-than-air craft, railroads, *voice* telegraphy with *and without* wires, horseless carriages, they were an old hat. Here, they are still wonders. Or wondered about."

Inventions and gadgets, decided Knecht. Those were Vonderberge's secret passion, and Kelly had described a technological faerieland. No wonder the Kommandant was entranced. Knecht was less in awe, himself. He had seen the proud ranks of the 18th New York mowed down like corn by the Pennsylvaanish machine guns at the Battle of the Raritan. And he had not forgotten what Kelly had written in his notebook: There were bombs that destroyed whole cities and poisoned the land for years after.

Vonderberge sighed and rolled up his list. He tied a cord around it. "It is difficult, Rudi," he said. "Very difficult. Your general, he only wants to hear about the inventions. He does not wonder why there are so many. Yet, I feel that this is an important question."

"Can't Kelly answer it?"

"He might. He has come close to it on several occasions; but he is . . . confused. Ochsenfuss sees to that."

Knecht noticed how Vonderberge's jaw set. The Kommandant's usual bantering tone was missing.

Vonderberge pulled a watch from his right pants pocket and studied its face. "It is time for my appointment with Kelly. Why don't you come with me. I'd like your opinion on something."

"On what?"

"On Kelly."

Knecht sat backward on a chair in the corner of the cell, leaning his arms on the back. A cigar was clamped tightly between his teeth. It had gone out, but he had not bothered to relight it. He watched the proceedings between Kelly and Vonderberge. So far, he did not like what he had seen.

Kelly spoke hesitantly. He seemed distracted and lapsed into frequent, uncomfortable silences. The papers spread out on his table were blank. No new equations. Just doodles of flowers. Roses, they looked like.

"Think, Kelly," Vonderberge pleaded. "We were talking of this only yesterday."

Kelly pursed his lips and frowned. "Were we? *Ja*, you're right. I think we did. I thought it was a dream."

"It was not a dream. It was real. You said you thought the Victorian Age was the key. What was the Victorian Age?"

Kelly looked puzzled. "Victorian Age? Are you sure?"

"Yes. You mentioned Queen Victoria . . ."

"She was never queen, though."

Vonderberge clucked impatiently. "That was in this world," he said. "In your world it must have been different."

"In my world . . ." It was half a statement, half a question. Kelly closed his eyes, hard. "I have such headaches, these days. It's hard to remember things. It's all confused."

Vonderberge turned to Knecht. "You see the problem?"

Knecht removed his cigar. "The problem," he said judiciously, "is the source of his confusion."

Vonderberge turned back to Kelly. "I think we both know who that is."

Kelly was losing touch, Knecht thought. That was certain. But was he losing touch with reality, or with fantasy?

"Wait!" Kelly's eyes were still closed, but his hand shot out and gripped Vonderberge's wrist. "The Victorian Age. That was the time from the War Between the States to World War I." He opened his eyes and looked at Vonderberge. "Am I right?"

Vonderberge threw his hands up. "Tchah! Why are you asking *me?*"

Knecht chewed thoughtfully on his cigar. *World* wars? And they were *numbered?*

"What has this 'Victorian Age' to do with your world's inventiveness?"

Kelly stared at a space in the air between them. He rapped rhythmically on the table with his knuckles. "Don't push it," he said. "I might lose the . . . Yes. I can hear Tom's voice explaining it." The eyes were unfocused. Knecht wondered what sort of mind heard voices talking to it. "What an odd-looking apartment it was. We were just BS'ing. Sharon, Tom, and . . . a girl, and I. The subject came up, but in a different context."

They waited patiently for Kelly to remember.

"Critical mass!" he said suddenly. "That was it. The rate at which new ideas are generated depends in part on the accumulation of past ideas. The more there are, the more ways they can be combined and modified. Then, boom." He gestured with his hands. "An explosion." He laughed shrilly; sobered instantly. "That's what happened during the Victorian Age. That's what's happening now, but slower."

A slow explosion? The idea amused Knecht. "Why slower?" he asked.

"Because of the barriers! Ideas must circulate freely if they're to trigger new ones. The velocity of ideas is as important to culture and technology as, as the velocity of money is to the economy. The United States would have been the largest free trade zone in the world. The second largest was England. Not even the United Kingdom, just England. Can you imagine? Paying a toll or a tariff every few miles?"

"What has commerce to do with ideas?" asked Vonderberge.

"It's the traveling people who carry ideas from place to place. The merchants, sailors, soldiers. At least until an international postal system is established. And radio. And tourism."

"I see . . ."

"But look at the barriers we have to deal with! The largest nation on the Atlantic seaboard is what? The Carolina Kingdom. Some of the Indian states are larger, but they don't have many people. How far can you travel before you pay a tariff? Or run into a foreign language like English or Choctaw or French? Or into a military patrol that shoots first and asks questions later? No wonder we're so far behind!"

Knecht pulled the cigar from his mouth. "We?" he asked. Vonderberge turned and gave him an anxious glance, so he, too, had noticed the shift in Kelly's personal pronoun.

The prisoner was flustered. "You," he said. "I meant 'you.' Your rate of progress is slower. I . . ."

Knecht forestalled further comment. "No, never mind. A slip of the tongue, *ja?*" He smiled to show he had dismissed the slip. He knew it was important; though in what way he was not yet sure. He took a long puff on his cigar. "Personally, I have never thought our progress slow. The horseless carriage was invented, what? 1920-something, in Dusseldorf. In less than fifty years you could find some in all the major cities. Last year, two nearly collided on the streets of Philadelphia! Soon every well-to-do family will have one."

The prisoner laughed. It was a great belly laugh that shook him and shook him until it turned imperceptibly into a sob. He squeezed his eyes tight.

"There was a man," he said distantly. "Back in my hometown of Longmont, Colorado." He opened his eyes and looked at them. "That would be in Nuevo Aztlan, if it existed, which it doesn't and never has . . ." He paused and shook his head, once, sharply, as if to clear it. "Old Mr. Brand. I was just a kid, but I remember when the newspapers and TV came around. When Old Brand was a youngster, he watched his dad drive a stagecoach. Before he died, he watched his son fly a space shuttle." He looked intently at Knecht. "And you think it is wonderful that a few rich people have hand-built cars after half a century?"

He laughed again; but this time the laugh was brittle. They watched him for a moment, and the laugh went on and on. Then Vonderberge leaned forward and slapped him sharply, twice.

Knecht chewed his moustache. What the prisoner said made some sense. He could see how technological progress—and social change with it—was coupled with free trade and the free exchange of ideas. Yet, he wasn't at all sure that it was necessarily a good thing. There was a lot to be said for stability and continuity. He blew a smoke ring. He wondered if Kelly were a social radical, driven mad by his inability to instigate change, who had built himself a fantasy world in which change ran amok. That made sense, too.

He glanced at his cigar, automatically timing the ash. A good cigar should burn at least five minutes before the ash needed knocking off.

Suddenly, he felt a tingling in his spine. He looked at the cigar as if it had come alive in his hand. It had gone out—he remembered that clearly. Now, it was burning, and he could not recall relighting it. He looked at the ashtray. *Yes, a spent match. I relit it, of course. It was such an automatic action that I paid it no mind.* That was one explanation. It was his memory playing tricks, not his reality. But the tingling in his spine did not stop.

He looked at Kelly, then he carefully laid his cigar in the ashtray to burn itself out.

"You just wait, though," Kelly was saying to Vonderberge. "Our curve is starting up, too. It took us longer, but we'll be reaching critical mass soon. We're maybe a hundred years off the pace. About where the other . . . where my world was just before the world wars."

That simple pronouncement filled Knecht with a formless dread. He watched the smoke from his smoldering cigar and saw how it rose, straight and true, until it reached a breaking point. There, it changed abruptly into a chaos of turbulent streamers, swirling at random in the motionless air. *Then we could do the same,* he thought. *Fight worldwide wars.*

Afterward, Knecht and Vonderberge spoke briefly as they crossed the parade ground. The sun was high in the sky, but the air held the coolness of autumn. Knecht was thoughtful, his mind on his cigar, on alternate realities, on the suddenness with which stability could turn to chaos.

"You saw it, didn't you?" asked Vonderberge.

For a moment he thought the Kommandant meant his mysteriously relit cigar. "Saw what?" he replied.

"Kelly. He has difficulty remembering his own world. He becomes confused, disoriented, melancholy."

"Is he always so?"

"Today was better than most. Sometimes I cannot stop his weeping."

"I have never heard him talk so long without mentioning his Rosa."

"Ah, you noticed that, too. But three days ago he was completely lucid and calculated columns of figures. Settings, he said, for his machine. They take into account, ah . . . 'many-valued inverse functions.' " Vonderberge smiled. "Whatever that means. And, if he ever sees his machine again."

"His machine," said Knecht. "Has anyone handled it?"

"No," said Vonderberge. "Ochsenfuss doesn't think it matters. It's just a collection of knobs and wires."

"And you?"

"Me?" Vonderberge looked at him. "I'm afraid to."

"Yet, its study could be most rewarding."

"A true scout. But if we try, four things could happen, and none of them good."

Knecht tugged on his moustaches. "We could open it up and find that it is an obvious fake, that it couldn't possibly work."

"Could we? How would it be obvious? We would still wonder whether the science were so advanced that we simply did not understand how it did work. Like a savage with a steam engine." The Kommandant was silent for a moment.

"That's one. You said four things could happen."

"The other three assume the machine works." He held up his fingers to count off his points. "Two: In our ignorance, we damage it irreparably, marooning Kelly forever. Three: We injure ourselves by some sort of shock or explosion."

"And four?"

"Four: We transport ourselves unwittingly to another world."

"A slim possibility, that."

Vonderberge shrugged. "Perhaps. But the penalty for being wrong is . . ."

"Excessive," agreed Knecht dryly.

"I *did* examine his 'calculator,' you know."

Knecht smiled to himself. He had wondered if the Kommandant had done that, too. Knecht had learned little from it, himself.

"It was fine work: the molded plastic, the tiny buttons, the intricate circuits and parts."

"Not beyond the capabilities of any competent electrosmith."

"What! Did you see how small the batteries were? And the, what did he call them? The chips? How can you say that?"

"I didn't mean we could build a calculating engine so small. But, is it a calculating engine? Did you see it function? No. Kelly says the batteries have gone dead. Which is convenient for him. Our regimental electrosmith could easily construct a copy that does the same thing: mainly, nothing."

Vonderberge stopped and held him by the arm. "Tell me, Rudi. Do you believe Kelly or not?"

"I . . ." Well, did he? The business with the cigar was too pat. It seemed important only because of Kelly's toying with another cigar a few weeks before. Otherwise, he would never have noticed, or thought nothing even if he had. Like the prophetic dream: It seems to be more than it is because we only remember them when they come true. "I . . . have no convincing evidence."

"Evidence?" asked Vonderberge harshly. "What more evidence do you need?"

"Something solid," Knecht snapped back. *Something more than that I like the prisoner and the Kommandant and I dislike the Hexmajor.* "Something more than a prisoner's tale," he said. "That becomes more confused as time goes on."

"That is Ochsenfuss's bungling!"

"Or his success! Have you thought that perhaps the Hexmajor is *curing* Kelly of a long-standing delusion?"

Vonderberge turned to go. "No."

Knecht stopped him. "Heinrich," he said.

"What?"

Knecht looked past the Kommandant. He could see the sentries where they paced the walls, and the cannon in their redoubts, and the gangways to the underground tunnels that led to the big guns fortified into the mountainside. "Real or fantasy, you've learned a lot about the prisoner's technology."

"Enough to want to learn more."

"Tell me, Heinrich. Do you *want* to learn to make nuclear bombs?"

Vonderberge followed Knecht's gaze. A troubled look crossed his face and he bit his lower lip. "No, I do not. But the same force can produce electricity. And the medical science that produces the miracle drugs can tailor-make horrible plagues. The jets that fly bombs can just as easily fly people or food or trade goods." He sighed. "What can I say, Rudi. It is not the tool, but the tool-user who creates the problems. Nature keeps no secrets. If something can be done, someone will find a way to do it."

Knecht made no reply. He didn't know if a reply was even possible. Certainly none that Vonderberge would understand.

When Ranger O Brien brought the news from the Nations, General Schneider was away from the fortress, inspecting the outposts on the forward slope. Knecht received O Brien's report, ordered the man to take some rest, and decided the general should hear the news immediately. He telegraphed Outpost Three that he was coming and rode out.

The crest of Kittatinny Mountain and all the forward slope had been clear-cut the distance of a cannon shot. Beyond that was wilderness. Ridge and valley alternated into the distant north, dense with trees, before rising once more into the Pocono range, where Wyoming had her own fortress line. Legally, the border ran somewhere through the no-man's-land between, but the main armies were entrenched in more easily defended terrain.

Knecht reined in at the crest of the Mountain and looked back. The valley of the Lehigh was checkerboarded with broad farms. Farther away, he could discern the smoke plumes of cities at the canal and rail heads. There was a speck in the air, most likely an airship sailing south.

When he turned, the contrast with the land north of the Mountain was jarring. He must have gazed upon that vista thousands of times over the years. Now, for just an instant, it looked *wrong*. It was said to be fertile land. Certainly, enough blood had manured it. And some said there was coal beneath it. He imagined the land filled with farms, mills, and mines.

At that moment of *frisson* he knew, irrationally, that Kelly had been telling the truth all along. Somewhere the barbed wire was used only to keep the *milch* cows safe.

And the bombs and missles? What if it were a rain of death from the other side of the world that we feared, and not a party of Mohawk bucks out to prove themselves to their elders? A slow explosion, Kelly had said. The inventions would come. Nature kept no secrets. The discoveries would be made and be given to the petty rulers of petty, quarreling states. Men with dreams of conquest, or revenge.

Knecht clucked to his horse and started downslope to the picket line. Give Konrad Schneider that, he thought. His only dream is survival, not conquest. Yet he is desperate; and desperate men do desperate things, not always wise things.

"Hah! Rudi!" General Schneider waved to him when he saw him coming. He was standing on the glacis of the outpost along with the Feldwebel and his men. The general's staff was as large as the platoon stationed there, so the area seemed ludicrously crowded. The general stood in their midst, a portly, barrel-chested man with a large curved pipe clenched firmly in his teeth. He pointed.

"Do you think the field of fire is clear enough and wide enough?"

Knecht tethered his horse and walked to where the general stood. He had never known Schneider to ask an idle question. He decided the real question was whether Vonderberge was reliable. He gave the cleared area careful scrutiny. Not so much as a blade of grass. No force large enough to take the outpost could approach unseen. "It seems adequate," he said.

"Hmph. High praise from you, Rudi." The general sucked on his pipe, staring downslope, imagining ranks of yankees and knickerbockers charging up. "It had better be. But you did not ride out here from Fox Gap only to answer an old man's foolish questions."

"No, General."

Schneider stared at him and the smile died on his face. He put his arm around Knecht's shoulder and led him off to the side. The others eyed them nervously. When scouts and generals spoke in secret the result was often trouble.

"What is it?"

"Friedrich O Brien has returned from the Nations."

"And?"

"The League has voted six to two to join the alliance against us."

They paced together in silence. Then Schneider said, "So, who held out?"

"Huron and Wyandot."

The general nodded. He released Knecht's shoulder and walked off by himself. He turned and gave a hollow laugh. "Well, at least some of our money was well spent. In the old days, it would have been enough. League votes would have had to be unanimous. Do you think they will fight? The two holdouts, I mean."

"Do you think they will split the League, General, over Pennsylvania?"

"Hmph. No. You are right again. They will go with the majority. But, perhaps, the fighting on the west will be less what? Enthusiastic?"

"At least it is too late in the year for an offensive."

"Perhaps, Rudi. But the crops are in. If they think they can knock us out in a lightning war before the snows, they may try anyway. How long can they hold their alliance together? It is unnatural. Yankees and knicks and longhousers side by side? Pfah! It cannot last. No, they must strike while they have Virginia with them, as well. What do you think? A holding action along the Fortress Line while the Lees strike up the Susquehannah and Shenandoah?"

"Will Virginia bleed for New York's gain."

Schneider nodded. "A two-front war, then." He rubbed his hands together briskly. "Well, our strategy is clear. We must stir up problems behind them. In New England or Carolina or Pontiac. And perhaps we have a few surprises of our own."

Knecht looked at him sharply. Schneider was smiling. It was a small smile, but it was a real one, not forced. "What are you talking about?"

Schneider pointed to the wires running from the outpost to the Fortress. "Suppose there were no wires to be cut or tapped. Suppose there were voices in the air, undetectable, sent from anywhere a man could carry an instrument. We would not need messengers or pigeons, either. Think how quickly we could learn of enemy formations and mobilize our own forces to meet them. The right force in the right time and place is worth regiments a mile away and a day late. Or airplanes, darting among the airships with machine guns and bombs. We could carry the fighting all the way to Wilkes Barre and Painted Post."

"Kelly."

"Ja." The general chuckled. "Vonderberge tells me of these gadgets, like radio. Crazy notions. But I wonder. What if it were true? Kelly's waking mind does not remember the details of the sort of, hmph, primitive inventions we could hope to copy. And from your report I suspect he would not help us willingly. Oh, he is friendly enough; but he does not like the military and would not help us prepare for war. Especially a war none of his concern. A problem. So, I seize the moment." He clenched his fist and waved it.

"You pass along the information to Ochsenfuss and ask him to find the details by prying in his unconscious mind."

Schneider looked at him. "You knew?"

"I guessed."

"You never guess. You're offended."

"No."

"You are. But I had to leave you out. You would have cut to the truth too quickly. I knew you. If you found that Kelly was mad, well, no harm done; but I was speculating that he was just what he said he was. If that were the case, I could not allow you to prove it."

"Why not?"

"Ochsenfuss, that old plodder. He will not mesmerize except for medical reasons. If you had proven Kelly was, well, Kelly, our friend the Hexmajor would have bowed out and Kelly's secrets would have remained secret. No, I needed Ochsenfuss's skill at mesmerizing. I needed Vonderberge's enthusiasm for technofiction, so he would know what questions to ask. And, for it to work, I needed Kelly's status to remain ambiguous."

"Then the Hexmajor does not know."

"No. He is our protective plumage. I read his reports and send them to a secret team of scientists that OKP has assembled at Franklin University. Only a few people at OKP know anything. Only I, and now you, know everything."

Knecht grunted. Ochsenfuss *did* know. At least he knew something. His remarks at the officers' club had made that clear.

"Vonderberge said we lack the tools to make the tools to make the things Kelly described."

"Then Vonderberge is shortsighted. Pfah! I am no fool. I don't ask for the sophisticated developments. Those are years ahead. Decades. But the original, basic inventions, those are different. As Kelly described it, they came about in a world much like our own. And, Rudi?"

"*Ja*, Herr General?"

"This morning I received word from Franklin. They have sent telegraphic messages *without wires* between Germantown and Philadelphia. They used a special kind of crystal. The pulses travel through the air itself." He grinned like a child with a new toy.

Knecht wondered how much difference such things would make in the coming war. There wasn't time to make enough of them and learn how to use them. He also remembered what Ochsenfuss had said in the officers' club. Something had to break. The question was what. Or who.

Knecht took a deep breath. "It's over, then. You've learned how to make radio messages. Ochsenfuss can stop treating him."

Schneider would not meet his eyes. "The mesmerization must continue. There are other inventions. We need to know about airframes. The details are sketchy yet. And napalm. And . . ."

"Between Ochsenfuss and Vonderberge, Kelly's personality is being destroyed. He hardly remembers who he is, or which world is real."

"This is war. In war there are casualties. Even innocent ones."

"It is not Kelly's war."

"No. But it is yours."

Knecht's mouth set in a grim line. "*Ja*, Herr General."

"You make it look so easy," said Vonderberge.

"Shh," hissed Knecht. He twisted his probe once more and felt the bolt slide back. "These old-style locks are easy, and I've had much practice." He pulled the storeroom door open and they stepped inside.

"Schneider will know you did it. Who else has your skill with locks?"

Knecht scowled. "Every scout and ranger in the corps. But, yes, Schneider will know it was me."

Vonderberge began searching the shelves. "Does that bother you?"

Knecht shrugged. "I don't know. It should. The general has been . . . like a father to me."

"Here it is," said Vonderberge. He stepped back. Kelly's rucksack in his hands. He looked inside. "Yes, the belt controls are here also. I don't think anyone has touched it. Schneider has the only key."

"Do you suppose it still works?"

Vonderberge's hands clenched around the straps. "It must."

They crossed the parade ground to the brig. It was dark. Knecht felt that he should dart from cover to cover; but that was silly. They were officers and they belonged here. They took salutes from three passing soldiers. Everything was normal.

The night guard in the cell block shook his head sadly when he saw them coming. "In the middle of the night, sir?" he said to Vonderberge. "Hasn't that poor bastard spilled his guts yet? Who is he, anyway?"

"As you said, soldier," Vonderberge answered. "Some poor bastard."

While the guard unlocked the cell door, Vonderberge hefted the ruck-sack, getting a better grip. He stroked the canvas nervously. Knecht could see beads of perspiration on his forehead.

Well, he's risking his career, too, he thought.

"We will never have a better chance, Rudi," Vonderberge whispered. "Kelly was very clear this morning when I told him what we proposed to do. He had already calculated settings several days ago, using his new 'formula.' He only needed to update them. I arranged a diversion to keep Ochsenfuss away from him, so he has not been mesmerized in the meantime. Tomorrow he may relapse into confusion once more."

"As you say," said Knecht shortly. He was not happy about this. For Knecht, his career was his life. He had been army since his teens. A scout, and a good one—perhaps the best. Now it was on the line. A scout observes and listens and pieces things together. He does not initiate action. How many times had he said that over the years? He had said it to Kelly. Why should he break his code now, for a man he hardly knew?

Knecht didn't know. He only knew that it would be worse to leave Kelly where he was. An obligation? Because he brought him here? Because of what they might learn from him?

Perhaps I could have argued Konrad into this, he thought. *And perhaps not. And if not, there would have been a guard on that storeroom door, and restricted access to the prisoner, and so I have to do this by night and by stealth.*

The guard came suddenly to attention. Knecht looked around and saw

Ochsenfuss entering the corridor from the guardroom. Vonderberge, already stepping inside the cell, saw him, too. He grabbed Knecht's shoulder. "Talk to him. Keep him out until it's too late."

Knecht nodded and Vonderberge pulled the door shut. Knecht had a momentary glimpse of Kelly, rising from his cot fully dressed. Then the door closed and Ochsenfuss was at his side. The guard looked at them and pretended to be somewhere else. Knecht wondered what he would say to the Hexmajor that would keep him out of the cell.

"Up late, *Herr Doctor*," he said. *Clever, Rudi. Very clever.*

"Insomnia," was the reply. "A common malady, it seems. You might ask who is *not* up late, whiling away the hours in the guardhouse. Do you have a cigar?"

The request caught Knecht by surprise. Dumbly, he took out his pocket humidor. Ochsenfuss made a great show of selecting one of the cigars inside. Knecht took one also and offered one to the guard, who refused.

"Fire?" Ochsenfuss struck a match for Knect, then lit his own. After a moment or two, he blew a perfect smoke ring. "I had an interesting experience today."

"Oh?" Knecht glanced at the guard, who decided this would be a good time to patrol the outside of the building.

"*Ja*. I had a message from Outpost 10. The farthest one. One of the men was behaving oddly. Confinement mania, perhaps. But when I arrived, no one knew about the message. Or, more precisely, no one *acknowledged* knowing about the message. Odd, don't you think?"

"A hoax." Dimly, through the door, Knecht could hear a low-pitched hum. The floor seemed to be vibrating, ever so slightly. He thought he could detect a faint whiff of ozone in the air. He studied the doctor's face, but saw no sign of awareness.

"Certainly a hoax. That was obvious. But to what purpose? Simply to laugh at the foolish doctor? Perhaps. But perhaps more. I could see but two possibilities, logically. The message was to make me do something or to prevent me from doing something."

Knecht nodded. "That does seem logical." The night air was cool, but he could feel the sweat running down his back, staining his shirt. The humming rose in pitch.

"Logic is a useful tool," Ochsenfuss agreed inanely. "As nearly as I could tell, the only thing the message made me do was to ride down the Mountain and back up. That did not seem to benefit anyone."

"Is there a point to this, *Herr Doctor?*" Knecht felt jumpy. Abruptly, the humming rose sharply in pitch and dropped in volume, sounding oddly like the whistle of a railroad train approaching and receding at the same time. Then it was gone. Knecht suppressed the urge to turn around. He swallowed a sigh of relief.

"What remains?" Ochsenfuss continued. "What was I prevented from doing? Why treating Kelly, of course. And who has been my opponent in the treatment? The Festungskommandant. So, since my return, I have been watching."

Knecht took the cigar from his mouth and stared. "*You* spied on *me?*"

Ochsenfuss laughed. A great bellow. He slapped Knecht's shoulder. "No, I pay you a high compliment. No one could watch you for long without you becoming aware of the fact. A sense shared by all scouts who survive. No, I followed Vonderberge. When you met him at the storeroom, I retired. It was obvious what you intended to do."

Knecht flushed. "And you told no one?"

Ochsenfuss sucked on his cigar. "No. Should I have?" He paused and pointed the stub of his cigar at the cell door. "He's not coming out, you know."

"What? Who?"

"Your friend, Vonderberge. He's not coming out. He's gone."

Knecht turned and stared at the door. "You mean he took the equipment and left Kelly behind?"

"No, no. They left together. If they stayed close, if they hugged, they would both be inside the field."

"Guard!" bellowed Knecht. "Open this door!" The guard came pounding down the corridor. He unlocked the door, and he and Knecht crowded inside. The cell was empty. Knecht saw that Ochsenfuss had not bothered to look. The guard gave a cry of astonishment and ran to fetch the watch-sergeant. Knecht stepped out and looked at the doctor.

The doctor shrugged. "I told you he would reject reality if he could."

"Explain that!" Knecht pointed to the empty cell.

Ochsenfuss blew another smoke ring. "He ran from reality." With a sudden motion, he kicked the cell door. It swung back and banged against the wall. "This is reality," he said harshly. "Vonderberge has fled it. How else can I say it?"

"Obviously, the other worlds are no less real. The evidence is there, now."

"What of it? It is the flight that matters, not the destination. What if the next world fails to please him? Will he reject that reality as well?"

A squad of soldiers came pelting from the guardroom. They pushed past Knecht and Ochsenfuss and crowded into the cell. Their sergeant followed at a more majestic pace.

"How long have you known," Knecht asked Ochsenfuss, "that the other worlds were real?"

Ochsenfuss shrugged. "Long enough." He laughed. "Poor, dull-witted Ochsenfuss! He cannot see a fact if it bit him on the nose." The Hexmajor's lips thinned. "Granted, I am no physical scientist, but what Kelly said went against everything I had ever read or heard. Later, I came to know I was wrong." Another shrug. "Well, we grow too soon old and too late smart. But I ask you, why did Vonderberge believe? He was correct from the beginning, but he believed before he had proof. He believed because he *wanted* to believe. And that, too, is madness."

"And Schneider?"

"Schneider never believed. He was making a bet. Just in case it was true. *He was playing games with my patient!*"

Knecht could see genuine anger now. The first real emotion he had ever seen in the Hexmajor. He saw the general for a moment through the doctor's eyes. It was a side of Konrad he did not care for.

They spoke in an island of calm. Around them soldiers were searching, looking for tunnels. Schneider would be coming soon, Knecht realized. Perhaps it was time to leave, to postpone the inevitable. He and the doctor walked to the front of the guardhouse but they went no farther than the wooden portico facing the parade ground. There was really no point in postponement.

Knecht leaned on the railing, looking out over the parade ground. A squad of soldiers marched past in the dusk: full kit, double-time. Their sergeant barked a cadence at them. Idly, Knecht wondered what infraction they had committed. Across the quadrangle, the Visiting Officers' Quarters were dark.

"So why, after you knew, did you continue to treat him?" He looked over his shoulder at the doctor.

Ochsenfuss waved his hands. The glowing tip of his cigar wove a complex pattern in the dark. "You read his journal. Do you really suppose he has found his way home this time? No, he goes deeper into the forest of time, hopelessly lost. And Vonderberge with him. Six worlds he had visited already and in what? In three of them, he was in danger. The next world may kill him."

"But . . ."

"Tchah! Isn't it obvious? He was driven to try. He had friends, family. His darling Rosa. Left behind forever. He could not bear the thought that he would never, ever see her again. How could he not try? How could he not fail? With me he had a chance. I saw it and I took it. If I could make him accept *this* world as the only reality, forget the other, then he might have adjusted. It was a daring thing to try."

Knecht looked back out at the parade ground. There had been a fourth possibility, after all. A refugee, but one slowly going mad. Lightning bugs flashed in the evening air. "It was daring," he agreed, "and it failed."

"Yes, it failed. His senses worked for me: everything Kelly saw and heard told him this world was real; but in the end there were too many memories. I could not tie them all off. Some would remain, buried under the false ones, disturbing him, surfacing in his dreams, eventually emerging as psychoses. I restored his memories, then. I could do no more to help him, so I made no effort to stop you."

Knecht's mind was a jumble. Every possible action was wrong. Whether Kelly had been the person he claimed to be, or a madman, Schneider had done the wrong thing. Ochsenfuss had been wrong to try and obliterate the man's true memories. As for himself, all he and Vonderberge had accomplished was to turn him out into a trackless jungle. *Oh, we all had our reasons. Schneider wanted defense. Ochsenfuss wanted to heal. Vonderberge wanted escape. And I . . .* Knecht wasn't sure what he had wanted.

"We could have kept him here, without your treatment," he told Ochsenfuss. "So the general could have learned more." Knecht was curious why the doctor had not done that.

As if on cue, the door of the VOQ burst open. Knecht could see Schneider, dressed in pants and undershirt, framed in its light. Schneider strode toward the guardhouse, his face white with rage and astonishment.

Ochsenfuss smiled. "Kelly would have lost what sanity he had left. If we had not given him the way home, we have at least given him hope.

And . . ." He looked in Schneider's direction. "While I am a logical man, I, too, have feelings. Your general thought to make me the fool. So, I made a medical decision in my patient's best interest."

Knecht could not help smiling also. "Perhaps I can buy you a drink tomorrow, in the officers' club. If we are both still in the army by then." His cigar had gone out. He looked at it. "I wonder what world they are in now."

"We will never know," replied Ochsenfuss. "Even if they try to come back and tell us, this world is a twig in an infinite forest. They will never find us again. It will be bad for you, Rudi, if you cannot bear not knowing."

Knecht threw his cigar away. He was a scout. It would be bad for him, not knowing.

ABOUT "THE FOREST OF TIME"

I wrote "The Forest of Time" in airports. My quality-management consulting had me flying so much that year that I personally staved off the bankruptcy of several major air carriers. I also had a lot of otherwise unproductive time on my hands aboard planes and in hotel rooms. Stan Schmidt at *Analog* had been foolish enough to buy one story from me ["Slan Libh," November 1984]. Perhaps, he could be tricked into buying more. There wasn't all that much else to do in a motel room in Paducah,* so I resurrected a yarn I had written in college. Very little besides the maps, some character names, and the basic idea of a hopelessly lost cross-time traveler survived the transition. "The Forest of Time" appeared in *Analog* (June 1987) and was reprinted in Gardner Dozois's *The Year's Best Science Fiction (5th Annual)*. It was my fourth published story, and it made the Hugo ballot.

I had wanted to write a "parallel Pennsylvania" story ever since reading H. Beam Piper's "Gunpowder God" in high school. Growing up in Easton, Pennsylvania, the historical themes were all Revolutionary, so it was only natural that when I thought alternate history, I thought of that era. Sometimes we forget how revolutionary our Revolution was; in many ways, more so than any that followed. How many others have slipped from republicanism to bonapartism and wound up with a Napoleon, a Lenin, or a Khomeini? A *written* constitution, one in which the *people* told the *government* what it was allowed to do? Alone among constitutional states, ours does not *grant* rights to the people. Read the Bill of Rights, especially Amendments Nine and Ten. People *possess* rights under the Natural Law, and the government is forbidden to interfere with them. If you think that that is only a semantic quibble, think again: The "right to privacy" is mentioned nowhere in the Constitution.

---

*You have a dirty mind.

But what if this Union had never happened and North America had filled with squabbling petty states—"as many Nations in North America as there are in Europe," as John Adams once feared? The innumerable tariff and custom barriers would strangle trade and commerce, and with it, the spread of new ideas. Until the Constitution eliminated tariff barriers among the states, little England was the *largest* free trade zone in the world. So I imagined a pre–World War I milieu, full of what Winston Churchill called "pumpernickel principalities."

Speaking of pumpernickel, could Pennsylvania really have become German-speaking? It is home today to Pennsylvaanisch, a Swabian dialect, but in Revolutionary times fully half the colony spoke German. Towns in the Lehigh Valley bear names like Schenkweilersville, and hills are called Swoveberg and Hexenkopf. As late as my grandfather's time, German newspapers in Easton still outnumbered English; and he, himself, bore the unlikely sobriquet of "Dutch" Flynn because of his accent. (His mother was an Ochenfuss.) In the 1930s, German was still a required course at my mother's elementary school, and our parish church had native-born German pastors until after I went off to college. I was raised on "German Hill," where you could toss a rock and hit five Deutschers before you hit an Italian or a Gael. Decouple the Commonwealth from the other English-speaking colonies, throw in some anti-Yankee enmity, and what do *you* think might have happened?

But all this is background. The story is not *about* an alternate Pennsylvania. That is only the setting. My one halfway original notion was that the departure and arrival of a cross-time traveler were themselves events which spawned new parallel worlds, and which therefore changed the "paratime" distances between them. One little slip in the quantum foam and— hey, presto!—you would be lost amid an infinity of worlds. The story was born of the single image of a man unable to find his way home and slowly losing hope and sanity because of it. Like the blind men and the elephant, Vonderberge and the Hexmajor, General Schneider and Rudi Knecht, each found something different in Kelly. Dour, dogged, dutiful Rudi remains one of my favorite characters.

"Great, Sweet Mother," which follows, is another kettle of fish entirely.

Great, Sweet Mother

I didn't really want to be disturbed, but as long as you're here, sit down.
The sand is free; and it's cool and soft at night. You can listen to the breakers with me. There's food in the hamper; help yourself. No, not the steel
one. That's cryogenic. You don't want to snack on what's in there. Yes, that's
right. Those two. Hot dishes are in the red one and cold dishes in the blue.

No, really. Go ahead. I don't mind the company. It's one more experience to top off, and you're probably dying of curiosity.

"   "

Sure, you are. You stopped, didn't you? Can't say I blame you. I must
be a curious sight, sitting out here on the beach in the middle of the night,
with baskets of food and a stack of books. I must be up to something odd,
mustn't I?

Sit and listen. Close your eyes and still your breathing. Hold yourself as
quiet as ever you can.

"   "

Hear it? That soft, rushing sigh? Waves breaking on a midnight beach.
The breakers whisper, don't they? A low, sibilant murmur, as if the world
were slowly breathing in its sleep. Quite restful, really. And at night there
are no gulls or shrieking children to drown it out. Just the ocean's slow
susurration, the voice of a distant crowd. There are spirits in the sea, you
know. What Andersen called "the people under the sea." I think that is why
the wave tips glow at night.

Did you ever wonder what they were saying? The waves, I mean? Did
you ever think that if you listened long enough and listened hard enough,
the voices would come clear?

"   "

Whose voices? Oh, I don't know. Davy Jones. The Little Mermaid. The crew of *Titanic* or the *Thresher.* Sandy. All those people under the sea. It's their chorus the waves whisper as they burst into spray. A thousand distant voices.

"   "

Who is Sandy?
Oh.
Did I mention Sandy?

"   "

Look at how black the sea grows toward the horizon! Black and cold and heavy. So dark you can't see the seam between sea and sky. Homer wrote about the "wine-dark sea," but he never saw the Atlantic. A stern ocean. There's nothing soft or gentle about it. Its islands are few and harsh and rocky. Iceland. The Hebrides. The Falklands. The very names conjure bleak, gray shores lashed with spray. There are no Tahitis out there.

Sandy is . . . a dream, perhaps. A memory. The reason is why I am sitting here in the night on the cool, soft sand, listening to the hissing waves. Sandy is, or was, half my life. Soft curves and hard planes and a smile like a summer's dawn. Strong when strength was called for; gentle when gentle was right. Muscles smooth and supple. Sandy was a swimmer, did I tell you? Sandy loved the sea.

The sea loved Sandy.

"   "

What am I talking about? Sometimes I wonder myself. Do you have time?

Of course, you do. Hiking along the sand at this time of night, you're in no great hurry to be anywhere. And it's probably just as well that someone knows what happened. Later, you can decide if you want to pass it along. There's no one I care to make my explanations to, anyway. Except Sandy; and Sandy will know soon enough. After that, I don't care who knows.

Hand me a sealed plate from the red hamper, would you? Number 127. It's baked chicken breasts à la Russe. Marinated in a paste of sour cream and paprika. And the wine from the blue hamper. Yes, the matching number. The right wine for the right meal. This one is a 1959, a good year for the Moselles, almost as good as '21, though well past its prime, now.

"   "

What else do I have in there? Oh, a little bit of everything, I suppose. Beef, mutton, pork. Vegetables and fruit. Done every way imaginable. Sautéed. Baked. Broiled. Stir-fried. And wines, and juices and sherbets, of course. Everything except sushi. I hate sushi; and I hate sashimi. Ironic, when you stop to think about it.

"   "

Oh, no. Just a taste of each; not a full meal. I'd never get through the list if I forced myself to eat a full meal of each. No, I just wanted the savor. I wanted the smells and the tastes.

"   "

I have my reasons. And, yes, as a matter of fact, I did spend a long time planning this outing.

This cove . . . It was one of our favorites. The cliffs provide a bit of privacy, and they reflect the sound of the waves. A little crescent spit of sand. A "sandy strip," we called it when we went skinny-dipping here. There's a rock out there. You can't see it now, but if you close your eyes and listen, you can hear how the combers dash against it and split apart and wrap around it like lovers after a quarrel. The shape of the sea gives an accent to the waves.

Where to begin . . . It's all a seamless whole; so I'll just grab a thread and start unraveling.

Sandy had two great loves in life. Well, three, I suppose. One was the sea. Those boundless horizons and hidden depths. Waves that come crashing from across half the world, like the messengers of God.

The other was biology.

"   "

Marine biology, of course. I'm surprised you asked.

That was how we met. Doing postdoc at Woods Hole. I was into cetaceans; Sandy was into cephalopods.

Whales and octopi, friend. Whales and octopi. Those secret rulers of the sea.

It was mutual respect, at first. Professional regard. But respect deepened into admiration, and admiration blossomed into love. I've always felt pride in that. That we were friends before we were lovers.

It began with a few touches. Tentative, half-accidental; both of us ready to pull back. Afraid to admit to the trembling thrill those touches triggered. Then, finally, one long, tender night, a discussion of cladistics and gene sequences somehow tumbled into one of hopes and fears, and of aches and longings. I don't remember exactly when our lips first found each other.

Have you ever made love under the water? Have you ever floated in the calm, lazy world beneath the surface and locked your rhythms into the rhythm of the sea? Swathed in the moist, cool, lubricating sea, stroked by the currents and the kelp; the world cast a deep blue-green. Inside and outside and inside-out inside the abiding womb of the planet. What is love between a man and a woman but a desperate attempt to push back into that small, dark ocean where we floated before we were born? The sea is the great, sweet mother of us all. We were born there; tottered out of it like newborns on stiffened fins into a strange and arid realm. We still carry it with us, inside us. Our blood is a saltwater soup in a bag of skin. It's the sea that's real. Only the sea.

"   "

Yes, I suppose I do wax a little mystical at times. I've always bent that way. Archetypes and symbols and resonance. Whenever I read *Moby Dick*—

"   "

Of course, I've read *Moby Dick*. I am a cetologist. It's in that stack of books there. No, the larger stack. Those are the ones I've finished rereading. *Moby Dick* and *Lord Jim* and *Twenty Thousand Leagues Under the Sea* and all of *Hornblower*, naturally. Cousteau. Odysseus wandering across the face of that wine-dark sea of his. But *Huckleberry Finn* is in there, too. And Kipling, and *Angels at the Ritz*, and *The Sign of Four*, *The Witches of Karres*, and *Beggars in Spain*, *The Cowboy and the Cossack*. Every book that ever made me laugh or cry. Or while away an idle hour. Or think, long into the night.

"   "

What's so funny? That I'm sitting on a deserted beach at night, nibbling at gourmet meals, and rereading every book I've ever loved? Can you think of anything more worthwhile?

"   "

Well, yes. Love under the water. There is that.

Sandy and I joined the Human Genome project together. By that time, we were "an item." Neither of us could imagine life without the other. I still can't; even though Sandy is down there and I'm up here. I've thought about it a great deal, ever since Sandy went overboard. That was the night my heart cracked.

Damn.

Oh, damn . . .

I . . .

" "

I'm sorry. I can't help it. When I think about Sandy's face gazing up through the tossing waves . . . That look of utter surprise and utter longing. Then, only a pale underwater shape, sinking farther and farther, growing paler, finally vanishing.

We had kissed one last time. A passionate, longing kiss. A last, tender caress. Then, while Sandy stood at the rail gazing out at the swell, I pushed and . . . Well . . .

" "

No, we hadn't quarreled. Not exactly.

" "

Listen, I don't care if you understand or not. I was minding my own business and you butted in and I've got books to read and meals to taste and I haven't got that much time left. So why don't you keep on going wherever it was you were headed.

No. The hell with it. I don't need to explain anything to anyone.

" "

To myself? Why would I . . . ? Oh, hell. All right. You might as well stick around and hear the rest of it.

Hand me Number 128, would you? It's a Kentucky Hot Brown. No, no wine. Beer with this one.

Thank you. You know, no one outside Kentucky has ever heard of this . . . Just a bite, now. Mmm, yes. Sharp. It's best with a sharp cheese. I've used cheddar.

" "

Go ahead and laugh. But tell me. If there was something you loved, something you cherished; and it was something you knew you could never do again, ever . . . What would you do the night before?

Well I like good food and I like a good book. So . . .

" "

Okay, you tell me. Why do you think I'll never taste good food or read a good book ever again? Why do you think I'm sitting out here on a midnight beach?

"   "

Not even close.

Where was I?

Yes, the Genome Project. That was just after SingerLabs became prime contractor. Watson was long retired and most of the original flush of enthusiasm had passed, but Jessica Burton-Peeler revitalized things.

"   "

Yes, the cure for Huntington's chorea. And the cure for sickle cell anemia two years later. Once the right part of the code was cracked, tyling the nanomachine to repair it was straightforward engineering. SingerLabs made a bundle, of course; but the marketing rights were part of the contract.

But Sandy and I didn't work on that end of the project. We played with the junk.

"   "

Junk genes. Introns. Ninety-nine percent of the human genome doesn't code for anything.

"   "

I know it sounds like a waste. All those nucleotides not doing anything, unread by the body. It's like reading a few meaningful sentences strung through a mishmash of words, phrases, fragments, and random letters. Like those acrostic puzzles where you're supposed to find the words in a grid of letters. You have to read in all directions. Up, down, left, right, diagonal. And the words in any particular sentence don't even have to be consecutive. A gene consists of a mosaic of nucleotides scattered here and there throughout the DNA strand. Somehow, the body reads it. Creates amino acids and all the rest. Don't you find that curious? Don't you find that remarkable? I do.

Think of the way files are stored on computer disks. Files needn't be written to consecutive addresses. There are flags and pointers that let the operating system hopscotch from address to address. When you erase a file, you don't actually erase the information; you only remove the flags. As time goes on, and files are erased, added, expanded, your disk becomes a mishmash of readable address mosaics—the currently saved files—and unreadable ghost bits—remnants of old saves and forgotten files.

"   "

Yes, exactly. It does sound a lot like "junk genes." That's what we thought. Addresses correspond to locations on a DNA strand; genes, to files. The geometry is different, but the concept is the same.

Yet, why should file storage on a computer disk—which humans invented for human convenience from cumulative prior art—why *should* it behave like gene storage on a DNA strand?

I don't know. Maybe it's only a coincidence that we learned to store data and crack the genetic code at the same time. Maybe it's nothing more than enthusiasm imposing the paradigm of one field onto another. Or maybe we have stumbled upon a fundamental truth of the universe?

Our idea was to search through the junk for recognizable gene fragments. Old genes are eventually overwritten by evolution, as Mother Nature recruits unused nucleotides for new purposes. But fragments—perhaps even whole genes—might survive amid the junk. "The shattered ruins of ancient genomes," I called them.

"   "

No, it wasn't easy. But a journey of a thousand miles begins with a single stumble. . . .

I suppose it would have made more sense to look for apelike genes. We share 99 percent of our genetic information with the chimps, you know. But, we were marine biologists; we knew that territory. So, we looked for leftover gene fragments from the days when we lived under the sea. Genes we shared with whales and octopi and the like. Especially the whales; because they lived on the land for a while; then they went home, to their great, sweet mother.

We didn't have much hope of finding anything, really. It was purely blue sky. The sort of wild speculation that Dr. Peeler encourages. After hundreds of millions of years of evolutionary overwrites, we'd be lucky if there was anything left of those ancient, marine genomes other than a few useless fragments, impossible to reconstruct. Impossible even to recognize.

Talk about your luck.

We did find a few recognizable gene fragments. Sandy recognized them. They coded for certain details of fine development and gill structure. Similar to, but not quite like, analogous genes in familiar marine species. You see, different species don't always use the same nucleotides at the same addresses to achieve the same results. Mother Nature is an opportunist. She uses whatever materials are available. So, in one species a nucleotide is recruited into one gene; in another species, into a different gene. Think how many different ways you could paraphrase the assembly instructions for a bicycle. Imagine trying to do it using only the words you have left over from other, discontinued instruction manuals. Different words; same results.

What made Sandy's discovery so exciting was two things. First, it gave us a hint of the kind of creature we once were.

"   "

No, not fishes. We were never fishes. Today's fish have as many years of evolution under their belts as we do. But, Once Upon a Time, we were something very much like fish. Something that doesn't exist anymore; something that may never have left a fossil for us to find. Something we have no name for.

Don't you feel it? Don't you feel the slightest shiver? This wasn't a glimpse of dead bones—of the petrified casts of dead bones—but a glimpse of an ancient, living world. Like finding the scrap of an old, old photograph in the bottom of your trunk.

"   "

The second reason?

I hate whalers. I hate them with a passion. I work with whales. I know them; and I love them. Those giant, gentle, humming beasts with their sad smiles. Singing through the oceans; nursing their children; dancing and playing in our bays and inlets. They shoot them with giant, explosive arrows. Arrows with barbs, so the more you pull against them, the more they dig into your body. Then, after you've exhausted yourself in hopeless escape, they shred you into strips for rich Japanese businessmen to nibble on, and boil down your fat for lotions, and—

Like I said, I hate them. Let them eat cow. A cow's destiny is to lie between two buns. It's what they were born for. A whale's destiny is to swim free and plumb the ocean depths. So—

"   "

What have whales to do with our discovery?

Did you ever wonder why babies are sometimes born with webbed fingers and toes?

Sometimes, the body runs one of those old, old programs.

Carry the computer analogy a step further. What if we could restore the markers to those fossil genes? Could we reactivate them, perhaps? The body sometimes does it by accident, by misreading a flag. Couldn't we do it on purpose? I guess in the backs of our minds was the notion of doing the genetic equivalent of a "hard drive recover." If only enough of the older genomes have survived overwriting . . . If only we could tyle a nanomachine . . . Think about it. Doesn't it excite you? No species need ever be "endangered" again.

" "

How? Reassemble the lost genome from the fragments surviving in "cousin" species. Our very own introns may contain most of the working blueprints for Neanderthalers.

And the whales . . .

Whales are mammals, like us. Our common ancestor is more recent than those ancient, maritime genes Sandy and I found, so similar fragments are almost surely buried in the whale genome, too. If we could infect the whales with the right nannies, they could grow gills. They would never need to surface, never need to blow. They could stay in the ocean depths, safe from the harpoons.

" "

No, they wouldn't be whales anymore. But they would *be*.

It could work. A genius could make it work. A genius could see how scattered nucleotides locked together, like a Chinese puzzle. A genius could perceive which nucleotides in the ghost gene were missing. Envision the whole from the fragment in hand. Ninety-nine percent of the genome is junk, so there's plenty of material on hand that the body doesn't need, material that could be recruited to flesh out the missing parts. A genius could set the flags to restore continuity so the body's operating system could read the fragments as a single gene.

I'm a genius, did I tell you? I'm a genius. So was Sandy. Genius times genius is genius squared.

Sometimes, I wish we hadn't been. Sometimes, I wish we had been as dull as ditch water. Other times . . . Other times . . . I don't know. Sandy and I both loved the sea. Loved the waves and the whales and the coral and the kelp. So maybe there was a rightness to what happened. A wyrd.

Even genius can grow careless. Even Neptune nods.

We were trying to tailor water-rabbits. To discover if we could reactivate the ancient genes in another mammal. Gill-bunnies, we called them. . . .

" "

No, it's not horrible. We were trying to save the whales, remember? And if, in the process, a few bunny rabbits learned how to breathe underwater, it was no harm to them.

We've been bio-engineering species for millennia. Do you think that sheep are natural? Do you think the Holstein cow existed in nature? How many different dogs have we created? Evolution gave maize three or four puny seeds; the Olmecs gave it row after row of great, juicy, golden kernels.

We did it the old-fashioned way, by patient breeding and hybridization, and it took generations; but we did it. We did it.

We do things much faster now.

It was an accident. The syringe was wrong way around in the tray, and Sandy reached without looking and was pricked on the hand.

At first, we thought that everything was okay, that not enough nannies had been injected to set up a self-sustaining population.

But, Sancta Maria, I do good work.

We took blood samples every day; and every day, they showed the nanny population growing, building strength, splicing new instructions into the cell nuclei. Then, as old cells died and new cells grew, they grew . . . differently.

I tried tyling new nanomachines, ones that could counteract those at work in Sandy's body. But there was not enough time. Not enough time.

Sandy spent more and more time here, by the breast of the sea. Sitting in the sand, facing out toward the deep; back turned against the land, listening to the waves. There was a longing growing inside, something that Swinburne had sensed when he wrote:

> *I will go back to the great, sweet mother.*
> *Mother and lover of men, the sea.*

Symptoms began to appear. Webbing between fingers and toes. Gill slits appeared and deepened on the lower chest. Sandy began to have trouble breathing—the instincts were all wrong. I filled the bathtub with water. Sandy could sit in it, keep the gills wet and still work.

It was nearly fatal. Fluoridation in the water . . .

We both knew how it would end. Dear Lord, when I think how calmly Sandy took it all. Maybe the lure was overpowering even then. Sandy had always loved the sea. One day, the song of the Lorelei became too strong. We rented a sailboat, and skimmed out beyond the gulls and the breakers to where the sea gently rocked us and the swells danced in the sun.

At the very end, Sandy hesitated, clung to me. Eros can sing as loud as Lorelei. So I had to push.

The gills worked fine. It's all a matter of learning new reflexes, of not breathing through the nose or mouth. Sandy surfaced after a while, treading water effortlessly, gazing at me with longing eyes. Then . . . Then, the ocean won. I stood at the railing for an hour afterward, gazing into the depths. Then, when it was growing dark and the wind began to turn, I tacked back to shore.

Have you ever lost your lover to another? To a great, good friend that you've known all your life? For a long time, I didn't know whether I hated the sea or not. I wonder what it's like down there in the octopus's garden, down in Fiddler's Green. Sandy has to contend with barracudas and sharks. Drift nets. God, I hope the dolphins help. Dolphins have always helped. They say they were once the mermen and mermaids of legend, that they used to be part human back in the Age of Magic.

"   "

Still alive? Yes, I think so. There have been reports. Sightings. Some cod fishers out of Reykjavik dragging their nets off the cold coast of Greenland. An oil tanker west of the Azores. A cruise ship nearing Aruba. Wild reports. No one believes them. No one credits them but me. Maybe you can tell them after I've gone.

"   "

Yes, of course, I'm going, too. Did you think I was sitting here mourning my loss? Did you think I was going to kill myself? No, not while Sandy and I can still be together, under the waves. What do you suppose is in that cryogenic cooler? What do you think these welts are on my abdomen?

No, go ahead and look. By tomorrow morning, when the sun crests the waves, they'll be full-fledged gills.

"   "

Yes, it is a big ocean. But we'll find each other. I'll have a whale sing across the sea. I'll sweep the Gulf Stream from Carib to the Isles. And someday . . . Someday . . . Sandy knows I'll come. We'll ride the currents together and dance among the seaweed and kelp. We'll make love under the waves until age or shark does for us.

I'll miss the books, though. Paper wouldn't last a minute down there. And the food . . . You can't cook in Fiddler's Green, and there's no sub-tlety of taste or smell, not for us humans—everything will smack of brine. Not much conversation, unless we broach and fill our shriveled lungs with air again. Nor even much sound—just squeaks and whistles and clicks, and the distant, mournful songs of the humpbacks.

Hand me number 129, would you? I want to remember the tastes. I want to remember the smells. From now on, it will be raw fish we snatch for ourselves from passing schools.

And, dear God, I do hate sushi.

ABOUT "GREAT, SWEET MOTHER"

". . . Mother" is one of the few stories I've written in which I consciously Tried To Do Something stylistically. Usually, I just start writing and wait to see what happens. Sometimes What Happens isn't too awful, so I slap on a coat of paint, varnish it, and ship it off to someone who may be deranged enough to send money by return mail.

I heard Terry Bisson read "They're Made Out of Meat" at the Barnes and Noble "superstore" in Paramus, New Jersey. Like some other stories he has written, ". . . Meat" was all dialogue, no narrative. It was like a Dare.

Push the idea a little farther. How about *half* a dialogue? Since, in current literary slang, "texts speak to us," the readers could supply the unspoken parts. If somewhere along the way your eyebrows went up because the text responded to a question in your head, then I was modestly successful.

The other stylistic quirk is gender. Nowhere in the story is the gender of Sandy or the narrator specified.

What do you mean, you didn't notice? It wasn't easy writing a story without third person pronouns. The least you could have done was notice the omission.

I would be interested to know how many of you thought the narrator was male and how many, female; and ditto for Sandy. Among those who read or heard the story before publication, guesses split about fifty-fifty, and I did not notice any bias distinguishing male from female readers.

And another thing, what makes you think that the narrator and Sandy are heterosexual . . . ?

No, I wasn't trying to Make a Statement. I just wanted the story to be free of all gender stereotypes. If you saw any there, you put them there yourself.

Or, God forbid, a copy editor . . .

The "fossil genes" business comes from Richard Dawkins's *The Blind Watchmaker*. Reading such nontechnical science books is a good way to troll for Ideas. (Ideas are a dime a dozen. Turning them into Stories is some-thing else.) When I read *The Blind Watchmaker* I was struck by the anal-ogy between file storage on disc and gene storage on helix and Dawkins's notion that "fossil genes" could be "reactivated." Might we be able to do a "hard drive recover" on our genes? About a year later, when I was trying to imagine what that "semi-dialogue" story might concern, the fossil gene angle came to mind.

For those who are interested, ". . . Mother" fits into the *Nanotech Chron-icles* story mosaic, between the time of "Remember'd Kisses" and that of "Werehouse." At Boskone a few years ago, I discovered to my amazement that there were actually people in this world trying to unearth the con-nections among my stories. I'm flattered, folks. And I don't think you've found them all, yet.

On the High Frontier

1. I see the wrong end of Big Jim's phaser.

It was in the Luckenback Wheel, falling around the sun behind Uranus, where I first heard tell of Slim Wittelsbach and his harebrained scheme to drive a thousand jellybellies into the sun.

I was having myself a drink in Hard-luck Hashimoto's bar, a dead-head dive in the butt end of the Number Three spoke. The clientele there was never too savory, but the spin gravity was just this side of tolerable and Hard-luck never watered the drinks enough so you'd notice. I was standing there minding my own business and thinking harm to no man when another spacer give me the elbow in the ribs, real deliberate-like; and so naturally I spilled my drink. In his face. Real deliberate-like.

Well, right off, I seen I made a mistake. It was Big Jim Callaghan; and he already had the drop on me. He was grinning ear to ear, and the aperture crystal on his phaser looked to be as big as the Ganymede light cannon. I kept my hand well clear of my own holster. I'm fast, mighty fast; but there ain't no one faster than the speed of light.

"Jim," says I with a nod, by way of sociable greeting.

"Ollie," he replies, "you are one clumsy spacehand. Give me one good reason why I shouldn't burn you down right here."

Now, offhand I could think of three or four good reasons; but I held my peace figuring Big Jim wasn't really all that interested.

Oliver Wendell Hatch is my handle. Mostly I go by Hatch, sometimes Dell; but somewhere or other Big Jim had found out how much I hated my front name and he never missed a chance to "Ollie" me. Which just goes to show he wasn't near as smart as he thought he was. If he wanted to goad me into fighting, he should have tried "Wendy."

I looked around that barroom with tolerable interest. A man's fights are his own, but I wouldn't have minded one bit if someone wanted to borrow a piece of this one. Share and share alike, my Pa always said. But the other spacers in the bar seemed terrible interested in their drinks or in their poker games or in being somewhere else. Some had hid themselves under their tables; and one or two were taking bets. I wondered what odds they was giving. Long ones, I suppose. I didn't blame them none for minding their own business. Big Jim was nasty, but he was the *nicest* of the three Callaghans. Sergei and Konrad would not think kindly on anyone who interfered with their baby brother's fun.

There was one fellow, a thin, olive-skinned stranger in the corner, studying us with narrowed eyes. He wore a red-and-white-striped skinsuit that I didn't recognize, wet with condensation, like he'd just orbited in from the Big Empty. He was toying with a set of balls and watching with what I took to be a professional interest.

Hard-luck himself was just a-waiting. Violence weren't new to him. He'd been in twenty, maybe thirty fights outlawing down to the Trojans back in the nineties with nary a scratch to show for it. But since he retired and opened his bar, he's lost three fingers and his right ear, all as a bystander. There wasn't a fight took place anywhere in Luckenback that didn't wing him somehow. Like they say, Hard-luck.

Big Jim was trying to rile me up by talking about my family; but it didn't bother me none, not being hot-tempered like my brother Sheridan. And truth-to-tell, my sister Felicity *did* have some mighty peculiar ways about her. Big Jim was grinning and laughing. He was having himself a powerful lot of fun. Me, I've had better times.

Pretty soon, though, Big Jim would realize that I wasn't about to draw to a stacked deck, say the hell with it, and burn me down anyway; so I fell to considering. The idea was to get him to point his phaser somewheres other than at my belly button. But it wouldn't do to point behind him and say, "Looky there!" Big Jim had his faults, but dumb wasn't one of them. If he thought I wanted him to look to the side, he'd never have done it. But let him think I didn't want nothing of the sort, and he'd just kind of naturally get curious. So I let my eyes drift ever so slightly over his right shoulder, my intention being to make him think I seen something I didn't want him to see.

Wouldn't you know it. I *did* see something I didn't want him to see. I jerked my attention back to Big Jim's ugly face just as the olive-skinned stranger whupped his arm around and let fly. Old Jim, he scowled and turned his head to the right just a little bit.

And that was enough.

I given my *kiai* yell and pivoted into a *mawashi-geri* kick to Big Jim's gun arm just as the stranger's bola wrapped itself around his neck. The phaser discharged, but missed me by an easy centimeter. I grabbed his gun arm and twisted and the phaser dropped to the deck, followed a moment or two later by Big Jim himself, choking and clawing at the bola. Everyone in the place, Big Jim excepted, let out a deep breath.

The man in the red-and-white come over to the bar. He wore a pencil-thin moustache and, underneath it, one of those quiet smiles you see on folks who have just accomplished a difficult task. I nodded to him. "That was mighty fine rope work, stranger. I sure would admire to buy you a beer."

He made light of it. "It was not the most difficult cast I have ever made, senhor. My target was in the same acceleration frame as I was; and he was not even moving. A slight correction for the Coriolis and . . ." A polite shrug of dismissal. "It was not a fair fight."

I wasn't sure which part he meant; but I wasn't about to waste no tears on Big Jim Callaghan. He'd come looking for trouble and he found it. Not many men achieve their goals so quickly.

Hard-luck brought two beers over. He was limping slightly, for Big Jim's light pulse had ricocheted off'n a mirror and caught him in the left buttock. For himself, Hard-luck would probably not have a mirror in the whole place, but most spacehands have a hankering to know who's behind them.

The stranger introduced himself. "I am Dom José Fernando da Silva Rodriguez y Yamamato, from Alto São Paulo." He bowed slightly, equal to equal, and offered me his card. I took it, using only one hand, and glanced at it, as politeness required. Strictly speaking, I should have used both hands, but I never did have a good sense of *wabi*, and I never like to have both my hands occupied anyway.

"Mighty proud to make your acquaintance, senhor Rodriguez-san." I handed him my own card, completing the *meishi* ceremony.

Rodriguez studied my card and his smile broadened. "*O senhor* Hatch! Such good fortune. You have ramrodded jellybellies, I have heard. For Stan Mitsui up in Mim's Reach."

"Off and on," I admitted.

"And later, you were segundo for Mercedes Nakamura-Jones. She spoke highly of you."

"You seem to know a lot about me, senhor."

"Enough to know you may be the sort of man we seek."

Now, when a fellow tells you that, it's always a sure sign of trouble, so I should've known better. But I was curious and full of good humor due to not being dead; and besides, it don't hurt none to be polite. "So, what's the job?" I asked, and took a long pull of my drink.

He leaned close and whispered. "We propose to take a herd of jellybellies down to the Saturn ringhead."

I choked and damn near sprayed him with the beer. "Drive critters to Saturn?" I said. "That's plumb loco! Why, the solar wind'll tear them apart." In those days no one had ever taken critters farther down than trans-Neptune.

"Quiet, please," José said between clenched teeth. His eyes darted around the barroom. Then he took me by the elbow and steered me into a private booth. "Cloud has men everywhere," he said when he had pulled the privacy shield and settled into the seat across from me. "I may have been followed here."

"Cloud?" I said leaning closer and dropping my voice, as folks generally did when Cloud's name come up. "Cloud is in on this?" Henri Cloud owned the Starwheel spread, up trans-Pluto way. He ran the biggest herd of jellybellies this side of Aries and was a man to walk carefully around.

"No, senhor. But if Cloud knew what we were attempting, he would do his best to stop us. My employer is *o professor* Federico 'Slim' Wittelsbach." José sat a little taller at the name. "He who discovered the method of producing stardust from jellybellies."

Stardust. Just say the word in any saloon or teahouse on the high frontier and heads would turn and eyes would narrow with thoughts of riches. Stardust did something—don't ask me what —that slowed down aging. Taken regular, a body need never die; leastwise of old age, which I didn't expect to apply in my case. It was the elixir of immortality. It tasted pure awful; but I never heard no one complain.

"Slim Wittelsbach," I said, running the name around the inside of my mouth. I washed it down with a beer. "Never heard of him," I decided. Leastwise, his name was not in my ship's computer, which I had accessed through my skull implant and tongue switch. "And besides, it was Cloud who come up with the stardust."

"As most people have been led to believe," José murmured. "Cloud and the professor were once partners. Senhor Wittelsbach-sama made the discovery; but Cloud made the riches. You understand how it is with some men."

José filled me in. It often happens that a man real smart in some ways is a damn fool in others; and the professor had been a fool in his choice of partners. Cloud was a sharp operator. He could gut a man faster with a piece of legal paper than most others could with a phaser. Wittelsbach had gone to Cloud for his seed money, but before he knew it, he was on the outside looking in. And no spacehand likes to be on the outside looking in. "So, your professor sees a chance to even the score," I guessed. Real shrewd guesser, that's me.

"*Sim,*" said José. "The professor has been quietly breeding wind-resistant critters on his own ranchero. A strain that may withstand the rigors of the seventh orbit. As you know, the ringhead is nearing Saturn. If we can establish a herd and a processing plant there, we can ship stardust by ion train anywhere in the Inner System. I am sure you see the financial advantages of such a move."

That José was a smooth one; I give him that. Most of the herds run out cis-Pluto way, where the orbits are powerful slow. So, a lot of times a customer's habitat would be behind the sun; and the ranchers either had to wait so the shipment could rendezvous at conjunction—and waiting cost them bank money; or they would try shipping to quadrature or even opposition, which was tricky and used up a lot of ΔV. Either way, it was expensive. But down in the Inner System, the ion trains ran through the boosters on a regular schedule. A ranch set up near a ring station could ship anywhere, anytime—and undercut everyone's prices, Cloud included.

Cloud would be unhappy.

José give me the eye. "Well?" he says. "What do you say to my proposition?"

I snorted. "It is the craziest dang notion I ever did hear. The High System is wild country, full of Oort storms, hawkingholes, and anhydrous deserts. No one's ever taken a herd through it. And a critter's instincts is all against going down-System. For which I can't say I blame them, seeing as how the flux density would kill 'em. They'd panic for sure, spread their wings, and stampede up-System with the wind at their backs. I'd say the odds in favor of pulling off your drive are mighty low, and once Cloud cottons on they'll drop down a black hole."

"It will take a special breed of hand to keep them headed nose down," José agreed. "Men with the bark on them."

I shook my head. The professor was fixing to pull a fast one on the most powerful man in the High System by driving a thousand critters where they did not want to go. Hell, a spacer would have to be plumb crazy to sign on for a drive like that. I was right flattered he'd thought of me.

I opened the privacy shield just in time to see two of Hard-luck's boys dragging Big Jim off to the recycler. Seeing as how Jim had no more need for it, José retrieved his bola. I watched the body out of sight. We all die someday; only Big Jim had had the rare privilege of picking the day himself. There wasn't anyone would miss him.

Excepting only his two brothers.

Thinking on them two made me suddenly wishful of being elsewhere.

I considered it some; and, you know, next to the thought of those Callaghans a-gunning for me, driving a thousand giant space-dwelling ameboids halfway across the Solar System was looking like a right fine idea.

2. I torch out of Luckenback with unseemly haste.

José and me split up when we reached the Hub. The way I figured it, them Callaghans would be looking for two spacers traveling together, so our chances would be better if we orbited separately. José agreed and give me a chiplet with the professor's orbital parameters and we agreed to rendezvous there.

Then I grabbed hold of the tow cable and rode it out along the north hitching pole. Them hitching poles was quite a sight. The tubes ran for miles out either end of Luckenback Hub, but were decoupled from its rotation. Most spacers berthed their cyberships there rather than park them in the livery dock. A body never knew when he might need to leave town in a hurry.

Like now.

When I was close enough to my slot, I tongued my implant and hollered for Belle. "Light the torch," I said. "We're cutting loose!"

"What's wrong, Hatch?" Belle transmitted back. "Someone's husband finally catch you?"

"No joking, Belle. There'll be a pair of Callaghans after me too soon for liking. And that's a pair I'd not like to draw to." Not that anyone in the bar had anything against me personal, but by now someone had surely called Big Jim's kin. For the entertainment value, if for nothing else.

"A pair is one Callaghan less than I remember," she said.

"You're a lightning calculator, Belle."

"Aren't I just. They didn't wire my brain into all these circuits for nothing. Tell me, turning three Callaghans into two is a tricky bit of arithmetic. Did you perform the subtraction yourself?"

"No, but I helped out some."

I let go the tow cable and momentum carried me toward the lock. Belle popped the hatch on cue, and I sailed through the umbilical right into her couch. I seen her readouts was all green, but I never expected less. Belle is a good ship. We'd been through tight times together more than once.

In a peculiar way, she and I were mirror images of each other. I had a computer link implanted in my brain, while Belle was a brain implanted in a computer. Belle never spoke of what it was that made her have the ultimate transplant. That was The Subject We Don't Discuss. For some folks it was body damage so bad that not even nanomachines could repair it; for others it was the adventure of being "wired-in." Belle never said, and I wasn't one to pry. She'd tell me when she was good and ready. Meanwhile, she was the best cybership I'd ever teamed with.

I was already wearing my skinsuit, so as soon as I was buckled in, Belle dropped the magnetic tether, blew the umbilical, and hit the jets. We must have torched out of Luckenback at three gees. Leastwise, that's what my ribs told my backbone. It was a killing pace, and neither Belle nor I could stand it for long, but what I craved most just then was kilometers.

That was my good-bye to Luckenback Wheel and the whole Circum-Uranian Republic. I'd had some good times there and was right sorrowful to see it in my aft viewscreen. But I was tolerably fond of my own skin as well, and meant to keep it with no more holes in it than I'd started out with.

After a few minutes of boost, Belle cut the torch and we coasted through Hydrogen Flats, a cluster of cheap habbies balanced on Uranus's forward libration point. "Where to now?" she asked.

I fed José's chiplet into her memory and let her think about how to get to the professor's spread. A spacehand setting out into the Big Empty must give it careful thought. Madeira's constant boost torch put the Solar System within reach, but it ate hydrogen at a prodigious rate. Best to travel at a moderate boost and conserve hydrogen. Many a hand has come to grief with his ship tuckered out megaklicks from the nearest gas cloud. The Big Empty is mighty big and mighty empty; and a spacer lost or a ship wind-blown can be powerful hard to find, bright-colored skinsuit and beacon or no. For the same reason, a spacer must also be aware of where the nearest air and water could be found and lay orbits so they was never too many ΔV's off.

Belle laid out our orbits, but I put my own mind to it as well, casting our horoscope by downlinking through Belle's astrogation sensor array. A good spacer always keeps the zodiac to hand, lest he become lost; and astrology is something he just naturally soaks up with his mother's milk. We were starting out near the forward edge of Virgo, with Earth just east of the sun and Saturn entering Pisces. The professor's habbie was in Sagittarius, in cis-Pluto. Call it, oh, forty-five hundred megaklicks, straight trig. Belle could maintain a constant boost of one deci-gee almost indefinitely without tiring, provided she could drink enough hydrogen along the way. Since we'd been ballistically coupled with Uranus, we had a starting velocity of 6.8 kisses. Add a little Kentucky windage and I figured it to be a seven-week trip. By the time I reached the professor's spread, Earth would be in conjunction and, from that angle, Saturn would be in Aries.

Seven weeks was plenty of time to bone up on jellybellies. I told Belle to get me a library link; then I sat back and waited. The main library was in Jovian orbit, but there was relays scattered all around the High System. According to the ephemeris, the nearest one was Nyeschastye Light, a navigation and booster laser for lightjammers. Belle would find the shortest relay path through the system; but even if the DataBank was in conjunction, I'd have to wait four hours for a reply, so I selected a *koan* at random and meditated upon it. I had no *roshi*, of course, but what better place for *za-zen* than the Big Empty?

When the link was finally established, my mind was in a proper state of readiness, having been emptied of conscious thought. The files could download holographically. There are some spacers can't handle their implants that way. They bring the data in linearly, like they was being read to. That's powerful slow. Pa, he taught us the *zen* way. In his younger days, he'd spent time back down to the Inner System, and he'd picked up some of their ways. *Matsushita-Bandierantes* and the *keidanren* no longer dominate space like in colonial days, but many of the old Nippo-Brazilian customs still lingered on the frontier.

Pa had always insisted that his kids be literate, so he taught us how to read, write, cipher, and hack. I knew some damn fine spacers couldn't do none of that, but I had it in me to better myself in life. Down-System, it mattered a lot if you was born into the right families and had the right manners; but up here there was no limit to what anyone could make of hisself.

When the jellybelly file dumped into my head, I "remembered" things I'd thought I'd forgotten; plus I learned a sight that was new. Which weren't no surprise. Quantum-biologists are always discovering new things about those critters. I mean, what *can't* you learn about something that's part jellyfish, part whale, part tent caterpillar, and part radio set; and not one bit like any of them? Scientists were still arguing about how to classify them. Me, I just called them critters, when I wasn't calling them a damn sight worse.

It used to be folks thought chemical reactions couldn't take place in open space. There wouldn't be enough energy to move the molecules over the activation barrier. But even back in the twentieth century, a Russ named Vitaly Goldansky showed that quantum tunneling through the energy barriers between potential wells would allow chemical reactions to proceed even in the cold of outer space. Some folks even synthesized formaldehyde and other long chain molecules at 4° Kelvin, which showed that organic compounds, maybe even life, could evolve in the Big Empty.

Still, space life took most everybody by surprise; though the biggest surprise of all was that it was related to Earth life. At some deep down level, men and ferns and jellybellies was kin. Of course, compared to a jellybelly, men and ferns are practically twins. The pan-Spermians had always held that life on Earth (and, later, on Titan) had been seeded from space, and it sure looked like they'd had the straight skinny all along. Somewhere down the line a few hardy spores must have made it through the Inner System and dropped into the Earth's chemical soup, precipitating all kinds of stuff, like dinosaurs, roses, wombats, and pretty girls.

However it happened, the High-up System, where the solar wind is weak and space is near flat, was full of things that acted like plants and things that acted like plant-eaters, just a-drifting abouts in the Big Empty. It stood to reason that there must be predators, too. There weren't near as many jellybellies as there ought to have been, so something must be harvesting them. No one had ever seen a "space-wolf," but then no one has seen everything. And there *were* stories that made the rounds whenever spacers gathered. About things heard and not quite seen. About spacers who had shown up missing.

Some folks called those tales foolish and laughed at them; but there were others as said nothing, and they didn't laugh at all. For myself, I kept an open mind, a wary eye, and a fully charged phaser, that being a good idea in any case.

Now the jellybelly is a somewhat comical critter, though in its native habitat it could be darned majestic. The two are not so different. It was shaped like an enormous jellyfish, but it wasn't multicellular. On the other hand, it wasn't exactly single-celled, neither. There was something topologically peculiar about it, something to do with the quantum dimensions of Nagy's hypospace. So, the scientists, they called it semicellular, just like they knew what that meant. Me, I only knew what scraps of quantum biology and hypospace physics I picked up in saloons from other spacehands. My implant could give me plenty of data, straight from the Jovian DataBank if I put my mind to it; but understanding was quite another matter.

Jellybellies grazed mostly on skycrop, the plantlike things that drifted about the High System. One feller told me skycrop was like plankton in the seas of Earth and the jellybellies was like whales, which may be true for all I know. But critters could feed right off the hydrogen, too, which my implant tells me whales cannot. The nutrients are carried by supercooled helium, which crawls like a kind of living blood around the outside of the critter's membrane and fluoresces all over the spectrum. A downright eerie sight to behold.

Jellybellies moved by expelling digestive gasses. They traveled in herds and called to each other on radio frequencies, singing songs somewhat like Titanian ice flowers, or those Terran whales I heard tell of. When they moved, they lined up along each other's magnetic fields. If you could get the lead bull headed the way you wanted, the rest would generally follow. Critters wasn't very smart, ranking in intelligence somewhere between a turnip and an overripe melon; but, hell, I'd known a few people here and there who'd gotten by on less.

If you can imagine hundreds of neon jellyfish farting through space with their noses stuck up each other's arse, playing their favorite tunes to each other on the radio, you can see how a spacer riding herd might develop a peculiar outlook on life.

3. I am cut off at the pass.

Meanwhile, I'd been keeping a sharp lookout on our backtrail. I didn't think for one minute that those Callaghans would give up. Say what you will about them—and I've said plenty—they took care of their own. But, after a couple days with no sign of pursuit, even with my sensors at maximum gain, my mind was resting somewhat easier.

Belle and I decided we would need water before we reached the professor's habbie. Torching out of Luckenback, we had used up a lot of mass, and, even though Belle's hydroponics produced some water and we recycled all of it, there was always losses, and the levels in the tanks were giving me concern. Besides, a spacer is always mindful of what his drinking water is recycled from; so the desire to freshen our stock was in me, and I commenced to give thought as to how I might do that.

We were passing near a stonebuster's habbie, but we did not slow down nor call out, since I was not wishful of drawing attention. What a man notices, he may repeat to others, even unwittingly. Anyway, a stonebuster would have little water to spare, even if his ballistic sling could match my orbit and speed. He was growing wheat and would need every drop of ice he could mine from his asteroid. He had upgraded his rock with a hawkinghole, which gave him enough gravity to hold an atmosphere; and sunlight he collected with a lens-and-mirror assembly ballistically coupled to his habbie. A hard life and a lonely one; and one that didn't need me dropping in to make it harder.

However, finding water was not that difficult. There was plenty of ice locked up here and there around the system. The trick was knowing where to look.

When spacers get together in saloons or teahouses, they naturally talk about the places they've been and the people they've seen. Where they'd found water ice or hawkingholes; or who was building a reputation as a rough man. The rest of us would be of a mind to listen and remember, since a body never knew when such knowledge would make the difference between life and death. Maybe computer implants didn't help us think better, but they sure did a wonder for the memory. Spacers who had never been there could describe the orbits of Mendoza's Moonlet and Deadman's Hole or say where the water-ice fields lay on Charon; and could detail down to the last scar the face of Toshiro ten Boom, the outlaw-turned-lawman who was now town marshal in Tokkuri Kosho Wheel.

So I knew there was four asteroids and two cometheads holding water-ice that lay near our present orbit. Two of them we could access without a major alteration of vectors. I asked Belle her opinion.

"Threadneedle Comethead," she told me, with even less delay than usual for her. "It has the lowest ΔV."

Now, I did wonder a might at that. Threadneedle had a bad reputation. It was part of a ballistic triplet with two black microholes that were slowly consuming it . . . plus anything else that got too close. A dang sight more spacers had gone up that pass than ever come down. "The gravity cliffs there are awful steep," I reminded her, as if, being a computer, she needed reminding. "I wouldn't want to fall down a hole."

It used to be they called microholes "cold, dark matter," before they learned better. Microholes didn't evaporate like they was supposed to because most of their structure was curled up in Nagy hypospace, underneath the floorboards of the universe. The Nagyists say that microholes are scattered randomly through hypospace, like the Big Bang says they ought to be, but they still form galaxies and clusters and such-like because we can only see them "edge-on." Like if you splatter a passel of dots on a sheet of paper, then look at the paper from the edge, the dots will blend into a line. Well, the edge is our space-time, and the rest of the paper is hypospace.

Leastwise, that's how Belle once explained it to me. There was some spacers who said that if'n you went down one hole, you would just pop out another somewheres else in the universe. I plan to wait for one of them folks to come back and tell me which one, which ain't happened yet.

Belle told me her plan. "It's simple, 'Dell. We come up from the west, behind Threadneedle, and follow the pass, where the three gravitational fields balance. That takes us directly over the north face of the comet-head — or under the south, if you like. We blow off a chunk and scoop it up without slowing down, then go straight out the spinward pass."

It was a tricky bit of maneuvering. Our constant boost had built up a respectable velocity, which wouldn't leave much reaction time to correct errors. "You're saying you can do it."

"Hatch, I wouldn't have recommended it otherwise."

Another point in its favor: Being so treacherous, Threadneedle did not attract crowds. Folks didn't exactly line up to be sucked into holes. Since I was signing up for a suicide critter drive and had two vicious killers a-chasing me, one more crazy risk hardly seemed to matter.

Over the next few days, as we boosted toward Threadneedle, an uneasy conviction grew on me that the Callaghans would be there a-waiting. I couldn't prove it, but I *knew*. Sometimes it's hard to tell intuition from subconscious hacking over the datalink. Calculations showed that they could beat me there easy if they boosted their ships ragged; but even if they *could* beat me to Threadneedle, how would they know I would go there when I hadn't known myself until a few days ago?

Now, the notion was so unlikely that I worried at it some, trying to get at the root of it. Common sense said that the Callaghans were far behind us, cutting for sign; or maybe even following José, instead. Insiders and Downsiders don't rightly appreciate how easy it is to track another ship across the Big Empty. They forget that our senses are slaved through our ship's EM sensor array. We can "see" by laser — though you have to know where to aim the laser pulses — and we can "hear" by radio. With neural implants, it *feels* like seeing and hearing. And out in the Big Empty, there's a lot to see and hear.

Most spacers grew up reading sign. Space is not a pure vacuum. It is full of gas and dust which can be disturbed by the wake of a ship's passing. It's powerful thin stuff, but a top hand can give study to the dust and figure how many ships have passed through, how long ago, and in which direction. Such things being often a matter of life and death, it can concentrate the attention remarkably. Of course, being downlinked to your ship's mini-cray helps a lot when it comes to doing the figuring.

A tracker also gives thought to emissions. No two engines are alike. They differ in their nozzle configurations, their state of repair, the impurities in their fuel, and so on; so that every jet plume leaves a unique spectrographic footprint, one that can linger for months before the solar wind or an Oort storm erases it. A top hand can tell from the impurities in the exhausts where the ship last took in hydrogen; and from the density and spatial pattern of the plume what ship it was and whether it had fired its orbital transfer jets. The size and shape of the footprint, as we say.

A spacehand also listens hard, since sound carries in space. Well, not sound, but EM noises, like I said. You can hear things quite a ways off: radio chatter between spacers, ships beacons, even casual sounds accidently picked up and transmitted. A spacer learns to identify the natural sounds around him: the hiss of the hydrogen, the chuckle of Uranus, background noise from nearby habbies, and so on. An out-of-place sound or radar echo may be the only warning he gets of danger.

Belle and me, we'd been almighty sly and left precious little trail to follow. When we transferred orbits, you never saw such tiny puffs of reaction mass; and we fought shy of settlements, lest someone there remark our passage. We even avoided hydrogen clouds, 'less Belle needed a drink. Belle took us through a sunstring—the remnant of a solar flare—drifting across our orbit. Slowed us down a might; but its spectrum had so much junk in it that the Callaghans would need some right fine instrumentation to pick out our particular pattern. A top tracker might still be able to follow us, but he would lose a lot of ΔV doing it. Truth to tell, I'd no idea whether those Callaghans were good trackers or not, but I was not terrible eager to find out; and there sure weren't no point in making it easy for them.

Yet, for some reason, some advice my Pa had given me kept running through my head. He'd been a canny man, given to good advice, which I kept in a locked ROM directly hardwired to my implant. After Ma died, Pa had gone yondering up Oort way and he never come back. I missed him something terrible. A machine persona ain't nothing like the real thing.

A *man leaves a trail*, his voice whispered in my brain, *not only in space, but in his mind; and the best way to follow him is to follow his thoughts.*

I didn't know why he was telling me that, since I wasn't following no one; so I guessed that a neural do-loop had got stuck somewheres on a random bit.

Like I said before, I wasn't born stupid, but I've had years of practice. It was only several days later that I realized what Pa's machine-ghost was trying to tell me. I commenced to cussing, something I am right good at.

"Problem, Hatch?" said Belle. "Or are you just trying to improve my vocabulary? I didn't even know that last one was possible."

"Only for hermaphroditic clones," I told her. "I must be suffering from terminal stupidity. Link me up to the Library's diagnostic programs."

"Done and done."

I hacked for two days straight, waiting after each query while the radiowaves crawled down to Jupiter and climbed back. I cut for sign through the pseudo-memories and finally picked up the ghost of a trail, which I followed to its end. When I was through, I knew three things I hadn't known before—at least, not consciously.

It was a matter of public record that José Rodriguez was segundo for Slim Wittelsbach's jellybelly station.

It was also a matter of record that I had downloaded the jellybelly file a few days after José and me left Luckenback.

Both those records had been accessed by Sergei Callaghan.

So, they had followed my mind. They knew I was headed for the professor's place. They knew I'd left Luckenback without time to top off my water tanks, which meant I'd have to water up along the way. And they knew that only a damned fool would take water at Threadneedle.

So naturally, they'd be there waiting for me.

I mentioned it to Belle and she agreed. "But we still have to go through Threadneedle," she said.

I put my mind to it and saw she was right. We had already passed the point of no return. The other water sources were no longer accessible from our trajectory. Too much ΔV would be needed to change orbits. Nor could we bypass Threadneedle entirely, since we would run dry long before reaching the next watering hole. That would only be an elaborate form of *seppuku*; and, while I am not afraid of dying, when my time comes I'd rather go down fighting than running.

"If we go up the pass, we'll be sitting ducks," I told Belle. "Even expecting trouble like we are, we'll come out the short end of it."

"Hatch, we've *got* to go to Threadneedle."

There was an odd catch in her voice when she said that. I wondered about it some, then thought I understood. If we went into Threadneedle to water up, we would both be killed. If we went on past, I would die of thirst, *but she wouldn't*. What right did I have to ask her to risk her life with mine?

"Maybe we *should* just mosey on by, Belle," I said, feeling noble and self-sacrificing as hell.

I waited for Belle's answer, but she was silent. Lights flickered on the control panel. When she finally spoke, her voice was angry.

"Well, I never thought I'd see it! Of all the ill-mannered, evolutionary dead ends taking up space in this system, Wendell Hatch, you surely do win the prize! You have no concern for me at all, do you? No solicitude for my feelings!"

Now, seeing as how I'd offered to sacrifice myself for her, I thought that what I'd just said showed more than a little solicitude for her feelings. "What do you mean, Belle?"

"Just how do you think I'd feel boosting all the way to Sagittarius with a thirsty corpse inside? Did you ever think of that? No, of course not. It wouldn't bother you at all."

Actually, I thought it would bother me considerable, so it was just as well she wasn't going to take me up on it. "All right, Belle. You win. If you want to get yourself killed along with me, why I'd be right pleased for the company." I felt real good that Belle was going to stand by me. Even if she wouldn't come right out and say so, I think she liked me some. A man out in the Big Empty had best have his ship for a friend, or else he may never need another.

"So, Belle, I guess we go in shooting; though I 'spect that'll be only a different form of suicide."

"No, we won't, Hatch."

"We won't go up the pass?"

"No."

"And we won't bypass the comethead?"

"No."

"Well then, tell me, Belle, seeing as how we're both going to die real soon, just how we plan to do it?"

She did have a plan. It weren't much of a plan, but then I wasn't in any position to be real choosy. Her plan was to slingshot around the sunward microhole and not come up the gravity pass at all. If we vectored around the hole just right, we could dip into it and get us some extra ΔV. Then we'd pop up over the ridge — the lip of the gravity well between the hole and the comethead — blast off a fragment, suck vapor, and be gone before the Callaghans even knew we were behind them.

It sounded to me like a third and even more elaborate form of suicide, and we would wind up wherever it is folks wind up when they get sucked into holes. I'd heard stories from other hands about spacers who had tried the same maneuver at one hole or another, trying to show how they had the Right Stuff; but the stories were always told in the third person, past tense. Still, it didn't look like I had much choice.

"No one's ever done it before," I pointed out.

"Just once. At Threadneedle."

That surprised me. "I never heard. Who was the hand that done it?"

"It was me, Dell."

Well, that shut my mouth right quick. Belle and I had yakked up a storm over the years we'd been together, but she'd never mentioned this before. Which meant it was tied in with The Subject We Don't Discuss.

"You mean, Threadneedle's where you . . . I mean, where your body . . . Uh, that is . . ."

"I'll save you the embarrassment, Hatch. Yes. Threadneedle is where I became eligible for cybership status."

Well, that was one way to put it.

I gave it some thought. She had tried the maneuver once before, which was good. On the other hand, there was nothing left of her but her brain, which was not so good.

"How'd it happen, Belle?"

"Prying, Hatch?"

"No." Yes, I was. Not many women take up the spacing life. Those that do are special. Belle had once been a real woman, with dreams and ambitions; ambitions that were now beyond any hope of fulfilling. Her consciousness had been saved, but was that a kindness? What kind of life could it be wired up to a ship's software? Still alive, sure; but alive as a *thing*. Seeing and hearing and speaking through hardware, and never, ever touching another human being.

I ran my hand along the frame of the console. Was it even worth living?

Not for me, I thought. Yet, who was I to decide for another what sort of life was worth living? We each plot our own orbit, and our Final Docking depends on our own skills as pilots.

I discovered that I wanted to know Belle better. But I held my tongue. In space, people did not pry into one another's lives, lest invited. What matters is who you are, not who you were. Still, I couldn't help but wonder. We were returning to the place where Belle had lost everything: her body, her future, her dreams, nearly her life. What sort of scar might that have left upon her mind? And was that scar healed, even now? Would she hesitate at just the wrong moment, fearful of repeating the misstep of her previous visit? Had she, in fact, maneuvered me into coming to Threadneedle only to prove something to herself?

Naturally, I assumed she had fallen off the cliff into one of the holes and barely managed to escape. Which just goes to show how wrong a body can be.

4. I pass water at Threadneedle.

Belle made the course corrections that would whip us around the sunward hole. As we drew closer, I kept a sharp watch. Radar and visuals showed nothing on the western pass, but that was natural. There was enough junk—small asteroids, cometary fragments and such—to provide plenty of cover for anyone mindful of staging an ambush; and naturally, any bushwhackers would have their beacons turned down as low as they dared. Belle and I had cut our own beacon down to minimal just before we came in range.

I paid close attention to the pseudo-sounds. Like I've said, a spacer learns to distinguish natural from unnatural sounds. Right then, all I could hear was natural. The 21 cm. hiss of the hydrogen, the distant hum of Jupiter and Saturn, the electric halo of Uranus far behind me. The chatter of habitats all over the System blended into indistinct murmuring and chirping, from which individual sounds emerged only on occasion. From Nyeschastye Light and High Bakaskaya, which were closer, I could make out fragments of words. Far off, the sound of a rogue jellybelly drifted to my inner ear. I scanned the frequencies up and down the spectrum.

"There!" said Belle. "Did you hear it?"

Often a man's ship, having keener senses, will hear things first; and a spacer learns to trust his ship's reactions. So, when Belle's ears pricked up, I knew that something was out there. I played the vernier until I found it: three faint echoes. Ships' beacons, on minimum. At this distance, I couldn't make out the identifying patterns.

"What do you think, Belle? I can't read the brands."

"There are three beacons," she pointed out, "and two Callaghans."

I shrugged. Odd as it might seem, the Callaghans did have friends. Men as rough as they were. Men so rough they wore out their skinsuits from the inside. And hell, all modesty aside, there wasn't any shortage of men willing to brag as how they'd burned Oliver Wendell Hatch. There's always those wanting to prove themselves fast. Me, I'm still here. I've always been fast enough; but it's accurate that counts. Accuracy and the sand in your belly to take it while someone else is shooting back. I don't draw my phaser often, but what I point at I generally hit.

I tongued my implant and fixed the locations of those three beacons in my mind since, when we topped the ridge next to Threadneedle, I wanted to know what direction the shots would come from. At that point we'd be making enough electromagnetic noise it wouldn't matter if beacons were on or not.

Space began warping and dropped away in front of us as we headed toward the hole. Light passing so close to the hole was warped, so even if they seen us they wouldn't see us where we were. But when we came back around, we'd be skylined sharply against the event horizon. I swallowed hard. I was scared, and I don't mind saying so. Anybody'd tell you different would be a liar. A slight miscalculation and we'd spiral all the way down to the bottom.—And a hole has no bottom.

Just as we started in, Belle spoke. "Hatch? Remember what I said. No matter what happens, trust me; and keep your finger on the triggers. I know things about this place."

Before I could reply, she let out a shriek that near to blew my earphones out. A horrible wail at maximum gain: the distress call of a jellybelly. Those three beacons, they winked out right away, which shows their intentions wasn't friendly at all.

Well, we slid around that gravity well faster than a politician around a question. What with the acceleration from our turn and the acceleration from the hole's gravity, I didn't know which way was down. Belle's body hummed and popped from the stresses. Somewhere aft I heard a sharp crack and prayed it was nothing vital.

Then we were up and over the ridge. The nose gun popped out of its scabbard, and I let loose a blast. A small mountain on the comethead sublimed into vapor and Belle roped it in with the magnetic scoop before it could disperse. After all the trouble we had gone through, I surely did hope that it contained a goodly amount of water.

Belle spun on her gyros and lined us up on the eastern pass, all the while screaming like a wounded jellybelly. I figured her first screech might have fooled the Callaghans into thinking we were a critter fallen down the hole; but now, after vaporizing part of the comet, we'd be showing up clear on their radars, and they surely knew who we were. So I couldn't figure out why she was still screaming.

It was just dumb luck that saved us. A chance reflection on the radar caught my eye. I slapped the steering jets and Belle shied off just as a streak of coherent light intersected our trajectory. I located the bushwhacker in my aft screen and my implant gave me his orbit. I laid three quick shots ahead of him and, just for luck, two more to either side, and that fellow, he rode right into one.

It opened his ship up like a can of beans, but I couldn't find it in me to feel sorry for him. He'd picked the game and set the rules, and if he'd gotten what he'd planned to give, why that was just too bad.

His two friends were coming up fast and we taken out of there, all jets firing. Our trick had sure fooled them, for they'd expected us to come up the western pass. Now I had water and a lead on them, which was good; but they were giving chase, which was not so good.

I started to tell Belle she could stop her screeching when I saw something I hope never to see again. It come up out of the Oort-ward hole with a growl of static that wiped out half the spectrum and like to paralyze me with fright and surprise. It was about a quarter the size of a jellybelly and made of the same shimmering stuff, but it was spitting particle beams. A gossamer tiger with high-energy fangs.

It missed me by a fraction of a second, though some of Belle's circuits shorted out from the umbra; but it got one of those Callaghans dead on. It was Sergei Callaghan, to judge from the faint beacon. I saw his ship flare briefly in my screens; then it drifted there, dead and silent, until that thing swallowed it up. I never set much store by those Callaghans, but I surely hoped Sergei was dead.

I also hoped he would give the beast indigestion, which would be the only favor any of that crowd ever did for me.

I didn't see what happened to the third ship, which I guessed to be Konrad Callaghan, the third brother. He might have reined aside and fallen into the hole, or he may have boosted free entirely.

Belle rotated on her gyros so we were flying backward, facing that monstrosity. "Kill it, Dell!" she shouted. "Kill that God damned son of a bitch!"

Well, that seemed like a real top-notch idea to me, so I commenced to shooting. Belle threw in random vectors with her steering jets, trying to keep us out of the beast's particle beams. She was wasting reaction mass like there was no end to it, and to tell the truth, I wasn't minded to ask her to go easy. Linked by implant like we were, I could compensate for her bucking and, like I said earlier, what I point at I generally hit.

It seemed like the fight went on for hours, but the chronometer tallied only fifteen minutes when it was over. Somewhere along the line, I must've hit something vital and eventually the news that it was dead reached whatever served the creature for a brain. It cried out one last time, and my radio fell silent.

There wasn't a sound, except for my own breathing and the background murmur. Then, hesitantly, Nyeschastye and Bakaskaya began chirping questions. I wondered what they had made of the ruckus, which surely had reached them, being only light-minutes away.

"Keep shooting," said Belle in a flat voice. "I want that bastard deader than dead."

I started to say something, then I shrugged. I loaded a scout missle into the launcher and let fly. When it had penetrated the monster, I set off the auto-destruct.

There wasn't anything left of the creature.

"Satisfied?" I asked Belle.

There was no answer. I looked at the readouts and saw that many of the panels were dark. One of the engineer boards was sparking where a circuit breaker had failed to trip. I hit the manual backup. We must have taken a few near misses in the fight. My skin tingled where the edge of a beam must have brushed it.

"Belle?" I asked again. This time there was real concern in my voice. To be out in the Big Empty without a ship was certain death. That's why ship rustling was a vacuum offense. Kinder to kill a man outright than to set him adrift. Even if Belle was only lamed, the symbiosis between human brain and ship's hardware was so intense that physical damage to the latter could cause psychological trauma as well. In extreme cases, euthanasia was the only alternative. I've never had to shoot my ship before. Belle and I had been through too much together for that possibility to sit easy with me.

Finally, she spoke. "Yes. I'm all right, Dell. I've . . . lost a few functions, is all. You can probably jury-rig most of them yourself, but I'll need a mechanic when we reach cis-Pluto. Those Callaghans gone?"

"Two of them are deaders for sure," I said. "Konrad might have gotten away."

"I've analyzed the gases we took on at Threadneedle. There's enough H and O to make water and enough H left over for me to burn until we find ourselves a cloud. I used up a lot of mass in that fight. We're nearly empty."

Damn! She was near apologizing for saving our lives. If it weren't for her maneuvering during the fight, Sergei Callaghan and I would be doing lunch together. "There's a hydrogen cloud," I said, "about two weeks from here, to the Oort-Oort-east. It's along the way."

"Good. We can make that, no trouble. Ready to boost?"

It was obvious she wasn't going to talk about what had just happened, and I wasn't about to press her. I could hear the tension in her voice. She was dealing with some powerful emotions of her own and needed time to sort them out.

I checked around. There were papers and odds and ends strewn around. Drawers had spilled open during our run through the hole and the fight afterward. I put the thongs back on the gun triggers and began tidying up. When I picked up the papers, I saw my hand was shaking.

"You going to fuss around like some old bachelor," asked Belle, "or are you ready to ride?"

"Why, let's ride," I said.

We showed Threadneedle our jets and taken off down the eastern pass. When we were back down in flat space, we set orbit for Professor Wittelsbach's habitat and lit the torch. We boosted high, to make up for lost time.

Now, it didn't need no kind of genius to realize that I'd fought whatever it was that preyed on jellybellies. Evidently it hid out behind the ridge of bent light, where it was electromagnetically invisible, waiting for victims, somewhat like the trapdoor spider back on Earth. Evolutionary adaptation is surely a wonder. I allowed as how I would be more wary in the future when passing anything larger than a hawkinghole.

Nor did it require a genius to realize that Belle had lured the creature out of hiding by imitating a wounded jellybelly; and, putting $2 \times 10°$ and $2 \times 10°$ together, I figured to know how she'd been almost killed on her last visit. And why she'd been so ready to bring us here.

It must have left a terrible knot of hate and fear buried in her mind, and I couldn't say as I blamed her. Many folks have suffered losses, but few as terrible as hers. Considering how easy she could have let go and fallen into the hole of madness, it showed a great strength of character to have held on and crawled her way back to sanity. Being a ship may not be much compared with being a human; but life does go on and you either go with it or not.

I wished I'd known Charity Belle a lot earlier, but I was proud to be with her now.

She still wasn't ready to talk about it, but she would be someday. Now that the monster in the hole had been put to rest, the monster in her mind could be, too. Sharing a hurt is part of the healing, and there weren't no one more ready than me to shoulder that share.

For now, it was just good to be alive. There's nothing like not being dead to improve a fellow's outlook, so I threw my head back and commenced to singing. I can carry a tune as well as most, though not so well as my brother Simpson; but Belle, she shut off all her internal audio pickups.

That didn't bother me none and I lit into some of the old songs, wrestling with "Pomnyu Ya" and "Red River," and coming out, on the whole, victorious. After what we'd been through, driving those jellybellies down to Saturn would be a Sunday picnic.

Though if I'd known then that I'd be riding orbit with a waldo, a clone, and a freemartin, I might have had second thoughts entirely.

What's a frontier without a tall tale or two? I always wanted to write a cowboy story and throw in every gol-danged cliché I could think of. I missed the obvious one, though. Hatch does not ride into the sunset at the end. No sunsets in space, you see . . .

There are a lot of SF standbys in there, too. The cyborg ship, the space cattle, the implanted computer link, the skinsuit. There may not be a single original idea in the entire novelette. . . .

I wrote this story shortly after selling "The Forest of Time." Its initial rejection broke my string of successes (if you can call five in a row a string). For a while, whenever I mentioned this story to Stan Schmidt, I would identify it as "the one you rejected." (There have been others since, alas.) But there is an important lesson here. **No rejection is ever final.** In its original incarnation, ". . . High Frontier" was rejected by everyone. It finally saw print—but only after an extensive rewrite that, among other things, cut its length by a third. (Hmm, I sense an Important Principle here . . .)

There will always be something in a rejected story you can rebuild around. Maybe a character, or a scene, or an idea. The character was good, but it wasn't the right story for her. Or the idea was great, but those characters couldn't make it gel. A while back I mentioned a three-page rejection letter from John W. Campbell, Jr. I eventually sold that story—after further rejections and much rewriting. It appeared in *Analog* as "Ashes" (December 1986). I made a solemn vow when I started into this game that I would sell every story I ever wrote, even if I had to rewrite it from scratch, with new characters and a new plot. . . .

The Common Goal of Nature

It was not clear to him, even afterward, exactly why he had decided to ask for help. It might have been the woman gang-raped in Central Park. It might have been the addict sprawled out dead of an overdose on the corner of Maiden and Nassau. It might have been the sea of shiftless beggars that had inundated Washington Square Park; or the miasma of urine and cheap booze that permeated Penn Station. Whatever it was, he had reached the conclusion that humanity was being buried under a pile of living detritus; that the situation was clearly growing worse; and that there was nothing any human being could do about it.

Any human being.

PROLEGOMENON

What Ralph Hugo Winterman hated most of all about arriving at work in the morning was entering the Winterman building. Not that he hated the building itself, of course. It bore his own name, after all; and was, in a manner of speaking, the child of his loins—the reminder of a happier time, when he had had some hope of making a difference. Nor was it exactly that the building which had once been a symbol of hope had become instead a symbol, if not precisely of defeat, then of irrelevance. The human flotsam that clogged the City had parted briefly during the building's construction, lapping around the edges of the work site like a pool of acid; then it had closed up again and reclaimed the street, the plaza, sometimes even the lobby itself, as indifferent to the aspirations of the new structure as it was to the despair of the old.

No, all that was bad enough, that walk from the limo to the building's doors. The ragged, dirty men living in cardboard boxes set helter-skelter atop the steam grates, hurling vulgarities and sometimes feces at those who stopped and stared. The importuning of the beggars, hands outcupped, fingers twitching gimme, gimme, gimme. The hookers, brazen even in the daylight, hawking their morning specials while they waited for the noon rush. The pushers and their druggies—the small packets of white powder furtively exchanged; the thick wads of soiled bills bound with rubber bands. Yes, all that was bad enough.

But the worst part always came just before he opened the bright, glass, ten-foot doors.

"Morning, captain."

Winterman froze, as he always did, with his hand on the polished brass handle and his arm muscles tensed to pull the door open. Around him, a flock of aides hovered. The new ones awaited orders. The older ones simply waited.

Winterman turned his head and looked down on the man sitting on the newel block of the granite steps that fronted on the Winterman building. Spindly legs dangling from cuffed jungle shorts. Brown and yellow teeth smiling through a slovenly, unkempt, salt-and-pepper beard. Khaki bush jacket, stained and torn and smelling of too-long a usage; darker on the sleeve, where the shadows of three chevrons and three rockers conjured the past.

"Gunny," Winterman replied with a nod.

"Nice day, captain. Wouldn't you say?"

"There's a high-pressure front moving in from Ohio, Oakes," Winterman told him. "The rainstorms tracked south of us, over Virginia."

"Why, thanks, captain." The lips parted into a gap-toothed smile. "I don't know what I'd do if it weren't for your weather reports." Oakes's breath was foul and smelled of cheap wine.

"It will be hot today. In the nineties. You shouldn't sit out in the sun."

Oakes mopped his brow. "Aw, hell, captain. You and me, we've been out in hotter weather than this. Remember Bluefields? They could have scraped the sweat off'n us and sold it for irrigation water." He grinned at Winterman.

Winterman smiled briefly and yanked open the door to the lobby. The cool air inside rolled out and over him like an Arctic blast. Oakes rapped his messkit cup against the granite, a tinny sound that seemed somehow far away. "How's about a little something to see me through the day, cap'n?"

Winterman would not meet his eyes. "Get a job," he said, and stepped into the cold.

He could hear the whispered voices behind him. *"Who was that?" "Why did The Man . . . ?" ". . . Mosquito Coast . . ."* Winterman set his jaw and waited before the private elevator while eager hands reached out and stabbed the buttons for him.

The morning was busy. Mornings were never his own. He sat at the head of the broad, mahogany conference table and passed sentence on the proposals of a succession of Bright Young Men and Women—BMWs they were called by the Dull Old Men and Women who had long since passed that phase of their lives. The BMWs were all eager and aggressive and ambitious and determined to show Winterman how they were different from the rest of this year's crop.

(It was not that Winterman disapproved of eagerness. Once, a long time ago, he had been eager himself, and so he had a certain tolerance for it. But those he kept around himself would outgrow it, just as he had. They would remain aggressive and ambitious and determined, of course; but it would be a patient aggression, a cold ambition, a calculated determination. It was a cutthroat game he played. The game board was the world; and the tokens were economic giants and Household Names, bargained and exchanged with other Players as wily and as clever as himself. Patience and strategic thinking were required, never eagerness.)

"One does not win at chess," Winterman told the BMW who sat flustered among a shuffle of printouts at the distant foot of the board table, "by seizing every opportune pawn."

"But . . . this company is decidedly undervalued," the BMW protested, holding forth a printout that Winterman did not bother to read. "If we buy in now we could . . ." His voice petered out as he saw that Winterman was not listening.

Winterman nodded and, in the polished tabletop, a shadow Winterman nodded at shadows. "Don't take it so hard . . ." He touched a button and the screen inset in the mahogany blinked the young man's name. ". . . Bill. The investment does look good—on the surface." He let his voice stress the last phrase just a bit. "The company is new and undercapitalized. Its Current Ratio is quite high, as is its Quick Ratio. On paper, it appears to be a very good acquisition. We could easily secure a senior interest by leveraging some of the more nervous investors. However . . ." And he raised a finger, schoolmaster fashion. "However, if you had dug more deeply you would have discovered that the ratios are not, in fact, as favorable as they appear. Their management have committed a substantial portion of the company's liquid assets to speculative research ventures in ZG production. Perhaps laudable as a point of human pride; but the odds are heavily against them, wouldn't you say?"

"The potential is great," the young man insisted, "and even if they fail, our losses would be minimal."

Secretly, Winterman admired the young man's grit. It took sand to stand up to the Old Man that way. Winterman did not care for sycophants, and those who caved in too quickly, he sent packing sooner than any of the others. Those who stood up to him too long, went packing later. That line, between obsequiousness and defiance, was a fine one to walk, especially for the inexperienced; but the winnowing process had to be swift and ruthless. The Game was hardball; the competition, fierce. Only the fittest survived. Those who could not cut it must themselves be cut—for their own good, as well as the company's. Later, the culls would thank him for diverting them from careers in which they had no future. Society had many worthy tasks; tasks in which they could be more useful. There was always a need for good salesmen, bus drivers, comm techs. Just as every species had a niche in which it contributed toward the entire ecosystem, every person had a destined niche in which he could contribute toward the whole of society. Usefulness, as Lewis Thomas once said, was the common goal of nature.

"Perhaps, Bill. Perhaps," he answered the young man. "Yet The Winterman Companies did not achieve its present position by acquiring losers, no matter how small the loss. If you could show how the assets currently slated for research could be diverted to advertising to increase sales or, better yet, directly to dividends, your proposal might be worth a second look."

When the young man had gone, Winterman turned to the woman who had been sitting quietly at the side of the table. "Well?" he said, rubbing his hands. "What did you think of Bill's proposal, Dr. Morton? Is there a chance of success?"

Bright red nails tapped against lacquered tabletop. "Is that why you had me sit through his presentation?" She shrugged with her hands. "No, Mr. Winterman, there is no chance of success. A human company cannot hope to compete with the Hraani in zero-gravity manufacture."

Winterman nodded slowly. "Yes. Deep space is their milieu, after all. But that was not what I meant by 'success.' Success is when The Winterman Companies makes money on a venture. It does not depend on the outcome of the venture itself."

Morton looked at him. Large, liquid eyes, made larger by the clever use of cosmetics. "I am an anthropologist," she said, "not a businesswoman. You retained my services because of my studies of the Hraani."

"Yes." Winterman leaned back and studied her face. "To business, then. What I want from you is a daily briefing on the Hraani for myself and my senior staff. A seminar, if you will. There will be five of us. Will a half hour a day be sufficient?"

She smiled with half her mouth. "One hour is more traditional. Three times a week."

Winterman believed in giving rein to experts within the scope of their expertise. "Very well. The time can be found. Arrange with my secretary for a convenient block."

Morton leaned her elbows on the table, twisted her fingers together as if in prayer. "Do you plan on doing business with them, Mr. Winterman?" she asked bluntly.

"With them—?"

"The Hraani. Because if you do, I strongly advise against it. What we know for certain about them would fit on a file card. A small file card. We know they have two major races. We know they can use sunlight, like plants. We know that their language has certain structural similarities to the Semitic tongues. We know that their senses differ from ours in various ways, especially in their lack of proprioception. But we know little of real importance. What are their social arrangements? Their literature? I've read some of their poems—I think. But I have no idea *why* they are poems. What is the significance of the dagger they wear? 'To cut the strings,' they say: but what does that mean? And why do they toss pixie dust in the air?" She threw her arm out in a familiar Hraani gesture; held it a moment; then shrugged and sagged into her chair. "We know so little about them," she repeated.

He waited her out patiently. "We know that they are a disciplined, military people," he said.

"Do we?"

"I have never seen a hran out of uniform," he told her. "Have you?"

"Johnny Starbuck."

A wave of dismissal. "He doesn't count."

Morton puckered her lips and gazed thoughtfully into the distance. "No," she admitted. "No, I haven't. But what does that mean? How many Hraani have we seen down here? A few thousand? There are millions of them in the TransPluto artifacts."

Winterman shrugged. "Even if they do have civilians up there, they only send their military down-system; and those are the ones we must deal with."

Morton frowned and studied her nails. "If you are asking me for my advice," she said, "my advice is don't deal with them at all."

"As you said, you are an anthropologist, not a businesswoman." They locked gazes for a moment, and Morton was the first to look away.

"If there is nothing else?" she suggested.

"There is. One thing I must settle this morning."

"What is that?"

"Are they honest?"

She gave him a quizzical look. "Honest?"

"The Hraani. If they make a bargain, do they keep it?"

She raised an eyebrow. "I suppose they are like other people. Some will and some won't. They are individuals, you know, not racial stereotypes. They vary, just as we do."

"But they have the *concept* of honesty, do they not?"

"They have a word of sorts in their major language. But—"

"A word 'of sorts'?"

Morton sighed. "Does the seminar begin now? Do you want a language lesson in *B'niirë*? If you do, I am not prepared. My materials—"

"I want my question answered." Winterman spoke sharply. He was not patient with hirelings who dithered. "Just explain what you meant by a 'sort of' word?"

Morton tapped her nails against the wood for a moment. They made a sound like tiny pebbles. "As nearly as we can tell from Johnny Starbuck and the others like him, *B'niirë* consists entirely of nouns."

"Nouns."

"Yes. Words that describe things."

"I know what a noun is," he snapped. He leaned back in his chair. "How do they describe actions, then?"

"They verb their nouns."

"What the devil does . . . ? Oh. I see."

"Yes. Take a word, like . . . oh, like 'table.' " She rapped the shining mahogany with her knuckles. "That would be *lf't*. The word *alf't* would mean something like 'the building of a table' and *alfeit*, 'the placing upon a table.' *Lfet* connotes 'tablelike' or perhaps 'flat.' And so on. There are sixteen forms of the word, each putting a different spin on the basic concept. They are modified by altering the vowels."

"I see. It sounds very logical." Rational, he thought. Ordered. Exactly what he would expect from a disciplined folk like the Hraani. "And honesty?"

Morton folded her hands into a ball on the table. "That's where we enter a grey area. Their psychology. A people's outlook — their soul — is found in their adjectives; and the Hraani have none, *per se*. A language consisting entirely of nouns implies a rather literal imagination, does it not? One that lacks — or that may lack — abstractions. There is a word that might mean 'honesty': *X' rt*." (It sounded to Winterman as if she had cleared her throat.) "But most scholars believe it means something more like 'an honest act.' Again, the tangible rather than the intangible. *X'rit* is the so-called 'adjectival' form. It could be taken as 'honest' or, more precisely, as 'the features of an honest act.' "

"I see."

"There is another word, *sgl*, which means 'an agreement' or 'a bargain.' So 'an honest bargain' would be *sgl x'rit*." She hissed the words and spat them.

Winterman smiled. " 'Seagull krit.' Well, there it is. Thank you, Dr. Morton. I wasn't sure if the concept existed in their language or not."

"Yes," said Morton. "But *sgl x'rit shu x'rt sgöl*."

Winterman thought a moment, then he smiled thinly. "I shall keep your advice in mind." He pulled a slip of paper from his vest pocket, unfolded it, and smoothed it out. He read the words he had scribbled on the slip. "One more question, Dr. Morton," he said. "What is the meaning of 'advaydy shew chosen'?"

Morton looked blank. "That doesn't make any . . . Oh. You must mean *adveidy shu-ch'sen!*" She cocked her head. "Why?"

He looked at her across the conference table. "That is none of your concern. I hired you to answer questions."

"You would be better served had you hired me to *ask* questions."

"Just answer me, please," he snapped.

Morton's eyes tightened. "It is one of the more tasteless Hraani concepts. It means 'useless people.' "

Winterman returned her gaze calmly. "And why do you find that concept so tasteless? Surely you cannot deny that there are useless people in the world. One must climb over them to enter this very building. Failures. Washouts. Parasites."

"I realize that there are such unfortunates—"

"Come, Doctor. A spade is a spade; and useless is useless. Let us not mince words."

Morton looked away. "I would not call any person useless."

Winterman shook his head. "You are a sentimentalist, Doctor. It doesn't matter what you decide. Nature decides. Gaea. Natural selection. She tests us constantly for fitness. Those who fail the test drop by the wayside. Heartless? Perhaps; but then Nature *is* heartless. You or I may not care for the process; paste over it with sticky, human emotions. We may mourn the passing of some vestigial organ, species or person; and even mount some well-intentioned, but ultimately futile program to halt the process. In the end, however, Nature always wins."

"And you, I suppose, like to be on the winning side."

"Of the two possibilities, I find that the more amenable. No one likes to lose."

"That wasn't what I meant."

"No?"

"No. I mean that if Nature always wins in the end, She needs no assistance from us."

"I see." Winterman felt a moment's unease. *Did Morton know?* Impossible. She had only arrived today. No, she was merely reacting to his opinions. He should not have spoken so freely in front of her. Most people refused to face the harsh realities of life, the ruthless winnowing that Gaea insisted upon. They were too sentimental. He had often thought that sentimentality itself was a weakness; a trait ill suited to living in harmony with Nature. "Advaydy shew chosen," he repeated, returning the discussion to the language lesson. "Advaydy means 'useless,' then?"

Morton hesitated; then accepted his verbal lead. Winterman could see the distaste on her lips, in the corners of her eyes. So what? He was not in business to be liked; even by attractive women.

"No," she said. "It is the entire phrasoid that must be translated; not the individual words. *Adveidy*" — she emphasized the pronunciation — "means a 'role or function.' *Ch'sen* means 'the attribute of existing.' *Shu* is the general negator. So the phrasoid is literally 'role or function nonexistent.' "

"I see." Winterman folded his hands as if at prayer. Sixteen forms of the basic word, she had said. The vowels modify the basic word. Then "adveidy" is a variant form of . . . "Tell me, Dr. Morton. What does, ah, 'dvd' mean?"

She bit her lip, and the cherry color brightened under the pressure. " 'Dv'd' is a person," she said. "An individual."

"Useless people," Winterman said. He said it slowly. His tongue and lips shaped the phrase carefully. "Adveidy shu-ch'sen." He made a deliberate effort to exorcise the phantom vowels that his throat insisted on. "Thank you for setting my mind at ease on Hraani thinking," he said, and rose from the board table.

Morton sat for a moment longer, watching him. Then she pushed her chair back, picked up her briefcase, and stood. Winterman took her hand briefly, noting how firm her grip was.

She walked to the door, but paused with her hand on the knob. "Mr. Winterman, I am not sure that I *want* to set your mind at ease. I've told you that *B'niirë* contains words for 'bargain' and 'honesty.' That does not imply that the individuals you plan to deal with will themselves be *esygl x'riit*, honest bargainers. Nor does it imply that 'an honest bargain' means the same thing to them as it does to us."

With the door closed firmly behind her, Winterman swiveled in his chair and gazed toward the window. He leaned his elbows on the arms of the chairs and steepled his fingers together. So, the Hraani word for 'function' was a modified form of the word for 'person.' Winterman smiled. Alien? Why, the Hraani were no more alien than he was.

I: THESIS

Winterman held his coffee cup in his hand and sipped from it from time to time as he watched the swarms on the street far below. Not so much the busy ants, going about their affairs — not the bankers and messenger boys and Met Ed repairmen — but the others. The ones who sat in the alleyways and the recesses of the buildings, like rocks or debris in a flowing stream. Work required movement—that was basic physics—and there were too many figures down there blocking movement. Not simply resting, no. They were not in motion at all. Not *going* anywhere, and impeding those who were. It would be better if . . .

The muted echo of a police siren filtered up to him from the distance and the scum on the street began to drift casually in the opposite direction. Winterman grunted without humor. Stimulus and response. It was almost as if he were observing some sort of bacterial culture. Some organisms groped toward the light. Phototropic, wasn't that the term? There should be a word for an organism that shrank from police sirens.

Failures, he thought. Parasites. Useless, and worse than useless. They were dangerous. A disease, a cancer, eating into the body of society. Hanging around the fringes, feeding off of us. Selling drugs or sex—selling disease, really. Or begging for handouts. Producing nothing of lasting value themselves. Darwin was right. Survival of the fittest improves the breed. But what happens when the unfit are supported, pampered—dammit, even encouraged?

Degeneracy, that's what. So that decent women could not walk the streets without fear of rape. So that good, productive citizens could be caught in the cross fire of a gang war. So that passengers could be jeopardized because the motorman or pilot is high. That oil spill up in Alaska. The first one; the big one. When had that been? '90? '89? The skipper had been an alky, hadn't he? Another parasite. And look what had happened: fisheries ruined, the shoreline, the wildlife. Millions diverted to cleanup and repair instead of income. Yo-ho-ho and a bottle of rum.

He drank the rest of his coffee and placed the empty cup and saucer on the credenza. He checked the time with a quick twist of his wrist. It was 10:50, and he had set the meeting up for eleven. *They* should be here by now. He thrust his hands into his pockets and began to pace.

Things had been different in the Corps. No human parasites there; no "useless people." Those had been weeded out quickly and efficiently by the jungle, by the enemy, or by fellow marines. Everyone had done their part; helped each other survive. Those who wouldn't pull their weight hadn't lasted long. Bullets. Booby traps. Poisonous snakes. Endless mangrove swamps of steaming moss and soft mud sucking you down. . . . There were plenty of ways to buy it when your buddies didn't look out for you.

At Bluefields . . . Well, Bluefields had been bad. And Greytown. And Monkey Point. The confusion of the Sandinista counterattack. The screams and shouted orders. Men darting this way and that. The mortar shells raining dirt and fire left, right, behind. The flash turning the night a brilliant white. Gunnery Sergeant Oakes—

His intercom buzzed.

"Yes, Janet?" he asked from his post at the window. The circuits were voice-activated. He folded his arms across his chest.

"Mr. Winterman?" (Winterman heard the catch in her voice.) "You have some Hraani visitors. They just now stepped off the elevator."

He checked the time—It was 10:59:55—and smiled. Punctual. Efficient. Courteous, too. They could have "beamed down" directly into his office, but had chosen to materialize in the closed elevator car and arrive like normal human visitors. He patted his vest pocket, felt the folded paper within. *Adveidy shu-ch'sen.* He thought he and the Hraani would see eye to eye on a great many issues.

One hran sported the silky, blue-green needles and the other, the broad, flat "oak leaves" that distinguished the two major Hraani races. One furry; one flaky; both decked out in flamboyant uniforms, looking around at their surroundings like tourists. Their rolling eyeballs, coupled with the stiff formality of their carriage, gave the Hraani a perpetually comic appearance. Winterman caught his lower lip in his teeth to keep from laughing.

There was a third visitor with them; and Winterman did smile when he saw who it was. "Hey, Johnny," he said. " 'What's the use?' "

It was hard to think of Johnny Starbuck (of Las Vegas and Atlantic City) as a hran. The beachcomber had lived on Earth for so long—his face and his antics, and especially his famous tag line, so familiar from his late-night television show—that he seemed almost a native. He sported a gold lamé leisure suit, unzipped to show his furry chest down to where a navel should have been, and his neck and arms were heavy with gold rings and chains. A familiar, clownish figure. Half the country "went to bed" with him five nights a week.

Janet had followed them in with a barely maintained professional aplomb. She tried to look at Winterman and the Hraani at the same time. "Will you require Dr. Morton?" she asked.

Winterman waved a dismissal. "No, we won't need her. I asked that the

Hraani bring their own interpreter, and . . ." A smile. "Look who they brought!"

Janet blushed. "I know. Do you think he would give me his autograph?"

Winterman nodded, and Janet pressed her appointment book on the TV star. Johnny looked at the book, then at Janet; then he rolled his eyes around in his head. "What's the use?" he said, and Janet laughed and clapped her hands. The two Hraani officers looked on while Johnny signed the book, in both English and B'niirë characters. Their faces were unreadable. Dog faces. Bear faces. Like both. Like neither.

When Janet had gone, the Hraani visitors favored Winterman with a long silent stare. In a human, it would have been considered rude or insolent; but a slow, mute appraisal, Winterman knew, was the normal Hraani greeting. Johnny always got big laughs when he used it on new guests, especially on female guests.

To be polite, Winterman returned the stare. Uniforms fascinated him, and the Hraani decked themselves out in costumes that would have shamed a grand duke. They used colors, sashes, badges, stripes, ribbons, heraldic devices: a mad potpourri of emblems and styles. Human military uniforms paled in comparison. The one on the left, the furry one, wore a bright red jumpsuit thick with insignias of various colors and shapes. Shoulders, sleeves, breasts. It seemed as if every inch of the uniform contained a badge of some sort. The hran even wore a "merit badge sash" over his left shoulder—like some manic, overachieving Eagle Scout. A ceremonial dagger with a jeweled hilt hung from the center of his belt. The "flake" was adorned in a similar fashion, except that he (she? it?) wore a powder blue smock cinched at the waist with a black cord.

Both Hraani reached into pouches at their belts and, with a flick of the wrist, tossed "pixie dust" into the air. The clouds glittered and winked with subtle colors as they slowly faded. No one knew why the aliens surrounded themselves with the floating, microscopic particles; but human children loved it. They would tag along after every hran they saw on the street, laughing and applauding whenever he scattered the sparkling material.

After a few minutes, the flake tossed his head like a horse. "J'wn ab'nsé ot'ngut."

Winterman smiled and, as best he could, repeated the greeting. "Jewán ábensay óatingut."

The flake hissed. Starbuck turned quickly and clasped a furry hand around the wrists of both Hraani before they could pull their daggers more than halfway from their scabbards. The blades shimmered in the sunlight from the window, sparkling as if they were electrically charged. Winterman backed away in sudden alarm, staggering into the sharp corner of his desk. Adrenaline jolted his body.

Starbuck spoke to them in low snarls, spits and coughs—B'niirë was not a pretty tongue—and gradually, the two Hraani relaxed, resheathed their knives, and showed Winterman their empty palms. Winterman swallowed, not daring to respond.

Starbuck turned and faced him. "Hey, one dumb critter, nicht wahr? Mon Dieu. Listen: the speech of the interpreter. Query: why flap your gums, bud?"

Johnny's bizarre vocabulary and grammar had made him a big hit on the lounge circuit even before he had gotten his own show. People got a kick out of his fractured syntax; but just now Winterman wondered how well he really understood the beachcomber.

"All I—" He stopped and swallowed. "All I did was repeat their greeting."

"Deadly insult, man. Winterman stew."

"Would they really have killed me?" *Me? Ralph Winterman? Dead over a grammatical error?*

Starbuck held up his hand. The two opposable thumbs approached each other like the jaws of a micrometer. "This close," he said. "Winterman vis à vis non-Winterman. Comme çi, comme ça. Qué será, será."

"But why? I don't understand?"

Starbuck looked at him, made a very humanlike shrug, and spoke briefly with his principals. The "furry" pulled a paddle from his pouch and flipped it back and forth. Three rapid clacks: the tinkling of a wooden bell. Then Starbuck led them to Winterman's two plush visitor chairs, which they studied carefully. The furry actually measured his chair with a tape measure before closing his eyes, spinning, and dropping into the seat with his arms outspread. The flake watched him do it and responded by clicking his tongue rapidly. Winterman felt the sweat cool on his forehead. *We don't know these people: not at all.* Not even after all these years.

He wondered if he had been too hasty in calling for this meeting. Perhaps he should have waited; held more discussions with Morton. But, no. Hesitation was the mother of second thoughts. And Morton was too sharp.

Winterman trembled to realize how much she might deduce from their one short conversation.

"Hokey doke," said Johnny Starbuck, the ridiculous caricature Vegas lounge lizard; the castaway beachcomber with the everlastingly silly grin. *And what*, Winterman wondered suddenly, *did grins mean on Hrana?*

Starbuck gestured with his hands. "A pausing in the action. Cut!" He clapped his hands together, and the flake turned and looked at him with his hugely black eyes. "Their arrival," said Starbuck. "The sight of you. No badges. No rank. A pig in a poke. Their wonder. Their query: who are you? Your query back, despite their uniforms." He shook his head slowly, a human trait he had picked up. "Deadly insult." He looked briefly at his fellows, then looked away again, his eyes blank.

Winterman relaxed slightly. *I should have worn my old uniform.* It hadn't been a greeting so much as a demand for "name, rank, and serial number." Some things were universal. The Hraani were military and preferred dealing with the military. They wore their ranks and functions on their uniforms. Winterman wore none; so they had asked. Repeating the demand could easily be taken as an insult. "Did you explain that I don't know how to read their ranks and campaign ribbons?"

"Hraani word. Means dumbshit."

Winterman pulled his head back. Normally he did not countenance such language, especially directed at him; but under the circumstances . . . Given his own lack of facility in B'niirë, he could hardly quibble about the speech habits Johnny had picked up.

"What should I do now?" he asked Starbuck.

"Show-and-tell time. What's my line? Let the mystery guest sign in, please. The Importance of Being Winterman."

"They want to know all about me. Is that it?"

"Life consists of doing one's job. Nature's question."

Winterman blinked, startled at hearing his own thoughts echoed from Starbuck's dark blue lips. "That's a Hraani belief, isn't it?" he asked. "About usefulness and Nature. I've heard rumors. Drawn conclusions from some of your monologues. It's why I asked for this meeting."

"The Advocates' impatience." Starbuck gestured toward the two officers.

With Johnny's prompting, Winterman carefully explained high finance, arbitrage and LBOs. He told of his long struggle to achieve his present em-

inence on "The Street." His guests listened impassively to Starbuck's trans-
lations, asking no questions, giving no feedback. Their eyes were in constant motion, rolling in their sockets, flicking here, there. Glancing at
Winterman, at the floor, even at their own arms and legs. It was not inattention. Winterman knew that from watching Johnny on his show. The
Hraani seldom made lasting eye contact.

But, after he had been talking only a few minutes, Winterman was startled to notice that the flake was leaning distinctly out of plumb; and that
the furry's left arm was waving as if it were caught in an ocean current.

"Big compliment," Starbuck told him when he asked. "Full attention.
The strings are loose."

The explanation meant nothing to Winterman. But if that was the Hraani
equivalent of nodding politely, he could accept it, disconcerting as it was.
He wondered momentarily if he should return the gesture; but remembered
what had almost happened following his previous sally into interstellar communication. Let Starbuck handle the interface. He had a foot in both camps.

Winterman finished his résumé and waited; but the two Hraani made
no response. He turned to Starbuck. "Do they understand what I've told
them?" he asked. "Do you *have* corporations and high finance on Hrana?"

Starbuck said nothing for a few moments. Then he said, "*Dvaadi-q'pang-
eq'panga-erds.* Our name for them."

"Good. Then they understand what it is that I do?"

"*Dv' d-q'png-ubsn.* People share ownership. Buy-sell ownerships. Your
function: Buy-sell ownerships, en masse. Nicht wahr? Big deal; big wheel.
Hey, what's the use?"

Winterman chuckled. "You have a way of putting things, Johnny." Absently, he rubbed his hands together, a gesture that seemed to fascinate the
two Hraani. One of them leaned forward and stared, first at Winterman's
hands, then at his own. Winterman gestured toward the two. "Now what
about your friends? Are you going to introduce me?"

Starbuck tossed his head. "No names."

Winterman pursed his lips. "I see. Perhaps that would be best. But . . ."
Sudden alarm. Sweat staining his shirt. "They know who I am. Can I trust
them to keep this meeting confidential? They do know the concept 'confidential,' don't they?" He had forgotten to ask Morton that earlier. He had
been too precipitous; had let his enthusiasm get the better of him. Hasty.
Not his wonted modus operandi, at all.

"They are Advocates. Those-who-argue-a-proposal."

"Lawyers?"

"Yes-no. Lawyers. Dicks. Scholars. Se-cret Aaaa-gent Man—" (Starbuck sang that one.) "The entirety of the wax ball."

"But they *will* keep this confidential?" Winterman stressed the point. He wanted no misunderstanding. "This is privileged communication. Our own advocates are not permitted to reveal what is told to them by their clients." If the Hraani did not respect privacy, he would have to call the meeting off. Would that be an insult to them? He pulled his handkerchief from his breast pocket and wiped his brow.

"Surprise!" Starbuck clapped his hands, and Winterman jumped. "Client *shu* Winterman; Client *aa* Proposal. The Proposal! What's the use, baby? It's good; it sucks. Who said it? Who cares?"

"Wait a minute. Wait a minute." Winterman gestured with his hands. "Do I understand you right? It doesn't matter who makes the proposal? They will argue for it purely as an abstract principle?"

"Argue pro; argue con. Run it up the flagpole and see who salutes." He pointed to the flake. "The Advocate for Change." To the furry. "The Advocate for Status Quo. Opening day." Starbuck held a hand to his mouth, like a microphone. "Your role: the out-throwing of the initial ball. The Advocates' volley. A duel. Choose your weapon." Starbuck held a paw up, one finger and one thumb simulating a pistol. He grinned. "Winner *eq'png adveid*. Forms company. Sells stock. Starts business."

"And my name stays out of it entirely?" Winterman allowed himself to smile. Why, this might work out better than he had hoped!

He took his guests to the window and showed them the throngs on the street below. "Do you agree," he said, pointing, "that, if society is to prosper, everyone must contribute something useful?"

Starbuck conveyed this sentiment to the Advocates. The furry one looked at Winterman and stroked his sash. "Dv'd aa adveidy," he said. "Jwn ch'seno; drak T'raani."

"The Advocate for Status Quo agrees," said Starbuck.

Winterman nodded and licked his lips. He returned his gaze to the window. He did not look directly at the Hraani, but at their reflections in the glass. There was no way of telling how his arguments were being received. The body language was all wrong. Hyperactive eyes in stiff, awkward bodies. None of the aliens was standing plumb. They leaned; they held their arms at odd angles. What did that mean?

"There are too many humans," he said after a moment, "who contribute nothing to our society. Or who contribute harm. Bums. Criminals. Addicts. Street people. The useless. Do the Hraani have such?"

Johnny hesitated. "Sometimes," he told Winterman. "Adveidy shu-ch'sen."

Winterman suppressed a smile. He nodded, still staring out the window. "Many?"

Starbuck was silent for a long time. Winterman turned from the window and looked at him.

"Not many."

The Advocate for Change said something. Starbuck listened; touched himself on the breast. "The Advocate's query. Get to the point, mac."

"All right. The point is: What do you do with your 'advaydy shu cho-sen'?"

"Usefulness one-way, two-way. You scratch my back, baby; I scratch yours. Action, reaction. Tit for tat. Your tit; society's tat. No tits; no tats. The off-cutting from society." He made a snipping motion with his fingers. "The health of the whole equals the pruning."

Winterman nodded. "Pruning. Yes. An apt description." He thrust his hands into his pockets; watched the crowds on the street. "We have places where we remove such people. Prisons. Asylums. But there are too many human advaydy shu chosen; too many, and not enough places to put them; so they roam the streets. We can no longer prune them ourselves. We . . . lack the discipline these days. I have wondered . . ." He looked di-rectly at the Advocates; at Starbuck, who stood between them and behind them, returning his gaze over their shoulders. "I have wondered whether the Hraani would contract to do the pruning for us. Take them away. Re-move them from the street." He took a deep breath and let it out. There. He had said it. "That's the proposal," he concluded. "As you can see, there is nothing for me, personally. No hidden deals. No strings attached."

Starbuck said nothing. He stared at Winterman until he began to weave like a belly dancer and the furry Advocate turned and barked something and they exchanged rapid words.

"Well?" demanded Winterman. His palms were moist, and he rubbed them surreptitiously on his pants.

The two Advocates slapped their breasts suddenly. Starbuck hissed at him, "The swaying of your body. A mandatory response."

Winterman hesitated for a fraction of a second; but, recalling the Hraani's earlier touchiness, he quickly complied. He pretended he was dizzy, or drunk. "Why am I doing this?" he asked Starbuck through a clenched smile.

"Their saluting of you. The selflessness of your proposal. Yrapl aa yrapílo."

"Does this mean that they accept my proposal?" His heart hammered and he leaned forward slightly.

"For the sake of argument. The winner? Who knows? Stay tuned, sports fans!"

It took only a short while to hammer out the details. Winterman wanted assurance that the Hraani did not regard children, students, or pensioners as "useless." The first two presented no problem. "The potentiality of the trainee," Starbuck said. "Great value." But the notion of retirees seemed to puzzle them, and he had to explain the concept of pensions and Social Security several times. "Amortization of personal surplus for extended use," was how Starbuck finally explained it.

To Winterman's surprise, the Hraani would not discuss price. At first, Winterman thought that was because they hadn't yet costed the job; but Johnny assured him otherwise. "Public benefit," he said. "On the house."

Winterman had been prepared *in extremis* to pledge the assets of his entire company to the task. But as much as he yearned to improve the quality of life, the fact that he could do so at no cost came as a certain relief.

As the Hraani were leaving, the flake paused at the office door. He turned to Starbuck and spoke a few words, placing something into Starbuck's hand. Then he joined his comrade at the elevator.

Winterman turned to the beachcomber. "Aren't you going with them?" he asked.

But Johnny was staring at his palm, swaying back and forth like a willow in a breeze. His fur rose and fell in ripples, and he made rapid, high-pitched squeaks. He saw Winterman looking and held out his paw.

Winterman looked at the outstretched palm and saw a small circular patch made of a light, flexible material. The patch was white, with a blue lozenge-shaped symbol. He looked from the patch to Starbuck's face and could see nothing there that made sense.

"Dovdy ng-ádveidy-echsan," Starbuck said. "Ng-echsan." And he resumed squeaking.

II: ANTITHESIS

Morton was waiting for him in the lobby and saw the whole incident.

Winterman breasted the tide of bums and beggars and climbed the steps, surrounded by his convoy of aides. He could see Morton ahead of him, behind the glass doors, waiting in the air-conditioned coolness. Her face was fashionably pale and the red of her lips stood out like a wound. She wore a dark, pin-striped business suit, skirt hemmed at mid-calf; and she held her briefcase in both hands, her arms forming a V across her body that accentuated the whiteness of her blouse. The morning sunlight, secondhand reflections from nearby towers, splashed a glare across the glass, surrounding her with a white-hot aura.

Winterman was so struck by the sight that he failed to notice Oakes, until the latter, sitting on the steps at his feet, tugged at his trouser cuff as he walked by.

Winterman pulled away at the unfamiliar touch and one of his aides moved to interpose himself between the boss and this unwelcome intrusion. But Winterman saw who it was and held out an arm to restrain him.

"It's all right," he said.

"Well, captain," said Oakes. "No hello for your old messmate?" Oakes clenched a torn and soiled paper bag in his fist.

"Good morning, gunny. I'm afraid I was distracted."

Oakes's grin split his face, showing his blackened, yellow teeth. He jerked a thumb over his shoulder. "Yeah, I saw her, too. She sure is a looker, isn't she? Be afraid to touch something like that, 'cause you'd leave fingerprints or smudges. Pull something out of place. Too delicate . . . no . . ." A thoughtful frown. "Not delicate. She's a hard-looking one, she is. Too . . . careful. Yeah, that's it. Careful. Look, but don't touch." He cackled suddenly. "Not like the Miskito women, eh, captain? Touched a few of them; but, Jeeze, you'd want to put a bag over their heads first. Brown and squatty, wasn't they?" He shook his head, shoved the paper bag to his face, and drank from the bottle inside. "That was 'Touch, but don't look.' Right?"

Winterman pursed his lips. He could sense his aides taking it in. Won-

dering. Humping bare-asses in the jungle? *Did the Old Man really . . . ?*
Inappropriate thoughts, really. And it was too long a time ago to matter anymore. "It will be cloudy later this afternoon," he told Oakes. "You should
get a break in this temperature." He brushed with his hand at a swarm of
gnats.

"Captain?" Oakes looked into the neck of the bottle hidden in his bag.
"What?"

"Forget the weather report. Take me in."

"What?"

"Take me in?" Oakes turned pleading eyes to Winterman.

"In." Winterman glanced briefly at the bright, sanitary building. "Why?"

"Because it ain't safe out here no more. It . . . People been disappearing the last couple nights. Not a sign. Not a trace. Jimmy Quick and his
two girls. Nobody seen 'em. Clarence that lives over there by the bank.
Gone. A dick and his push went up that alley last night at oh-three hundred. They never came back out. No blood. No screams. No sign." Oakes's
hands were shaking, and he set his bottle down carefully on the stone pave-
ment. "It's like it was at the forward base, at Greytown. Remember how
the government's tame *zambos* used to infiltrate the camp each night? You
never knew . . ." He grabbed his left hand convulsively in his right and
steadied it, hugging it to his breast. "You never knew who wouldn't be
there in the morning."

Winterman smiled. "I'm sure there are no *zambos* in New York."

Oakes stabbed a finger at him. "You think I'm still sick, don't you?" he
shouted. "You think I'm flashing! Well, I ain't! I tell you people are disappearing off the streets!"

Winterman pursed his lips and ran his tongue across his teeth. He
looked up and down the narrow lane. *So soon?* he thought as he reached
for the doors. It had only been three days since his meeting with the Hraani
Advocates. Could they have decided and acted this quickly? Perhaps. They
had struck him as a decisive, no-nonsense folk. Military efficiency. No time
lost in foolish debates. No politics. "I'm sure nothing has happened to
them. In fact, I can assure you that they have merely been 'removed' somewhere far away." Where? he wondered briefly. The Hraani Artifacts in
TransPluto were immense—an embryonic Ringworld someone had told
him, whatever that meant. You could lose a thousand Earths in them, let
alone the street sweepings the Hraani were collecting. With a mental

shrug, he dismissed the speculations. He didn't much care where the Hraani stacked the human deadwood they collected.

"Who was that man?" Morton asked when the doors had eased shut behind him. "Do you know him?" She looked once, quickly, over her shoulder at the plaza; then fell into step beside him.

Winterman looked at her. "I knew him once, a long time ago."

"Incoming, captain! Duck!"

Star shells throwing the camp into a ghastly, colorless illumination. The sewing machine sounds of assault rifles. Tiny geysers of dirt where the bullets hit. The dull, meaty thump when they hit flesh. The whistle of incoming rounds. The screams and shouted orders. Men darting this way and that. The mortar shells raining dirt and fire left, right, behind. The flash directly in front of him turning the night a brilliant white. Lifting, flying, falling. The earth rearing up and striking him across the back like a hammer. The sight of distant stars through the gaps in the jungle canopy. Gunnery Sergeant Oakes's face staring down into his own—

"A long time ago," he repeated. "In another life."

"Was he a friend of yours?"

Winterman looked at her; considered telling her it was none of her business. The elevator sighed open, and they stepped inside. Winterman waved his entourage off and let the doors seal him in with Morton.

"A friend," said Winterman, watching the floor numbers light up in succession. "Yes, he was. He was my sergeant. We were in combat together. Most of us came out of the fighting without any psychic damage; but Oakes hasn't 'readjusted' well to civilian life."

Morton's eyes shaded over and her mouth formed an "oh."

Winterman could not abide understanding from those who could not possibly understand. Morton hadn't been there, and that was that. "There was no braver man than Jonathon Oakes," he said, "when it came to open combat. But we each have our Achilles' heel, and his was the zambo attacks." *Stealthy. Never any sign. Just haul out the bodies each morning. And ask yourself why the man on your left or your right? Did they flip a coin to decide which ones they killed?* "The zambos utterly unnerved him. He wouldn't sleep at night. He became nervous, jittery, undependable. In the end, he cracked; and I was forced to evacuate him. He has not been the same man since."

"And you won't help him out now?"

"A handout isn't a helpout."

"Very glib."

"I think you are overstepping your bounds, Doctor. You should confine yourself to anthropology."

"Still, if he was your friend—"

The elevator chimed and Winterman leaned on the "doors closed" button. "My friend," he told her, "was a brave, practical soldier. He was sharp, both mentally and in his personal hygiene. He was *not* a bum or a drunkard. He did not sit on street corners, half-crocked and flea-infested, wheedling dollars from strangers!"

"There must be something you can do for him."

"He has to do it for himself." Winterman studied the elevator panel. He ran his finger over the Braille dots. "I did try," he said after a moment. "When he first showed up on my steps out there. I gave him a job in security. He would have been good at it. He *should* have been good. But it didn't work out."

"What do you mean, 'It didn't work out'?"

"It is time for our briefing, isn't it?" He jabbed the "open" button. The doors parted, and he stalked out without waiting to see if Morton followed.

"The Hraani," Morton told the managers at the morning briefing, "are blind."

Winterman folded his hands, fingertips to fingertips. He glanced at his staff, saw them whispering or simply looking puzzled. "Doctor Morton," he said, "I have dealt with the Hraani. They are not blind."

Morton favored him with a challenging look; one that said she dearly wanted to know what that deal had been. "Tell me," she said. "Did you notice how still and awkward their bearing was? How they constantly looked around themselves to the point we would consider rude? How, on occasion, their arms or entire body seemed to 'wander'?"

It was, of course, a rhetorical question. Winterman leaned forward on the table. "Yes. Why is that?" He was still irritated over their quarrel in the elevator; but he had hired her for her knowledge, not her personality.

"Because they *are* blind," she told him, "but in a very special way. Would you all close your eyes, please? Thank you. Now, at arm's length, bring the tips of your forefingers together. You see? You have little trouble 'finding' your fingers, even with your eyes closed. The Hraani cannot do that, because they lack a sense that we take so much for granted that we seldom notice it at all. Sherrington called it 'our secret sense.' It is the constant and automatic sensing and adjusting of the position and tone of our bodies. We call it 'proprioception,' from the Latin *proprius*, meaning 'one's own.' It is the sense by which we feel 'ownership' over our bodies. It tells us we live just behind our eyeballs." She tapped her skull with a pointed nail. "The Hraani do not have this sense. And that colors their whole outlook." She smiled, as if at a secret joke. "Literally, their 'out-look.'"

"There was something about that on PBS last year," said O'Donnell. "But I didn't understand it at the time." A few other heads around the table nodded at the recollection. Winterman waited for the answer. He preferred to let his managers ask the questions. Let them appear ill informed. Silence was construed as understanding.

"Yes," replied Morton. "That was when we first realized how different the Hraani senses were. A neurologist watching Johnny's show was struck by the similarity of his behavior to that of body-blind people he had been treating. Until then, everyone assumed that he acted that way for the laughs."

"Body-blind," Winterman repeated. "An apt phrase."

"I am an anthropologist," she told them. "But that is what the neurologists have concluded. The Hraani would consider what you just did with your fingers to be a supernatural power."

"Interesting," said Gunn. "The Hraani usually make us feel inferior. It's nice to know we've got something over them. Why isn't it better known?"

"Because, as usual, people are caught up in superficialities. In photosynthetic fur, or uniforms." She looked at Winterman when she said that and Winterman returned the gaze without reacting. "We are so accustomed to the idea that we 'live inside our bodies,'" she continued, "that it never occurred to us that the Hraani did not. And, of course, the Hraani never mentioned it for the same reason. In fact, I doubt that they understand the issue any more than an eye-blind person understands orange."

O'Donnell looked up from her notepad. "I'm not sure what you meant, Doctor Morton, when you said that the Hraani do not 'live inside their bodies.'"

Morton nodded slowly. She clasped her hands behind her back and walked slowly to the window. "Body-blindness is unusual among us humans, but it does happen. There was a classic case many years ago of a woman, 'Christina,' who became body-blind while in the hospital awaiting surgery. No one was ever quite sure what triggered her condition, but the results were startling and dramatic. She could not stand upright; her hands wandered. When she reached out for something, she would miss wildly. Her face became slack; her voice, flat. 'I can't feel my body,' she told the doctors. 'I feel weird—disembodied.' "

"Disembodied," Winterman repeated.

"Yes. An insightful comment. She had lost—literally—the sense that she lived within her body. She was *not* numb or paralyzed. She could feel, see, speak, move her arms. But, the 'seeing' had become something akin to watching a monitor; the 'hearing,' to listening to speakers. In her own words, her body had become 'blind and deaf to itself.' If 'Christina' had been any less the person she was, the psychological effects could have been catastrophic."

"What happened to her?" asked Vermeers. "Did she ever recover?"

Morton shook her head and turned away from the window. "No, she did not. But she eventually learned how to cope. And therein lies the only clue we have to understanding the Hraani *Weltanschauung*. Like other sense-blind people, 'Christina' learned to compensate for her loss by using her remaining senses. For the now-missing *proprio*ception of body position, she learned to substitute her visual *per*ception. She actually had to watch where she put her arms and legs." Morton demonstrated by walking toward the table, glancing repeatedly at her feet before she moved them. Winterman recognized the similarity to Hraani behavior. No wonder their eyes were in constant motion! They were constantly taking bodily inventory.

"Similarly," Morton concluded, " 'Christina' learned to use her hearing to modulate her voice; and her vestibular sense took on more of the chore of balance. But she never lost that disembodied sensation. Everything she did became a pose; every motion, an artifice. The fact that, with practice, it became subconscious and automatic does not hide the fact that she was not 'wearing' her body, but 'operating' it."

"Like a puppeteer," said O'Donnell, "operating a puppet."

Morton thought for a moment and nodded. "That is a very good image, Ms. O'Donnell. We believe that, from the Hraani point of view, their consciousness lies 'outside' their bodies. They manipulate their bodies. The distinction between 'Christina' and Johnny Starbuck is that what for us is

a dysfunction of the spinal cord is for them natural. They have evolved—
what should we say?—a more intense concentration, faster reflexes. Still,
they cannot rely on the unconscious and automatic coordination of their
bodies that we take for granted. And when they *are* distracted or concen-
trating on another object, they 'lose' their limbs and posture. The reason
they never apologize for knocking things over is because they take occasional clumsiness for granted."

"Oh!" That was Gunn. Morton looked at him. "I wonder. Could that
be why they attend so many concerts, ballet performances, and such? I
mean, you cannot play music properly if you have to decide even semi-
consciously where to place your fingers for each note. And the same goes
for dance. Perhaps even more so."

"Or sport," said O'Donnell. "Remember Wimbledon last year? The
Hraani packed the stands. Playing tennis or basketball must seem almost
supernatural to them."

Morton nodded. "That's true, and many of us in the research community believe that the Hraani are interested in us primarily because of our
'super powers.' But think—" She leaned on the table and looked at each
one of them. "What might their congenital disembodiment imply about
their beliefs or their value systems? Their interpersonal and social relationships? We don't know. Perhaps we *cannot* know. All that we do know
is that their 'out-look' could not possibly be the same as ours, no matter
what the superficial resemblances may be." And she again caught and held
Winterman's gaze as she said it.

III: SYNTHESIS

It was not that the crowds on the street grew sparser. They did not. But, as
the days went by, Winterman's practiced eye noted a thinning around the
edges. One day there was a ragged old woman sitting on a heating grate
arguing angrily with herself. The next day, she was gone. Removed quickly
and quietly. There was a gang of black youths who hung around the mouth
of the alleyway, shaking down passersby for change. Day by day, their numbers grew fewer; and those who remained bore a haunted look.

All in all, Winterman thought, the pruning was proceeding quite satis-
factorily.

Eventually, the media noticed.

There was a spate of articles and news bites on the sudden drop in homelessness and crime. Politicians were interviewed. (They showed how their policies were responsible for the improvement.) The police were interviewed. (They showed how efficient, no-nonsense law enforcement was responsible.) Sociologists were interviewed. (They showed how their theories and studies were responsible.) Once or twice, even "street people" were interviewed—though they told wild stories about unexplained vanishings, and goblins that appeared and disappeared in the flickering of an eye. Too incoherent, really, for the evening news.

"Good morning, Gunny," Winterman said cheerfully as he bounded up the steps.

Oakes turned wet, red-rimmed eyes to him. He squinted at Winterman for a few moments. "Oh, it's you, captain." He swayed gently on his seat on the newel block.

"You don't look well, sergeant."

"I ain't slept in days," he replied. "Can't sleep. Not with the zambos sneaking around." He swatted idly at a swarm of gnats.

"There are no—"

"Saw one, th'other day," he slurred, angry, triumphant. "Saw one. Early morning. Still dark. He was dressed in camouflage, all covered up with leaves. Never saw him 'til he was right there next to me. He pointed to my sleeve and an' said, 'What function? What function?' Just like that. Knew it was a zambo 'cause he hadda weird accent."

Winterman ran an uneasy hand across his lips. "What did you tell him?"

Oakes sat up straighter and cocked his hand to his eyebrow. "I gave him my best fuckin' USMC salute an' said, 'Gunnery Sergeant Jonathon Oakes, Fifth Marine Engineering Battalion, at yer fuckin' service.' Bastard tried to throw sand in my face. He said, 'What's the use?' Then he was gone." Oakes's tongue wet his lips. He squinted again into Winterman's face. "I run him off, captain. I surely did. Faced up to that fuckin' zambo and he backed down."

Winterman felt ice in his belly. "You surely did, Gunny. You surely did." But . . . *How long will they be fooled,* he wondered? *How long before they find that Oakes no longer has a productive function?*

"Incoming, captain! Duck!"

Star shells throwing the camp into a ghastly, colorless illumination. The sewing machine sounds of assault rifles. Tiny geysers of dirt where the bul-

lets hit. The dull, meaty thump when they hit flesh. The whistle of incoming rounds. The screams and shouted orders. Men darting this way and that. The mortar shells raining dirt and fire left, right, behind. The flash directly in front of him turning the night a brilliant white. Lifting, flying, falling. The earth rearing up and striking him across the back like a hammer. The sight of distant stars through the gaps in the jungle canopy. Sergeant Oakes's face staring down into his own. Arms lifting him up: carrying him. Hanging down over Oakes's shoulder gazing into the churned and smoking earth. A shell explodes and splatters them with mud and rock. Oakes staggers but doesn't fall. Jarring bounds that jostle him from side to side. Then—

Winterman made a decision. "Come with me, sergeant. I'm taking you in."

"You mean I'm being relieved? 'S'about fuckin' time." He slid off the newel block and wobbled unsteadily on his feet. Winterman put an arm around his shoulder to steady him. "Careful." Behind him, Winterman heard the buzzing voices of his aides. His lips formed a grim line. Let them gossip.

Winterman led Oakes toward the huge, glass doors. While he fumbled with the handles, Oakes tugged on his sleeve. "You know, they aren't so tough, after all, captain. Those zambos. I can't believe I was ever afraid of them."

He took Oakes up the elevator and into the executive offices, where surprised and puzzled staffers peeked cautiously around the edges of their partitions. He and Oakes brushed past Morton just as she emerged from her own office with a thick manila folder in her hands. She drew back, startled from the filthy, foul-smelling apparition, holding her arms up to avoid touching. Winterman paused.

"What's wrong, Dr. Morton?" Winterman asked sardonically. "You told me I should help him."

"Yes, but . . ."

Yes, but somewhere else. At an approved charity, perhaps. Something not so messy. Or so close. Winterman did not wait to hear her reply. He was probably not being fair to Morton. Still . . . *What if I had carried him up here on my shoulders?*

Janet sat transfixed at her desk and stared at Oakes. "Mister Winterman!" she said.

"Don't fret yourself about it, Janet." He turned to Oakes. "That's my office through there. There's an executive washroom all the way in the back. It has a stall shower. Why don't you go wash up." He slapped Oakes on the shoulder.

Oakes turned and looked at him. "It sure is good to be posted with you again, captain." He held out a cracked hand with torn and blackened fingernails. Winterman hesitated fractionally and took it.

"It's good to have you in the company." He turned back to Janet.

She had his appointment book open, her finger marking the place, but she was looking after Oakes where he had vanished into Winterman's office.

"Janet," he said sharply.

"Oh!" She glanced down at the appointment book. "Two of your meetings today are canceled. Mr. Rollins's secretary called to cancel the A.M. conference call. And when I called Ms. Thurlow's office to confirm your P.M. they told me that she hasn't been into her office since the day before yesterday."

"Never mind that, now," he told her, thinking briefly that he would have had to cancel those meetings anyway. "Get me Johnny Starbuck on the phone immediately. Tell him it's urgent. I need to modify the proposal. Tell him that. Then have someone shop around for some clothing for Sergeant Oakes. Casual, I think, will do."

"Yessir." Janet began punching buttons on her console. "You know, I haven't cared much for Johnny the last week or so."

Winterman paused at his door. "Eh?"

"His show." She held the handset to her ear with her shoulder so she would have both hands free to flip the Rolodex. "His ratings are down, I heard. Somehow, 'What's the use?' doesn't sound funny anymore. The way he says it, I mean. You simply don't say that about the king of England, not even for laughs."

Winterman shook his head. The ratings for *The Johnny Starbuck Show* were the least of his concerns at the moment. He strode into his office.

The door to the washroom was slightly ajar. He could hear the sound of running water. Streamers of mist curled around the edge of the door. Winterman went over and pulled the door closed, muting the rush of the water.

Oakes. He had never intended that Oakes . . . But, what else could he have intended? Useless? Of course. Oakes had given new meaning to uselessness. But, somehow, whenever he had considered the problem of the street people, he had never thought explicitly of Gunnery Sergeant Oakes. A blind spot. Why? *And why the sudden urgency now?* Oakes would probably be better off with the Hraani, anyway. A new start. Sentiment? If Nature had decreed Oakes surplus, what was the point of struggling against it? Hadn't he done that once before? Hadn't that been the very lesson that brought home to him the pointlessness of appealing Nature's verdict? He glanced at the washroom door. He could just hear Oakes's voice, but could not make out the tune. Did it matter what he did today? In a week, Oakes would be back where he had found him.

Just like the last time.

The intercom buzzed. "Yes, Janet?" he spoke toward the desk.

"It's only five A.M. on the Coast," she said. Her voice sounded tinny and distant. "Nobody's at Johnny's studio but the night guard."

"See if you can track him down through his service," he told her. *Do I have to do all the thinking around here?* "It's extremely urgent."

"Yessir." Janet clicked off and Winterman found himself standing in the middle of his office with nothing to do but wait. Wait until Oakes finished his shower. Wait until Janet located Starbuck.

He shifted from foot to foot, decided there was no help for it, and sat down at his desk. He had picked up his first briefing folder and was already refreshing himself on the details of the buyout when he remembered what Janet had told him. Rollins's secretary had canceled.

Was Rollins trying to welsh on the deal? Six months to set this up and he—Rather than distract Janet with another task, Winterman grabbed the phone himself and punched in the call.

"Rollins, Corona, and Moffett," said a pleasant voice. "May we help you?"

"Yes, this is Winterman. Let me speak to Rollins."

There was a moment of shocked silence as the receptionist came to grips with a principal placing his own call. Then he evidently decided that protocol required passing the buck. "Let me connect you with Mr. Rollins's secretary."

There was the briefest of buzzes before the secretary answered. "Mr. Rollins—?"

"No, this is Winterman, at The Winterman Companies. I am calling about the meeting we were to have this morning."

"Oh, Mr. Winterman, I already called your office and canceled it."

"I know that," he replied firmly. "I was calling to discover why. May I speak to him?"

"He's not in yet."

Winterman checked his watch and snorted. "Nonsense. Jim Rollins is always in position before seven and it is now after eight. The markets will open soon."

"I know that, sir. But he hasn't come in. We've called his home, but his staff says that he was gone before any of them awoke. Frankly, Mr. Winterman, we are worried sick about him."

"I see. Has there been word of an accident? He comes in on the Sawmill River Parkway, does he not?"

"No, sir. No word of anything."

"Well . . . When you do hear, I would appreciate a call."

"Yes, sir."

"Thank you."

Winterman cradled the phone slowly. He pursed his lips. His eyes fell on the second folder. The deal with Thurlow. And she hadn't been seen for two days, according to Janet. Rollins. Thurlow. Winterman had the sudden sensation of falling. He laid his hands upon his desk to steady himself. Then he pulled the phone in front of him and began pressing the quick-call buttons.

Fifteen minutes later, he had finished. Of the twenty-three other arbitrageurs and financiers that he dealt with frequently, thirteen were not in their offices as of 8:22. Six of those had not put in an appearance for two days; and four, not in three days. Winterman clasped his hands into a ball on the desktop; studied how the edges of his nails turned white.

Adveidy shu-ch'sen. Useless people.

He pressed the intercom button. "Dr. Morton?"

"Yes, Mr. Winterman. What may I do for you?"

"Another phrase, if you will." He closed his eyes and concentrated, trying to remember. "Dvaadi-q'pang-eq'panga-erds and, ah, dv'd-q'ping-ubesn. What is the precise distinction?"

"Could you repeat that? You must mean 'ubsn,' not 'ubesn.' Just a moment. Let me consult my notes." There was a short silence before she came back on. "Here we are. Dv'd, as you already know, denotes a person, an individual. Q'png is an association, Dvaadi-q'pang are individuals having the attribute of association. A limited liability company, perhaps; although the German *Gemeinschaft* or *Gesellschaft* would be closer."

"And erds and ubesn? What do they mean?"

"An initial vowel in the first declension denotes the creation of a thing. *Erds* means the creation of *rds*, or product—production; while *ubsn* means the creation of *bsn* or possessions—acquisition. So the first phrase means 'a company that produces goods' and the second means 'an individual who possesses associations.' What is this all about?"

"Then the Hraani make a distinction between possessing and producing."

"Of course. Doesn't everyone?"

There are people out there who produce nothing. They are useless. They have no function. "Ah, but the nuances, Doctor," he said sadly. "The nuances."

He cut the intercom and sat for a long moment, not looking at anything in particular. He felt nothing. No surprise. No outrage. He wondered if, in some secret corner of his mind, he had always expected this; intended it, even. Then he pushed himself away from the desk and strode to the washroom door and banged on it.

"Oakes? Oakes!" He stuck his head inside. "If a hran ever asks you your function, tell him that you are my scout. Tell them that you sat on my steps because you were undercover, watching for street crime that might affect me. Tell them that that was your *adveidy*." He shouted to be heard above the rush of the shower. "Do you understand me, Oakes?"

There was no answer but the hiss of the showerhead. Winterman stepped inside the washroom. "Gunny?"

He could see nothing through the glass of the shower door. Placing an apology on his lips he pulled it open. "Gunny?"

The stall was empty.

The water streamed from the showerhead. It splashed on the tiles, sprinkling Winterman like a priest's aspergillum. It roiled on the basin of the stall; swirled down the drain, foaming and bubbling. Winterman leaned his face against the glass. It was cold and wet. "Jonathon," he said.

IV: APOTHEOSIS

Winterman found that, at this point in his life, he could take pride in very few things; and then only in small things. One was that, after so many years, his old dress uniform still fit. He stood before the full-length mirror in the dressing room of his Connecticut estate and smoothed the creases. Carlos had done a fine job cleaning and pressing it. He could hardly smell the cedar.

He straightened the white saucer cap on his head. The eagle-globe-and-anchor affixed to the front was black brass. He wondered briefly what his household had thought of his abrupt return from the City; about his request, phoned ahead, to ready his uniform. *The Man has finally snapped,* he could imagine them saying.

He stared into the mirror. Into his eyes. Then abruptly, he turned and marched off.

The house was silent—he had given the staff the rest of the day off—and he waited in the downstairs living room. There were photographs and plaques lining the walls. Winterman with presidents. Winterman with sheiks and movie stars. Awards. Tributes. Winterman walked from one to the other, standing for a few moments before each.

There was a featherlike disturbance in the air. A puff. A light draft tickled his cheek.

"Hello, Johnny," he said to the room. "I've been expecting you."

He turned about-face; and Starbuck was standing there in his gold lamé leisure suit. The white badge with the blue lozenge was affixed to the right breast. On his left was a larger, square badge Winterman had not seen before. It was filled with twisting lines and slashes, like a Chinese ideogram. The Hraani ceremonial knife was snug in its scabbard, hanging from the center of his belt.

"You're reverting to type, aren't you, Johnny?"

The Hraani TV star looked blank and did not answer. He flicked his wrist and scattered pixie dust; something Winterman had never seen him do before. Tiny particles floated in the air like a swarm of gnats.

"What are you?" Winterman asked. "An adventurer? Remittance man? Ne'er-do-well second son? Never mind; it doesn't matter. I suppose slumming among the natives has its charms, but it must feel good to be accepted in civilized society again. To get back into uniform."

Johnny fingered his badges. "Ng-ádveidy-echsan, Winterman-dv'd. My functions. My place. My place or yours. Interpreter . . ." He touched the lozenge, which Winterman now realized was a stylized rendition of a pair of Hraani lips. "The time, the place, the purpose, n'est-ce pas? The read-ing of it. My life. My pride. The knowing of me by others."

Could that much detail, Winterman wondered, be encoded in such a simple emblem? Perhaps. If one were attentive enough to notice the sub-tleties of size, curvature, hue. And, according to Morton, the Hraani had evolved a merciless degree of attentiveness. Still, that explained the long slow greeting. New acquaintances needed time to "read" each other's ré-sumé. Even after the Hraani had developed higher technology, the badge-reading custom would persist; as handshaking had survived the need to prove empty-handedness. "And the larger badge?" he asked.

Starbuck stroked his breast. "Entertainer of Earthlings. New function. New niche. First badge." He pointed to a single dot in the upper-right cor-ner. "Jean le Premier. You may kiss my feet."

It struck Winterman suddenly that Starbuck did not understand much of what he said; that, like a parrot, he only repeated phrases. Black boxes. *These* words elicit *that* response. But as to what lay inside the boxes . . . The deeper meanings of the words eluded him.

Winterman smiled sadly. It was a melancholy thought to realize that Johnny had never been trying to be funny. "What's the use?" had always been a serious question.

Starbuck tossed his head. "J'wn ab'nsé ot'ngut, Winterman."

Winterman straightened. "Ralph Hugo Winterman, Captain, Fifth En-gineers, USMC." He pointed to the cross. "Marksman rating." To the fruit salad. "Mosquito Coast Expeditionary Force. Unit Citation for the assault on Corn Island beachhead. Good Conduct Medal." Winterman could feel the sweat of uncertainty on his body. "Silver Star for breaking up the San-dinista tank attack at Monkey Point. Purple Heart, wounded by a mortar shell at Bluefields. The same battle," he added, "in which Gunnery Sergeant Jonathon Oakes received the Congressional Medal of Honor."

"Former Captain," said Johnny Starbuck, simply and finally.

Winterman closed his eyes briefly. He had not really expected it to work. The Hraani were very methodical, and they learned fast. But he had felt compelled for some reason he could not name to put on the old uni-form. "I suppose you've come to take me away," he said.

"The proposer proposed. An honest bargain."

Winterman felt the shiver run through him. Echoes of Morton's warning. Second thoughts too late. Rolling downhill, picking up speed. Humpty Dumpty: When I use a word it means exactly what I want it to mean. That is not what *I* mean by success, he had told Morton. Talking to the Advocates, but not connecting, not connecting. Saying one thing; but hearing another. Person and function were two sides of the same coin. Useless people. But not Oakes! Not useless. He saved my life once. *And I was ashamed to have been saved by the likes of him.* The truth of the thought was a knife in the heart. Too proud; too proud. "What . . . ?" He swallowed. "What is an honest bargain?"

"Truth or consequences. Truth and consequences. Truth *is* consequences. Honesty *aa* the self-acceptance of the consequences." Johnny looked at him. His green fur rippled. "Achtung! The salute." Johnny stroked his breast.

Winterman smiled quietly and put his hand to his visor, pulled it down sharply.

"The greatest unselfishness," said Johnny. "The launching of the proposal at oneself. The removal of useless people from the street. Winterman the Big Man on the Street, hein?" He held a finger to his head, one thumb as the hammer, the other as the trigger. "The honor: Its delivery my privilege."

Winterman stood at parade rest. "Did you request that? To deliver my 'honor'?"

Johnny was silent. His body tilted slightly. "Be it ever so humble. Hi, honey, I'm home! Five years, T'rran. Five years here on T'rrana. The thinking of the Hraani. The thinking of the T'rranni. The arithmetic sum." A slap on the chest. "The thinking of the t'rran-hran." He paused; hissed like a steam boiler before it bursts. "I knew what your proposal meant, Winterman."

Winterman was so startled by the sentence delivered in clear English that he did not respond for a moment. When he found his voice, all he could say was, "What it meant?"

"Remove them from the streets," Johnny quoted. "Take them away. That's the proposal. Nothing for me, personally. No hidden deals. No strings attached." He stroked his breast once more.

Winterman took a breath and released it. He took another long look around his house. The richness of the woods; the softness of the carpeting. The elegance of the fixtures. Bright crystal; burnished brass. The black, polished piano in the corner, reflections in the curve of the casing weirdly distorted, as if by a fun-house mirror. Now he would go to dwell among those he had always despised. The bums, the prostitutes, the addicts. Gunnery Sergeant Oakes.

He held himself straight. He owed it to Oakes, to Jonathon. To himself. It was justice, after all, for his dereliction. He would take his punishment without whining. You made pickup on your fallen comrades, dammit; and that obligation did not end when the uniform was removed. No matter how ashamed you might be to acknowledge a vagrant as your creditor. If that was mere sentiment, a futile striving against Entropy and Nature, so be it. "I'm ready to go now."

Johnny tossed his head. His right arm moved and the crystaline knife snaked out of its sheath. Starbuck advanced toward him. Winterman's heart skipped. *But* . . .

But what? Taken to the TransPluto habitats? Why should he have believed that? No hran had ever told him so. "Remove them." He knew what he had really meant; what he had always meant, in that dark and frozen part of his heart that he had never dared explore. "Remove them." He had never inquired too closely into the Hraani plans so that he could deny, even to himself.

Still, he had to ask.

"What is the knife for, Johnny?"

"To cut the strings," Johnny told him. "No strings attached. You want nothing for yourself."

EXCURSUS

"Are you sure about that?" Cynthia Morton asked.

"As sure as I can be, Cyn," replied the voice on the telephone. "We did a complete image comparison by computer and checked it with a random visual sample. There's no doubt about it. Some of the differences are very subtle, but no two Hraani uniforms are alike. At least, among those we've seen."

Morton thanked her caller and cradled the phone. *So,* she thought. *They aren't really uniforms at all; at least, not in the sense we think of them. They are expressions of individuality, not of uniformity.* She glanced out her office window toward Winterman's office. She couldn't wait to tell the fascist bastard.

They would need a different name for the costumes. "Uniform" was not really appropriate. A new word. If "uniformity" gives us "uniform," "individuality" gives us . . .

Individual.

Dv'd.

The excitement raced through her like a fire. Yes, yes! The word did not simply mean a person. It carried nuances, resonances. "That which makes a person distinct." It must refer as much to the costume as to the person wearing it!

She pulled her notebook to her and opened it to her notes on *dv'd* and scribbled hastily. She had long been puzzled by the distinction between dv'd and hrn. Why the aliens called themselves "Hraani" rather than "Dveieida." The accepted explanation was that the two words were analogous to "Terrans" and "Humans." Yet, she had never been satisfied with that explanation. She had a nagging intuition that there was an important, subtle shading that was being missed because of the psychological differences between the two species. The words were tied into concepts of personhood; and what sort of concept would body-blind "persons" have? Morton was convinced that only Terran scientists could hope to understand the dichotomy between the two species. The Hraani could barely comprehend that the dichotomy existed; and even then, the comprehension was rooted in the physical fact of Terran "super powers" rather than in the abstract notion of a "secret sense."

"You are what you do," she scribbled into her notebook. She paused a moment and read what she had written. Her stream-of-consciousness notetaking often produced white noise, but sometimes . . .

Yes, it fit. You are what you do. The concrete versus the abstract. Dv'd. But person-ness was an abstraction; the mind experiencing itself. The Hraani concept must be more concrete. Was "person" no more than "uniform." Was that why "person" and "function" were virtual synonyms?

But each Hraani mind must experience itself as a concrete entity, as a dv'd. (She imagined a "Hraani Descartes" saying, *I think: therefore I am,* and was startled to realize that, in B'niirë, the aphorism was tautological.) That was concrete enough; but, what about other individuals? The Hraani mind could not experience others concretely.

Well, neither could humans. So what was the difference? Did it make other minds somehow less real?

Not for humans. Humans lived inside their heads, so they *knew* from direct experience that every body contained a self. I think: therefore *you* are. But the Hraani did not live "inside" their bodies. They sensed their bodies as things, possessions. As a *hrn*, she thought triumphantly, to be manipulated by a *dv'd!*

Yes. Hrn and dv'd. Body and self. Similar concepts, but rooted in utterly different perceptions.

Could any dv'd really conceive, down in the gut, that other hraani— friends, companions, acquaintances, strangers—were anything more than physical objects? Perhaps. But only as an abstract principle, generalizing from one's own self. And the Hraani were notoriously weak at abstractions.

Dear Lord, an entire race of solipsists!

What must it be like never to contact another person, save through the mechanical intermediary of two hraani? Could you make love by interfacing two machines? Reach out and touch someone, the old ads had said. But you could only do it because you *knew* that what was at the other end of the comm link was a person like yourself. Because your proprioception told you that every body contained a self. But what if other people had never been anything but voices in a diaphragm or phosphor dots on a screen?

They must be, she thought, *the most lonely race in the galaxy. They cannot touch one another the way we humans can.* Even though (she glanced briefly at Winterman's office) we often find it difficult ourselves. So they drape their hrn with concrete representations of their dv'd-ness, as if they were waving a flag from the window. Desperately hoping to make contact? Or was she starting to anthropomorphize? If you have never made contact with another soul, could you ever miss it?

She could see the outlines of her monograph taking shape. It would be a seminal paper, one that would establish her eminence in the field. It would tie so many things together. The now moribund Hraani religions had held a common belief in transmigration of souls. Yes, of course. It would be a logical conclusion for a "disembodied" people. And the complete lack of funeral practices. Death could mean no more to them than engine failure does to a truck driver. Easy to believe when you directly experienced the body as a machine; something to be "operated," like a puppet on strings.

She glanced again at Winterman's office, wondering where he had gone

in such an agitated hurry; wondering when he would be back. It was already past time for the regular briefing. She gathered her notes together.
Then she took up the current copy of the *Journal of Anthropology* and settled back to wait. When he did return, she would tell him about her de-
ductions. She wondered if he would find them as fascinating as she did.

ABOUT "THE COMMON GOAL OF NATURE"

Aliens are a staple of SF. They hold a fun-house mirror up to humanity. So why aren't there more aliens in my stories? "Eifelheim," not included in this collection, involved aliens; but they remained offstage. "Common Goal . . ." remains my one and only story *about* aliens.

I suppose one reason is that there are enough aliens among us humans. Winterman, for one. But another reason was John W. Campbell's old challenge: to create aliens that think as well as humans, but differently. If I was going to do an alien story, I didn't want humans in rubber suits.

To create an alien that thinks *differently*, we have to know how we ourselves think; and we don't, not really. Fundamentals go unnoticed. "Fish aren't aware of water." Give you an example: I look out the window here in my home office and I see . . . a tree.

Now, all I can actually see from here is the trunk. (It is a rather tall tree.) But why do I not think "trunk" when I look at it? Or even "bark"? For that matter, why do I not think "gum tree," since that is what it is? Or "Northeastern forest"? In other words, we humans recognize things first some level between the very specific (bark of lower trunk of gum tree) and the very general (a plant). We perceive the entity, not its parts and not the whole of which it is a member. We would look out the window and say, "I see leaves," only if the leaves were not attached to a tree.

Now, I have an alien here with me. (Trust me on this.) I pointed out the window. "What do you see?" "An ecosphere," it replied. Such an alien, seeing the set before seeing the members of the set, would have to *know* things in a different way than we do. How would that perception translate into behavior and into culture? And what kind of story would that require? I don't have the answers yet; but my alien friend here is anxious to get on with life.

(I do have another alien waiting in the wings: the Sh'thanrigk. They belong to the same mosaic as the Hraani and will make their appearance in "The Seanachy" if and when I figure out how to finish that story.)

The inspiration for the Hraani came from *The Man Who Mistook His Wife for a Hat*, by Oliver Sacks. My esteemed agent, the keen and crafty Eleanor Wood, gave it to me at lunch one day. She complained that she was never able to finish the book because she kept giving her copies to friends before she was finished. (Although, as an agent, she only needs to read 10 percent of the book, anyway.) The book is a treasure trove of ideas. Gene Wolfe mined it for *Soldier of the Mist* and Nancy Kress for *Brain Rose*. The chapter about "body blindness" led me to wonder about the thought processes of a creature that had evolved without proprioception.

But an alien does not make a story; it must be relevant to the story. In what sort of tale might the nature of the Hraani be peculiarly appropriate? Then I thought of Winterman. (Winter-man is cold, but I did not pick the name for that reason. Though, images of ice and cold permeate the story, so there must be something to this subconscious thing, after all.) The hran's disconnection from his body counterpoints Winterman's emotional disconnection from humanity, especially from his old friend, Sergeant Oakes. Oakes and Johnny Starbuck are also disconnected, in different ways. Perhaps Morton, too, who gives advice but never acts. The story is about Winterman reconnecting. The ending should come as no surprise, but as an inevitable juggernaut rolling down on Winterman from the beginning. Repentance came too late, but it came; and that is the important thing. Was the ending justice or tragedy, or both? Damned if I know, I just write the things.

Grave Reservations

by Rowland Shew

Tony Fanculli cast a sour eye at the Reservation Police and resigned himself to a long wait for the tour bus coming from Jersey. The police were searching cars as they exited the tunnel, and the traffic was backed up all the way to Secaucus.

He hated drawing tour duty. It was worse than jury duty. At least jurors dealt with New Yorkers—often officials high in city government. Tour guides had to deal with hicks. He sighed and reviewed the tour package instructions for the hundredth time.

By the time the bus arrived at the tour dock, he knew what to expect. It was a mixed group from most of the Nine Nations: a couple of Dixiecans, a Breadbasket family, a Texan, some Sunbelters, three Westerners, and a pair of Ecotopians. He recognized the latter when they disembarked: they were clad in hiking boots and backpacks and were chewing something which Tony assumed was granola. He shuddered. If the Good Lord had meant for people to eat granola, He would never have given us The Hoagie.

He could tell from their white faces and shaky gait that the bus had taken them on the Jersey Turnpike Thrill Ride. The Ride was often included with the tour package since the OSHA people had ruled it sufficiently safe. New Jersey drivers were the best in the world. They had to be, to drive the way they did and live to tell of it.

The tour leader, Gayle Possit, approached him. He had dealt with Gayle many times before and found her to be tolerable, for a hick. She lived out in the country somewhere, in a place called New Haven. "Sorry we're late," she said. "What was the delay?"

Tony gestured toward the roadblock where the Reservation Police were still stopping cars. "Sales tax check," he said.

One of the hicks heard him and frowned. From his flashy and vulgar clothing, Tony judged him to be one of the Dixiecans. The man was actually wearing a *checkered* jacket. "What do y'all mean, sales tax check? You mean it ain't a search for an escaped convict or one of them there Mafiosi we read about?"

Before Tony could answer, a police whistle blew, and they all turned in time to see the police drag a driver out of her car. The trunk lid was sprung, revealing a color television set. One of the policemen read the sales slip.

"It's Joisey, awright," he announced.

His partner shook his head sadly and addressed the woman. "Yer ID sez you're a City resident. Don'cha know it's illegal to buy somethin' widdout payin' the sales tax?"

"But I did pay the sales tax!" she protested. "I bought it in Joisey and paid Joisey taxes."

"Don't matter where ya bought it. City people gotta pay City taxes. Ya owe the City the difference between what'cha paid Joisey and what'cha shoulda paid the City. That's been the law since the 1980s." He waved his baton. "Take her in, Charlie. Sales tax evasion." He turned his attention back to the cars still in line, many of whose drivers were now looking rather nervous.

Tony nodded in satisfaction. Another desperate criminal brought to justice. New York's Finest never slept. He turned back to the tour group, who were still watching the tunnel blockage goggle-eyed. "Welcome to da City," he announced.

"Hold on thar!" bellowed a man ridiculously garbed in string tie, cowboy hat, and tooled boots. "Is that true, what we jest heard? No matter whar a New Yorker shops, he pays New York taxes?"

Tony was nettled at having his Welcome Speech interrupted. "Certainly," he said curtly. "It ain't right to cheat the City. People only go shoppin' in Joisey to escape paying their Fair Share of taxes; so when we catch 'em, we make 'em pay the difference. That takes the incentive out of buying outside the City. The merchants are all for it."

One of the Ecotopians spoke up. "What if that lady had bought her TV in Portland? There's *no* sales tax in Portland."

Tony was so stunned at the thought that there was a place with no sales tax that he didn't even ask where Portland was. All he knew was it was somewhere in the vast wastelands west of the Hudson.

Gayle spoke up, soothing the group. "Now, remember we signed a paper before we left, pledging not to criticize native customs, no matter how bizarre they appear. After all, each of the Nine Nations has customs that seem strange to the other Eight. The New York Reservation is even stranger. In this case, New Yorkers believe that a person's money really belongs to the government, a belief once widely held in the old U.S.A., mostly in the Northeast; but now restricted to the New York and Washington Reservations. It's a quaint belief; but the City only has sales tax agreements with the Foundry States of New Jersey and West Connecticut. New Yorkers are not sure even that other states exist."

Tony fumed while he listened. Gayle was OK, but somehow she always sounded patronizing when explaining City customs to the hicks. Personally, Tony did not feel any need to explain anything. After all, New York was The Greatest City in The World. One of the radio stations said so every morning. He cleared his throat and started his Welcome Speech over.

"Welcome to da City. Da Big Apple. Da Greatest City inna World." He always started the speech in his native tongue, because the hicks loved to hear it; but he always made an effort to conduct the tour in something approaching Standard English. "Me, I'm Tony Fanculli, yer guide for the next eight hours. We'll start the tour here at the Port Authority and head Downtown, go up the East Side, through Midtown, down the West Side, and have you back here before dark. That's if we're lucky." He laughed at his own joke. Actually, there was seldom a problem with schedule. Tour groups always had right of way, even over taxi cabs. The City needed the hard currency the hicks brought in—especially Western currency, which was gold-backed. Everyone recognized this, even the street gangs, who limited their tourist predation to the obligatory purse snatching. (Tourists were provided with special "breakaway" purses for just this purpose.) Tony checked his itinerary. The Lords of Death were supposed to snatch two purses from this group down in the Village.

Gayle interrupted. "One word of warning, if I may. If you become separated from the group, proceed immediately to the nearest public phone and call the Tourist Board. There are bound to be a few public phones in working order. Do *not*, repeat not, attempt to ask a native for directions. Only one in three will give you the correct directions, and, of course, you have no way of knowing which one. The natives have a quaint belief that if you don't already know how to get somewhere, you don't deserve to go there."

Tony double-checked his itinerary. "Oh, there's one change to the tour. We will not be able to attend a meeting of the City Council. City Hall has been recently relocated to Riker's Island, which was the only place that all the officials could meet conveniently." He looked at the group. "So, regretfully, we must skip that part of the tour; although we still do plan to meet with Victor Steinmetz, who, before he retired, spent an entire career in City Government during the 1990s without once being indicted." He folded the papers and returned them to his jacket pocket. "Now, are there any questions before we begin? I am an experienced tour guide, as Ms. Possit has undoubtedly told you. I've been just about everywhere there is to go."

"Oh? Have you ever been to St. Paul?" That was the Breadbasket mother. She was clad frumpishly in a shapeless print dress and had an obvious need, Tony thought, to visit Seventh Avenue.

"St. Paul?" he said. "Sure. It's up on 117th St. I told you, I been all over."

The Breadbasketer blinked in confusion, and a Sunbelter asked, "What about New Mexico? Ever been there?"

"Nah," Tony admitted. "I ain't never been outa the old U.S.A."

The Sunbelter looked offended, though Tony didn't know why.

"Well, then, where have you traveled?" asked a Westerner.

"I tol' ya, I been all over: SoHo, TriBeCa, the East Village, the Fashion District. I been all the way up to Washington Heights. I go to Brooklyn almost every week. I been to Staten Island a couple times; and once I even went to Joisey."

"Hell, son," drawled the Texan. "You call that travelin'? I go fu'ther than that just to reach the front gate of my ranch."

Gayle interposed herself and explained smoothly. "When a New Yorker says *everywhere*, he or she usually means 'everywhere in New York.' Actually, compared to many other natives, Mr. Fanculli really is well traveled. Many people on the Reservation never even leave the neighborhood where they were born. They spend their whole lives in The Village, or on the Upper West Side, or wherever. They claim that, since all their needs are met within walking distance of their 'flat' or 'loft' or 'walk-up' that there's no reason to go anywhere else. So they think their own small corner of the world *is* the world. . . .

"Some of you may remember the so-called 'crack epidemic' of a while back. To hear the New York-centered media tell it, crack was everywhere. Yet, when the statistics were finally analyzed the police found it was largely concentrated in New York and its Miami and Los Angeles connections. Since the media never went anywhere else, the problem naturally appeared to be 'everywhere.' "

They boarded the electric tram and wound their way down the specially cleared tourist lanes toward Wall Street. Tony kept pointing out sights and the hicks kept craning their necks and gawking. Occasionally he overheard comments:

"Have you noticed how *filthy* the streets are," a Westerner commented. "Not clean like Denver or Salt Lake City."

"Narrow, too," replied his companion. "Our *driveway* is wider than most of these lanes. And why do they drive such big cars when the streets are so narrow?"

"I don't understand what's so interesting about Chinatown," one of the Ecotopians said to the other. "They should come to San Francisco if they want to see a Chinatown."

"Daddy," said the Breadbasket child. "Why does the man keep talking about The City. Does he mean Kansas City?"

"No, honey. He means New York City."

"Then why does he only say The City?"

Gayle, the tour coordinator explained. "All primitive peoples think of themselves as special. Often, their name for themselves means simply The People. The Navajo call themselves Na Dene; the Eskimo call themselves the Inuit. The implicit meaning is that other tribes are not really people. Well, in just the same way, New Yorkers talk about The City as if it were the only real city and other cities, like Dallas or Chicago or San Francisco, don't really matter. Whenever you hear a New Yorker say 'The' you know he's talking about New York. Like The Met, The Guggenheim, The Street, and so on. You see, they are very parochial here and know next to nothing about life anywhere outside the Reservation."

When they passed the World Trade Center an Ecotopian noticed the name of the hotel nearby. He looked puzzled. "Vista International?" He looked up toward the top of the building. "Why do they call it the Vista *International?*"

"Because," Tony told them. "From the top, you can see Joisey."

The purse snatching in the Village came off as planned. The Death Lords were right on schedule, grabbing the purses and disappearing down Bleecker Street. It was professionally done and Tony made a mental note to raise the gang's tip. The hicks were all buzzing about law and order.

"Oh, my!" said the lady from St. Paul, "Is that what it's like to be a crime victim? That's never happened to me before."

"I wish they hadn't made me check mah shootin' irons at the tunnel," complained the Texan. "I'd show them punks a thang or two."

"I'm afraid you can't bring guns into the City, sir," explained Tony patiently. "We have gun control here."

"Why's that?"

"Why? To cut down on crime, of course!"

"Oh?" asked a Westerner. "Is that why New York is so safe at night?"

"The City ain't all that dangerous," Tony protested. "You just gotta know where you can go, and when."

The Breadbasket lady was knitting. She looked up at him. "Tell me, young man. You've lived here your whole life, have you not? Perhaps thirty years? Well, how many times have you been a crime victim yourself?"

Tony pursed his lips and shook his head. "Not often." He counted on his fingers. "I've been mugged once, burglarized twice, and had my car stolen once."

"Well, that's not much in thirty years."

"Oh no, that's *this* year."

The Ecotopian boy raised his hand. "I read in the paper how a businessman and his Mafia partner set up a dummy corporation with a black politician as a front man to take advantage of the minority contractor law. Why did the jury let them go free?"

Tony frowned. "Why not? That law is just a technicality. Besides, it's hard to convince a New Yorker that an action is criminal if it doesn't actually involve someone sticking a gun in your face."

"And yet, since they walked away with your tax money, shouldn't you

consider yourself a victim of *that* crime, as well? Why do you only count
street crimes, committed by poor people?"

In the Wall Street area they marveled at the fleets of stretch limousines and
other luxury cars parked up on the sidewalks of the narrow lanes. Somehow it seemed appropriate that the largest cars of all were saved for the nar-
rowest streets of all. Maiden Lane looked like a Mercedes Benz showroom.
Pedestrians streamed around the cars, oblivious to the obstructions in their
paths. The hicks noticed that many of the limos were occupied by men
and women speaking animatedly on their car phones.

"What are they doing?" a Sunbelter asked.

"Doin' business. They're calling The Exchange or their brokers. Sometimes it's too crowded on The Floor. They can't get in the building, so they
sit in their cars and work by phone."

"Why can't they just stay home and work by phone?" The Sunbelter was
genuinely puzzled. "Don't you people have a DataNet yet? You can, like,
plug in and download data, interface with anybody else on the Net."

Tony looked on him with pity. "But if they stayed home in Darien or
Short Hills, *they wouldn't be doing business in The City!*"

There seemed no way to answer that. The Sunbelter fell silent, but
Tony caught him later making whirly motions with his finger around his
head.

They were just passing one of the Wall Street banks when a man flew
abruptly through the main door and landed on the street in front of them.
Two other men stood dusting their hands off in front of the bank building.
"And don't come back till ya loin ta dress!" one of them said.

The object of their scorn stood up and brushed himself off. He saw the
tourists looking at him and hung his head in shame.

"What's wrong with the way he's dressed?" asked the Texan.

Privately, Tony thought that a man wearing a string tie and cowboy
boots would never understand the answer. Nevertheless, he tried to explain.

"Just look at his suit," he told the group. "A *brown* suit. How can anyone take seriously a man wearin' a brown suit? And woist of all . . ." He let
the words drag out. "He's not wearin' a *power tie!*"

If he had expected a gasp of outrage, Tony was disappointed. All he saw
were blank stares. "You see," he continued lamely, "a businessman in

Manhattan must wear a black, blue, or pinstripe suit with a white or pale solid shirt and a power tie."

"Why?" asked a Sunbelter girl decked out in bright-colored shorts, sunglasses, and tan. (Tony wondered if her garb passed for business dress in San Diego or Albuquerque.) "Like, what has a person's clothing got to do with, y'know, his skills as a businessman or the values of his ideas?"

Once again, Gayle came to Tony's rescue. "Another feature of primitive tribes," she explained, "is the presence of sumptuary laws—often unwritten—regulating the sort of clothing tribal members are allowed to wear. For example, at one time in Europe only kings were allowed to wear purple clothing. The same is true of business garb in New York. Appearances count for more than substance. There is no logical reason for it. You or I might not refuse to deal with a person because he was wearing a brown suit, *or even if he was not wearing a suit at all,* but New Yorkers retain many old and quaint customs. For example, have you noticed the businesswomen in their fashionable suit dresses, but wearing Adidas or Nike walking shoes? They change into their heels after they get to their offices."

"Hell, little lady," said the Texan, "that's the first thing I've seen today that makes *sense!*"

"Because it's difficult to walk across the grates in heels?"

"No, to outrun the muggers."

The businessman slunk away, hiding his face, and the tram proceeded to South Street Seaport, which one of the Dixiecans likened to Baltimore Harbor—except it didn't have the water taxis like Baltimore had. Tony was scandalized that anyone would compare The City to a hick town like Baltimore, but he held his tongue rather than risk offending the Tourist Dollar.

Since the group would leave the tram for a while and walk around the shops, Tony decided it was time for the Safety Lecture. He gathered them in a half circle around him by the curb.

"Remember to be careful when crossin' the street. Wait for the light and look both ways, then run like hell to the other side. That won't guarantee success, but you'll have a better chance that way. If any cars honk at you—and many will—be sure to bang on their hoods with your fist. The drivers will expect it. The odds are only one in fifty that the driver will shoot you."

"In California," a Sunbelter said, "pedestrians have the right of way. Like, if a pedestrian, y'know, puts a toe into a crosswalk, cars have to stop."

Tony smiled. "It's not that way here." To demonstrate, he put his toe out into the street and immediately two passing automobiles and a gypsy cab swerved to run over it. Tony yanked it back safely in time. "Do not try this maneuver on your own," he admonished the group. "Remember, I am a trained professional."

The hicks walked around the Seaport for a half hour and Tony was stunned when they returned without having bought anything. When he asked, all he got was shrugs. "There are bookstores and clothing stores and stuff back home," was the answer they gave him. "We can buy the same things there for less."

The whole idea of the Tour Program was to suck in the hick dollars; but he had been noticing the reaction more and more lately: Why come to The City to buy things you can buy anywhere else? Tony bit his lip, thinking about the letter he would get from the Merchants' Association. With some misgivings he rounded them up and the tram set off for the trip up the East Side.

They had gone about a block when a car suddenly drove up on the sidewalk, cut in front of them, and stopped. The driver hopped out and ran into a store. Since the street was only one-lane wide and there were cars on both sides, the tram was unable to move. Tony waited patiently, but some of the hicks were angry.

"What did he do that for?" complained a Dixiecan. "Why, that's just flat out rude. Why did that fellow have to block the street like that when there's a parking garage just down the block?"

Tony gave him a blank look, not understanding the word "rude." "In The City," he told them, "no one can tell whether the streets are blocked or not. There's no difference in the flow of traffic. The guy wanted to run into the store. Why should he park half a block away when he can double park right in front? Parking garages cost money. Besides, there aren't that many residents like him."

"What do you mean?" asked an Ecotopian.

"Residents who drive in the City. Very few actually drive cars. There are many who don't even have licenses."

"That's right," recalled the Texan. "My company hired a New Yorker one time. The poor feller was totally lost. The first time he tried to drive a car, he got in and grabbed the strap and waited for the door to close. Couldn't help feelin' sorry for him, the feller was so naive."

"Naive? New Yorkers have Street Smarts!" Tony protested.

"Only for your streets, though. He just couldn't adjust to life off the Reservation; so pretty soon, he gave it up and scurried back where he come from."

Tony shook his head angrily. "That's impossible. This is The City. If You Can Make It Here, You Can Make It Anywhere!"

"Is that so?" The Texan looked amused. "Can you run an oil rig?"

"Or bring in a wheat crop?" asked the Breadbasket father.

"Or sail the Straits of Juan de Fuca?" That was the Ecotopian.

"Or run a herd of white-faces on the open range?"

"Or design a new LSIC chip?"

"Or tag 'gators down in the 'Glades?"

"Or survive a night on the Alaskan tundra?"

"Or pour steel in the Foundry?"

Gayle saw how the talk was headed and interrupted. "Excuse me, Tony; but if not that many New Yorkers drive, where do all those cars come from?" She waved at the unbroken lines of parked automobiles. They sat along both sides of the street, next to the fire hydrants, and under the No Parking signs.

Tony shot her a look of gratitude for the planted question. "Oh, those, I said New Yorkers didn't *drive* cars; I never said they didn't *own* them. Many of these cars have been parked there for decades. See there? That's a 1955 Chevy Bel Air. Its owner, Morris Katz, who lived in the upper forties, found a parking space down here in October of '57. So he parked it here and took the train home. Neither his son nor his grandson have moved it since then, because they don't want to risk losing the space."

"Shoot. They couldn't move it nohow, son," the Texan drawled. "She ain't got no tires." (Actually, he said 'tars' but Tony caught his meaning.) In the City, a parked car—or even one that was moving slowly—usually wound up being stripped.

The Breadbasket child pointed to the cars. "Are those parking tickets in the windshields, Mister?"

"They sure enough are," interjected a Westerner. "How cum some cars have 'em and some don't?"

"Because the cops only write the tickets if the car's from out-of-town."

"But there aren't any No Parking signs!"

Tony shrugged. "So what? We don't need signs. Everyone knows you're not supposed to park there."

"Even the out-of-towners?"

"Oh, *they* don't. We do. Unmarked No Parking zones are one of The City's main sources of revenue."

The Ecotopian woman wrinkled her nose. "What's that smell?"

Tony smiled. He could usually expect to get a lead-in from one of the hicks at about this point in the tour. "That smell," he announced, "is one of the most historic sites in the entire City. As the tram turns here to follow the East River, if you would all look to your right, you will see *The Flying Trashman*. The legendary garbage scow that sailed the seas back in '87, fated never to reach port. They say that seven states and five foreign countries refused to berth her because the garbage was from New York and they believed, in their prejudice, that that meant it was dangerously toxic."

"Then why didn't you-all unload it when it finally returned here?" asked a Dixiecan.

Tony stared at him in pity. "Are you nuts? It's probably dangerously toxic. Besides, Brooklyn and Islip couldn't agree on which particular articles of trash belonged to each municipality."

"Wait a minute, son. You mean grown men and women stood there like a passel of young'uns and said, 'I won't pick it up because I didn't put it there!'?"

Tony shook his head. "I didn't say anything about grown men and women. These were City politicians."

"What you may not realize," Gayle added, "is that New York is the last major city on the East Coast that still dumps untreated sewage directly into the sea."

Tony shrugged. "Sure, but the currents take it away from land."

The Ecotopians began to chant, "Save the Whales! Save the Whales!" But Gayle calmed them by pointing out that the currents that carried the sewage away from New York carried it to the Jersey Shore, where it washed up regularly on the northern beaches and in front of the governor's summer house. The whales were in no danger; and nobody but Jerseyans cared about toxic waste in Jersey.

"Wait a consarn minute!" interrupted a Westerner. "You mean New York can do whatever it damn well pleases, and New Jersey can't do a thing about it?"

"Yes. In fact, once the entire country had to change because New York wouldn't. Years ago, each state used to set its own drinking age. New York's was set at eighteen, while New Jersey and Connecticut were at twenty-one. Thousands of teenagers would drive into the City every week to get drunk and then drive back, killing themselves and others. The other states tried for years to get New York to do something about the 'Blood Border.' But, the people who were complaining were not New York voters, while those who sold the liquor were. Finally, the old Federal Government stepped in and mandated that *all* states had to raise the drinking age to twenty-one, even if they did not border New York. Many of the Western states protested that they had no trouble at all with Blood Borders, and that they had a sensible, two-tier drinking system, with 3.2 beer for the eighteen-year-olds; but a *federal* law was a way out for the New York politicians."

They passed a group of tall buildings along the East River. "Oh, look!" said the foreigner from New Mexico. "Ain't that the U.N.? Does the tour go there?"

Gayle answered his question. "No, sir, I'm afraid we don't go there. The admission fee that you paid at the tunnel coming in only covers admittance to the Reservation. The U.N. is covered by an additional fee. A sort of Reservation within the Reservation. And besides" — she smiled quietly — "if you have a hard time dealing with New York customs, you'll *never* believe what goes on in there!"

They cruised past enormous office towers that had once been the headquarters of major corporations. Now, they were virtually empty, their windows smashed and their walls ablaze with graffiti. Tony told them about the Battle of the Tunnels, in which the mayor, real estate speculators, and other paragons of civic virtue had thrown up barricades to prevent the last of the corporations from leaving. It hadn't worked, however, since they forgot to blockade the Staten Island Ferry and the corporations sneaked out the back way.

"But," he said brightly, "We still got the Mets an' the Yankees an' the

Jets. Every year the Mets an' the Yankees play the Subway Series for the World Championship of City Baseball."

"What about the Giants?"

"The Giants?" he asked with a sneer. "The *Joisey* Giants? They were one of the first to leave, the traitors. Nah, Joisey got 'em. An' it soives 'em both right! Back in 1987, when someone said to Mayor Koch that The City should hold a ticker tape parade for the Giants in case they won the Super Bowl, he said no, an' his aide said that 'some rube mayor in Moonachie' should throw a parade instead."

"Which they did," added Gayle.

"I remember that," said one of the Westerners. "Denver held a ticker tape parade down Eighteenth Street for the Broncos, who lost the Game, and more people showed up for that than showed up for the Giants."

Tony looked at him, bug-eyed. "They congratulated the *losers?*" Didn't these people know *anything* about sports?

The Breadbasket mother tugged at Tony's sleeve. "Young man. If all the corporations left back in the nineties, then what is that they're building over there?"

They all looked where she pointed. A framework of girders and brick was climbing to the sky. Hordes of workers ate their lunch or sat on large pieces of equipment or walked the girders, carrying things from one place to another so that other workers could carry them back.

"That," said Tony proudly, "is the new Koch-Trump Memorial Office Tower, named after the two men who, more than anyone else, made New York what it is today."

Men with clipboards ambled among the workers. The men with the clipboards outnumbered all the others. They were City inspectors, checking the plumbing, the wiring, the construction, the finances. They were signing licenses, stamping approvals, receiving kickbacks. There were inspectors from the buildings department, the roads department, the parks department, the Parking Authority, the Environmental Protection Agency, and the Mafia.

The Mafia inspectors were there to make sure that only substandard materials were used on the job and also that the graft was fairly distributed. Tony and the others watched while the pouring of a concrete caisson was interrupted so that the remains of Eduardo "Fat Eddie" Scutari could be added to the mix. Tony explained that the Mafia had run out of room in its retire-ment home under the East River. City legends had it that Jimmy Hoffa him-self was resting in the foundations of one or more of these buildings and had not ended his days, as many others supposed, as an impurity in a steel ingot.

Just then, a workman tripped over a piece of pipe. He picked it up to throw it in the scrap bin. Immediately, all work on the site came to a halt. The first man froze, looked at the pipe in his hand, and dropped it as if it had become red-hot. But it was too late. A wildcat strike had begun.

Thirty-five shop stewards, each representing a different craft union con-verged on the gang boss's trailer, shouting and waving copies of their con-tracts.

"What's going on thar?" asked the Texan.

"Jurisdictional grievance," Tony answered. "That man there, he picked up a pipe."

"Well? The pipe was a hazard, wasn't it?"

"But the man wasn't a pipe fitter!"

Again, all he got from the hicks were blank stares. Didn't they realize how important craft boundaries were? If people were allowed to do work outside their craft, the result would be chaos. Before you knew it, one man would be doing the job of three and the cost of construction work would plummet. "It's a union rule," he explained lamely.

"Unions?" asked a Sunbelter. "You still have, like, unions here?"

"I bet they still have managements, too," sneered an Ecotopian.

"Well, if you have the one, you generally have the other," the Sunbel-ter told him. "They go together, like herpes and cold sores."

They broke for lunch at a "deli" and had bagels with cream cheese, New York's contribution to *haute cuisine*. Everyone agreed that the food was one of the high points of the tour. The Breadbasket mother turned and signaled. "Oh, waiter!" None of the young men and women scurrying about the din-ing area paid the slightest attention. Instead, they chatted with one another or read *Variety*.

Tony smiled and shook his head. "You hafta know how to call a City waiter." He turned and cupped his hands around his mouth. "CASTING CALL!"

Immediately, seventeen waiters and waitresses surrounded their table, 8 × 10 glossy publicity stills in their hands.

"You see," Tony explained to the group, "there are no waiters or wait-resses in New York, only unemployed actors and actresses."

"Currently between engagements," one of the young ladies corrected him.

"Are they *really* actors and actresses?" asked Mama Breadbasket.

"Well, yes and no. Most of them have probably appeared off-off-Broadway and some off-Broadway; but I doubt more than one or two have actually appeared on Broadway."

"I've never understood that," said a Dixiecan. "Why the distinction be-tween what street a theater is on?"

"It's not that," said Tony. "Some of the Broadway theaters aren't actu-ally on Broadway. It's a distinction of class, or prestige. You Haven't Made It Till You've Made Broadway. This is The Heart of The Theater."

"Oh? I thought most of the new plays these days were coming from Lon-don, and New York was just a stop for the road companies." That was the Ecotopian girl. Tony scowled at her.

"What would someone from Ecotopia know about The Theater?"

"Why, don't you know? Even back in the 1980s, Seattle was premiering more new plays than any city in the old U.S.A. except New York. Care to guess who's Number One now?"

"A play that premieres in Seattle doesn't count."

"Why not?"

"Because the New York Drama Critics haven't reviewed it!"

She shrugged. "Who cares what they have to say?"

Tony's jaw dropped and he looked around. "Be careful! Someone might hear you!"

As they left the building, Tony noticed the headlines on the *News*. Nearly unique among newspapers, the back page of the *News* was a second "front page" featuring sports headlines. "Hey! How about that! The New York Gi-ants won the game today!"

The Texan raised an eyebrow. "I thought they were the Jersey Giants."

"Only when they lose," explained Tony. "When they win, they're the New York Giants. It's a fine point of City grammar first popularized by Hiz-zoner Mayor Koch back in the 1980s."

As they cut through Central Park, Tony saw that they were in for a treat. The bird was singing and the flower was blooming.

They paused in the Fashion District and watched workers manhandle racks of clothing between buildings and into the backs of trucks. The trucks were parked on the sidewalks and in the middle of the street.

"Aren't those rather primitive production methods for the twenty-first century?" asked a Sunbelter.

A Westerner answered her. "Why, this whole town is still stuck in the nineteenth or early twentieth centuries. Didn't you notice back in that buildin' where we ate lunch? They still have human elevator operators."

"And their banks close at three o'clock," said an Ecotopian. "I saw a sign in a bank window."

"There's a sound economic reason for that," protested Tony. "You see, if the banks are closed, people can't deposit their paychecks, so they cash them out at work. That means every Friday a large amount of cash is walking around the streets, which gives the muggers a fair chance to make a profit. . . ."

"Cash?" asked a Westerner, goggle-eyed. "Don't you have ACH or debit cards?"

"My word! What is that?"

Tony welcomed the interruption from Mama Breadbasket. They all turned to look where she was pointing. An incredibly thin and bony woman was walking down the street. Her skin had all the color of those fish species that lived their whole lives in dark caves. She was dressed bizarrely, in clothing that constricted her movements and which did not hang well unless she struck the most unnatural poses. Parts of her dress were of clear plastic, and not always the parts that one might suspect.

"That," said Tony proudly, "is This Year's Look." He saw the blank faces again and elaborated. "This is the Fashion that all the women will be wearing this year."

The Texan scratched his chin. "I doubt that, son. Most women have better sense than that. What makes you think so?"

"Because New York is Where Fashions Are Made."

"You are very mistaken, young man," said the Breadbasket mother. "Nothing becomes a fashion until it is adopted in the Breadbasket. Until then, it is only a fad."

As they made their way down the West Side, a sound began to make itself felt. The Sound had always been there, in the background. A muted humming. Faint and indistinct. Now it grew louder and clearer: the sound of a hundred automobile horns blasting all at once. Tony passed hearing protection around.

"What you are hearing," he said through the throat mike, "is the world's first and only Permanent Traffic Jam. It was created in 1998 when Betsy Amato of Ozone Park tried to run a yellow light southbound on Ninth Avenue and got caught in the intersection. This Blocked the Box for the westbound traffic on Forty-fifth Street, which then backed up into the intersection on Eighth Avenue, stopping the northbound traffic there. The blockage ran back across Forty-fourth Street, plugging up southbound Ninth. At that point, none of the four streets could move."

The electric tram rolled down the sidewalk. A few cars in the traffic jam had tried to get around it by driving down the sidewalk themselves before getting stuck, but there was plenty of room for the narrow tour cars.

The drivers in the cars waved to the passing tourists, who waved back and clicked holographs to show the folks back home. One driver began to beat out a syncopated rhythm on his horn and others took it up with him. Soon the whole street was jamming to a monotonic tune.

"There was some thought given to crushing the cars *in situ* and paving over the whole mess; but everyone sorta hoped the jam would break up someday. Many of the drivers you see today are the children and grandchildren of the original drivers. They report to their cars at 9:00 every morning, honk their horns at the car blocking them, and leave at 5:00 each night."

"Do they get breaks?"

"Of course! They got a union. After a while a mathematician at Columbia showed that topologically the knot was permanent and the jam could not be untied in four dimensions. By then, however, it had become a permanent attraction."

"Why do they honk?" the Sunbelter girl asked. "I mean, like, it's obvious that honking at the car in front of you isn't going to do any good at all."

"Because it always seemed to work in the past," said Gayle, once again explaining the native customs. "Whenever a New Yorker was in a jam, he would honk his horn. If he honked long enough, the jam would break up. It was an easy step from there to the belief that honking the horn *caused* the jam to break. It's called *post hoc, ergo propter hoc,* or beating on the tom-toms. Many primitive tribes have similar beliefs. For example, if you beat on the tom-toms during an eclipse of the sun, it will restore the sun. Try it. You just have to remember to keep beating long enough."

When they reached the Port Authority Terminal, Tony gathered the hicks together for good-byes. He asked them what they thought about The City.

They told him.

New York just didn't measure up. Seattle was much nicer. Or Denver was. Or Albuquerque. Or Minneapolis-St. Paul. New York was too crowded, too dirty, too crooked, too dangerous. Its people were too rude. What did New York have that San Francisco or New Orleans or dozens of other big cities didn't have? Finally, Tony could take it no more.

"Hicks!" he exploded. "None of those places of yours have half of what New York has!"

"Well, we don't have half the crime."

"Or half the garbage."

"Or half the crooked politicians."

"Or half the traffic."

"Yeah, sure. And you don't have half the theaters; or half the museums; or . . . Just where do you come off actin' so superior?" He pointed at a Dix-iecan. "Are you sayin' Atlanta don't have urban decay?" To a Sunbelter: "Or Los Angeles have traffic jams? What's the difference between Broad-way hype and Hollywood plastic?" To the Texan: "Does Houston have any more urban planning than The City? Ain't there no crime in Dallas?" To a Westerner: "No pollution in Denver?" There were tears in his eyes now. "Why you gotta pick on New York, The Greatest City Inna World? What makes The City so special?"

They stared at him, half-astonished, half-embarrassed. Finally, Gayle cleared her throat. "Because New York *is* special. It's a vanishing way of life. We had to take steps to preserve it, *so that people would remember how bad things could get.* New York is our object lesson. Of course, all those other cities have the same problems, but the memory of New York helps us keep them from getting out of hand." She paused and patted Tony on the cheek. "Sometimes, though, it's easy to forget that New York is some-one's hometown, too; and that people can love their hometown in the teeth of all logic and reason. You're a dear, Tony, and you've worked your heart out for the Tourist Board. I've noticed how tired and overwrought you've been the last couple of tours. You need a vacation."

Tony brightened. "Coney Island?"

"No, farther than that."

"The Hamptons?"

"No. I'd like you to join a tour group I'm putting together. We're going to visit La-La Land, the Southern California Reservation."

Tony glanced at the discomfited Sunbelters and his smile broadened. Now *that* sounded like fun!

ABOUT "GRAVE RESERVATIONS"

———◆◆●◆◆———

David Hartwell has included this story as a concession to my good friend, Rowland Shew. The first real sale I made to *Analog* was on Rowland's behalf ("The Quality Throop," *Analog*, February 1984). We had just moved to New Jersey.* My new employer threw an office party. "You'll love it here," everyone said. "Just think how close you'll be to New York!" Our friends in Denver gave us a going away party. "You'll hate it there," they said dolefully. "Just think how close you'll be to New York!" What is it about New York that inspires such sentiments? Los Angeles gets some of that love-hate thing, too. But not Chicago, not San Francisco, not Seattle, not a whole host of other cities with their own individual personalities. Is it because of TV and Hollywood? Are NY and LA different because they are onstage and the rest of us in the audience?

While traveling on business the year before we moved I read a book called *The Nine Nations of North America*, by Joel Garreau, in which he described the Native Cultures of the nine nations. I had been forming many of the same impressions during my assignments in Seattle, Paducah, Detroit, and elsewhere. Consider the following sets:

{Boston, Providence, Augusta, St. John, Halifax . . . }
{Buffalo, Pittsburgh, Detroit, Windsor . . . }
{Atlanta, Birmingham, Memphis, Charlotte, Dallas . . . }
{Miami, San Juan, Nassau, Havana . . . }
{Minneapolis, St. Louis, Kansas City, Fort Worth, Winnipeg . . . }
{El Paso, Juarez, Santa Fe, Los Angeles, Tijuana . . . }
{Juneau, Vancouver, Seattle, Portland, San Francisco . . . }
{Denver, Calgary, Salt Lake City, Fairbanks . . . }
{Quebec, Montreal, Trois Rivieres . . . }

———

*From Colorado, and don't ask.

The cities in each set "taste" similar to one another; but each set has its own "flavor." Attitudes in Calgary and Cheyenne are much alike. But Los Angeles and San Francisco are on different planets, *Weltanschauung*-wise. Garreau listed New York City as an aberration, not fitting in with the rest of The Foundry. So Rowland incorporated this notion into a satire on The Greatest City in the World. (And no fooling, one of New York's radio stations really does use that line, and they really do believe it.)

Mammy Morgan Played the Organ; Her Daddy Beat the Drum

An idle breeze was all it was. It was all it could have been.

Hilda Schenckweiler raised her head and looked around the business office. A sound? The old library building creaked at night, as its century-old foundation snuggled deeper into the soil. It popped and groaned with voices that went unnoticed during the bustle of the day, but which caught the attention during the still evenings. And the other librarians told certain stories, absurd stories on the face of them, that became more uncertain and less absurd as the night deepened. She laid aside the correspondence she had been answering and sat very still.

Yes, definitely a sound. But what? A soft, sliding sound, like the breath of a sleeping child. Familiar; but that nagging sort of familiarity that defied recognition. A shuddery feeling crawled like spiders up the back of her head, and she brushed instinctively at her hair.

The sound seemed to come from behind her. She rose from her seat, hesitated a moment, then walked to the doorway that led to Interlibrary Loan. The illumination spilling from the business office spread a fan of light into the darkened work areas, teasing the dim shapes of tables and arching doorways from the shadows. Her own shadow, elongated and angular, was a spear thrusting into the shrouded gloom. Open doorways were cave mouths along the left-hand wall. Directly ahead, across the workroom, the entrance to Aquisitions & Processing was a blacker rectangle, barely discernible in the stray light from the desk behind her.

She held her breath and listened. It was a quiet, almost casual sound. It seemed somehow idle, diffident.

The clock in the boardroom next door began to chime. Seven notes spaced in slow cadence. She caught her lower lip between her teeth and backed away from the yawning mouths of the dark doorways. When she bumped into the desk her heart froze for an instant. Without taking her eyes off the open workroom door, she probed behind herself with her right hand.

And knocked over the pencil cup. Pencils, pens, and paper clips clattered to the floor, and Hilda watched as, in slow motion, a gum eraser bounced soundlessly out the door and into the workroom, where it lay neatly centered in the wedge of light.

Her heart timed the long seconds that followed. With every beat she became more certain that someone—something—would emerge from one of the doorways.

But no one came to pick up the eraser. No shadow fell across the doorway. And, after another minute had passed, she realized that the sounds had stopped.

Slowly, she untensed, releasing a breath she hadn't known she was holding. Alone at night in a large building . . . It was easy to get spooked. She had been warned about it when she had volunteered for the overtime. The building was too dark. There were no windows in the business office to admit the streetlights or the moonlight or the comforting sounds of evening traffic.

She stepped boldly into the darkened workroom. Darker shadows limned huge and silent shapes that she knew—*she knew!*—were book racks and furniture. Yet, behind the veils of darkness she could imagine—things.

She turned left and glanced inside the boardroom. Shadows of tree branches played black lightning across the window. A reflected streetlamp glimmered in the surface of the broad, polished conference table, like the moon on a midnight pond. The Empress Maria Theresa stared back primly from her portrait on the wall.

Hilda left the boardroom, closing the door carefully behind her, and continued across the Interlibrary Loan workroom. The floorboards complained beneath the carpeting. As she passed the entrance to Cataloguing, a blue-green flash teased the corner of her eye. A flashbulb? An electrical short? She stood in the entrance peering at the dim shapes looming in the darkness.

Nothing.

No flash. No sparks. Yet, she had seen something. She was sure of it. She groped for the wall switch and the overhead fluorescents flickered on. Squinting her eyes against the sudden illumination, Hilda took a careful step into the room. To her right was the huge, incongruous brick fireplace, a reminder of a time long ago when this had been a public reading room. (Reading in those days had been a serious business, conducted in comfortable, quiet surroundings.) To her left was the long worktable with the scissors and the paste and the Dewey reference books. Backed against the far wall stood the row of five-foot-high wooden catalogues. She saw nothing out of place.

But, when she turned to go, she froze. The fireplace was flanked by two doors: the one she had just come in and another on the farther side. Between the other door and the fireplace itself stood two, small, nine-drawer cabinets, one atop the other. The center drawer of the top cabinet hung halfway out.

She approached it with tentative steps, circling around to her left. That was what the sound had been. The familiar sound of card drawers opening and closing. That was all it had been.

Except that she was alone in the building.

A damp cold enveloped her, and her breath was mist in the suddenly frigid air. Hilda wrapped her body tightly in her arms, and the sigh of an old wind ran up her spine. Someone was watching her. Someone behind her. She felt it. She could feel the eyes on the back of her head; twin spots like the pressure of two fingertips where her neck joined her skull. It was not a menacing feeling, exactly. She felt no menace, but a cold disinterest that was far more chilling than any threat could be. Her breathing was loud and hoarse in her ears. She did not want to turn around. She did *not* want to turn around. She . . .

Felt a hand run through her hair.

And screamed.

And when she did turn, she saw there was no one behind her, after all. Nobody.

So it must have been a breeze. What else could it have been?

II

"What else?" Leo Reissman asked. "A hysterical reaction," he told her, "brought on by the isolation and the dark. The human mind is a strange and wonderful thing. The neural impulses that we interpret as sights or sounds can be triggered without any external input. By a migraine, for example." He folded his hands across his vest and beamed at the two women. He wondered if this might be the case that would make his reputation; restore his respectability in the department. Odd—to chase over half a country in search of the bizarre, then to find it, almost literally, in his own backyard. More likely, though, it was nothing. Another false alarm. Night fears of the sort he was already too familiar with.

"I saw what I saw," Hilda Schenckweiler insisted, twisting her hands together. "The drawer was open. That was no hallucination. I shoved it closed myself. The rest of it. The sound. The light. The cold. I don't know. But that drawer was open."

"Ah, but what was the significance of its being open?" he asked. "Perhaps it had been hanging open the whole while."

The director was sitting behind her desk, turning Leo's business card over and over in her hands. She looked up at him. "Everything is properly put away when the library closes."

Leo shrugged. "Carelessness does happen," he reminded them.

"It's not the first time," said Hilda suddenly. Leo looked at her with surprise; the director, with annoyance. She flushed. "I mean odd things happening at night, not carelessness."

Leo raised his eyebrows. "Indeed?"

"It is very eerie sitting in the old building at night," the director told him, and Leo wondered briefly why she insisted on answering for her librarian. "We've all gotten 'the willies' at one time or another. Dr. . . ." She glanced briefly at the business card she was twisting in her hand. "Dr. Reissman. That doesn't mean there is anything, well, supernatural taking place."

Leo blinked and lifted his head. "Oh, dear. I should think not!" he said.

The director seemed confused. She looked at Hilda. "But the patrolman said that he would send around a man who . . . Hilda, how did he put it?"

"A man who has had experience with this sort of phenomenon," Hilda quoted carefully.

"He said that?" Leo chuckled. "Oh, Sam was just being mysterious. That's his nature. I helped him out once with a little problem he had, but there was nothing supernatural about it. I don't believe in the supernatural."

"But . . ." The director flicked her finger against his business card. "Aren't you a psychic?"

"What? Oh, *that's* why you're confused." He gestured toward the business card. "If you would read it again?" he suggested.

The director frowned at him, frowned at the card. "Physicist," she read. She looked up at Leo. "Physicist?"

Leo smiled at them again. "Certainly. Nothing supernatural about physics, I assure you."

"I don't understand," Hilda said to him as they stood together at the entrance to the Cataloguing Room. "Why would a physicist be interested in ghosts?"

Leo studied the layout of the room from the doorway. Yes, there was the catalogue, nestled between the fireplace and the other doorway. The accused looked innocent enough. Hardly the sort of thing to frighten a librarian.

Yet, hardly the sort of thing to open and close of itself on a dark, lonely night.

Probably just a case of nerves, he told himself. Nerves and fright accounted for more apparitions than anything physical. That was the problem with this sort of thing. It was often a struggle to establish whether anything had happened at all. And most often of all, he knew with a glum satisfaction, nothing *had* happened. That would explain so much. It was an answer he hungered for with an intensity that sometimes frightened him. If it *were* true, then he was most assuredly alone; but he would know, at last, why he was alone.

"Ghosts?" he answered her at last, though with more force than he had intended. "There are no such things as ghosts." Something harsh must have come out in his voice, because Hilda backed away from him.

"Then, do you think I'm crazy? That I imagined it all?"

"I didn't say that," he assured her. "Perhaps you did see something. But if you did, then it was something real, made of matter and energy, not a ghost." He shrugged his shoulders and pushed his hands into his pants pockets. "No, I don't believe in ghosts," he continued. "But I don't believe that the edge of the universe or the inside of the nucleus are the only frontiers of physics, either. There are still discoveries to be made in the odd nooks and crannies of the workaday world." He turned his mouth up. "Other physicists study quarks. I study quirks."

She smiled tentatively at his joke.

"I think," he continued, "that what you saw was a natural phenomenon that has never been properly studied. Like *Kugelblitz*. That was once dismissed as folklore, too." He realized abruptly that they were both still standing in the doorway, like two kids afraid to enter a haunted house. "Well," he said, rubbing his hands, "shall we get started?"

He crossed the room and began examining the card catalogue. It was a very old, dark wood cabinet about three feet by three feet, and it sat atop a second, similar cabinet. The dark wood shone from decades of rubbing hands. Leo touched the little brass fingerhook on the front of one of the drawers and it slid easily in and out. "Was this the drawer?" He wondered if the drawers could slide by themselves. From traffic vibrations, perhaps. Unlikely, but . . . Experimentally, he shook the heavy, wooden unit, but it did not budge and the drawers stayed put.

"No," he heard her say. "The one I saw was the center drawer, second row, but I heard the sounds for several minutes. More than the one drawer might have moved."

Or none, Leo thought. He turned and saw with surprise that Hilda was still standing in the doorway. "Aren't you coming in?" he asked.

She hugged herself and shook her head. "I'm frightened."

"There's no need to be frightened."

He had meant to comfort her; but—unexpectedly—she flared up at him. "What do you know about it? You weren't there!"

"I—" Memories bubbled beneath his thoughts. The birds blackening the sky. The half-heard fragment of a word. Lying awake sweat-soaked in the heart of the night. He pressed his teeth into his lower lip. "I've studied a fair number of snugs," he said finally.

"Snugs?"

"SNGs. Standard Nighttime Ghosts." He found quick refuge in the jargon. "The acronym is less semantically loaded. If you use the word 'ghost,' you make assumptions about what the phenomenon is."

She turned up her mouth. "And if you use the acronym, you make assumptions about what it *isn't*."

"I'm sorry," he told her. "I never meant to sound patronizing. Whether your snug was a real phenomenon or not, your fright certainly was."

"Don't trivialize it!" She hunched over her folded arms. "My fright was more than just a 'real phenomenon.' It was something I *felt*. That I still feel."

"Would it help," he asked quietly after a moment, "if I told you that I know exactly how you felt?"

Hilda raised her head and studied him for a few moments. Her mouth parted slightly, and Leo was afraid that she would ask him how he knew how she felt; but she said nothing. Finally, she unfolded her arms and stepped into the room. As she approached the catalogue, she sidestepped to her left and pointed to a file drawer. "That's the one I saw open."

Leo sucked in his breath. She had walked *desail*. . . . The Dundrum Effect? If so, how to test it? As casually as he could, he walked to the fireplace and pretended to look up the flue. He pulled his head out. "Ms. Schenck-weiler," he said, "would you come over here a moment?"

She gave him a frown. "What is it?" He watched her turn and take a step and . . .

"There! You're doing it again!"

She stopped and looked around herself with a bewildered expression. "What?"

"Just now, and earlier, when you walked toward the catalogue, you turned—right about there." He pointed to a spot half a meter in front of the catalogue. "As if you were stepping around an obstacle."

Hilda stared at the empty air, then she turned wide eyes on him. "Obstacle?" she said. Her voice rose in pitch, and she took a hasty step backward away from The Spot. "Do you mean the ghost is still there?" Her hand sought her mouth.

Dammit, now I've frightened her. Leo raised his hands, palms out. "Now don't—" He stopped himself. He had almost said *don't be frightened*. "It's a common experience. I call it the Dundrum Effect, after the Irish village where Conway first described it. I believe that it is due to a sort of 'peripheral vision' that some especially sensitive people possess. Perhaps a sense much as the blind develop, when they can 'feel' the presence of a wall or of another person."

She lowered her hand slowly. "It does help a little."

"Eh? What does?"

"Your dry-as-dust explanations. You make it sound so ordinary. That . . . takes the edge off." She kept staring at The Spot.

Dry-as-dust? Leo grunted. He took a tape measure and a small notebook from his jacket pocket and measured The Spot's location from several benchmarks around the room. He entered the figures in the notebook. "SNGs," he told her as he worked, "generally recur within well-defined loci. So, it is always there, even if it is not always manifest."

"What do you mean?" Hilda responded. "They don't move?"

Leo was kneeling on the floor. He released the button on the tape measure and the steel strip snaked back into the spool. He rocked back on his heels and considered her question. "Well, not exactly," he said. "Some are mobile. . . . That is, some do move. But they move along well-defined trajectories; always repeating the same actions."

"I see," she said. "Like an obsessive-compulsive personality disorder."

He cocked his head. "Actually, more like a stuck record. Don't jump to the conclusion that snugs have a personality to be 'compelled'; or that they are even 'conscious,' in some sense. Those are some of the assumptions we make when we say 'ghosts.' When you think about it, the ocean tides show the same sort of 'compulsive' behavior."

"How do you *know* that your 'snugs' don't have self-awareness? Aren't they the spirits of the dead?"

Leo hesitated a moment. He rubbed his left hand absently with his right. *The flutter of birds blackening the sky. The faint echo of an unheard voice.* He took a deep breath and buried the memories that threatened to break surface. "I don't know that they are. Carpenter's Conjecture is that souls and ghosts are equivalent entities; but that has never been proven. Back in 1906, a Boston physician named MacDougall weighed six people on platform scales as they were dying, and recorded a weight loss of ten to forty grams at the moment of death. So it would seem that *something* physical leaves the body at death. However, no one has ever repeated the experiment under proper controls, so we cannot be sure. The weights Mac-Dougall recorded are about the same as for the snugs I've measured; but the similarity of mass may be coincidence. There may be snugs that are not souls; and souls that are not snugs. And even if there is a connection of some sort, the snug may be nothing more than a . . . a holographic recording of the soul, lacking volition or awareness."

Hilda leaned forward and waved her hand tentatively through the air above The Spot. "I . . . don't feel anything."

Leo rose and brushed at his pants. "No, you wouldn't. Snugs have extremely low density. About a tenth of a milligram per cubic centimeter. You could walk right through them and never notice. Go ahead. Take a step forward."

She looked at him and hesitated. "Go ahead," he urged her. "It can't hurt you."

She closed her eyes and took three abrupt steps. Then she opened her eyes and slowly unclenched her fists. "Nothing." She looked at him. "No feeling of avoidance."

"Exactly. The Dundrum Effect only occurs when you don't consciously think about where you're walking."

"I didn't feel a thing," she said.

"I told you snugs have low density."

Hilda laughed a short, high-pitched laugh that caused Leo to give her an uncertain look.

"What is it?"

"The old proof that ghosts are invisible. You've never seen one, have you? Then that proves that they're invisible!"

III

The director stopped him as he passed through the business office on his way out.

"May I see you for a moment?" She stood in the doorway to the secretary's office. Leo shifted the overcoat draped across his arm and glanced toward the hall door where Hilda Schenckweiler waited for him.

"Certainly," he said.

"Hilda, you may wait for Dr. Riessman downstairs."

Leo followed the director through the secretary's office and left into the librarian's office. He noticed a fireplace in the corner, the twin to the one in the Cataloguing Room, and surmised that these two offices had been built from a second reading room, a mirror image of the one on the other side of the building. The director sat behind her desk, leaning forward in her chair, elbows planted on the desktop. Leo waited for her to say what she intended to say.

"This 'investigation' of yours needn't last long."

He was not sure if she was making a forecast, expressing an opinion, or giving an order. Leo had heard the quotation marks in her voice. "I will try to be expeditious," he said.

She picked up a pencil from her desk and twisted it in her fingers. "I doubt that there is any more to this incident than simple hysteria."

"Most of the cases that I have examined," he said carefully, "have turned out to be nothing more than wild imagination. A few have been deliberate hoaxes."

The director tapped the eraser end of the pencil on her desk blotter. "I don't believe Hilda would deliberately hoax anyone."

Something about her voice pricked Leo's curiosity. "But . . ." he probed.

The woman sat back and brushed a hand at her hair. "It is really not my place to say. . . ."

But you'll say it anyway.

"Hilda *has* had a few problems in her life recently. Her mother, you understand. She had to put her in a home. She has been seeing a psychiatrist about it."

"Seeing a psychiatrist is not—"

She broke him off with a flip of her hand. "I know that, Doctor. I know that. These days it is almost a status symbol. But—" She paused in thought. "What I am trying to say is that the Library Ghost is an old tradition with the staff here. Every time a new girl is scheduled to work evenings, she is told all sorts of stories. You know the kind I mean. Well, the old building is genuinely creepy at night, and you do hear sounds and feel light drafts. Someone with, well, with an uncertain imagination, may magnify them into—who knows what?" She laid the pencil down; picked it up again.

Leo nodded curtly. "I understand Ms. Schenckweiler may not have seen anything. That is certainly a possibility that I will keep in mind." He straightened his overcoat and turned to go.

The director's voice stopped him at the door. "It will all turn out to be a hyperactive imagination. You'll see."

He turned and looked at her. Her fingers were twisting and turning the pencil. Leo locked eyes with her for a moment. Then he nodded. "More than likely," he told her.

Hilda was waiting for him when the elevator doors chimed open on the first-floor lobby. She took him firmly by the arm and guided him toward the front door, past the odd-looking flag in its glass display case. "The First Stars and Stripes of the United Colonies—July 8, 1776." It resembled the Besty Ross flag, save that the stripes were in the canton and the stars were in the fly. Leo waved his rumpled, felt fedora toward the rear door. "But, my car . . ." he started to say.

"I thought you told me you wanted a tour of the grounds outside."

Leo didn't remember saying that at all. He looked at her and opened his mouth, but then thought better of it. There was a crease on her forehead, above her nose, and her face had a tight, closed-in expression. He shrugged. Whatever it was she wanted to tell him, he would learn in due time. So, he followed her lead. Outside was a bracing October afternoon, and a walk around the building would do him no harm.

They stepped out into a swirl of wind; red and gold leaves chattered in their faces. Leo clamped his hand firmly to his head to keep his hat from flying off. The sidewalk was bounded on the left by the "new" annex and on the right by a brick wall retaining the bank of a grassy knoll. The wind, trapped in the pocket, struggled to escape.

Leo strode briskly forward, out of the whirlwind. At the point where the sidewalk cascaded down flights of steps to Church Street, he turned and faced the building. The library grounds occupied the entire block of Church Street between Fifth and Sixth. The original building, a dark brick Carnegie-style structure, sat atop the crest of the knoll in the center of the block. Attached to its east face and extending to the corner at Fifth, was the annex that now housed the Circulating Collection. Behind the two loomed the massive, tree-shrouded, stone knob of Mount Jefferson.

A side path branched off the sidewalk and wound west toward the old building. *The original entrance*, Leo surmised, studying the arched portal with its decorative scrollwork. *They don't make 'em like that anymore.* It was sealed up now; the old, grand staircase was a platform for shrubbery planters. *Too bad.* The old building *looked* like a library. Its facade was distinctive; not like the anonymous structures they put up nowadays. Stone benches were spotted here and there about the grounds. Leo wondered if anyone ever used them.

Hilda was waiting for him at the point where the sidewalk forked. Beside her, atop the grassy knoll, was an odd-looking stone structure. It was flat, like a table or a bench; but it was too low for the one and too wide for the other. And it was surrounded by a wrought-iron fence. Leo frowned at it. He felt he should know what it was: that, in another setting, it would be instantly recognizable. "What is that?" he asked her.

Hilda turned her head. "What, this? Why, it's only Billy."

The surprise in her voice was overdone. *She wanted me to see this,* he thought. *It's why she led me out this way.* Leo hunched his shoulders against the wind and walked up the side path and around on the grass to look down on the object.

It was a flattopped sepulcher. A grave.

Of course. Instantly recognizable; but not something that one would expect to find sitting beside the town library's main entrance. Leo knelt and brushed away the dirt and leaves that obscured the horizontal slab. *William M. Parsons, Esq.,* he read. *Born May 6,* 1701. *Died December 22,* 1752. *He rocked Easton in her cradle and watched of her infant footsteps with paternal solicitude.* He ran his fingers across the slab. The stone was cold and rough. Old. It was strange to think that this grave was nearly a quarter century old when certain men had pledged their lives and fortunes at Philadelphia.

He looked up and saw that Hilda had joined him. "This is a grave," he said, which was stupid because she knew it was a grave. "A grave on the library grounds. Why did no one mention this earlier?"

Hilda rubbed her palms together against the chill. She glanced briefly at the windows overlooking them. "The director thought it would be best not to bring it up."

"Why ever not?" He stood and brushed at his trousers.

"Because she doesn't want any sensationalism attached to the library. She doesn't want us on the cover of the *National Enquirer.*"

He grunted. *Then why did you insist on leading me right to it?* He wanted to ask her straight out, but something in her face made him hesitate. Some deep-seated worry that gnawed within her. Best to approach the issue sideways. If at all. What did Hilda Schenckweiler's state of mind have to do with his investigation? Perhaps nothing. Perhaps everything. He remembered what the director had told him just before he left. Then he wondered if Hilda might have waited outside the office and overheard the comments. Showing him the grave might be nothing more than an act of defiance on her part. "I can appreciate her fears; but I really do need all the facts of your case."

"My case." She gestured toward the sepulcher. "Parsons was the city's founder. He did the surveying and laid out the plots for Thomas Penn." She gazed toward the far corner of the building; at the Cataloguing Room windows. "Do you think that he was doing late-night research or something?"

Leo laughed. "No, I don't know that he has anything to do with what happened last night; but, then I don't know that he hasn't, either. Unless I have all the data, I cannot decide what is important and what is not."

Hilda glanced again at the oversize windows of the Librarian's Office, and Leo turned and saw the slat of a venetian blind flick closed.

"Is there anything else you haven't told me?"

Hilda took a deep breath. "Follow me."

The second grave was less elaborate. It was little more than a rock surrounded by an iron rail situated in the little park on the west side of the driveway. The rock was about two feet high and was worn and pitted. Leo thought it looked a bit like a meteor. A large concavity on its top had collected a pool of stagnant rainwater, in which floated a brown, curled leaf.

Elizabeth Bell Morgan, stated the small plaque. *"Mammy Morgan" Died October 16, 1839. Aged about 79 years.* Leo grunted. He squinted at the plaque. "Mammy Morgan. Is that the same Mammy Morgan—"

"That the hill was named after? Of course. How many Mammy Morgans do you suppose there were?"

"Just asking." He shaded his eyes and looked south across the rooftops. From Mount Jefferson, Mammy Morgan's Hill was a motley of orange and gold and red in the October-lit distance. "Who was she? When I moved out here, Magruder took me around and showed me all the sights; but they're only names to me."

Hilda folded her arms against the chill. "I suppose you could call her a foundress of our library. Her donations of money and law books helped get the library started back in 1811."

"Law books? She was a lawyer? Wasn't that unusual for a woman back then?"

Hilda shook her head. "She wasn't a lawyer, but she was probably better educated than most of the lawyers in town. She was born and raised a Quaker in Philadelphia, but her parents sent her to school in Europe. She had fallen in love with a soldier boy and they hoped to 'cure' her. That was before the Revolution. She came here later, in 1793, when the yellow fever epidemic swept Philadelphia. Her husband set her and the children up in a hotel on the hill"—she gestured toward the south—"then he went back to Philadelphia, and wound up in a mass grave."

"What? Why on earth would he go back?"

"Why? He was a doctor. That's what doctors do during epidemics. History is full of forgotten, everyday heroes like Abel Morgan. Afterward, the Widow Morgan bought the hotel and ran it for fifty years. She had a fine collection of books from her European studies and her favorite pastime was reading law."

Leo chuckled. "Light reading, eh?"

Hilda scowled. "It beats soap operas. She kept her law books on a bench in the hotel's public room. Her neighbors kept asking for her opinions on disputes, so she began to 'dispense law,' as she put it."

"Like Judge Roy Bean," said Leo. "The Law South of the Lehigh."

She turned her mouth up. "Without the arbitrary hangings. She was a woman. She ruled so wisely that people seldom appealed their cases to the regular courts. The Germans began to call her *Die Mommie*. When she died, the funeral procession stretched over two miles, from here all the way to Lachenour Heights. The Indian corn mill"—she gestured toward the tombstone—"was added later."

"One of your folk heroes, I see. But there's more to the story," he prodded. "Isn't there?"

Hilda rubbed her arms and looked at the stone. "You know how people are. An educated woman, living alone, supporting herself. Especially in those days. The local bar tried especially hard to discredit her, spreading malicious stories about her character and about goings-on in her hotel. Some people said . . . Well, they said she was a witch."

He looked at her. "A witch."

She look back. "Nonsense of course. But people love to spread malicious rumors. There was a children's rhyme: '*Mammy Morgan played the organ/Her daddy beat the drum.*' It was no more than rhyme play on her name; but some tried to make it sound as if she was involved in powwow magic."

Leo pursed his lips. "So, there are two graves on the library grounds, then."

Hilda cocked her head. "Follow me," she said.

Leo stared at the indentation in the northeast section of the library's driveway. "Eighty-eight?" he asked incredulously.

"There's a vault under there," Hilda told him.

"Eighty-eight bodies?" He still couldn't believe it. He looked around: at the buildings, the parking lot. There was an old man sitting on one of the park benches, reading a book. Children were playing in the dead-end of Sixth Street. The rocky knob behind him rose steeply into a whispering shroud of trees. "What is this, a cemetery?"

"Yes."

He gave her a sharp glance. "Are you serious?"

"Quite serious," she replied tartly. "You might as well know it all. When they started construction on the library in 1901, the cheapest land available was the old German Reformed Cemetery, on this hilltop. There were 514 bodies in it then, and they exhumed them all."

Leo's breath caught in his throat. Digging up hundreds of rotted corpses . . . The gaping skulls; the bones fleshed out in tatters . . . What was it like to turn over the earth and find . . . No, he was letting his imagination get the better of him. The bodies—the "remains"—would have been in coffins, and the coffins would have been largely intact. Most of them, anyway. He took a deep breath and glanced at Hilda. "What . . . What did they do with them all?" he asked huskily.

She gave him a quizzical look. "Reusing old cemeteries was fairly common around the turn of the last century. People weren't as uptight about 'disturbing the dead' as they are now. The city wrote letters to all the relatives and descendants they could locate, asking them to come and claim the remains. Most of them were reburied elsewhere." Her eyes dropped to the concavity in the asphalt. "All but these eighty-eight. They were put in new wooden caskets and buried together in a large underground cavern."

"I see. And were there any, ah, unusual events reported during the construction?"

"She said I shouldn't tell you."

Leo looked at her. "The director."

"Yes. But . . ." She shrugged heavily. "What's the point? You can look it up in our own archives. It was never kept secret. There were even newspaper features about it over the years." She pointed toward the end of the driveway. "The people who lived along North Fifth claimed they saw moving lights at night; and—" She paused and made a face. "A headless woman."

Leo stifled a sudden laugh. The lights were a possibility; but the headless woman was too much. Too Gothic. Although, he reminded himself, this part of Pennsylvania had been heavily settled by Germans, so Gothic images might be expected. He studied the row houses along North Fifth Street at the end of the driveway. The site of the vault would have been clearly visible back then. "You're not pulling my leg, are you?" Some people thought it was great fun to try to fool him with tall tales. Hilda didn't seem the type, but you never knew.

"Of course I'm not," she said. "But I can't answer for the local residents a hundred years ago. *They* may have been pulling every leg in sight. You know the German sense of humor. The next night, people came from all over town, hoping to see 'die shpooken'; but nothing happened. Then, after everyone left, the locals claimed the ghosts came back."

Leo smiled. "You're right. It sounds like they were having some fun."

"I'm sure they were; because no one reported anything unusual in the mid-sixties."

"Oh? What happened then?"

"That's when the annex was built." She gestured toward the newer building. "The weight of the construction equipment broke the vault open. Caskets disintegrated and there were bones and skulls rolling all over."

It took him by surprise. Death images clawed their way to the surface of his mind. Whitened skeletons robed in rotted, worm-eaten flesh. Hanks of colorless hairs; eyeless sockets. *Gonna roll them bones.* He sucked in his breath. "My God! That's terrible!"

"Yes, it sounds like a scene from a bad horror movie, doesn't it?"

Leo mopped his brow against the chill autumn air. "But for one difference."

"What's that?"

"In the movies, that sort of scene is always a prelude to something grisly and horrible. But in the real world, when you 'disturb the dead,' nothing supernatural happens."

One side of the parking lot opened onto the park by Sixth Street; the other was bounded by the wooded knob of rock—private property, Hilda told him. A castellated stone wall marched along the backside of the grounds, from the stone knob all the way across the dead end of Sixth. Gravel crunched beneath their feet as they walked together toward his car.

They stopped beside his car and Leo fished in his pocket for his keys. Hilda glanced toward the library building. "Do you think you can explain what happened to me last night?"

There was an odd tightness to her voice, and Leo studied her as he jug-gled the car keys in his hand. "I don't know," he replied honestly. "We don't have all the answers. We never will."

"Oh," she said, and fell silent.

He paused with his keys out and gazed across the roof of his car. Leafy branches reached up and over the stone wall. In the distance he could see the trees and houses covering the slopes of College Hill. He frowned. There was something wrong with the vista. Foreground and background; but no middle ground. "What's on the other side of that wall," he asked.

"Nothing."

"Eh?" He froze, dreading what she would say next.

"Unless you count 120 feet of air as something."

Leo glanced from her to the wall and back. There was a sudden void in his chest. He knew what she meant. He knew. He pocketed his keys and walked slowly to the back end of the lot. Every step was torture, but he had to see for himself. When he reached the wall, he craned his neck and looked down without leaning over.

A heavily shrubbed, rocky cliff dropped in a near vertical line to the black asphalt ribbon of Bushkill Street. Toy cars hummed below across his field of vision. Farther west, the slope was more gentle and ribbed with trees growing out of the side of the hill; but here, at the east edge of the parking lot, it was a straight drop. A *stumble, Falling, falling. Leo! Hands grabbing. Bushes torn out by their roots.* The scene below seemed to turn slowly counterclockwise. He backed away and stared at the comforting so-lidity of the rocky knob that capped Mount Jefferson. It added, he judged, another thirty feet; and the drop-off was just as sheer. The high-dive plat-form.

Hilda joined him. "It's a long way to fall, isn't it?"

Leo started. What macabre impulse had prompted her to say that? "Not really," he said. "It would only take about three seconds to reach the bot-tom. It would be over with quickly."

"Three seconds?" she said. "Long enough to realize what was happen-ing to you." She braced her hands on the top of the wall and leaned over. Leo gasped and grabbed her by the arm.

"Hey!"

"Don't do that!" She pulled her arm from his grasp. "What's the matter with you?"

"I . . . don't like heights," he said. His heart was pumping heavily. *Long enough to know.*

She gave him an odd look; but stepped away from the wall and folded her arms. "It's getting cold. I'd better get back inside."

"All right."

"I'm sorry. Did I make you nervous, leaning out like that?"

"No. Yes." Some people had no grasp of physics; no conception of the forces that could kill them. Their knowledge of force and motion came from Hollywood movies and television shows. Not more than a few meters away, the planetary mass was waiting to smash her like a bug onto a windshield; and she leaned out over the wall and dared it.

They walked together back to his car, and Leo fumbled again with his keys. A cliff. He hadn't known that the library backed so close to the cliff.

"Do you think anyone could survive?"

"What?" He looked at Hilda. "Survive what?"

She was gazing toward the back end of the parking lot. "A fall. Off the cliff. You said it would only take three seconds to reach the bottom."

Good Lord! He refused to turn and look with her. "It's not how long you fall that matters," he told her. "It's how fast you're moving when you hit. Free-falling one hundred twenty feet, under gravitational acceleration . . ." He thought it through, doing the calculations in traditional units so she would understand. Numbers were a comforting abstraction, hiding the reality of the drop; the terror of the fall. "You would hit the ground traveling eighty-eight feet per second. That's roughly sixty miles an hour."

She looked at the wall. "Oh." She thought for a moment. "It would be horrible to die like that, to *watch* it happening to you. Can you imagine what it would be like to know that you were going to die?"

Branches snapping; shrubs uprooted; stones clattering loose beneath flailing hands. Leo gave a backward glance at the wall. "But it would be so much worse to remember afterward."

He sat in the car after she left him and let the engine idle, grumbling and complaining in its mechanical way about the mild chill. He glanced around while he waited for the car to warm up. The old building, the annex, the park, the depression in the driveway. Everywhere but that awful drop behind him. Hilda's remarks. So thoughtless; so callous. Gallows humor. He fought to expel it from his mind. He concentrated on the problem at hand. The haunt. If it was a haunt.

So, the library was built on deconsecrated ground. And there's the body of the town's founder, who watched over it all his life—and maybe longer. And the body of a woman who was certainly not a witch, but who loved to read books. And the bodies of eighty-eight poor souls thrown into a common grave and later spilled all over like a game of pick-up sticks.

Yes, this could be an interesting case. If only there hadn't been a cliff.

IV

Hilda felt the director watching over her shoulder as she wound the roll of graph paper into a tube. She wished the other woman would not stand so close and hunched her shoulders as she strapped a rubber band around the tube.

"What is all that?" asked the director.

"I told you. It's a strip recorder for the thermocouples. Leo . . . Dr. Reissman asked me to bring the tracings in today." She put the graph paper into her purse and snapped it shut.

"Does that mean he's finished?" The director's lips pressed together as she surveyed the equipment set up around the room. "I don't like my library cluttered up this way."

"I don't know. I'll ask him."

The director muttered something.

"What did you say?"

"I said he was a crazy old coot. Wasting his time—and ours—on this foolishness."

"He isn't that old."

The director looked at her. "Nor that crazy, I suppose."

"He's nice," Hilda told her. "A gentleman. Maybe a little stuffy. And shy because he's stuffy. And he's afraid of heights." She hefted the purse and slung it over her shoulder. "I think he is very sad about something, an old hurt. Sometimes, when he doesn't know anyone is watching, he forgets to smile."

"Does he." The director made a moue with her lips. "Well, he's kept this business out of the newspapers. I'll grant him that. But what has he discovered after two weeks? People have been seeing and hearing and feel-

ing things in this library for years. You weren't the first to hear card drawers sliding. Or the first to feel a hand in your hair." The director's hand
made a half-conscious move toward her own coiffure.

"I know. I've talked to Andy, Barbara, and Lynn and some of the others
who used to work here. They would tell each other ghost stories whenever
any of them had to work late."

The director cracked a smile. "I imagine half the nighttime experiences
here have been because of those stories."

"And the other half?" Hilda asked.

The director's face went hard. "It was just a manner of speaking."

Leaving the library, Hilda felt her car bounce through the depression in
the driveway. She had driven over that spot hundreds of times before.
Now, every time she did so, she remembered what lay under it. Restlessly,
perhaps?

She thought for a moment about the thermocouples that Leo had installed around the Cataloguing Room. Physical evidence, he had told her.
*Our first priority is to establish whether the phenomenon is internal or ex-
ternal.* A fancy way he had of hinting that it might have all been in her
mind. It was easier to believe that than to believe that ghosts might be real.
. . . *From ghosties and ghoulies and long-legged beasties and things that go
bump in the night, Good Lord, deliver us.* If ghosts were real, what else
might be? What horrors might lurk in the shadows around us?

Yet, what if it *had* all been in her mind? In many ways, that was even
more frightening, because that would mean it was herself and not reality
that was cracking. *The breakdown of the universe I can deal with.* The other
was a road she had no desire to travel. She had already seen what lay at the
end of it.

She tightened her grip on the steering wheel; and, when she turned right
onto Fifth, she cut much harder than she needed to.

The college had perched atop the hill overlooking a bend of the Bushkill
Creek since 1826, and its older buildings had had ample time to acquire
the customary mantle of ivy. Cliffs dropped to the Bushkill on two sides of
the campus, while city streets and residential housing hemmed it in on the
east and north. Hilda found herself a parking place on McCartney, close

by the campus gate. When she entered, she encountered the marquis, himself.

"Lafayette, I am here," she told the statue.

A passing student showed her the way to the physics building, where the department secretary told her which office was Dr. Reissman's and said she could go inside and wait. "It isn't as if there were anything worth stealing in there," she said with a sniff.

Hilda found Leo's office cluttered, but neat. One entire wall was taken up by shelves stuffed with books and technical journals arranged according to some obscure logic. On one shelf sat a black box with a set of funny-looking lenses. A cable connected it to a computer on a side table. A plain wooden desk facing the far wall was stacked high with papers, each stack held in place by machinists' blocks of various shapes.

She lifted the paperweight from one of the stacks and saw that on top was a typewritten manuscript: "On Possible Mechanisms for a Thermophotonic Effect," by Leo M. Reissman, Ph.D. Paper-clipped to it was a handwritten note: *Sorry, Leo, but the referees just couldn't buy it.* Beneath that paper she found another: "Frequency and Duration of SNG Sightings, with Reference to Boltzmann Statistics." This time the attached note read: *Is this a joke?*

Hilda replaced the papers and paperweight and wandered idly around the office. A small, framed snapshot sat on the right-hand corner of the desk. She picked it up and looked at it. Two teenage boys—identical twins—dressed in scout uniforms smiled back at her. They had their arms around each other's shoulders and they looked like younger versions of the physicist. Leo's sons? The twin smiles frozen in time gave her no answer.

She set the snapshot down and peered into the corner between the bookshelves and the desk. A dollhouse? She bent over and lifted it. Yes, a dollhouse. The plastic kind, made with snap-together panels. Cheap. Not like the one her grandfather had built for her in his workshop. (Sometimes she wondered what had ever happened to it. Why did the adult always yearn for the treasures that the teenager spurned?) She studied the dollhouse she held. Each room was filled with a clear, gelatin-like plastic. Now what—?

"What would a grown man want with a dollhouse in his office, right?"

The voice behind her made her jump, and she nearly dropped the toy. She turned and saw Leo standing in the doorway. "L—Dr. Reissman. You startled me."

"I'm sorry." He waved a hand toward the chair beside the desk. "Have a seat, Ms. Schenckweiler. I hadn't expected you so soon."

Hilda sat holding the dollhouse in her lap. She looked at it dumbly for a moment, then she made an exasperated sound in her throat and started to get up; but Leo took it from her.

"Never mind. I'll put it back." He gave the toy an affectionate glance. "This is my main claim to fame, you know."

"A dollhouse?"

He cocked his head at her. "Oh, yes. You wouldn't know, would you? It's why the college keeps me around in my dotage. They're hoping for another apple to rap me on the head and reflect credit on them— presumably for granting me a spot under their tree. You see, I once devised a reliable and inexpensive method for projecting holographs. That was my field of specialization before I took up more arcane realms. Lasers and holography." He placed the dollhouse on the desk, with the open back facing Hilda. "Lasers and holography," he repeated to himself. He opened and closed the front door of the dollhouse. "Watch this."

He stepped to the bookcase, where he pressed something on the black box. Ghostly shapes flickered inside the rooms. Near-solid images of furniture and wallpaper appeared. Hilda leaned forward. Why, that was marvelous! He was projecting three-dimensional pictures of the furnishings into each room.

Leo tapped some buttons on the computer console, and the furniture in the living room changed style and color. The phantom wallpaper became a new shape and pattern. Hilda gasped.

He turned the unit off and the furnishings winked out. "What do you think of it?"

"I think it's very clever. Delightful. I wish I had known about this before I redecorated my house. I've always found it difficult to visualize an entire room from a sample swatch of wallpaper or carpeting. Decorators and architects must love this."

"They do, but that is just one application. I understand that some enterprising individuals in California are attempting a holographic motion picture." Leo lifted the dollhouse from the table. "Patent royalties and

tenure," he said. "Those are what grant me the freedom to pursue my somewhat unorthodox investigations. Well . . ." He returned the dollhouse to
its cranny. "Enough of my checkered past. What do you have for me?"

Crackpots, Hilda told herself, did not invent clever and useful gadgets.
Leo thought that ghosts were real — or, at least, that there was a reality that
people called "ghosts" — and Leo was a serious and practical scientist. She
took the rolls of graph paper from her purse. "I put fresh rolls into the
recorders and reset the timers the way you showed me. Was that all right?"

"Oh, certainly. Certainly." He rubbed his hands together briskly. "Now,
which one is the chart for The Spot?"

She handed it to him and he pulled off the rubber band and unrolled
it like a papyrus scroll. He studied it silently for a few minutes; then he
chuckled to himself. "Yes. Yes." He rapped the paper with his fingernail.
"Excellent."

"What is it?"

He spread the sheet across the table. "Look here," he pointed. "And
here." Hilda bent over the chart and stared at the wriggling pen line.

"There's your snug," he told her. "See those jogs in the plot? Those are
temperature drops."

She shook her head. The wriggling line was just a wriggling line. The
jog his finger pointed to looked no different to her than any of the other
random ups and downs; only a trifle deeper. "I don't see anything. Why is
that so important?"

He looked at her and blinked his eyes. "Why, it proves that there is something physical happening at that location. Something that caused the temperature to fall abruptly. It wasn't in your head."

"I never thought it was." *Liar.* The untightening she felt deep within herself belied that. *Oh, Mother . . .* She ran her finger along the graph. The
sharp spikes were icicles, sudden bursts of cold. Real, physical cold; measured not by a shivering librarian, but by an inanimate instrument. *Not
crazy. Not crazy.* Who ever said that objectivity was dehumanizing?

"I don't understand. What does the temperature have to do with the
gh — ah, 'snug.' "

Leo pulled a small rule from his shirt pocket and measured the slopes
of the lines. "When a snug lights up," he said, "it uses energy. My guess is
that it converts the thermal energy in the air directly to photons, somehow
tapping the 'high-energy tail' of the Maxwell-Boltzmann thermal distrib-

ution. The only spirit involved is Maxwell's Demon. Ah . . ." He looked
up at her and flushed. "I'm doing it again. Lecturing. You see, air molecules are not all the same. . . . Well, let's say that they are not all the same
'temperature.' That's close enough. There is a random distribution of tem-
peratures. Some air molecules are 'warmer'; and—"

"Wait a minute! Are you trying to tell me that ghosts are a lot of hot air?"

His flush deepened. "No, I am trying *not* to tell you that, because I have
heard it too often from my colleagues here." He hung his head and entered the numbers into a small desk calculator. "A thermocouple converts
heat energy into electricity. Why can there not be a similar mechanism—
a natural mechanism—that converts heat into light? It needn't be too en-
ergetic. The brightest snug I've ever measured has had an output of less
than twenty watts. Regardless . . ." He raised his head again and looked at
her. "If a snug uses the high end of the thermal energy curve to energize
itself, the temperature of the surrounding air will naturally drop. When the
dew point is reached, the moisture in the air will condense, so you would
feel 'cold and clammy' and the snug will be shrouded in fog. So, you see . . ."
He spread his hands. ". . . the traditional descriptions of ghosts match physical theory quite well. Even to the extent that 'shrouded ghosts' are more
commonly seen in the British Isles, where the dew point is high."

Leo blinked at the calculator display. "The temperature drops in the library averaged about 3.4°C per minute. That would make your snug's
power output . . ." His fingers danced on the keypad. ". . . around five watts.
Durations ranged from a few seconds to five minutes."

Hilda ran her finger along the plot trace. "It was real. That's all that matters."

He hunched over the rule, measuring the distances between icicles.
"Mean recurrence rate . . . 2,460 minutes, plus or minus a trivial amount
that could be instrument error. Let's see . . . Forty-one hours. Hunh." He
put the end of the rule in his mouth and chewed on it. "Diurnally out of
synch. That's interesting."

Hilda raised her head and looked at him. "What? You mean the ghost
reappears every two days? I don't believe it! More people would have seen
it."

"Not every two days. Forty-one hours. That would be . . . Got it! It's a
harmonic of the lunar month! One-sixteenth. So, each appearance would

be seven hours earlier in the day than the previous one." He stopped and blinked at her. "Oh. Why haven't more people seen it? Think. Most of the nighttime events would take place on weekends or holidays or in the wee hours of the morning, when no one was around to see them. And more than half the occurrences would be during daylight or early evening when the building lights would be on. A five-watt snug doesn't make much of a flash and the vast majority of the events would be too brief to notice. You were lucky that night, to have experienced such a long-lasting event."

Lucky? She supposed that, from Leo's viewpoint, she had been. But he hadn't been there. He hadn't experienced that horrid feeling. "What about the cold?" she asked, to avoid thinking about it. "Or the fog? People would notice that, even during the day. Especially in the summer."

"Would they? In an air-conditioned building? Or would they think it was a draft? Most thermoluminescent events would be very short—a few seconds, perhaps. Boltzmann statistics. The longer the event, the less frequently it occurs. Now, a 'bright' twenty-watt snug would trigger a drop of, say, ten degrees celcius per minute. That's a maximum, without convection or anything. So if the snug 'lit up' for two seconds, you would experience a local temperature drop of at most one-third of a degree. Who would notice? And the Library Snug is much dimmer than that. It only shows up on my trace because of the sensitivity of the instruments."

"Then it probably won't happen to me again," she said.

Leo sighed. "Probably not," he said with regret. "Reproducibility is such a problem in this field. Oh." He looked into her eyes and, surprised, she turned her face away. "It was a frightening experience, wasn't it?" His eyes grew distant. "Frightening," he repeated to himself. "I could prepare a schedule for you of the snug's expected reappearances. There is no way of telling beforehand whether an event will fall in the longer-lived tail of the distribution: but you can schedule your late-night work to avoid them."

"That would be nice. Thank you."

"Meanwhile . . ." He pulled a calendar appointment book from his shirt pocket and flipped quickly through the pages. "You first sensed the snug, when? The ninth, wasn't it?"

"Yes. It was seven at night." She shivered. "I still remember the chimes."

"Uh-huh. And the last event on the strip recorder was, hmm . . ." He ran his eye down the chart on his desk. "Six P.M. on the twenty-first."

"Hey!" she said. "That means there was one today, doesn't it?" She closed her eyes and counted the hours on the clockface. "At eleven A.M.!" She gasped. "I was in the room then!"

Leo was still studying his calendar. "Didn't notice anything, right?"

"I—No."

He waved a pencil at the graph. "Daytime. Short duration. If you weren't looking straight at it, you wouldn't know anything had happened. Even if you were, the overhead lights would probably have masked it. Here we go. The next one is at four A.M. the day after tomorrow." He shook his head. "Too soon. We won't be ready in time. It'll have to be nine P.M. on the twenty-sixth." He penciled a notation on his calendar and put it back in his shirt pocket. He reached behind himself to the desk, where he found a small booklet, which he opened.

"Ready? Ready for what?"

He picked up his telephone and flipped through the booklet. "I have a friend in aerospace engineering who doesn't think I'm too crazy," he told her. "He has some computer-imaging equipment he will let me borrow, if I'm not too explicit about why I want it. I'll tell him it's for a holographic experiment. He'll know I'm lying, but that will cover him with his chairman."

"You want to take its picture. The ghost."

"The snug. Of course. More than just a visual picture. With modern image-enhancement techniques I can study the snug at virtually every wavelength and obtain a pretty thorough electromagnetic footprint."

"You want to set up all this equipment in the Cataloguing Room? The director won't be happy about that."

"She won't care," Leo predicted. "Not too much, anyway. The twenty-sixth is a Sunday. No one will be around to be scandalized."

"Well, I'll ask her," she said uncertainly.

Leo smiled. "Tell her I will continue to pester her if she does not let us do this experiment."

Hilda looked at her watch. "Look at the time!" she said. "I've got to be going. I suppose your wife will be waiting supper for you."

"My wife?" Leo seemed puzzled, as if wondering whether he had forgotten if he had one. Then he blinked and said, "Oh, no. I am not married. I never have been."

"Oh." She pointed toward the desk. "I thought those were your sons."

"Sons?" He twisted his head to see where she was pointing. "Ah." He gazed at the picture for a long time before answering. "That picture was taken many years ago," he said finally. "A great many years ago. I am the one on the left." He stared at the snapshot a while longer before adding, "Harry and I did everything together. Read the same books, saw the same movies, earned the same merit badges." He smiled slightly, his head cocked in reminiscence. "Dated the same girl. You never saw one of us without the other. We dressed alike. We even thought alike. Sometimes he would answer a question before I even asked it."

"Where is he now?"

Leo sighed and turned his back on the picture. "Dead."

"Oh. I'm sorry."

Leo shrugged. "It was a long time ago." He made a ball of his hands, twisted his fingers together.

"I'm sorry," she repeated, unable to think of anything else worth saying.

Leo studied his hands. "It was the only thing we never did together."

V

He hadn't thought about Harry in a long time. Leo rinsed his mouth and spat into the sink. He put his toothbrush back in the rack: then he leaned forward and studied his own face in the mirror. It would have been Harry's face, too, he decided. They would never have grown too different. He tried not to think about reality; about what Harry's face must look like now, after all these years below the ground. Decay. Rot. Worms. He shuddered and turned out the bathroom light and went to bed.

And lay there unable to sleep. It was too hot with the covers on, too cold with them off. The dark and the quiet blanketed him. Far away, he could hear a faint, intermittent knocking. Only his own pulse in his ears. He had established that long ago, after innumerable and futile trips to his apartment door, peering through the spyhole at empty hallways. Only his own pulse, audible now that the world was hushed. He closed his eyes and tried to empty his mind.

As he relaxed into the borderland of sleep, the voices began.

Fragments. Soft, random syllables, chopped off, with long pauses in between. Seldom a complete word. Never anything that made sense. *Wonder-*, whispered a voice. And *Waysdi-*. Leo strained to hear the message, knowing there was none. *Beewith-* and *Verythi-*. The voices were without tone or inflection—not masculine, not feminine—bursting like shells in the silence of his mind.

Insensibly he drifted out of the borderland and the popcorn voices were stilled. As he lay there in the quiet he became gradually aware that someone was watching him. He was lying on his side and behind him was the wall and between the bed and the wall stood . . . something.

It watched him as he lay there. He could feel its height. It was black and featureless, with not even eyes to break its seamless shadow. Utterly silent, with no whisper of breath—its gaze neither threatening nor benevolent, but an implacable dispassion. It watched without feeling or interest.

Leo knew he had to see it, to confront it. He gathered his will from a dozen scattered points and rolled over on his back and opened his eyes. . . .

And awoke lying on his side in the darkness.

He contemplated the fact that he had dreamed about dreaming, and wondered if, even now, he was awake; because, if so, he had awoken into his dream, into the same dark bedroom, curled into the same position.

With the same monstrous feeling of being watched.

He twisted around and stared into the darkness between the bed and the wall, and there was nothing there save the darkness itself. Unless . . . was there, within the darkness, a deeper shadow, somehow solid? He could feel its inexorable presence pressing on his skin, brushing the small hairs of his neck and arms.

Leo opened his mouth to speak, but the words came out as a flaccid cry, a low-pitched moan that lacked the will to scream. He woke with a gasp and groped for the bedside lamp and turned it on, fearful that, this once, there would be a shadow its light would not dispel.

But, of course, there was not.

He sat up in his bed, with his back braced against his pillows, and listened to the hammer of his heart. Resolutely, his eyes sought out the familiar landmarks of his room. The chest. The hairbrush. The tie thrown across the chairback. Simple, ordinary objects. Anchors to reality. Comforting in their everyday intimacy. Slowly, his pulse stilled, and he lay back down again. There was no need to check the thermocouple. He had disconnected it a long time ago. In all the years, there had never been a quiver on it.

He went to sleep with the light on—something he had not done since he was a boy.

The next morning, Leo's nightmare faded while he installed the equipment in the library. That was the best therapy. Concentrate on the task at hand. Lose yourself in the details of a routine task; let the mind idle in neutral while the subconscious sorts things out. He started to hum.

Hilda picked up the loose end of a cable. "Where do you want this?"

"Here, give it to me. It goes in the computer port."

A *complete physical record*, he thought. At last, he would have a complete physical record. Electromagnetic, sound, temperature, and relative humidity. Everything. Let Magruder argue with that, if he could!

Leo stopped humming and grimaced. He probably would. What did physical evidence mean? There had been too many photographs of "flying saucers" and "Martian faces" and "Loch Ness monsters." Mistaken identity. Wishful thinking. Even outright hoaxes. Magruder wouldn't accuse him of hoaxing the department. At least, not aloud.

He set his jaw. This would be no blurred, half-focused snapshot. This was the best equipment NASA could buy.

"What's wrong?"

"Eh?" He looked up from his wiring and saw Hilda watching him. "What do you mean?"

"Well, you looked so happy there for a while. Then, all of a sudden, you were the face of gloom."

He twisted his smile. "I was just thinking about some of my colleagues, how they won't accept my findings, in spite of everything."

"I don't understand. They're scientists. They'll have to believe you if you show them the evidence."

Leo wiped his hands on a rag. He set the camera atop its tripod and screwed it in place. "You don't know scientists. If they already believe a thing is impossible, they'll refuse even to look at the evidence. If I had Magruder here and he saw the snug for himself, he would still refuse to believe it. A trick, he'd say. An illusion. He might even find a stage magician who could duplicate everything that happened. As if any phenomenon that *could* be duplicated by hoax must therefore *be* a hoax." He smiled sadly and looked into the distance. "I am an embarrassment to them. They think I am so far around the bend, that I cannot even see the bend any-more." He picked up a screwdriver. "They took away my freshman classes this year. I'm professor emeritus, now. E-meritus. That means 'without merit.' " He laughed at his own joke.

"And can you see it?" she asked.

"Can I what?"

"See the bend."

He paused and looked at her with raised eyebrows. Hilda had her hands half-raised and clenched at waist level. "As clearly as anyone else," he told her. He bent again over his work. Why was Hilda so concerned with *his* mental health? "You see, I don't have a problem with snugs—hell, with 'ghosts.' There is a class of phenomenon that needs explaining, that's all. I have no vested interest in the nature of the explanation. The problem with unbelievers is their dogmatism."

"What do you mean?"

He grunted. "They can't just disbelieve. They've got to disbelieve in a certain way: Orthodox disbelief! Talk with an atheist some time; you'll never get a clearer vision of the fundamentalist God. God, they'll tell you, wouldn't play games with fossils or light waves just to trick us into thinking that the universe was older than six thousand years. Now, *Loki* might very well do that, or *Raven*; but those aren't the gods that they disbelieve in."

"You don't really believe that—"

"That the physical universe was created in 4004 B.C.?" He made a face. "Of course not. Although the date does approximate the creation of our *cultural* universe. No. I was merely using it as an example, to show how even unbelievers hold certain unquestionable beliefs. My colleagues have a mental image of the *sort* of ghosts they do not believe in, and if someone like me comes along with a different paradigm—a materialistic one, unconnected with magic or superstition . . . Why, they'll denounce it as rank heresy! I try to talk about a mechanism for the thermophotonic effect, and they'll argue that spells and pentagrams vio-late conservation of energy. I try to describe the frequency and duration of certain odd events, and they'll point out that mediums and spiritual-ists are frauds. I wonder if there might not be *something* that needs ex-plaining, and they'll bring up crystals and pyramid power." He tossed the screwdriver to the table. It banged and rolled and dropped to the floor.

Leo made a face. "Sorry," he said. "Even we nutcases can grow exasperated with the stupidity of others."

" 'What am I doing in here with all these crazy people?' "

Leo chuckled. "Yes, exactly." But he looked at her and saw she wasn't smiling. "What's wrong?"

She folded her arms under her breasts and hunched over. She studied the equipment on the table. "I wasn't making a joke," she told the oscilloscope.

Leo stood quietly with the cable in his hand and waited.

Hilda unfolded her arms and lightly touched the knobs on the scope. "You would think that when a person's mind goes, she wouldn't recognize mental illness in others. But it isn't like that at all." She turned and looked him in the eye. "My mother and I were very close." She said it as a challenge. "Especially after Father died. We were the kind of mother and daughter who dressed alike and went places together. I look like her—I mean, I look like she did when she was younger. There isn't a trace of my father anywhere in my face. Even after I was grown, we did things together. I thought she was just so wonderful, and I wanted to be just like her."

"Then . . . ?"

She looked away, at the card catalogue, at the racks of books. "Then something happened inside her head. I don't know what it was. The doctors didn't know what it was. They talked about strokes and lithium imbalance and I don't know what else. But they didn't know anything, really. What it all came down to was that she wasn't my mother anymore. She was a stranger who saw things, who heard things. Sometimes the voices talked to her; and she talked back. Twice, she left my apartment while I was at work and wandered around the neighborhood. After a while, I couldn't deal with it anymore and I—" Her hands clenched again. "I had her committed. When I went back the first time to visit her, she gave me the most heartbreaking and bewildered look and asked me why she was in there with all those crazy people."

Leo saw a tear in the corner of her eye. "It was probably the best thing you could have done," he said slowly. "I mean, the professionals would know how to—"

"You don't understand." She shook her head slowly. "When I visit the

. . . place where she lives now . . . when I look at her, I see myself, only older. *I wanted to grow up to be just like her!*"

"Oh." Leo bent over and plugged the cable into the computer.

"So I've got to know, Dr. Reissman. I've got to know, am I starting to see things, too?"

He straightened and looked at her. Hilda's lower lip was almost white from the pressure of her teeth. "I told you you weren't. I showed you the traces on the temperature records. You saw something real."

She shook her head. "You showed me some lines on a chart. They could have meant anything. I don't understand things like that. I'm not a technical person. I just want to know if I can believe you. Or are you a nutcase, too?"

Leo wiped his palms on his pants lets. *What can I tell her? That I hear voices? That things visit me in the night?* He touched the computer with his forefinger, rubbing it along the top of the case. "The mind can see and hear things that aren't real. I'll grant you that. I think it happens to everyone at some time or another. The signals are blocked or scrambled or misinterpreted. But it doesn't matter what I am. Because this—" He rapped the computer with his knuckles. "This will only see a picture if there are photons; it will only record a voice if there are sound waves."

Hilda flexed her fingers, brushed at the sleeves of her blouse. "Then we'll let the machines tell us if we're sane," she said; but Leo pretended he hadn't heard.

VI

The ticking of the clock in the boardroom next door was a steady, distant metronome. *Funny*, Hilda thought. She had never realized how loud it was; unless its sound was magnified by the evening stillness, or by her imagination. She glanced to her right, where Leo sat quietly in the other chair studying the instruments that he had racked on the table before him. *How can he wait so calmly?* she wondered. He reached out to the oscilloscope and turned one of its knobs an infinitesimal fraction to the right. Hilda thought he had turned it to the left just a short while ago; so perhaps he was not as calm as he appeared. That made her feel fractionally better.

"How much longer?" she asked.

Leo pushed his sleeve up. "Five minutes. That is one minute less than the last time you asked."

Hilda blushed. She was acting like a fidgety schoolgirl. Yet the waiting was, in many ways, worse than the unexpected apparition of a fortnight or so past. Surprise could be numbing; but anticipation amplified everything, until the nerve endings stuck out a foot beyond the skin, and the least little event exploded on the senses.

In five—no, four—minutes, a ghost would appear. Or not. And she was afraid of either outcome, though in different ways. The unknown; or the known-too-well. Unless it was not fear, but another emotion entirely, that trembled in her body.

Leo rose and walked to the doorway, where he turned off the overhead lights. The room went dark, except for the dim green glow of his instruments and scopes. "We will be better able to see it with our own eyes," he said, "if the room is darkened."

Hilda turned from him and hunched herself in her chair. She clenched and unclenched her hands. The glow from Leo's instruments teased the corners of her eyes. She stared into the darkness, toward The Spot, waiting. "How much—"

"Sh!"

Dim shapes emerged from the black as her vision adjusted to the room. There was the work bench, the fireplace, and, yes, the old card catalogue. The only sounds were her own breath and the faint electrical hum of the equipment.

It seemed as if an endless time went by. Then a light winked in the air, as brief as a firefly on a summer's eve; a spark that was gone before it was even seen. Leo rose and walked toward the light switch. Hilda expelled her breath. "Was that it?"

Leo turned the lights back on. He returned to the instrument table and leaned over the scope. He pressed a button. "Yes," he said.

"Why, that was hardly anything at all." She felt peeved; as if the ghost had let her down. All that anticipation. All that buildup. It seemed anticlimactic. Only a fleeting glimmer in the dark. No sliding drawers. No hand in her hair. No piercing cold. She clasped her hands together. Had she imagined everything, after all?

She watched over Leo's shoulder as he replayed the apparition on his computer screen. She saw the spark flash again—a digitized memory of it. Leo froze the display and the screen showed a featureless smear of white.

Not what she had ever imagined a ghost should look like. Yet, the instruments *had* recorded something.

Leo scowled and advanced the record one frame at a time. Forward. Backward. Forward, again. Hilda could not decide what he was looking for. The whiteness wasn't there, then it was, then it wasn't. Like a light that had turned on and off.

When she leaned forward to see better, she placed her hand on his shoulder, and he jerked as if electrocuted. Hilda backed away from him. He gave her a distant, preoccupied look and turned back to the screen without speaking. His fingers made clacking sounds on the keyboard.

Finally, he sighed. "Here, look at this," he said.

Hilda stepped cautiously to his side. She did not know why he was so edgy, but she did not want to disturb him. "What is it?"

"I have enhanced the signal to show greater detail."

The freeze frame showed the same featureless blob she had seen before. She shook her head. "I don't see anything."

Leo made a sound in his throat. "Look more carefully. See the way it narrows into a head? And those dark spots near the top. Those must be eyes, wouldn't you say?"

"No. It's just a white smear."

"It's not only white. The spectral analysis shows some blue with some overtones of green. Auroral effects from the excitation of diatomic nitrogen and monatomic oxygen."

"If you say so," she said doubtfully.

"I have had more practice than you at image interpretation. Let me refine the image further." He again bent over the keyboard and the NASA equipment did whatever it was that it did. The image on the screen changed colors. Vertical wipes passed through it, changed it. The edges became sharper. The suggestion of contour emerged.

"There is a face there. I know it." Leo hit the keys several more times and features solidified out of the smoky shape. "There! There! Do you see it now?"

"I see a woman in a billowy gown," she said slowly. The balloon shape could be a hoop skirt. The halo could be a bonnet. And, yes, if she concentrated on it long enough, she could see the pits of eyes and the shadow of a long straight nose. She looked at Leo. Had the image been there in the shape all the time, waiting to be evoked by the computer; or had Leo, for some reason of his own, imposed an image upon it—an electronic Michelangelo creating a digital *Madonna?* She couldn't know. She couldn't. If you worried at it long enough, could your heart not find any form at all buried in formlessness? Weren't there bestiaries in inkblots; menageries in the clouds?

Leo straightened with a satisfied look on his face. "That proves it, wouldn't you say?" Hilda started to answer, but realized that he was not talking to her. "A human face couldn't be a coincidence. There must be a connection between ghosts and the souls of the dead." He folded his arms and studied the woman on the screen. "I wonder who she was? One of the women in the vault? Or Mammy Morgan herself?" He pulled out a chair and sat down and began scratching rapidly in his notebook. "I should be able to excite the ghost artificially. Increase its brightness and duration. With a laser, perhaps. The matrix appears to be a hologram of some sort; the light is naturally coherent. Yes. With a laser, I can amplify the signal; make contact." The point of his pencil snapped against the notebook page and he looked at it dumbly.

Ghost. He had said "ghost." Hilda wondered what had become of snugs. She realized suddenly that Leo was never going to settle the reality of her ghost or the stability of her mind. Everything he said or did could be colored by his own yearnings for . . . What? Vindication? Respectability? Something else? She had been foolish to rely on this old man and his facade of scientific objectivity. No amount of gadgetry could ever quiet her doubts, because the doubts had grown inside herself, where no instrument could reach.

"I could bring my own laser over. The projector. Create an excited state directly in the heart of the ghost." He flipped the pages of his notebook. "Damn!" He ran his finger down a column of figures. "The next two apparitions will be during the daylight on weekdays. Well, I've waited this long; I can wait a short while longer." He drummed his fingers on the table. Then he looked at her as if he had suddenly recalled her presence.

"Your director would be very upset if this equipment were still sitting here tomorrow morning. We must break it down and store it for a few days. Is there a room here in the library I can use?"

"Yes," she said. "There's a place in back of the closed stacks."

"Good. Good." He nodded. "Would you help me set it up again on Friday after the library closes? The next nighttime appearance is twelve o'clock that night."

"Midnight," she said without checking the calendar. "All Hallows' Eve."

The next five days passed slowly. A climax, Hilda thought (and a climax was coming, she knew) should not come after an intermission. There should not be such a lapse in which to think and doubt and wonder. The days seemed pointlessly spent, idle time. She discussed Leo's experiment with the director, who listened in prim disapproval, but did not forbid it. For whatever reason, Hilda said nothing of her doubts regarding Leo himself.

She read all she could about ghosts. Not the sensational things, the kinds of reports that smacked of showmanship and the need to be noticed; but the quietly understated tales of casual, everyday haunts. Most haunts, she discovered, did not involve grisly and horrible events. Instead, they were almost matter-of-fact. The sound of a ball bouncing down the hallway; when there was no such ball. A shadow on a wall, when there was nothing to cast it. They were almost comforting in their ordinariness. The Irish ghost scholar, Dr. Michael MacLiammoir, wrote that "it is the unbeliever who feels the greatest fear of ghosts; for the believer knows that they are harmless."

She made it a point to be in the Cataloguing Room on the occasion of both the predicted daytime events. She was not sure why, or what she expected to see—which was nothing in the first case and (maybe) a brief spark in the second—but she could not wait out the days doing nothing.

Then, finally, it was the night of Leo's experiment. Hilda drove to the library at ten P.M. Midnight, he had said; but, of course, he would need time to set up his equipment. The downtown was empty when she drove through; her tires hissed on abandoned streets. Stone veterans of Antietam and Gettysburg gazed down from their monument in Center Square. It was a ghostlit night. Black clouds streaked a silver-dollar moon. The wind shivered naked tree branches against the sky.

She turned onto Church and drove past the darkened library. A single light broke the black facade; the director's office, she noted with surprise. Why tonight, of all nights, had the director stayed to watch? Hilda turned right into the driveway and drove all the way to the rear parking lot. Her headlight beams cut across the night, picking out the colorless shapes of two other cars and, briefly, a solitary figure standing by the back wall.

When she cut her engine, she could hear the muted rush of the wind through the trees. She shivered. It was a cold sound, a lonely sound. Autumn was, in many ways, a colder time than winter. She unbuckled herself and got out of the car. The slam of the door closing behind her echoed in the nighttime silence. She peered toward the wall, where she had seen the figure, and saw Leo already approaching. His overcoat, unbuttoned, flapped in the breeze; and he held his hat in place with his left hand. The smile that cut his face tightened his skin like a drum.

"Well," he said. "Tonight is the night."

And that simply had to be true, because it could mean anything.

"All Hallows' Eve," she told Leo as they reconnected the monitors, "was the old Celtic New Year. New Year's Day began at sunset on the last day of October. The Celts believed that the spirits of those who had died during the year would roam the night, trying to occupy the bodies of the living. People dressed themselves in frightening costumes to scare the spirits off."

Leo grunted as he strung the cables. "I know that. It's all myth, though. Superstition. The dead go walking all year round, not just tonight."

There was no possible reply to a remark like that. And he had said it in so reasonable a tone. Still, if he was right that the recurrent, spontaneous light flashes were the souls of the dead, they did indeed go a-walking all year round. Every two days in the library workroom.

If there was any connection at all. She thought it was remarkable that, as she had come to think of the flashes as simple, physical events, Leo had gone the other way. Rather suddenly, it seemed to her. Between her visit to his office and their first test on the twenty-sixth. Something had happened to him over that weekend. Make contact, he had said after that first test. Contact with what? A flashbulb? A holographic recording? Leo was not setting up an experiment, she suddenly realized; he was conducting a séance. Not with trumpets or tambourines, though; there would be no holding hands in the dark. This was a modern séance, with all the modern, electronic conveniences.

She watched him hunched over his work. His lips were drawn tight against his teeth, and his hand trembled very slightly. *What was he thinking?* she wondered. She was not sure she wanted to know.

Everything was ready by eleven-forty, and the last few minutes seemed to drag by as slowly as they had five days before. Leo had rigged his laser to a photoelectric cell so that it would fire the instant the ghost appeared. The idea, he explained, was not to destroy the entity, but to amplify it through a kind of supercharging. Hilda did not understand what he said about energy levels and transitions and the like. She assumed that, in this one arena, at least, he was a competent gladiator.

She was not concerned with whether the ghost would appear. It would, and that was all there was to it. The sun rose and set; the moon ran through her phases; and the library ghost would make its regular appearance. As simply and predictably as that. And didn't that predictability argue against its being a 'person'? People always took you by surprise. Consider her mother, or even Leo. Things happened; people changed. Only the natural world ran forever in a predictable rut. "The stars in their courses . . ." So, it might not be a ghost as she had always thought of ghosts, as hauntings by the unquiet dead. It might be, as Leo had once told her, a stuck, holographic record. But that did not bother her. It wasn't *what* it was that mattered, but only *that* it was. It was that knowledge that made her safe within her own skull.

The director appeared in the doorway, bearing a tray. She carried it to the worktable against the east wall and set it down. "I thought you might want some coffee," she said.

Leo raised his head. "What? Who . . . ? Oh. No. No, coffee. Thank you." He ducked back into his work.

"I'll have a cup," Hilda said quietly.

The director poured from a portable electric pot into two china cups and handed one to Hilda.

"Thank you." Hilda sipped from the hot liquid. "Why are you here?" she asked bluntly.

The director shrugged. "Who can resist putting her beliefs to the test? Tonight is the denoument, isn't it? Tonight will settle things once and for all."

Hilda glanced at Leo. "Some things."

The director followed her glance. She raised her own cup to her lips. "Yes. Well."

Leo turned out the lights and they waited quietly in the dark while the clock crept toward midnight. Hilda could hear the hushed sounds of breathing and, occasionally, the sharp tink of a cup against its saucer. The director had said nothing more after the first brief sentences. She stood in the shadows beside Hilda, thin and proper and faintly disapproving, and asked no questions. Hilda resisted the urge to cross the room and sit beside Leo. Instead, she leaned back against the worktable. "Soon, now," Leo's voice announced from the gloom.

When the clock in the boardroom struck, Hilda jerked and leaned forward, peering into the dark. She held her breath as the soft chimes rang a slow, leaking drip of sound.

It happened suddenly on the tenth ring. A brightness flickered on the far side of the room and, simultaneously, a ruby red beam of light, straight as a steel rod, pierced its heart. In an instant, a phosphorescent sphere bloomed in the darkened room. It was white with a tinge of blue around its edges. It throbbed like a soap-bubble heart.

Hilda shivered in the sudden cold. Her breath made puffs of steam that glowed in the pale light emanating from the ghost. Campfire-shadows writhed on the walls. Hilda heard the director's coffee cup shatter on the floor; she saw Leo stand and lean across his table.

"Can you hear me?" Leo asked.

The pearly ball of light stretched and twisted like an amoeba.

"Can you take a message? For Harry? I must speak with him!"

The ghost pulsated and danced in the air.

The director grabbed her by the sleeve. "Do you see it?" she demanded. "Do you see it?"

Hilda disengaged her sleeve from the curled fingers. "Of course, I see it."

"Oh, it's wonderful! It's so wonderful!"

She turned and looked at the woman. The director's face was a crescent moon in the ghostly light. "Why?" she asked her. "Why is it so wonderful?"

"Don't you see? It means we go on. It means we don't end when we die!"

Across the room, Leo shouted question at the light. Hilda backed away from her companions. Were they both mad? The apparition was an iridescent soap bubble floating in the air. A strange thing, yes, a beautiful thing; but only a thing, as incapable of silent witness as it was of answering questions. Was she the only one who saw nothing more? Were they blind; or she?

The world was an enigma, a conundrum that everyone solved to their own contentment; and in the end, each person's world was as impenetrably individual as her mother's. The ghost was a perfect mirror, reflecting whatever images each imagination could project. The director saw eternal life glowing in the room. Harry saw a channel to his dead brother. She saw . . .

A light. Only a light. Mystery, but no magic.

Leo gave a shout and twisted something on his control panel. The instruments hummed louder and the ruby light brightened. The ghost waxed, shimmering with a thousand colors. Streamers of azure and crimson roiled through it. Silver bubbles drifted from the center toward the edge and fell back inward. The surface twitched and spasmed. Frost appeared on the windowpanes of the room, on the worktables. The cold bit into Hilda and her teeth chattered.

Then the ghost fell in on itself like a collapsing star. For just an instant, Hilda thought she saw it coalesce into a slim, fine-featured woman; then it shattered into a billion twinkling lights that exploded soundlessly into the corners of the room, dying like fireworks in the nighttime sky.

The room fell dark.

Hilda sucked in a breath. Beside her, she heard the director's soft "Amen." The hum of the equipment was the only other sound. The cold slowly faded; the frost dripped from the windows. The laser cast a small, red spot on the card catalogue. Abruptly, it, too, vanished. Across the room, she heard Leo sob.

Hilda hit the light switch and saw Leo slumped in his chair with his face in his hands. She went to him and put a gentle hand on his shoulder. "Leo?"

He turned a face toward her. "He'll never come back," he said. "He'll never come back." He pushed her hand away, rose, and staggered from the room.

"Who?" That was the director. The question was flat, unemotional. Hilda turned around and saw the same hard face she had always known. There was no trace of her earlier exaltation. "Who will never come back?"

Hilda sighed and hugged herself. Who? Everyone. Anyone. Leo's brother. Her mother. All the strangers we once thought we knew. "Harry," she said aloud. "Leo's twin brother, Harry."

The director pressed her lips together. "Of course, he won't. His brother is dead. I talked to his chairman. He told me that Dr. Reissman's brother had died while they were on a Boy Scout hike. He stumbled off a cliff in the dark." She shook her head. "Tragic. I imagine twins are very close."

Hilda felt the blood drain from her.

"Off a cliff? Oh, God!" And she turned and bolted from the room.

When she burst from the library's back door into the cold of the night, the wind bit through her blouse like a knife. It tore her hair loose and sent it streaming. It sucked the breath from her open mouth. She remembered what she had said to Leo that first day. *A long way to fall. Time enough to know.* How cruel her words must have been! But she hadn't known. How could she have known?

Time enough for a gulping breath; then she turned and ran to the parking lot. Halfway across the flat asphalt surface, she skidded to a halt. Leo was standing atop the stone wall at the east end, where the drop was nearly sheer. She did not want to startle him; so she walked slowly to his side and waited for him to notice her.

He was staring down into the black depths. Above, the moon glowed cold behind racing clouds. Hilda shivered in the icy wind.

"You should go back inside," he said after a moment. "You'll catch pneumonia."

"You will, too."

He shook his head. "I won't be standing here long enough for that to matter."

"Please, Leo. Harry can't want that."

He turned his head and looked at her. His cheeks drooped, pulling his mouth down. "He must."

"Why?" She forced her voice to remain as quiet and as reasonable as his. She wanted to shout, to scream at him. *Calm,* she told herself. *Stay calm.*

"Why? So we can be together, like we always were. Like we were meant to be."

She knew then that there was a third sort of fear. She knew that Leo would die unless she saved him, and she did not know if she could do it. Caring was not enough. She had not been able to save her own mother.

"You can't mean that." Did you argue with the suicidal? Did logic convince them? If not logic, what?

"I knew it the moment it happened." He spoke in a quiet, distant voice. "I woke up in the middle of the night, and I knew that something had happened to him. I roused the scoutmaster and told him that Harry was gone, that he needed help." He sighed and studied the cloud-shrouded sky. "It was just growing light when we found him. He was at the bottom of a hundred-foot cliff. He had gone off to take a leak away from the camp, turned the wrong way in the dark, and walked off the edge. When I closed my eyes I could picture every step he had taken. I could remember his hands flailing wildly, grasping vainly for handholds as he fell. Fingers breaking against the rocks." He looked again at the rocks below him.

"He was still alive," he continued. "If he had been dead already, it might not have hurt so much. But he was still alive. I saw him move an arm. It took an hour for them to find another way to the bottom. I sat at the top of the cliff and watched. Harry opened his eyes and he saw me up there looking down; and, for an instant, I saw myself seeing him. Then he closed his eyes and he didn't move again. A few minutes later, every bird in the forest took wing and circled above, blackening the sky, screeching. I knew that Harry had died. There was always a link of some sort, a channel that joined us; and someone had just . . . hung up the extension. That's as clearly as I can explain it. I could call out, but no one would ever answer again. I have never been happy since that moment."

"It must have been terrible." She thought her words were shallow, inadequate; but it did not matter. He continued as if she had not spoken at all.

"A few years later, I thought I heard a whisper over our private line. A few words spoken in the darkness as I fell asleep. I thought Harry was trying to reach me. To tell me something important. I tried to listen; but the harder I concentrated, the more elusive the words were. They were . . . 'peripheral' sounds. Every night, before I went to bed, I prayed that Harry would come back. But I had read 'The Monkey's Paw' and sometimes I was afraid that my prayers would be answered. Teenage boys don't like to cry; but I cried. I cried. Then, one night, while I was in college; he did come back. Or he tried to."

Hilda took a deep breath and hunched over. She knew she shouldn't try to grab him. If she did, he would pull away and fall; and she would never be able to hang on to him. "What happened?" Behind her, she could hear the library door open and footsteps clicking on the asphalt. She knew that the director had followed them—after first stopping sensibly for her over-coat. Without turning, Hilda gestured with her hand, and she heard the other woman leave, to—sensibly—call the rescue squad.

"I was asleep," Leo said. "I was in my dormitory room asleep when I felt him standing beside my bed. The prickling at the back of my head woke me up and, for a moment, I thought I had dreamed it. Then, I realized that I could still feel the presence beside me. I stared toward it, but I could see nothing. I tried to raise my arm to reach out, but I was paralyzed. I felt nothing over the channel Harry and I had shared—only a vast indiffer-ence—so I knew that, though he was trying to come back to me, he was unable to make it through all the way."

"Did it . . . Did you . . ." She let her breath out. "I know the feeling."

He nodded slowly. "Yes, so you told me. That was when I knew that ghosts were souls. When you told me that you had felt the same thing. That could not have been coincidence."

"But that mightn't mean that at all. You told me so yourself."

"I did. I *wanted* apparitions to be false, or that they not be souls. I needed to believe that."

"You never were objective about it."

He shook his head and studied the darkness below him. "If ghosts were real and they were souls, then why had Harry never come back to me?"

There was nothing she could answer to that. "What changed your mind?"

"Last Friday night, my haunt returned. I knew it wasn't real—I had set-tled that years ago—but I knew your library ghost was real. And that didn't make any sense. Why the library ghost and not Harry? I had to know."

How paper-thin was the barrier between thought and unreality. The slightest thing—a stroke, a psychic trauma—rips it through. She recalled that Leo used his laser to project images. What had they really seen in the workroom tonight? Did even Leo know? "I was close to my mother, too," she told him. "We could have been twins, too; except for the age."

He looked at her. "Your mother is still alive."

She avoided his gaze. "But I treated her as if she were dead. Your brother is dead, but you treat him as if he were alive. You won't let him go."

He turned and faced the drop once more. "I can't."

"How many years has it been?"

"A great many."

"It's too long ago to matter anymore."

He turned a tear-stained face to her. He looked older than at any other time she had seen him. "It will always matter. If I had gotten up with him, he would never have died."

So, that was it. Hilda felt like crying herself. "Or you might both have died. You can't torture yourself over things that might have been."

"Can't I? My brother is dead, and it was my fault. Now, my career is finished; my colleagues laugh at me. Why should I not take this one last step? It is such a small one."

"Because *I* don't want you to!" She cried it, shouted it into the night.

"Eh?" He gave her an astonished look.

She was angry with him, for what he had done to her and to her life; and for what he had done to himself. "Do you think I want to go through the rest of my life with the same load of guilt you've been carrying; always rerunning this night and asking myself what I could have done differently? Blaming myself."

He looked stricken. "But . . . But you mustn't blame yourself," he said. "You can not be responsible for what I do."

She held her breath, willing him to see the connection. She could not tell him; he had to tell himself. He stood there for two long breaths, studying her. The seconds seemed to stretch out forever. Then he nodded. "Yes. I see." He glanced once more at the abyss below him; then he stepped down onto the solidity of the parking lot. He began to shake. Hilda closed her eyes briefly and said a prayer of thanks. She opened her arms and he stepped into them and laid his head on her shoulder and wept. "There," she said. "It's all right now." She patted him on the back. "It's all right."

"I would have jumped," he said. "I would have."

"I know. It's all right, now."

"No, it is not all right," he said after a long silence. "I'm frightened of what I yet might do." He shook his head. "I'm not happy. I won't be anytime soon; but I think, perhaps, I can see happiness from here."

After a few moments, he disengaged himself. He rubbed his hand over his face and turned back to the wall. Hilda held one hand out to him, but he only approached the wall and gazed over its edge. The tears still coated his cheeks. Hilda watched him, her arms half-raised toward him, her hands clenched. The wind was bitterly cold. Winter was coming. All tears were ice; and winter must be brave.

ABOUT "MAMMY MORGAN PLAYED THE ORGAN; HER DADDY BEAT THE DRUM"

Everything in this story is true, except the parts I made up. And they might not be the parts you think.

The library is real. It's where I read all those SF books a long time ago; though the addition mentioned in the story hadn't been built yet. The library really is built atop a cliff on the site of a Dutch Reformed graveyard. And there really are bodies still buried on the grounds, including Mammy Morgan herself. And it really is supposed to be haunted.

Okay, not really. The librarians tell tales — the various events mentioned in the story (the card drawers, the hand in the hair) happened to one or another of them, but they don't actually believe in the ghost. It's all in fun.

Right?

My brother Kevin and I scouted the locale one summer when we were both in town visiting the folks. Kevin is a newspaper reporter (and also an author, though in the True Crime genre), so I suppose he had a feature story in mind. I kept wondering, how do I get a science-fiction story out of this?

That's science fiction, not fantasy.

A hard science-fiction ghost story . . . ? Yes, because it is all in the attitude, not in the stage props. Suppose there is some physical phenomenon that we call a "ghost." Something rare, like ball lightning. Years ago, Donald Carpenter wrote an article for *Analog* entitled "The Physics of Haunting," in which he showed that many of the reported features of haunts are compatible with known laws of physics. I used this background to imagine a researcher who is trying to study "a phenomenon" in a strictly materialist way and is trying very, very hard not to think about spirits of the dead, because . . . Sometimes, we don't know our own motivations, and Leo is no exception.

By the way, a death researcher wrote me to complain that I had painted death researchers as psychologically troubled. Now, Leo was not, in fact, researching death, but the larger point is that a character who pursues a particular line of work (or who is of a particular race, gender, or ethnicity, or who practices a particular religion, et ad nauseum cetera) does not necessarily symbolize all members of that subset. Please try to keep this in mind. Individuals are individuals. They do not take their identity, racists of the left and right notwithstanding, from their membership in a larger group.

When I showed "Mammy Morgan . . ." to Nancy Kress, she asked me if I'd had a brother who died. The answer is yes, though not in the circumstances of the story. It was cancer, it took a long time, and it hurt, a lot. Dennis was not my twin. He was 362 days younger than me; and we did do everything together (like writing science-fiction stories). We knew what each other was thinking; not from telepathy, but just because we knew each other. And one day, when I was playing street football with the other guys, I knew he had just died.

As for the birds . . . My Uncle Paul lived two doors up the street. (Of the six houses on our block, four contained relatives of one sort or another.) He had been ill for some time. One day, his twin brother rushed through an early dinner, saying, "I've got to go see Paul." When Ralph reached his brother's house, Paul said, "Is that you, Ralph?" Ralph said, "Yes." Paul said, "Good." Then he died. Whereupon all the birds in the world descended on the house and went crazy. It was like a scene from Hitchcock. They darted about madly, chirruping and banging into windows. The roof, the eaves, the rain gutter, the clotheslines were draped with singing birds.

My parents saw this out our kitchen window. They turned to each other.

"Do you think Paul is trying to tell us something?"

"Yes. I think he's saying it's all for the birds."

Spark of Genius

He was a mean drunk; the solitary sort who scowled for long minutes into the amber mirror of his liquor before tossing it off in a single spasm of the arm and throat. The kind whose empty glass struck the bar like a hammer, so that the other patrons would look and as quickly look away. They had left a careful number of vacant stools between themselves and him. A type like that—you never could tell what would set them off.

The barkeeper approached, wiping his hands on his apron. Whatever else it might presage, an empty glass striking wood was the sound of money in the till.

"Another?"

The drinker looked up. "Double," he said.

The barkeeper did not reply, but poured from the bottle. He used the bar Scotch. Subtleties of taste would be wasted on this one. The drunk grasped his wrist as he turned away.

"Leave the bottle."

"I'm afraid that is against house rules, sir." It was his house and his rules; and sometimes he left the bottle and sometimes not. His voice was polite, but his left hand felt under the bar for a length of steel pipe that he kept there. Not that he thought he would need it, but you never knew, and the insurance gave him a sort of peace of mind. It was a hell of a world.

The drunk released him. "The hell with it. The hell with you." The barkeeper relaxed and turned to go. "Hey!"

"Yes, sir?" *Sir* because even a surly customer is a customer.

"You've got to stay and listen to my troubles. Isn't that part of the job description? Priests, shrinks, cops, and bartenders. They all gotta listen."

The barkeeper nodded to his relief man to take over. He folded his beefy arms across his chest. "All right. I'm listening. So what's your trouble?"

The drunk seized the shot glass and tossed off its contents. "My problem," he said when he banged it down, "is I'm too damned successful."

The bartender grunted. "Sure, we all should have those problems."

The man clenched both hands into fists on the bar top. "You don't understand. I've just written a best-seller."

The bartender thought about it. Then he poured himself a glass of bottled water — water, because only a fool drank his own profits — and took a sip. "So, tell me about it."

Ward's desk was an old wooden rolltop. Its pigeonholes were stuffed thick with letters and memos. A stack of manuscripts, boxed and tied with string, filled one corner. The walls were lined with copies of the books Ward had bought — at least, the successful ones. In another corner of the office, a proofreader peered through thick-lensed glasses while she blue-penciled a set of galleys. All in all, it was what an editor's office should look like. Armitage waited uncertainly just inside the door.

"About my manuscript . . ." he said.

"Sit down, Ken, sit down." Ward waved to a dark wood captain's chair with a pillow seat cushion. "The reason I asked you to come into the city —"

"It's about the book I sent you, isn't it?"

Ward blinked. "Why, of course it is. I've read it and —"

"I understand. I had my doubts about it when I sent it in."

Springs creaked as the editor leaned back in his swivel chair. "What on earth are you talking about?"

"It's pretty awful, isn't it?"

"Awful? Awful!" Ward rolled his eyes up to heaven. "Now you see why you're the writer and I'm the editor. Ken, it is far and away the best work you've ever done. It's . . . well, it's magnificent. Definitely crossover material. I've spoken to the publisher about putting it out on our mainstream list; break you out of the genre ghetto. Ken, we're talking best-seller here!"

Armitage half stood from the captain's chair, then he slowly lowered himself back down. "Best-seller," he repeated.

"Well, I can't promise, naturally. Only the readers can decide that. But it is as good as or better than anything that has hit the list in the last five years. I think you have finally found your voice."

"My voice." Armitage knew he sounded like a fool, echoing his editor's remarks. Still, the comment rankled some. He had six previous books out, and two of them had done quite well in the genre market. To be told that he was only now "finding his voice" . . . and on *this* book! "What were my other books, Ward, chopped liver?"

Ward blinked. "What? Oh, no. Don't think that." Writers were so temperamental. "But you must admit that you were learning your craft. If you don't improve with each book, then what? No, all I meant was that it has all come together with *Neural Life.*" He patted the manuscript box in a paternalistic fashion.

Armitage shrugged. "To tell you the truth, I thought it read very stilted. Mechanical."

The editor smiled. "I sometimes felt the same way about stories of my own. Familiarity breeds contempt. Do you know what I liked best about your story?"

Armitage shook his head, but did not speak.

"The way you used neural nets."

Armitage scowled. He shifted in the hard wooden chair. "What do you mean?"

"You used them in three different ways. First, as the technology that linked the major characters together—you based their company on the Center where you work, didn't you? But you also used them as the structure of the plot itself, *and* as a metaphor for the interaction of the text with the reader. When I read that opening scene, I hated Justin."

Armitage nodded. "For shooting Melinda in the square."

"Yes, yes. It was a brutal and unprovoked act. I thought Justin was a sonuvabitch. But then, when the story cycled around to the same scene, this time from Francine's viewpoint, I felt . . . well, pity for him. Then, the third time . . . How many times did you replay that scene?"

"Six?"

"Six. Right. Each time from the viewpoint—and in the voice—of a different participant. And each time I felt a different emotion. Even elation, if you can believe it."

"That was after you had learned that Melinda was the drug pusher responsible for the death of Justin's son."

The editor's head bobbed. "It certainly put a different light on things. Hell's bells. Each time I read that scene it was in a different light. To find out afterward that Melinda had been forced into the drug trade by her boyfriend's brutality . . . That made me ashamed of my earlier elation. When I finished the book, I felt like I had been on an emotional roller coaster. I was drained."

"And neural networks was a metaphor for all that."

Ward gave him a shrewd look. "You weren't aware of it yourself, were you? Well, they say the subconscious is the cleverest part of the brain. Sure, it was a metaphor. Look, how does a neural net computer work? You explained it in the book—and by the way, Willi over at our mainstream imprint thinks the explanation is clear enough for nongenre readers. You explained it in the book; just give me the recap."

Armitage pursed his lips. He rose from the chair and paced the room, pausing a moment at the proofreader's desk. The proofreader—Arlene— looked up, recognized him, and smiled. Armitage gave her a brief smile in return. Then he faced Ward. "No one knows how a neural net works. Not even those of us in the AI game. It just seemed like a more promising approach to the study of the human brain than the so-called 'expert' systems."

Ward nodded. "Go on."

"The basic idea is simple. You set up a collection of nodes—circuits that fire like the neurons in the brain. Based on the input from other nodes, each node 'decides' whether to fire—to send outputs to other nodes—and how strong those outputs should be. Of course, the actual connections among the nodes can be quite complex."

"There. You see? That's the plot structure. Each character in the story is a node in a kind of sociological neural net. Based on the inputs received from some characters, they decide to act on other characters. The architecture of neural nets permeates every scene."

Armitage cocked his head. "I hadn't thought of it that way." He returned to the captain's chair and sat with his hand on his chin. "What was the third level? I am morbidly interested."

Ward smiled. "That relates to what you told me about programming neural nets."

Armitage grunted without humor. "What we say at the Center is that you don't program a neural net, you teach it."

"Meaning, of course . . ."

"Meaning that we present a pattern to the input nodes and 'clamp' a desired output to the output nodes. Then we let the net fire. It compares its actual output to the clamped output and varies the signal strengths of the intermediate connections to obtain a better match. Eventually, it 'learns' the pattern well enough that it can even handle variations in the input. Terry Sejnowski's NETalk learned how to read English from a simple input text. The sentences were entered into the input nodes and the correct phonetic pronunciation was 'clamped' to the output nodes. After reading the same text over and over for about ten hours, the net was doing as well as any second grader. It even made the same sorts of mistakes. And the fascinating thing was that it read just as well when new text was presented. Somehow, it had discovered the 'rules' for reading." Armitage shrugged again. "And NETalk was a primitive net, with only a few hundred neurons."

Ward slapped the desk with his palm.

"And there you have it! Your book takes the readers through six iterations of the same pattern, as they progressively learn what it means. It treats the reading audience as a neural net."

Armitage fingered his lip. "I . . . see. I hadn't realized that."

"What writer does? It wells up, out of the subconscious. Otherwise, we wouldn't need critics or English Lit departments."

Armitage did his writing at home, in a room that he had converted to an office. He stood there now and studied the array of equipment, touching each one briefly and gently. The trusty old word processor. The laser printer. Disk files and hard copy files. In the corner, gathering dust, an old Smith Corona manual. He remembered those days, when pounding out a story meant exactly that. Somehow, it had seemed more like *writing* than it did now, certainly more than it would in the future.

The future occupied one entire side of the office, where he had knocked out the wall to the spare bedroom. A complex maze of optical fibers and microcomputers occupied that space, glittering in the sunlight that filtered through the shaded windows.

Armitage shoved his hands into his pockets as he contemplated the neural net. No one knew how a net arranged its synapses to attain its outputs. It did not apply rules, not in an algorithmic sense. After all, what rule did the human brain use to recognize the letter A—to recognize it in any size and typeface, in any handwriting? To recognize it even when partially obscured? The rules were there, implicit somehow in the pattern of synapses.

He walked to the bookcase and ran his fingers along the spines of the books that stuffed the shelves. Austen. Melville. Hemingway. Faulkner. Trevor. The raw inputs and the clamped outputs. Milieu, idea, character, event—laboriously analyzed, transcribed, and entered on the input nodes; and somehow, somehow, the net configured itself to match the story clamped to the output. What went on inside the net? He doubted that he could describe the connectivity of the system any more. It had grown too complex.

It was hard work to isolate the plot elements. To describe the characters and settings. It was writing of a sort. Research had always been the most difficult stage of the creative process. That was still his own, no matter that the net had learned to take any input and create a story from it. That part of it was only the donkey work, after all. The tedious hours spent staring at a blank screen. He had always hated that. His back always hurt and his eyes felt dry and red when he was done.

So it wasn't as if he had somehow automated the creative spark of writing. It wasn't that at all. Setting the inputs was the essentially creative act. It was the ideas that mattered, not the wordsmithing.

A best-seller, Ward had said. A crossover book. Six books sweated out the hard way with little recognition save among a small clique of fans. Now, he had "found his voice."

Except it wasn't *his* voice, at all. It was the voice of a machine. The machine had found the words and the machine had put them together into brilliant metaphors and images; into crisp dialogue that crackled with irony. The machine had learned something by studying the works of the greats; some spark of genius that had always eluded him.

He turned abruptly and strode to his desk, where he yanked open the bottom drawer. He pawed through the screwdrivers and wirecutters and pliers that cluttered it, and pulled out a claw hammer. Then he approached the shining lattice, breathing heavily.

He cocked the hammer over his right shoulder. "You sonuvabitch!" he told the network. "What do you know about life? You aren't even alive! How can you write about it?"

He swung—but checked the swing halfway. He paused, took a deep breath, and swung again. But again, he could not follow through. The network glittered; light pulsed through its optical fibers as it stoically awaited his judgment.

He threw the hammer to the floor. He could not smash his net. It was not only a valuable research project—his "day job" at the Center, when he was not pretending to be a writer—but, it had, as Ward had said, a "voice." Dammit, that manuscript *had* been good. He could admit it. It was better than anything he had ever written before. Better than anything *he* had ever written.

"I can certainly see," the bartender said, "why you wanted to get drunk. It must be hell knowing that a bunch of chips and wires is a better writer than you."

Armitage pulled his face from his drink and glowered at the man. "It isn't that at all. Not that at all. I think I might have been able to live with that. No, it was something else."

"What was that?"

He slammed his glass hard on the countertop and the remaining liquor sloshed out over his hand. "*It won't even take the soul out of writing.* Don't you see? If a machine can create a story, the soul was never there to begin with. Everything we have ever called creativity was never anything more than a pattern of synapses in a neural net. Semiconductor net. Protoplasm net, it doesn't matter. We compare the outputs to the reactions of editors, readers, critics. Then we adjust the strengths of our connections to bring the output more into line. Somewhere along the way, we learned to call the process 'creativity' and we dared to think we were touched by the gods. Here." He waved the empty glass. "Call me a cab when I pass out. I'm going to drink until I forget why I'm drinking."

His hand shook when he lifted the refilled shot glass. "Here's to the human brain," he said. "We invented neural nets to find out how it worked. And now, God help us, we have."

The bartender shook his head. "I don't know anything about writing. I like a good thriller now and then, but that's about it. But I was told one thing about writing that I remember, and I guess this net of yours learned it pretty well."

Armitage stared into his drink. "What was that?" he asked without interest.

"You should always write about what you know."

ABOUT "SPARK OF GENIUS"

SF is the literature of Challenge and Change, and one consequence of Change is pain. Pulling out an old idea is like pulling out a tooth — without the Novocain. New ideas *hurt*, at least at first. Later you, or your children, wonder how you ever got along without them. (Recently, I tried typing a story on an electric typewriter. How did people *live* like that?) The very best science fiction is rooted in this pain — or in the relief that follows.

The *cautionary tale* focuses on the pain caused by change, as in the original tale of John Henry (cf. my story, "The Steel Driver," *Analog*, June 1988). In the *wonderful tale*, the change is shown as the solution to the pain. John Henry uses the new invention to drill through the rubble of a cave-in to rescue his friends. The third approach to change is the *alternative tale*. What if the change doesn't happen? If the steam drill was never invented, what becomes of John Henry then?

So, in writing a story about change, one important question to ask is, "whom does this hurt the most, and how?"

Neural nets are a new and exciting approach to Artificial Intelligence that mimic the way the human brain works. Inputs enter one end of the network, the neuron-switches fire, and outputs come out the other end. Neural nets are "taught," not "programmed." That is, they are not given an algorithm for solving a problem, but rather the inputs and the correct output. The net fires, compares its outcome to the prescribed outcome, and reconfigures itself through back propagation to achieve a closer match the next time.

I have watched a neural net "learn" how to aim a virtual cannon, without ever being programmed with the appropriate formulas. Of more interest to the laboratory where I saw this was a net that "learned" to design computer chips. The intriguing thing is that whatever internal rules the net creates for itself work even when the inputs are changed. For example, when Terry Sejnowski taught NETalk to "read" an input sentence aloud (via a vocoder) it went on to read new sentences with the same expertise

. . . and the same mistakes! Anyone interested in neural nets should read *Apprentices of Wonder,* by William Allman.

Now, who would be most affected by a computer that mimics the learning process? Creative people? Authors, composers, folks who "don't work according to prescribed rules like an assembly line robot?" If a net can learn the art of chip design, can it learn the art of plot design? The human brain is a neural net. It is the original neural net. If a protoplasmic net can learn to create art, why not an electronic net? And if so, what does it tell us about the "creative process"?

On the Wings of a Butterfly

The ship sailed into the Gulf of Guayaquil under a cloud of canvas and dropped anchor off the town of Túmbez. All the people of the town gathered on the beach to stare at the strange floating castle and to jabber excitedly to one another concerning who (or what) might live in it. Manco chose a vantage point for himself on the dunes so he could watch everything that took place. He shaded his eyes with his hand and peered at the vessel. Sailors danced in the yards, shrouding the sails. Gulls shrieked overhead. He saw a boat throw off its towline.

So, it begins, he thought.

The mayor of the town scrambled toward the fore of the crowd, hastily tying on his fringe of office. A visiting Inca followed him languidly, no doubt amused by all the provincial hubbub. The Inca, Manco knew, was Someone's Younger Son, sent off to visit the Lowlands, either to keep an eye on the local *curacas* or—what Manco thought more likely—to get him out of the parental hair. He led a pair of tame cats—a puma and a jaguar—on light golden chains, and was trying his best to look bored and unimpressed. But the biggest sailboats he had ever seen before were reed *balsas* on the shores of Lake Cuzco, and the caravel off the coast challenged even his aplomb. Manco waited patiently while the ship's boat rowed in. After waiting so long, what did a few more minutes matter?

The man who finally stepped ashore, Manco learned later, was the gunner, Pedro de Candia, which meant "Pete the Greek." He was a large man, of imposing stature, and wore sheets of black iron on his chest and limbs and a helmet of the same strange material atop his head. He was a man of such impressive physique that he would have evoked comment wherever he went. And, indeed, there was much discussion over his size. What shocked the crowd, though, and made them murmur and point was his face, which was white and hairy.

The Inca forgot to be unimpressed. He dropped his leashes in surprise and the cats, suddenly loosened, bounded toward the stranger. The crowd cried out in warning, and Manco could see the men lining the gunwales of the caravel also pointing and shouting. The Greek turned and saw the cats racing across the sand and crossed himself, right to left. Manco watched silently, with his arms folded.

The tame cats leapt upon the Greek, nearly toppling him with their momentum. They licked his face and nuzzled him. "Hey, hey!" Manco heard the surprised gunner say in his badly accented Spanish. "You cats like the Greek, no? Yes, you good omen. Hey?" He turned and waved to the ship off shore. "Is all right, *amigos!* They is friendly here!"

"For now," he added more softly as he turned to pet the jaguar.

Manco, watching from his vantage point, rubbed his hands together nervously. *Now, he'll go back to the ship and bring his capo.* Manco looked out at the ship and caught sight of a robust, white-haired man leaning over the rail. *Pizarro*, he thought. *That would be the one they call Pizarro.*

The folk of Túmbez loved a good spectacle, and Manco had to admit that the Spaniards put on quite a show. Swords flashed, and multicolored banners flapped in the sea breeze. The white-faced men knelt in the sands of Guayaquil and sang. It was a display the like of which the town had never seen before. Manco wondered how the admiring audience would react had they understood the words the Spaniards were using. *We claim these lands . . .* Most of them would not care, Manco decided. Why should they? What was one cruel and distant lord compared to another? But, the young Inca would hardly be amused to learn that they were claiming Tavantinsuyu for their absentee king.

Not that the Child of the Sun and his *coya* queen ever set foot in the Lowlands, either.

Manco watched the young noble as he stood there surrounded by the Iron Hats, grinning foolishly like the younger son he was, while the strangers talked gibberish to him and fingered his golden ornaments and traded significant glances with one another.

Manco decided it was time for him to intervene.

He walked toward the two older men. They were deep in conversation with each other, gesticulating and scowling. Both of them were white-haired, well into their fifties; but robust and full of pent-up energies. There was an aura of power around them both. Something that other men sensed and gave heed to. But there the similarity ended. As Manco came closer, one of their henchmen shouted something and they turned to watch him.

The one on the right, Manco saw, was missing an eye. He was small of stature and about as ugly a man as Manco had ever seen. Yet, his cheeks were full, and there were laughter lines at the corners of his mouth and eyes. He folded his arms across his chest and fixed Manco with a stare. "I wonder what this one wants," he told his companion.

"Probably wants to rub our skin to see if the paint comes off," the taller man answered, and they both laughed. The tall man was solidly built, big-framed, with a set to his jaw and an unblinking stare. There were no laugh lines on his face, but other lines, as though he bore the weight of the world upon himself, and knew it. There was something hard and cruel about his mouth.

Manco bowed low from the waist, courtier-style, and swept his arm out gracefully. "Have I the honor," he said in Spanish, "of addressing the *Adelantado* Francisco Pizarro?"

The two exchanged surprised looks. "You speak our language," said the short, ugly one.

Manco turned his bow toward him. "Allow this poor one to introduce himself. I am Manco Sanchez. My father was a shipwrecked Spanish sailor cast ashore near here many years ago. He married an Indio woman, but he raised me to be Spanish like himself. I knew that someday you would come, and I have waited many years for this. When I heard that your ship was nearing these waters, I hastened to Túmbez to offer my services."

"Túmbez," repeated the tall one. "Is that the name of this sty?" He seemed almost surprised that such a place would have a name. "Well-met, señor. I am Francisco Pizarro," he continued, "though I am no Adelantado. At least, not yet." He laughed and his companion shot him a covert glance. "I am but a poor explorer. This is my partner, Diego de Almagro."

Manco bowed again to the one-eyed man. So this was "Almagro Jake," a man whose strength and endurance were legendary. He could, it was said, outwalk even an Indio through the mountains and jungles, and battle with swords at the end of it. And still have the energy to carouse the night away.

"Save that bowing and scraping," said Almagro Jake, "for the Madonna-forsaken dons. We are all equals here." Manco noticed how his glance flicked again toward Pizarro as he said that. Almagro grasped Manco's arm and squeezed it vigorously.

"We will have great need of an interpreter here," said Almagro. "You do speak the heathen gibberish, don't you?"

Manco smiled and said something polite in Quechua and, just to show his versatility, followed it with a sentence in Aymaru. He doubted that the Spaniards would know the difference; or even that there was a difference. Like the Greco-Latin Empire of legend, the Inca realm spoke in two tongues.

Almagro laughed and nudged Pizarro with his elbow. "There! You see! This is what we need. He is just like that Doña Marino bitch that Cortez found up Mexico way, though not so pretty."

Manco thought that this squat, ugly man would be the last one to judge another's beauty, but he held his peace, not wishing to offend his new patrons. He wondered if they believed his story about the shipwreck.

"Perhaps," said Pizarro. He was a severe man, not much given to smiles. Years of privation had left their marks on his face. The look he gave Manco was so full of weariness that for a moment Manco felt pity well up inside him. "I would not condemn a good Christian to live one more day than necessary in this squalor," Pizarro said. "We will have need of an interpreter when we return here, and you may join our company if you wish it. But for now, we return to Darien."

"Don't be a fool, Francisco," said Almagro, and Manco had the sense that he was resuming an earlier, interrupted argument. "Look at the gold on that young dandy over there! And this is just a provincial town, not worth two bites of a Spanish thaler. I tell you, El Hombre Dorado, the Golden Man, must live near here somewhere. If we return to Panama now, with this news, 'Pedro the Jouster' will seize our ship and send his own lackeys here to take the wealth."

"Governor Pedr'arias sold us back his share . . ."

"*Don* Pedro Arias de Avila," said Almagro firmly, "is a grasping, conniving, traitorous man. Believe me, I know many such men." He laughed aloud. "Why, I am one myself; and you as well." Manco noticed a strange look cross Pizarro's face at that, but it was gone in an instant.

"When you left me on Gallo Island," Pizarro reminded him, "you said it was because we had not the numbers to strike inland. Look about you!" He waved an arm wide. "Have we the numbers now? No, we are fewer, yet, what with the losses and desertions. For what did we wait, there on Gorgona, I and my thirteen comrades, amid the ceaseless rains and pestilent mosquitoes; starving, because there was no food on that forsaken isle? We endured, because we knew you would be returning with the reinforcements." Pizarro turned to Manco. "And when he came—" Manco knew the words were addressed to Almagro and not to him. "And when he came, he brought but the one ship and crew and no additional men. Why must I endure the hardships alone, while he sails back and forth to Darien at his leisure?"

"Pest!" Almagro's face flushed. "Do you know why I brought no men with me, 'Cisco? Do you know why? Because no one would come with me; that is why! Because they laugh at us in Darien! What point is there in going back? Father Fernando can raise no more money. Fernando de Luque! The townfolk, they call him 'de Loco.' We have sailed south now how many times? And we lose men and we lose ships and we lose money and always we return with nothing. By Our Lady, I will return with *something* this time!" He crossed his arms and dared Pizarro to disagree.

Manco thought it best to say something; before Pizarro and Almagro could have a falling-out. If they argued, they would simply loot Túmbez and return to Darien, and Manco did not want that.

"Indeed, Señor Almagro speaks truth," he said. "When you return, you must return with gold dripping from your pockets, not with the few baubles and trinkets you see here. Then you will have all the volunteers you need." Manco saw how their eyes lit at the mention of the gold. If Manco could call what they saw about them "a few baubles," what might await them elsewhere? Pizarro licked his lips in a quick gesture. He glanced at the town, at the Inca, at the ship, at the mountain.

"We have not the men and arms to capture an empire," he said doubtfully.

"At this juncture, my captains, you may not need them. Now is the time to strike into the mountains. Without delay."

"Without delay." Pizarro looked at him with an icy stare. "And why is that, Sanchez?"

Manco swallowed. "They say that the Child of the Sun has died and that his two sons are fighting over his realm. My lords, the Inca domain is vast, far vaster than you may imagine and its armies are numberless. Even a large expedition might be overwhelmed by sheer numbers. But all commands originate with the Child of the Sun. Capture him, and you have captured the empire. At this juncture, a bold man might seize the initiative and rule them all. Delay, and the opportunity may be lost."

Pizarro ran his fingers through his beard. He looked at Almagro. "A civil war, you say? How old is this news?"

"The great Huayana Capac was alive no more than a month ago." That was certainly the case. The stones of Quito still smoked from the fighting.

"And how bitter is the conflict between the two brothers?"

"To the death. They hate each other. Huascar and Atahualpa are but half brothers. The one is legitimate; the other, illegitimate."

Almagro grinned. "I like the sound of this, Francisco. Did not Don Cortez say he owed his victory as much to Machiavelli as to cannon? Divide and rule. The Indios are like little boys at such games."

Little boys. Manco remembered how, when Huayana Capac put down the revolt of the Carangues, he had beheaded all of the men of fighting age and had thrown their bodies into the lake, declaring, "Now you are all boys." A ruthless man, perhaps as ruthless as Pizarro; and not to be trifled with. Atahualpa was not yet of the same stamp.

Pizarro stared out at the ship, where it lay upon the water. He pulled upon his beard. "Which brother is the more skilled with arms, would you say, Sanchez?"

"Atahualpa, without a doubt. His father made him viceroy of Quito, which is here in the north, because the Empire of Quito was but recently conquered and the Chimu folk on the coast are restless under the Inca yoke and need a firm hand over them."

"And which is he? Atahualpa. The legitimate heir?"

"No, he is the bastard."

Pizarro laughed. It wasn't coarse and hearty like Almagro's laugh. It was a cracked and nasty laugh. It snapped out once, twice, like a whip; then it was gone. "Then I suppose we must aid him. This Atahualpa."

"Certes," said Almagro. "We bastards have to stick together."

The climb up the western slope of the Andes was a long and arduous one. Manco had scouted routes over the past year preparing for this day; and there were Inca roads and bridges and *tambos* along the way. Even so, it was a difficult journey. The conquistadors had taken off all their armor save their helmets and their breast-and-backs, stowing the gear in the packs tied to their mules. Pizarro had given Manco the use of a horse and put him on the point to guide them.

"Mother of God!" said Sebastian de Benalcazár when they breasted the Ecuadorian foothills and first caught sight of the snowcapped peaks of the cordillera. "Those passes are higher than Alpine peaks!"

The others paused in their weary march to stare at the vista. Peak piled upon peak toward the distant sky. A wall, vast and mighty, crowned in snow and ice that sparkled a russet color. "We have as far to climb as we have already climbed," said Almagro Jake, and he looked at Manco when he said it.

Manco shrugged. "If that Inca boy in Túmbez can make the trip, it is surely no great feat for such men as ourselves."

"That boy was strangely built," mused Pizarro. "His chest seemed bigger than it should have been for a man his size."

"Small wonder," wheezed Pedro de Candia, the gunner. "It is to breathe enough of this thin air." They all laughed. It was true enough. All of them were panting hard and felt light-headed. Except Manco, of course.

"The Empire of the Great Sun," said Manco, pointing to the shining peaks, "lies in the mountain valleys between that range and the next. The Inca rules the coast as well, but all the wealth and riches are in the mountains." He stared at the mountains. Tavantinsuyu. The Four Quarters of the World. Such a vast world; and yet grown now so tiny. The world had more quarters than even the Inca could imagine. "There is gold there. More gold than you can carry."

Pizarro leaned over his horse's neck. "What are those mountains called, Sanchez?"

"Andes," Manco answered. "The Copper Mountains."

"Copper," said Pizarro, stroking his horse's mane. "No, they are the Golden Mountains."

"El Hombre Dorado," whispered Benalcazár.

They resumed their march, with Manco in the lead. Almagro quickened his step and fell in beside him. "I will believe in this El Dorado when I see him," he said, jerking a thumb at Benalcazár. "Always the Indios tell us he lives somewhere else. Not here, great lord, but way over there." He laughed. "As I would say myself were I them."

Manco looked at him. "I thought you believed in him yourself, this El Dorado."

Almagro shrugged and squinted at the distant mountains. "I believe in looking for him."

"There really is a Golden Man," Manco told him. "And he really does live somewhere else and not in Tavantinsuyu."

Almagro laughed and Manco shrugged. "He was a king of the Chibchas, a people who live in great cities on a plateau to the north. They say that in ancient times, the king killed his wife for adultery and threw her body in the lake. Ever since then, at a certain time each year, the king is covered with gum and then dusted with gold. Then he rows to the middle of the lake and washes the gold off as an offering to the dead queen."

Almagro looked at him. "All that gold, washed into the lake?" He shook his head, not believing such ignorance possible.

They walked their horses a while longer in silence, Manco watching the Spaniard for evidence of fatigue. He could see no sign of it. After a while, he said casually, "It is a wonderful thing how we have all come here together into these mountains, don Almagro."

Almagro spit on the road. "I am no don. And there is little enough to wonder at. You are here because your father was shipwrecked. I came here because there was no other place to go." He said nothing after that, and Manco wondered if he would answer. Then he grunted and laughed. "But we are all New Men here, you know. Why, I could style myself 'don' if I'd a mind to, and who would call me out? Even the poorest and most ignorant peasant lad can become an *encomendero* with vast estates. Francisco and Fernando and I, we have a thriving partnership back in Darien. Mines and farms. We are *vecinos*. What would we be in España, any of us? Nothing. Less than nothing. I left the village of Almagro because it was nothing. I could stand that numbing peasant labor no longer. So, I ran off and became a servant to one of the chief magistrates at the Alhambra. Then . . ." He spit again. "Then I was in a fight. A tavern brawl. Over a woman, or over a bet, or over nothing. What does it matter now? I had my knife and he had his, but I knew better how to use it. Now I am here."

"But why not stay in Darien with your mines and farms? Why come to these mountains to sweat and bleed? What more do you want?"

"What more do I want?" He paused and looked again at the peaks above. A condor circled in the air above them, and Almagro watched its arrogant flight until, with a screech, it banked away and vanished. "I want El Dorado," he whispered.

Manco called a halt when they reached the next *tambo*. This was a small rest stop, with only a single building and a storehouse, since the road they were traveling was only a feeder road from the Lowlands. The *tambos* were spaced every ten to twelve miles and contained provisions for travelers. Some of them, on the main roads on the High Plateau, were quite large.

The *chasqui* who was waiting inside looked surprised when he saw Manco enter with his party. While the rest stops were in theory for everyone in the Empire, few folks traveled, except on official business. The runner's eyes bugged when he saw the white men, and he looked to Manco for an explanation.

"What did you tell him?" Pizarro demanded after he had finished.

"Only that you are foreign lords coming to pay your respects to the Child of the Sun."

"Gold is the Child of the Sun," said Pizarro. "With gold, a man is wealthy and has the respect of his community. Without it, he is nothing. A chattel of the dons. Oh, yes, Sanchez, I am coming to pay my respects."

Manco did not tell him that the Incas called gold, "The Tears of the Sun."

The runner was busily tying knots in his *quipu*. It was a form of writing so different from what the Spaniards were used to that they did not even realize that the runner was making notes on their numbers and strength. Manco told the runner that the men also had *horses*. That these were beasts like giant llamas that men could ride. And that they possessed weapons made of the black metal, including a kind of sling called a *musket* that threw shots with great noise and speed. The man's face told Manco that he believed only half of what he was telling him, so Manco told him to go outside and see the horses for himself. The runner demanded to know by what authority he gave orders to a *chasqui* and Manco exposed the fringe he was wearing beneath his *poncho*.

The runner's face went pale, and he bowed and ducked out of the building.

"What was that all about?" asked Almagro.

"I told him of your horses, and he didn't believe me."

"Who is he, the innkeeper?"

"No. There is no innkeeper at small stations like this one."

"No innkeeper? Then who prevents the peasants from running off with the provisions stocked here?"

Manco shrugged. "No one steals in Tavantinsuyu."

"What? Nonsense." Almagro plainly did not believe him, and Manco was not disposed to argue. That valuable goods could be left unguarded was such an alien concept that it was easier to reject it out of hand. The Incas knew quite well that disaffection was rooted in poverty and idleness, so they took measures to assure that both were eradicated. No Indio, however low his station, ever lacked for food or clothing issued him by the government. Thus, there was no reason to steal.

"If not the innkeeper, then who?" That was Pizarro, who had come up behind them while they talked. Manco looked him in the face. Pizarro wanted to know everything, because who knew on what detail his survival might depend? He wanted to know how the Empire was put together so that he could take it apart and rebuild it closer to his own heart's desire.

"A royal messenger. *Chasqui*, they are called. You can tell from his uniform."

"Uniform?" interjected Almagro. "All these heathen costumes look alike to me."

Fortunately so, Manco mused. "The runners carry messages along the roads," he continued. "In fact, the roads were built for that purpose. Each runner goes from one way station to the next—about ten miles—and hands the message on to the next runner."

"Message? Have they writing, then?"

"No. The message is memorized."

Pizarro stroked his beard speculatively. "That will limit the complexity of their messages then."

Manco would have said something, but the sound of running feet drew them to the doorway. Pizarro looked out into the evening dark. "Who is it?" Manco came up behind him.

"Another runner," he said, looking over Pizarro's shoulder.

He saw the new man hand his *quipu* over. The two runners conversed quickly and lowly, with quick glances toward the building. Then the man who had been in the way station sprinted up the road toward the next *tambo.* The second man walked slowly to the building. He held a conch shell in his hand that he used as a horn.

When he came to the doorway he stopped and waited for Pizarro to get out of his way. It was expected. Everyone made way for the emperor's runners.

Pizarro looked him up and down slowly, then moved back a step and let the man inside. Then he returned to the doorway and watched the departing runner.

"The first man is going up the trail, toward the mountains," he observed. "This one must have come up from the coast, then."

"From the coast, eh?" said the Greek from the fire where the others were gathered. "I thinks word of our comings go before us, hey?" The Spaniards looked at one another and began to mutter.

Pizarro turned. "And what of it?" he demanded. "What if this whole Madonna-forsaken Empire knows of our coming? Don Cortez had little more than we when he toppled the Aztecs."

That seemed to cheer them somewhat. "Aye, we have the horses and muskets," said Benalcazár, "and they do not."

Pizarro smiled. "No, Sebastian. If it comes to combat, our guns and horses will make little difference. There are only a score of us. In a battle, could we reload before the fighting closed hand to hand?" He waved an arm in dismissal. "How much impact would twenty shots have in a battle involving thousands? And our horses? Did the Aztecs remain long frightened of them? No, my friends . . ." He slapped the hilt of his sword. "It is not our technology that gives us the edge. It is this!" And he tapped his skull.

Benalcazár glanced at his companions and grunted. "If brains are to be our weapons, I would wish ourselves better armed."

The next day they came to a chasm spanned by a rope bridge. The conquistadors looked nervously over the edge. Far below, a wild stream smashed itself against rocks. Manco estimated the drop at three hundred meters. The rope bridge swayed in the wind that hummed in the cañon below. The cables were woven of maguey fibers into bundles as thick as a man's body. The footing was a macramé of rope and wooden planks.

"We are to cross that?" asked Benalcazár. His face was white, and his throat worked convulsively.

"How did they throw the bridge across? That's what I'd like to know." That was Bartolomé Ruiz, the navigator. He was studying the construction of the bridge closely, running his hands along the coarse ropes, probing the knots with his fingers.

"What of the horses, 'Cisco?" Almagro asked gravely from the edge of the precipice.

"Blindfold them and lead them," Pizarro decided. "So they won't panic."

Manco had crossed such bridges many times, but even he was still careful not to look down when he did so. He warned the others that their weight in the middle of the bridge would make it stretch and sag, but that this was normal. Benalcazár laughed nervously.

"Who will be first across?" he asked.

They all looked at Pizarro, who twisted his mouth in a wry grin. "The price of leadership," Manco heard him mutter.

Carefully, Pizarro tied blinders onto his horse so it could only look straight ahead. The horse was nervous and stamped its hooves, blowing out its breath. Pizarro spoke soothingly to it and stroked its muzzle.

"A wrong step here could spell your doom," he told the others across his horse's neck. "But when in our misbegotten lives has that not been so? Whether crossing the sea or"—he laughed—"crossing Pedr'arias. Next to that risk, this bridge is child's play."

When he was ready, he led his horse out upon the rope bridge. He walked gingerly at first, until he had gotten the feel of it, then he stepped more confidently. "It is sturdier than it looks," he called back. He coaxed his horse along, talking all the while, keeping the animal's attention fixed firmly on himself.

Manco glanced at where the others stood. Almagro squatted on his haunches, watching Pizarro intently, rubbing one big-knuckled hand in the other. When Pizarro was safely across, Almagro let his breath out and closed his eyes. His lips moved silently. His right hand flicked quickly, almost furtively, making a cross on his chest, and he kissed his fingertips. Then he rose and began bawling at the others to line up and move across one at a time.

What a strange friendship, Manco thought. Two men so unlike, yet so loyal to each other. He thought of their quarrels and what the future might hold for them both. *I'm doing the right thing,* he assured himself, and not for the first time.

· · ·

That night they camped in another *tambo*. They were higher up the mountains now and the air was crisp and cold. Their breath came in white cotton clouds as they huddled close around the fires. "Not far," Manco assured them, slapping his arms around his chest. "Tomorrow we'll be through the pass. A few days more, and we'll be in the high valley of Quito."

He left them trading stories of El Dorado and walked out into the night. The breeze was chill and brisk, and Manco wrapped his cloak more tightly around his shoulders. He wandered away from the *tambo* until he found a large boulder; then he perched himself upon it, facing the pass.

The snow-lined peaks glittered in the evening sunlight. Condors floated lazily near the summits, seeking their nests. He thought about what lay on the other side. About all his preparations and what he was doing to Tavantinsuyu by bringing the Spaniard into the mountains.

It is better this way, he thought. The Incas had brought unity and prosperity to the high country. Famine, so common elsewhere, was unknown here. The Inca looked on his subjects as a kind father on his children. In the compulsory public labor, no one was assigned tasks beyond his ability. The laws were carefully directed toward the health and preservation of the people. The divine Inca would not permit his children to be miserable.

Yet, the realm must be destroyed.

Every benefit the people had—and they had many, compared to the Spaniards—they had as a grant from the god-king, not as a right. There was no such concept as private property. They could not engage in any work or amusement, except as provided by law. They could not change their residence or their costume without a license. Even their own husbands and wives were assigned to them by the government.

If the Inca would not allow them to be miserable, neither would he allow them to be happy, except as he permitted.

The realm was brittle. The least disturbance would shatter it. Individual initiative was stifled. Nothing happened except at the Inca's will. If the Inca decided, the Empire acted. If the Inca hesitated, the entire cordillera, from Quito to the Atacama, would be paralyzed with uncertainty. The realm lacked vitality; its people were frozen in a timeless stasis. The Spaniards would end all that—that top-heavy, frozen brittleness. They would bring vitality and initiative and change, along with their rough and greedy ways. The conquistadors were brutal, granted; but no less so than

Huayana Capac or Tupac Yupanqui had been. They were cruel, but the Inca laws were cruel as well. Their families would rule as aristocrats; but were the Inca *allyus* any less aristocratic? The difference was the difference between lords who ruled with an iron rod, and lords who ruled with a copper one. If anything, the Spanish state was more loosely organized than the Inca state. And that was crucial: when things were loose, movement was possible.

At least, so he had told himself.

He realized that he was trying to justify his plans to himself. Manco had known when he had started on his task, that uncounted men, women, and children would be deprived of life because of him. *It must be worth it. It must.* He had prayed—to Christ, to Viracocha, to anyone who would listen—for assurance; and had gotten no answer that would comfort him. The eyes of the unborn watched him in his dreams. Yet, the stifling hold of the totalitarian Inca state must be cracked; and the Spaniards were his hammer. Only, it must be just the right blow, delivered in just the right way.

He realized that he was more afraid of striking badly than of not striking at all.

A foot brushed the gravel behind him and he turned to see Pizarro standing there, his hands clasped tightly behind his back and his gray-marbled beard thrust forward. He looked older than he had at any time since Manco had joined him.

"That is a sight, for the poets, eh, Sanchez?" he said, nodding toward the glowing peaks. "Many a minstrel in Seville would give his life for such a vista."

Manco said nothing, waiting for Pizarro to say what he had come to say.

"These Inca warriors, how do they fight? Do they fight like the Aztecs?"

Pizarro had told him about Cortez and the Aztecs. Manco thought about it, then shook his head. "They are not such hard fighters as the Aztecs, but they are better. They are soldiers, not warriors. The Aztecs fought as a mob; but the Inca's soldiers are disciplined. They fight in ranks. Each tribe has its own regiments, with their own banners; all unified under the Rainbow Banner of the Child of the Sun. And they are better armed than the Aztecs. Their spears and battle-axes are copper, not stone. And their maces have copper spikes. They use wooden shields, sometimes bossed with copper, and wear thick, quilted jackets for armor. They carry slings, arrows, javelins, and lances. And two weapons you have never seen before: the *lasso* and the *boleadora*, or bola."

Pizarro nodded gravely. "Yes."

Manco had told him all this already. Pizarro's first questions back in Túmbez had been military. The captain had not come out into the night to rehash matters long settled.

"Soon we will find if the gamble was worth it, eh, Sanchez?" Pizarro's voice sounded nervous. And small wonder. A score of men to challenge an empire? It would be madness, if it hadn't been done once already. "Next month," he said, "we may be lords or we may be dead."

"Is it so important to be lords," asked Manco, "that the alternative may be death?"

Pizarro spit into the night. "There is nothing more important. A man takes charge of his own destiny, or he is as good as dead. I am a bastard. Did you know that, Sanchez? A bastard. Most of us here are. Diego, too. Outcasts in our own land. Less than nothing. My father would not acknowledge me, would not treat me as he did his legitimate sons, though everyone in Estremadura knew the truth of it." Pizarro's voice hardened, and Manco thought he saw his eyes narrow in the dusk. "He raised me as a peasant; set me to tend the pigs. I cannot read nor write, you know. Not even my own name. Sometimes I wonder how my life might have gone had I . . ." He shook himself.

"But that is milk long spilt. One day, I lost some pigs. Flies stampeded them. Oh, I ran after them—the pigs, that is—slipping and falling in the rank mud, and I rounded most of them up, but . . ." Again he paused. "I could not face my father's wrath," he concluded, "so I fled to the Indies, 'with a cloak and a sword.' "

"Flies," said Manco.

"Yes. You find that amusing?" Pizarro turned his head sharply, and his face said that there had better be no humor found.

"They say," said Manco, toying with the fringe of his cloak, "that a butterfly's wings flapping in Spain can create storms in France."

Pizarro scowled at him. "What do you mean by that?"

"Butterfly's wings," he repeated as if to himself. "It means that from small, unnoticed beginnings, great events may grow. Were it not for the buzzing of some flies in Estremadura, you would not be here now banging on the Inca's door."

Pizarro grunted. He hunkered down on his haunches and ran his fingers through the dirt. "Good soil," he commented. Manco said nothing, and after a while Pizarro threw the dirt down. He laughed bitterly, his forearms resting on his knees. "When I pause and consider it," he said finally, "I find it very unlikely for me to be here."

"Why is that? The flies, again?"

"No. That was but the first chance. There were others. Times when the least change in direction might have taken me to an altogether different fate. I was with Ojeda on his expedition to Cartagena and, so, I might have died there, and not here." He shook his head. "That Ojeda! There was a man for you! The Indios on the Cartagena coast are the fiercest anywhere. We took great losses fighting them. Juan de la Cosa died there, as fine a man as ever lived; died with a poisoned arrow through his throat, kicking and twitching and fouling himself. He had been Master of the old *Santa Maria*. The first man to see the Indies. Dead in the steaming mud of some tropical sty. Ojeda was wounded, too. He knew the arrow was poisoned, so he told the doctor to bind the wound with red-hot iron plates; threatened to hang the man if he did not." Pizarro shook his head again. "But I escaped unscathed from the battle.

"Ojeda left on a passing pirate ship and put me in charge until Enciso, his second-in-command, should arrive with the follow-up ship. When he did . . ." and here Pizarro laughed. "When Encisco finally arrived, he brought some rare wine with him."

"I don't understand," said Manco. Pizarro seemed to be struggling with some inner turmoil, some half-forgotten memories challenging him. For the moment, the hard ruthlessness had slipped from his face, and Manco saw that it was not Pizarro's future pulling him toward his fate, but his past, pushing.

"Vasco Nuñez de Balboa," he said, "was a stowaway aboard Enciso's ship. He had hidden from his creditors in España in an empty wine cask. And there was another turn of fate, because it was Balboa that saved us. We were in poor shape, barely surviving on that rank shore. Balboa led us to where there was food, but no poisoned arrows. Enciso was seething all the way; but the man was no leader, and Balboa was. We built a city there and called it Santa Maria la Antigua; but now it is called Darien. We proclaimed Balboa as *Alcalde*. Any real man," Pizarro declared, "recognizes another real man. The men loved him—I loved him—we would have followed him anywhere. 'I always lead from in front,' he used to say. I suppose," Pizarro concluded, looking at his hands, "that that was his secret."

Manco let the silence draw out for a while before asking: "And where is this Balboa now?" The hammer blows must be aimed just right.

Pizarro winced and gave Manco a quick glance. "Dead. For all the glory he found, being the first among us to espy the great South Sea, his head decorated the city gate of Darien. Enciso saw to that; though he took years with his revenge. And I . . ." Pizarro frowned and began drawing aimless diagrams in the dirt. The moonlight glittered off his helmet. Manco heard him sigh. "I was the one sent to arrest him. He was thatching his roof when I came. He was dressed as a common laborer and was working side by side with his Indios." Pizarro added a filligree to his design. "He was far from a tender man, but he always treated his Indios well. Once conquered, he said, the Indios were our own and should be treated decently. He saw me coming and he must have known why, for he climbed down from the roof and greeted me. 'You never used to come to me like this, Francisco,' he said, 'when we were on the Cartagena coast.' "

Pizarro looked at Manco. "But what could I do?" he demanded. "I had my orders from Pedro the Jouster, the Madonna-forsaken Royal Governor of Darien. What else could I do? Enciso had charged him with mutiny and . . ." He looked suddenly away. "And that is enough of this sort of talk."

Pizarro stood abruptly and dusted his hands. Manco stood also and bowed to the captain, peering closely as he did so. Pizarro strode off, and Manco looked after him. He had not been mistaken. There were tears in the old man's eyes.

Manco smiled.

There was a *tambo* set in the pass. A vast complex of many buildings with stout walls of dressed and fitted stone. Ruiz tried to fit his sword blade between two stones and could not; and he marveled that it could be done with no mortar. The buildings loomed over them, dark and ominous, the walls lined with feathered soldiers in burning red uniforms, who watched the Spaniards impassively as they stepped their horses over the cobblestoned highway.

Benalcazár looked up and shuddered. "How many are in that fortress?" he asked.

Manco reined in and studied the soldiers on the parapet. He shrugged.

"I do not know. Some of the *tambos* serve as garrisons for the Inca's regiments."

Pizarro turned to speak to Manco. "Why do they do nothing?" he asked.

"Because they have received no orders concerning us."

Almagro looked back from where he rode at the head of the column. Then he looked at the soldiers lining the walls and laughed. Pizarro frowned and shook his head. "I do not know if that is a good or a bad thing in a soldier."

He clucked to his horse and the column resumed its slow walk through the pass. Snow fell. Tiny flakes that melted before they struck. Manco looked up at the walls, at the soldiers who leaned there on their spears. That had been a lie, that part about them receiving no orders. Very specific orders had been given. But it was also true that, lacking orders from above, the garrison would still have done nothing.

Much like the soldiers of any totalitarian state, anyplace.

Or anytime.

The soldiers returned his stare with stolid lack of interest. *Like robots*, thought Manco. But the thought of robots made him think of everything he had left behind forever. Abruptly, he turned his horse and cantered to his post at the head of the column.

Bartolomé Ruiz, the navigator, was an inquisitive man. Perhaps it was because his work accustomed him to the close observation of nature; to measurement and calculation. Perhaps it was because he was simply curious about so many things. Whatever the reason, he was the closest thing to a scientist on the expedition.

Of all the conquistadors, Manco feared him the most.

The road trended downward, now, gliding toward the valley of Quito. They saw more terraces and irrigation canals. Indios tending the fields of maize paused in their work to stare as the white-skinned men marched past. They backed away in fear from the strange, giant llamas.

Ruiz quick-stepped his horse and fell in beside Manco at the point.

"Soon, now, eh, Manco?" he said. Ruiz was the only officer who called him by his first name.

"Soon," he agreed, and wondered what Ruiz wanted.

"Francisco has told me of your butterflies."

Manco looked at him. "We spoke of how small beginnings may build into great conclusions."

"Surely. I found it a fascinating notion, and have thought about how we here have reached this great conclusion of ours. It was a long, uncertain road we traveled. Did the Captain tell you that he was not Pedr'arias's first choice to head the expedition here to Birú? It was Don Andagoya that first raised these shores and heard rumors of a great empire. But he was too badly injured to attempt the return. The Jouster chose another captain to go in his place; but that man had the good grace to die before the expedition set sail. Only then was Father de Luque able to obtain the governor's sanction for the partnership to undertake the task." He gestured over his shoulder to where Pizarro and Almagro rode side by side, conversing in low tones. "So there you have a chain of chance. What if Don Andagoya had not fallen in the river? What if Pedr'arias's next choice had not died? What if de Luque had not convinced the governor to back Francisco?" Ruiz spread his hands in question.

"Chance guides us all," said Manco.

Ruiz shrugged. "Or God's Will. Which may be much the same thing." He twisted and untwisted the reins around his hand and looked off into the distance. "We set sail for the first time in December of '24. Just Pizarro and one ship, with one hundred men. Almagro was to follow us with a second ship." Ruiz shook his head. "That was a hard voyage. We named our encampments Burnt Village, Port Famine, and the like; so you can see that we had no enjoyable time of it, tramping through the swamps and the rain-soaked forests. That first trip was the begining of years of exhaustion, sickness, and starvation. And fighting. The captain was wounded no less than seven times by the Indios. Almagro never appeared; so we finally raised anchor and returned to Panama, though the captain asked to be put ashore at a small coastal village, and not at Darien. He declared he would set no foot in Darien until he had found the Golden Empire. That was when the two of them fought for the first time, he and Almagro. Almagro swore he had scoured the coast for us without success; and that he had lost an eye to the Indios as token of his efforts."

"A loss that did not add to his beauty," said Manco.

Ruiz laughed. "No. Though it did not subtract a great deal, either. The captain realized that no one surrenders an eye for appearance' sake, so they quickly became reconciled. But then there was further trouble. The Jouster was loath to finance another voyage, considering our losses on the first. But we argued the case with him, especially Father de Luque, who was friends with Judge Espinoza. He managed to raise twenty thousand *pesos de oro* for the effort. Pedr'arias laughingly sold us back his interest in the profits of our exploration, saying there would be no profits. So we weighed anchor a second time in early '26 and felt our way down the coast. We lost men constantly to hostiles. Primitive tribes that ran naked through the forest. Nowhere did we see signs of gold, yet everywhere we heard tales of it. Almagro returned to Darien and fetched more recruits and we continued south, still fighting bare-assed savages. The captain would have been killed at one engagement, save that he was thrown from his horse."

"Being thrown in battle is usually fatal."

"Aye. But the Indios thought that some strange beast had divided in two. They were thrown into panic, and we were able to withdraw. So there was another chance event that guided our course. Pizarro made camp on an isle beyond reach of the bare-asses' canoes while Almagro returned to Darien yet a third time. Shortly, ships came, not from Almagro but from the governor, offering to return us to Panama. The governor had decided there would be no more costly southern fiascos." Ruiz leaned over his horse and spit.

"I have heard this tale."

"But did you hear how the captain responded? He drew his sword and scratched a line in the sand and said that any who wished to wager his life against the hopes of gold and riches might cross the line and stay with him. As for himself, he declared, he would remain—alone if need be—and await Almagro's return." Ruiz grinned at him. "Thirteen of us crossed the line, twelve at my heels. Even those returning to Darien were moved by the grandness of the gesture. If you search for butterflies' wings, Manco, you will find them fluttering on that island on that afternoon. Never has so momentous a course of action been decided on so small a gesture."

Manco grunted noncommittally. "If you could change any of that, what would you change?"

"Change?"

Manco spoke carefully. "What if you could sail into the past as easily as you sail on the seas? Where would you go and what would you change?"

Ruiz gave him an odd look. "Why, I suppose I would wish that more of us had crossed the line to stand with the captain." He gestured over his shoulder at the weary column of men. "We are a thin line."

"The tip of a wedge is thin also," Manco told him. "Yet, hammered into a crack in the rocks, it may tear down mountains."

Ruiz grunted, but said nothing. Manco thought he was considering the problem of tearing down the Inca realm. Even simple machines, thought Manco, can accomplish great tasks. Though sometimes the machine is not so simple, and the task, almost insuperable.

"And how would you accomplish it?" he asked finally. "How would you induce more men to cross the line?"

"What? Oh." Ruiz frowned at him, then appeared to ponder. The horses' hooves made soft sounds on the packed earth of the trail. "I would need to work on the men long before the moment of decision came," he decided after a while. "Or, rather, knowing what I know now, I would have guided both the captain's and Diego's ships directly to Túmbez in '24. Then the first expedition would not have been such a dismal failure. The captain and Diego would not have quarreled. And the people of Darien would not have withdrawn their support." Ruiz's voice sounded almost startled. He was thinking new kinds of thoughts.

Manco nodded. "Yes, the outcome is often decided far in advance of the actual event. Always we find the roots in some small, unnoticed detail. It is like a lever, where a small push on one end moves great weights on the other. The Greek philospher, Archimedes, once said that given a place to stand and position his lever, he could move the world. What he did not say was that the true difficulty lay in deciding just where to position the lever to achieve the proper movement."

Ruiz thought about it, searching Manco's face. "You are right, castaway. It is one thing to say that your butterfly's wings could cause a storm; but quite another to know where to place the butterfly to create the particular storm you desire." Then he laughed. "But enough of this wild talk. We discuss the impossible. What is done is done and may not be undone."

"As you say," said Manco, smiling. "Provided one did not possess a caravel in which to sail the seas of time. But with such a craft . . ." He let the words linger in the air a moment. "With such a craft, it would be a different matter. Certes, the event we would wish to change is but the last link in a long chain. And yet, if one were to study on it, one might find the one weak link. The link that a single, ordinary man could snap, and so change all that came after."

Ruiz considered him with narrowed eyes. "And such a weak link is . . . ?" he suggested slowly.

"Perhaps a civil war among an emperor's sons. Or a line drawn in the sand of a tropical beach. Or a flock of flies in Estremadura." Manco spoke the lies smoothly. He did not mention the one link that was crucial. "It was a hard question, deciding just where the butterfly's wings should flap."

They rode a while longer in silence. Then Ruiz reached across suddenly and seized Manco's bridal. "Was? It *was* a hard decision? What are you trying to say? Who are you, Manco?"

Manco looked at him calmly. "A butterfly."

Ruiz swore an oath. He yanked hard on his horse's reins and galloped back to where Pizarro and Almagro rode. Manco watched them talk; watched Ruiz gesture and point. *Another blow struck*, he thought. Soon the structure would begin to crack. *But, will it crack properly?* The ghosts of family and friends not yet born whispered to him on the wind that scoured the altiplano. *You will kill us, Manco,* they said. *We will never have been. You will never have been.*

It was a chill wind, and Manco pulled his cloak tight about himself.

Pizarro, Almagro, and Ruiz took him aside. They shoved him up against a high stone Inca wall and hemmed him in. Almagro and Ruiz stood to either side with their arms folded across their chests, and Pizarro faced him directly with a dagger held close between his eyes. The point flashed in the noonday sun.

"What is this wild tale that Ruiz has brought me?" he said, his eyes as hard and gray as the stones around them.

"What tale is that?" said Manco, watching the dagger.

"That you plan to destroy our expedition! To save your heathen Empire!"

Manco turned his eyes toward Ruiz. "No. He misunderstood me. I spoke only of butterflies."

"You spoke of changing the past!" Ruiz accused him. "Deny it!"

"Change the past," said Pizarro. "What witchcraft is this? How are we to change the past?"

Manco shook his head. "Not the past. The future. You are the past."

Ruiz unfolded his arms and shifted his stance. Almagro traced a hasty cross over his body. Pizarro looked at him oddly, and the dagger sank a few centimeters. "We are the past," he repeated.

"Yes. I was born in these mountains four hundred and fifty years from now."

"Four hundred and fifty years?" Almagro whispered. "Mother of God!"

Pizarro braced Manco again. "I do not believe you," he declared. "You are mad. Why should I believe you?"

"Are you a magician," asked Ruiz, "that you travel through time?"

"Are you a magician," countered Manco, "that you sail the Ocean Sea?"

Ruiz blinked, looked thoughtful, then laughed. Pizarro turned his head and frowned a question, and Ruiz explained. "Surely our own devices," he said, "must appear as magic to the heathens."

"I've never been a wizard before," Almagro commented dryly.

Pizarro was unconvinced. He held the dagger closer and put his face into Manco's. His breath was foul and stank of rotted teeth. "Can you prove this wild tale of yours, Sanchez?"

"To what purpose? I am what I am. If you believe me or not, what is that to me?" It was a great deal, of course. But Pizarro was not to be pushed into belief. He must be led, one step at a time, until there was no turning back.

Pizarro hesitated. He licked his lips and he glanced once more at his two companions. Then he laughed his harsh and brittle laugh and put his dagger away. "True. And what is it to me?"

"He is leading us into the Indios's empire," Ruiz pointed out.

Pizarro shrugged. "He leads us where we wish to go."

"Does he? What if he is a madman? Should we follow him? And if he *has* come from the future somehow, then he must have some purpose of his own, this self-confessed butterfly." Ruiz turned on Manco. "Well? Speak, and speak plainly. What is your purpose here?"

"I seek," said Manco, "a better future."

Pizarro gripped his dagger hilt. "How?" Then he jerked his free arm up. "No. This is madness." He half turned away.

"He plans to destroy our expedition," declared Ruiz. "To save his Empire." The words were a challenge. Manco looked at the navigator.

"No," Manco told him. "The Empire must fall. Where there is no choice there is no morality. When everything is prescribed by law, there

can be nothing new. It has stunted my people, turned them into unthink-
ing cattle. Easy prey for brigands such as yourselves."

There was no insulting men like these. Words like "brigand" rolled off
them like the rain off of down. If they were brutal, it was at least an honest brutality; and they made no excuses, no mealy-mouthed euphemisms
either to others or to themselves. "Then for what?" asked Ruiz.

Almagro laughed. "Why, then, he must have come to assure our success, amigos. He wishes to smash his forefathers' empire and we are the
instrument he has chosen." He clenched his fist in an unconscious gesture.

"Does your history record this expedition as a failure then?" asked Ruiz.
"Are you here to change that fate?" Pizarro turned back toward them.
Manco could see the curiosity in his eyes. A part of him wanted to know,
and another part did not want to know. His lips parted, but no words came
out. If you speak your dreams aloud, they do not come true. But who can
resist to speak of them?

Manco addressed his answer to Pizarro rather than Ruiz. "Our histories
tell," he said, avoiding the specific question Ruiz had asked, "of how the
conquistador, Pizarro, conquered an empire with but a handful of men.
How he aided and befriended Atahualpa and then garrotted him for his
gold. How the king of Spain made him a marquis and a governor."

Pizarro seemed oddly unsatisfied with the announcement. If success is
foreordained, where is the savor? Ruiz and Almagro were puzzled.

"If you have not come to save the Inca," said Ruiz, "and you have not
come to save us, then tell us: just why have you come?"

Manco took a deep breath. This was a critical point in his plan. "There
is a limit," he told them, "to what an individual such as myself may accomplish alone. I spoke earlier of change. Of finding the right place to put
my lever. Of finding the the weak link in a chain of events. The time when
a small seed may grow into great fruit."

Pizarro looked at Ruiz, who nodded. "Yes, I remember."

"Then, attend me. The place for my lever is here, on this cold mountain trail, and now. I want to alter the Conquest. Not *whether* it happened,
but *how* it happened. The Spaniard is coming to these mountains. That
cannot be stopped, least of all by myself. Nor would I block it if I could
because, as I said, the Inca realm must fall. But, my captains, the Conquest

was too cruel. It destroyed and embittered the Indios. In my time," he told them, "the sad remnants of Tavantinsuyu are the poorest states in Latin America. Because of continual insurrection and political instability, our peoples, Hispanic and Indio alike, will live in abject poverty, illiterate, condemned to mind-numbing peasant labor, *tending pigs for their padrones.*"

That struck responses in both Almagro and Pizarro. The squat, ugly man nibbled his lip and frowned. Pizarro sneered. "Then let them do as I did," he challenged.

"The Incas," Manco said in a pleading voice, "will not accept your rule. Rebellion will follow rebellion: Manco Capac. Tupac Amaru. Tupac Amaru II. Down through the centuries. Long after the Aztecs and the Mayas have forgotten who they were, *we will remember!* In my own time, I was for a while a member of The Shining Path, an Inca society dedicated to the overthrow of the Hispanic Republic of Peru and the restoration of the Inca way, or Maoism, as it will then be called. That must not happen, that long history of hate and rebellion. We must forge a new destiny, one that will lead to a better future."

Manco suddenly realized that he was appealing to Pizarro's better nature; which was a mistake, because the man did not have one. Pizarro hated weakness, and Manco could see contempt for this pleading in the other man's eyes.

"There is a limit, you said, to what one man could accomplish." That was Ruiz, intent, as always with getting to the bottom of things. Manco turned to him once more.

"Yes."

"Then how did you propose to change that course of events you have outlined by accompanying us?"

"The Empire must fall." *Forgive me Tavantinsuyu!* "The Empire must fall; but it must fall in just the right way. There is no need for Spaniard and Inca to become enemies—"

Pizarro laughed sharply. "No need? Your Inca has an Empire and we mean to take it. Is that a basis for friendship?"

Manco could feel the sweat from the noon sun roll down his neck. The men facing him were tense, edgy. The wrong words now could mean his death. "If you have gold and power," he said carefully, "would it matter overmuch who it was had given it you?"

Questions of gold and power always interested Pizarro. "Say on," he said.

"I mean that the Child of the Sun can be no less generous than your own king when it comes to granting titles and wealth."

Pizarro and Almagro exchanged long looks. "Your Indio emperor would give us gold and make us nobles?" asked Pizarro, "And for what? Why should he do such a thing?"

"Why, for breeding your horses and teaching his men to ride them," Manco answered, pointing to the steeds where the other men sat waiting. "You have both stallions and mares in your train. And for smelting iron and teaching his smiths to work it. For teaching navigation and boat building. For a hundred skills which to you are commonplace but which are unknown here."

"And for staying here and never returning to Darien," said Pizarro dryly.

Manco shrugged. "Is that such a terrible price? Is there a greater prize for you if you return? No, only Spanish *dons* instead of Indio *Incas*."

Manco saw that Ruiz, at least, was half-convinced. The thought of playing Galileo to an entire world must be tempting to a man like him. And the others would follow where these three led. Benalcazár would make a fine general on the Empire's southern frontier. Pedro the Greek, the ship's gunner, was an amiable bear of a man. Set him to teaching ordnance and he would be happy. But Almagro and Pizarro . . .

"It will not work, Manco," said Ruiz, shaking his head. Almost reluctantly, Manco thought. "Surely, you know that we are not the only men in Darien who dream of conquest. Others will follow, whatever we decide here."

"Aye. Others will follow," Manco agreed. "But not for some time. Your treacherous governor is already disillusioned with southern ventures. Señor Almagro could raise no more volunteers on his last return voyage. If you fail to return this one last time, Tavantinsuyu will have a breathing space. A time to change and prepare, so that the contest, when it comes, will not be so one-sided. The Spaniard will still prevail, but there will not be a Conquest, but rather a blending of our two peoples." It did no harm to remind these men that Darien had forsaken them, that their governor could not be trusted.

Pizarro snorted. "I bleed for the Indios," he said. "If that was your intention, then you should have had Balboa here, and not I."

Manco looked at him. "Balboa is dead," he said distinctly. "That was a knot I could not unravel on my own. Too many forces were tangled up in his murder."

Pizarro flinched. "It was no murder. It was decided by the court . . ."

"A court perjured and bought. Judicial murder, perhaps, but murder it was. And I could not hope to influence the decisions of men like Pedr'arias, or Enciso, or Espinoza and save the noble Balboa."

"And you believe you can influence us?" Pizarro's eyes told him it was a lie.

Manco shrugged. "This expedition was a turning point of history. When things are in flux, their flow may be guided. History is being made here, on this trail, by a handful of bold men. The future turns on your decisions, my captains. Say now, which is it to be?"

He saw the crafty look come into Pizarro's eyes and knew that his persuasion had failed. "Why surely," the man said, "that is a vision worthy of us. A joining of our peoples. Eh, Diego? Lead us on to this Atahualpa, then. If we can be rich and powerful under the Inca, why concern ourselves with Darien?" Pizarro gathered in his lieutenants with a glance, and they turned to go.

Manco knew that the conquistador was lying. An overlord in distant Spain was one thing; an overlord in Cuzco was something else. If Manco could see that, Pizarro surely did. Manco began to feel the inertia of history. In his bones; in his aching muscles. It was rolling toward him as inexorably as Juggernaut's chariot.

One more blow, he thought. But aimed just right, lest the target shatter. "Wait a while. Don Pizarro. I have not told you all that would transpire if you continue down the path you have set your feet upon." The trio kept walking, Ruiz giving him a sad and disappointed glance. If the path led to conquest, what else mattered?

"What does history say of Pizarro's partner?" he called after them.

They stopped and turned. Almagro scowled at him and Manco, seeing that dark and ravaged face, thought that Diego's emnity was something he would never want to have. Almagro stared at him through his one good eye. "And what of Pizarro's partner?" he asked in a soft voice.

Manco watched Pizarro as he answered Almagro. "History tells us that, following the Conquest, Pizarro was named governor, marquis, captain-general, *Adelantado*, and Alguacil Mayor of Peru for life, with the revenues of Peru for his salary. 'Almagro Jake' was appointed simply governor of

Túmbez, with less than half the salary, and the Thirteen were granted the rank of hidalgos. That by a capitulation signed by the queen regent at Pizarro's request. History tells us that Almagro felt cheated of his rightful share and that civil war resulted. In the end, Almagro was betrayed and legally condemned by a tribunal chaired by Hernando Pizarro. He appealed for clemency to his old friend, the marquis, but the marquis, *don* Pizarro, refused to countermand his brother's judgment. And so, Don Almagro was hung. And it tells us how afterward Almagro's friends burst into the governor's palace at Lima and hacked the aged marquis to death with their swords."

Pizarro's face turned white, then red with rage. "You lie!" he shouted. He lunged toward Manco, but Ruiz and Almagro grabbed him and held him. Pizarro twisted and pulled in their grasp. The other men, alarmed at the spectacle, shot to their feet and one—Benalcazár, Manco thought— pulled his sword.

Ruiz waved them back. "It is nothing important. Just another argument."

"Christ damn you, Ruiz," spit Pizarro. "Release me and I'll slit yon liar's gizzard."

"Francisco," said Almagro, not relaxing his grip.

Pizarro looked at him. "Diego. Old friend. You know I would not do that to you."

Almagro shook his head. "Does today know what tomorrow will do? Who knows what fate holds for us?" He looked at Manco. "Do you swear it, Sanchez? Do you swear on your mother's grave that what you have said is the truth? Would it come to that?"

Manco locked eyes with him. "I swear it. It would have come down to that. Jealousy and rage. Betrayal and murder. Civil war."

Almagro sighed and cradled his partner in his arms. Ruiz let go and backed away and Pizarro sagged, no longer struggling "Ah, success," said Almagro. "It is the great corrupter, is it not, Francisco? So long as we searched, we searched together." He looked back over his shoulder, toward the Quito road. "Let us turn aside from this," he said. "Let us go elsewhere and continue searching for El Hombre Dorado. I never feared danger, on the sea or in the jungle; but I fear success, Francisco, and what it might do to you."

"No," said Manco. "You need not turn aside. Travel the other path, the one that I have laid out for you."

Almagro grunted. "That path, too, leads to success. And down that path, you have no map, no memory to guide our future. Can you tell me that the same fate does not await us at its end?"

Manco shook his head but said nothing. Almagro sighed.

"I wish you had never come, with your omens and warnings. Perhaps you are no magician, after all. Only a conquistador from out of time. God's ways are many and marvelous." Almagro shook his head again. "But there is magic here." He released Pizarro; but the captain merely slumped to the ground. Tears drew dark lines in the dirt on his face. "Vasco," the conquistador murmured. "Vasco."

Almagro looked from Pizarro to Manco. "There is magic here," he repeated.

"Do you suppose it will work?"

Ruiz asked him that as they rode side by side at the head of the column. Great towering cliffs rose above them on either side of the road. The thin cool air of the altiplano whipped through the cañon. Beyond it, framed by the cliffs, Manco could see the plains of Quito. "Do I suppose what will work?"

"The spell you cast on the captain."

"Spell?" Manco cast an amused glance at his companion. "Now who calls it magic?"

"Call it what you wish. It is but a name. What did you do to him?" Ruiz insisted. Then, with an edge to his voice he added, "I will not see him emasculated."

Manco laughed. "No, Captain Pizarro remains Captain Pizarro. As cruel and as treacherous as ever. I only helped him to confront himself."

"I don't know what you mean."

"And you must know, mustn't you?" Manco smiled thinly. "I know your type." He stared straight ahead, the reins loose in his hand. "The captain himself said it, back at the first *tambo* where we camped. Your advantage over the Indios lies not in your technology—in your mechanic skills," he added for clarification, "but in your organizational skills. Your software rather than your hardware." He knew that the terms puzzled Ruiz, but he did not explain. "I had software of my own," he continued. When Ruiz said nothing, he added, "The captain said that your secret weapon was Machiavelli."

Ruiz looked at him. "I remember," he said.

"You had Machiavelli," Manco told him, "but I had Freud."

Ruiz looked backward at the column, where Pizarro and Almagro rode side by side, talking and laughing. "They were drifting apart," he said. "Growing suspicious of each other. Arguing. Everything you told us would have come to pass. I know it. Now . . . I am not sure. Perhaps the breach has been healed. Who was this Freud? A magician who ensorceled men's minds?"

"Yes," said Manco, laughing.

Ruiz shook his head. "With our swords we slice up men's bodies. Your sword slices up men's souls. I think you are crueler than we, Manco."

"Pizarro had betrayed his friend and hero once before. Vasco Balboa, a man he sincerely loved and admired. He had rationalized his actions to himself; but deep inside his mind, in what we call the subconscious, he did not believe those rationalizations. They preyed upon him constantly; poisoned his friendships with anger. He knew that someday, somehow, he would betray Almagro. Not in his waking mind, but underneath it, in that subconscious. He knew it . . . He knew it in his dreams. I forced him to confront that."

"Why?"

"You know why."

"So that he would turn from his path to yours. So he could avoid betraying Diego."

"The shining path," Manco agreed.

"He will still destroy your Empire," Ruiz told him.

"That is his destiny. It must be done. The Inca will give you places, honored places. But you are men who do not know your place. The Inca people cannot conceive of the notion of ambition. I expect . . ." And now Manco glanced back also at the captain. "I expect that the captain will be the next Inca. Why steal an empire and give it to Pedr'arias? It will not take that crafty mind long to realize that no one in Darien will be coming soon; that his expedition will be written off as the final disaster; that he will have time to mold this country to his will."

Ruiz twisted his mouth. "Inca Pizarro. Must we then approach him barefoot and carrying a burden, as you have told us the Inca is approached?"

"No. That will change. Everything will change. Everything that ever was will become what might have been. As it was in the beginning, is not, and nevermore shall be."

Ruiz crossed himself. "And will it end as you have planned? In partnership rather than conquest?"

Manco looked suddenly away. "I do not know," he admitted. "I am not so wise as all that. I will never know. I smashed my machine, my time caravel, and threw its pieces down a great gorge. I had to. Because of what I have done here, my friends and family will never have been born. People I have known and loved all my life, and millions of others, strangers, will never have lived. Is what I have done so much different from killing them?" He shook his head once, convulsively. "No, I must never go back. I must remain here and tell myself every day that I have helped create a better future than the one I left behind."

Ruiz reached across and gripped his arm. "And you cannot cast a spell on yourself, can you, to relieve your own inner torment?"

"No, mine is the worst fate of all."

"And what if it doesn't work? What if, in spite of everything, Francisco calls on the men of Darien? You have told us how irresolute your Atahualpa is. Francisco may grow restive as a noble under him; may begin to wonder what he might accomplish with two hundred men and cannon. What is to stop him—or any of us—from seeking our way home?"

"I do not place all my eggs in a single basket," Manco told him. "You will not have the opportunity to reconsider."

"What do you mean?"

"I mean I have already been living in Tavantinsuyu for three years. I wear the fringe of office on my cloak, granted me by a grateful Inca. I had penicillin with me. Bartolomé, I neglected to say something earlier. It will make no difference if I say it now. Pizarro's second expedition *was* a failure."

"What!" Ruiz sat erect. "Then it was all lies, what you told us? About the Conquest? About Francisco's betrayal of Diego?"

"No lies. It all happened as I told you; but it happened on the *third* expedition."

Ruiz slumped in his saddle. He stared at Manco. "The third."

"Yes. In my history, you did return to Darien with the gold of Túmbez. Pizarro showed it to the queen regent in Toledo the day after Cortez had delivered the Royal Fifth of the treasure of Mexico. Men flocked to join your banner. You came here again in '29 and took an empire."

"And the civil war was not finished by then? You said that we would take advantage of the civil war between the brothers. You urged us into the mountains on that account. To reach here and exploit the conflict before it ended."

"The civil war?"

They broke from the cañon onto the altiplano. And there the thin, weary line of Spaniards halted in dismay. The cold, thin sun of the high country blazed down upon them. The condors circled above. And drawn up before them in rank after rank were the proud Inca regiments, fresh from the defeat of the Empire of Quito. Their numbers filled the plain with a countless mass of men, resplendent in their blazing feathers and quilted jacks, their proud banners snapping in the highland breeze. And above them all flew the Rainbow Banner of the Child of the Sun, where he stood arrogantly atop his platform, carried on the shoulders of his nobles: Huayana Capac Inca, a man of infinite resolution and decisiveness, the undisputed leader of an army that had never known defeat.

"The civil war," said Manco simply, "has not yet started."

I wrote this because my son, Dennis, didn't want to do his homework, which involved the Inca Empire. He demanded to know—in those lovely utilitarian tones that youth employs—"What will I ever *use* this for?"

Now, one answer is that it needn't be used for anything. When Hercule Poirot bragged that he had "got on very well without" a knowledge of the classics, Dr. Burton told him, "It's not a man's working hours that are important—it's his leisure hours." You would think that "What will I ever *use* this for?" would be an odd question coming from someone who can recite details of the lives of any number of rock musicians. . . .

At any rate, I wrote "On the Wings of a Butterfly" and sold it; then I showed him the check.

"This is what you can use it for."

If you want to be strictly utilitarian about such things.

Of course, I know for a fact that Dennis has written stories of his own. Horror stories, à la Freddie Krueger, et al. He won't show them to me.

In late-twentieth-century American academic thought, the story of Pizarro has been reduced to an assault by Evil Western Imperialists on Helpless Native Americans. Connie Willis has called this mind set "chronocentrism," the notion that the mores of our time and place are the supreme pinnacle of thought and ethics, and that benighted dwellers in the outer darkness of earlier times can be righteously judged, *ex post facto*, on our terms.

Reality was never so neat. Pizarro is not a symbol. He was a real human being, with traits both admirable and repulsive. The Amerinds were real people, too, not symbols for modern Western counterculture philosophies. The Incas were imperialists, who built on the blood of conquered and massacred peoples. The Spaniards' crime is that they were better at it.

The idea for this story came from Toynbee's *Mankind and Mother Earth*, in which he wrote: "If Pizarro had marched inland on his first expedition, he would have collided with Inca Huayana Capac, still alive, still undisputedly the sole sovereign of the Inca Empire, and still encamped in the north with the main body of the Inca Imperial Army . . ." Now *there* is an image to build a story around. I fudged a bit—I used the second expedition, and it is not certain Huayana Capac was still alive by then, but I wanted the psychology of Pizarro and his men to be at the right cusp of hope and desperation.

The story uses the conceit of the "butterfly." For want of a nail, a shoe was lost . . . That sort of thing. But, as I find myself protesting repeatedly when discussing science fiction, the story is not *about* chaos theory or the "snowball" effect of small changes. The story is about what people make of themselves, both in the sense of how they create their future and how they re-create their own past. And, oh, in doing so, they sometimes make or break empires.

The Feeders

It was in the bloody slaughter of the Ardennes that Heinrich Mauer first saw the creatures.

The company was advancing in a skirmish line through the dark, haunted forests when a battery of French 75s let loose. Fountains of earth erupted like geysers, and the skirmish line dropped in a flutter of trench coats, their spiked helmets bobbing as the soldiers scratched a hasty trench in the moist soil. The shells and the men screamed.

Heinrich scraped frantically at the earth. The smell of clay and loam was in his nostrils. He turned to the man on his left. "At the training school they taught us that the French did not use artillery to prepare an attack."

Karl grinned. "Perhaps their commander attended a different school. You feel betrayed? Dig! Their infantry will be coming."

The captain was running down the line. He pointed at Heinrich. "You! Lay down some barbed wire in front of us!" The shells whistled and crashed in the trees. One exploded nearby and the captain ducked.

Karl took Heinrich's rifle. "Come back when you are done," he said. "We'll wait."

Heinrich grabbed a spool of wire and ran parallel to the trench a few yards in front of it. The spool whirled on its handles and a cruel hedge of entanglement grew in his wake. Another soldier followed, bracing the wire with posts.

The earth suddenly heaved next to Heinrich and dirt and rocks sprayed in the air. There was a flash of light and a roar. Something hard struck him on the side of his head and his eyesight went double. As he fell he thought, *I am a dead man.*

He lay on the ground and waited for death to claim him. His breath came in short, rapid gulps. Flashes of memory: His *Gemeinde* and how cool the banks of the Neckar were. . . . And the university at Karlsruhe that he would never attend now. . . . And Magda and how smooth and white her skin was. . . . And what they did and didn't do together. Above him, a double set of trees stretched spinning skyward, converging into a blurred canopy overhead. The air was thick with the scent of pine.

The roar of the 75s ceased.

He thought, *Now their infantry will attack.* He put his hand to his head and it came away bloody. The dizziness passed, and he realized suddenly that he would live. For at least a short while longer.

A noise like the thrumming of a million bees grew in the background. It was the sound of hundreds of human voices joined in a great chorus, shouting desperately and loudly so that they would not be afraid to charge the enemy. Heinrich scrabbled in the dirt, crawling toward the safety of the trench.

Hands grabbed him and pulled him into the makeshift shelter. His rifle was thrust at him. "They're coming," he heard someone say. He raised his head dazedly and saw a great cloud of red and blue pouring through the trees. The French infantry. Their brightly colored uniforms made them stand out clearly against the background. With his vision still doubled, there seemed twice as many as there really were. The machine gun to his right began to chatter and the charging men fell like wheat.

My helmet! He had lost it when the shell hit. He looked around. And he saw the creature.

The creature squatted on the broken stump of a tree. It was small and bony, pale yellow in color and obscenely naked. It looked a little bit like a monkey and a little bit like a bat and a little bit like nothing he had ever seen before. The skin was shiny, with no trace of hair or scales, and hung on the beast in loose folds. The skull was narrow and pointed and the eyes glowed like two red coals. Its mouth was an open pit of blackness, gaping in a soundless shriek.

Heinrich was paralyzed, unable to move. It was like some old woodcut of a medieval Satan, done in miniature. For an instant he wondered if he really had died and this was hell.

The creature stretched. Two batlike wings thrust out from its shoulders. With a flap like the rustle of ancient paper, it soared into the air. Tracking its flight, Heinrich saw scores of the beasts. They were in the air. They were clinging to the trees. They were alighting on the French and German soldiers and appeared to be biting them.

Heinrich Mauer cowered in the trench. A whimper escaped his throat. What in the name of Heaven was happening?

No one else seemed to notice the creatures. A burly Frenchman charging straight at him had one wrapped tightly around his neck, yet he showed no signs that he knew it was there.

Heinrich shook the man on his right. "Do you see them!?"

But the man's face was a bloody ruin. Heinrich's stomach heaved even as he brought his bayonet up. He held it steady, fighting the urge to retch.

At training camp, the instructor had taught that hate was a vital element of the bayonet drill. Hate the enemy; despise him. There could be no room for compassion, or even for neutrality, in this most personal form of modern combat. A single moment's hesitation could be fatal.

Scream! Thrust! Tear!

But Heinrich could conjure no other emotion than numbing terror. When the Frenchman was close enough, he screamed and lunged. The scream was closer to desperation than hate, but the lunge was effective enough. A sea of red spread across the enemy's topcoat. Heinrich twisted the bayonet and the man collapsed across him, pinning him to the ground.

He choked under the weight of the body. He could feel the warm blood soaking into his own uniform. The Frenchman's face was pressed into his like a lover's. Heinrich tried to push him away and found himself staring into the other's eyes.

It was a young face, no older than his own. Not a hardened warrior at all. A few hairs sketched a tentative moustache across his lip. He stared at Heinrich with bewilderment. His mouth opened as if he were trying to say something, but all that escaped his lips was a drawn-out sigh. Then the eyes filmed over and stared not at Heinrich, but at some point a long distance off.

Heinrich became aware that, at death, a man's bowel and bladder relaxed. The thought of it made him gag. This time he did not hold back and the sour liquid drained into the earthen floor of the trench.

When he looked up again, he realized that the shouting and gunfire had stopped. He heard German voices. He pushed at the body and it fell away from him. He crawled to the lip of the trench and looked. Hundreds of bodies, both field grey and red-and-blue, carpeted the forest floor. Some of the bodies stood upright, held in place by flying buttresses of corpses. Heinrich saw the machine gunner, Georg, sitting dumb behind his weapon, staring at it in disbelief. Soldiers were sitting or lying, staring into space or weeping.

He did not know which sight affected him the most. The impersonal architecture of death, the grotesque cathedral of corpses that had been carved from the attacking infantry, or the lone man he had slain with his own two hands. He glanced at his hands and saw that the blood had run down them, and he wiped them on his jacket in a convulsive gesture.

He crawled to the lip of the trench and pressed his cheek against the cool earth. So this was war. That was the glory of battle. Hours of foot-numbing marches followed by a few moments of utter terror. He glanced at the boy he had killed. A man, he supposed. The army made a man of you, because it made you old, old.

He remembered the parades that had seen him off with his comrades. Bands playing *"Pariser Eintrittsmarsch"* and *"Der Jäger aus Kurzpfalz."* Girls running up to them, thrusting flowers into their lapels, throwing arms around their necks and kissing them. Old men and women weeping for joy that at last *Der Tag* had come.

The captain and a squad of five were stalking the wounded. Whenever they found a Frenchman who still lived, they shot him through the temple. Most of the soldiers averted their gaze in revulsion; but Heinrich could not tear his eyes away. The captain had one of the creatures riding on his back.

Heinrich looked wildly around the battlefield. They were everywhere. They clung to the trees or squatted among the bodies. Their heads darted from side to side. Heinrich thought of vultures and wondered why they did not fall on and devour the dead.

If he could still see them, he thought, then they must be real. Or he had gone irretrievably mad. And which alternative was worse? Were they then an illusion caused by his wound? Or had they always been there, unseen? Fluttering about him invisibly. Somehow that thought terrified him more than the actual sight.

Then the Skoda 305s laying siege to Namur opened up, and the horizon grew red and the ground trembled, even this far away. Smoky red devil eyes turned north and the horde of creatures took wing and soared, leaving the corpses and the smoking desolation.

•   •   •

The captain, of course, received a medal.

The Crown Prince himself came to the blasted village where Heinrich's company was resting. A platform was erected in the ruins of the town square and the prince made a speech from it.

Heinrich had tried not to think of the devil-bats. In the days since the battle their horror had faded, and he began to believe that he had imagined them. Once or twice he thought he had glimpsed one; but it was always at a distance and he could not be certain. He had spoken to no one about them — not to his comrades and not to the company doctor who certified him fit for duty. Best to say nothing, he had decided. Heinrich had no desire to be shut away in a madhouse. No, keep the horror to himself. Perhaps everyone had seen them. Perhaps devil-bats were as common as flies on a dunghill, and the same fear kept everyone silent.

So he stood in the square, his back ramrod-stiff, in ranks with his comrades, and listened to the prince drone. The flag of the Fourth Army snapped in the hot August breeze. Heinrich had already learned the old soldier's trick of surviving such speeches. He let his eyes glaze over. He tensed his thigh muscles alternately to keep the blood from pooling in his legs. Only snatches of the speech reached him. ". . . bravery of such fine officers . . ." ". . . French resistance smashed . . ." ". . . enemy in headlong retreat . . ." ". . . success in Belgium guaranteed . . ." "home before the leaves fall . . ."

Ah, now that was a thought! Home before the leaves fall. Would he and Magda picnic again in the Black Forest? He wondered if Magda would wait for his discharge, as she had promised. He imagined Papa meeting him at the train station, decked out in his old uniform and medals. The Kingdom of Bavaria, a country which no longer existed; a warfare that no longer existed. And yet, Papa must have stood in parades like this one; must have lived through terror as intense as his own. Suddenly he regretted not having listened more closely to the old man's rambling tales.

The captain and two other officers marched smartly to the fore, and the prince and his aides met them with a tray of medals. Heinrich sensed movement in the corner of his eye. The flapping of wings; and the faint sound of rustling curtains.

Heinrich turned his head, then quickly snapped it back. The devil-bats were coming. Six of them. They circled the town square, dipping and weaving. Two of the pale-skinned creatures alighted upon officers standing in the ranks, and a third draped itself around one of the Crown Prince's aides. The remaining three circled the medalists, settling first on the shoulders of the captain, then on those of the second officer.

The last creature wheeled slowly. It dipped toward the remaining man, then veered off and circled once more. Its companions watched its progress with their large red eyes. In the end, it perched upon a nearby tree branch. The burning eyes were expressionless.

Heinrich closed his own eyes and wished them away. *Dear God*, he thought. *Let them not be there!*

He opened his eyes.

The six were still there. Two of them seemed to be looking in his direction. Terror was an icicle in his heart. *Don't think about them. Think about anything else. Magda. The Kaiser. The soccer game the day before your induction.*

The creatures looked away.

The one in the tree took wing suddenly. It circled the captain. The creature already perched there watched a moment, then it raised its own wings and the two changed places.

How kind, thought Heinrich crazily. He felt dizzy and, despite his precautions, he did pass out at last.

"Heinrich? Heinrich? It *is* you!"

He opened his eyes. He was lying in a cot. Nursing orderlies strode about with an air of importance. *I must be in battalion hospital*, he thought groggily. He turned to see who had spoken.

"Sepp!" he exclaimed. "Sepp Zimmerman! So the Kaiser has gotten you as well."

The man in the next cot had his leg wrapped in bandages. He grinned at Heinrich. "I would guess that there are few enough men of fighting age left in our village. Just the old men and the cowboys left to bring in the harvest."

Heinrich grunted. "Ach, we will be back before harvest moon. The decisive battle has been fought, and we have won. That is how modern war is. All the books have said so. One decisive battle and everyone goes home. The French are beaten. All that is left for us now is to gather them up."

"Perhaps," said Sepp doubtfully. "But, if the French are beaten, I think someone has forgotten to tell them so. My unit fought at Onhaye. The French may be retreating, but they are not fleeing. They are taking their weapons with them. They are fighting hard at every bridgehead. My lieutenant was given a medal, but the enemy escaped nevertheless."

"A medal?" Heinrich remembered the ceremony; the creatures. "Was he one of the three today?"

"Yes. The one on the far right. Perhaps you saw him."

Heinrich remembered that the creatures had avoided that officer. He was suddenly consumed by an overwhelming desire to know why. "And what act of heroism did he perform?"

Sepp shrugged. "Who knows? A dozen. A score. He was a wild man on the battlefield. He was everywhere, rallying our men against the French counterattack. For myself, I believe he was terrified; but then the line between fright and courage is not always clear."

"Courage is doing what you must when you are frightened," Heinrich quoted.

"Perhaps." Sepp allowed the possibility. "Now he is a hero of the Reich." He hunched over conspiratorially. "But the plain truth of it," he explained, "is that the lieutenant agrees with you. He did not even want the medal. He told us that he had only done his duty, and no soldier should expect a medal for that. He was only happy that we were at last breaking the vicious Encirclement that England, France, and Russia had thrown around us."

"I thought we were fighting to avenge an Austrian archduke."

"So. We avenge a Serbian murder of an Austrian by attacking the Belgians?" Sepp laughed cynically. "No, my friend, the issues are much larger than that. *Realpolitik*," he said importantly. German was a fine tongue for building new words out of old ones. "*Realpolitik* and the struggle for African colonies and our rightful place in the sun that the decadent British have denied us for so long." His grin faded. He fell silent and looked away. "Could this slaughter be justified on any grounds less lofty? The machine guns." He shook his head. "My God, the machine guns. Who could have imagined it?"

The orderly came and released Heinrich for duty once more. Sepp accompanied him through the village. Sepp walked with the aid of a crutch, and Heinrich carried his friend's things for him. Rubble from the bombardment littered the streets. Heinrich asked a military policeman where his unit was bivouacked, and they turned their steps in that direction.

Heinrich found himself watching the sky. Sepp looked at him. "Expecting French aeroplanes?" he asked.

Heinrich started. "No," he said quickly. "Just daydreaming." They continued in silence for a short while. Then Heinrich spoke again. "Tell me, Sepp. Do you believe in spirits?"

Sepp gave him a puzzled look. "The priests taught us about devils and angels and souls and God. But that was a long time ago; and I was a child."

"I had thought myself an unbeliever also," said Heinrich abstractedly.

Sepp nudged him with his elbow. "What? Have you found God in the trenches, then?" His voice was mocking.

"Not God. Maybe devils."

Sepp's face turned serious. "You have that right," he admitted. "This battle has had horror enough for a dozen hells. I think the horses are the worst part. The way they scream and kick." He shook his head slowly. "The sights I have seen . . ."

Heinrich waited, wondering if Sepp had seen any sight like the one Heinrich had seen. The horses, he thought, were something short of being the worst. But Sepp was looking to the side of the road.

"Ach, but here is a bit of Heaven for contrast."

Heinrich looked also and saw a Frenchwoman. She was old, perhaps thirty or more, and was blackened with smoke and dirt. She was digging in the ruins of one of the houses. Her clothing was torn and ragged and, when she bent over, Heinrich could see her breasts.

"Hey! Pretty one!" called Sepp. The woman looked up and regarded them neutrally. "Come, Heinrich." Sepp tugged at his arm. "You don't need to report immediately, do you?"

Heinrich hesitated. "Well, Magda and I promised each other. . . ." Sepp laughed.

"Then imagine you are with her while you do it. That is how a soldier remains faithful to his girl."

"But she will wait for me."

"Surely, but she will wait on her back."

Heinrich drew himself up. "Magda is a virgin!" he said hotly.

"And I am Count Bismarck," Sepp replied. "Don't take it so seriously. Don't tell me you don't want to do it." He tugged on Heinrich's sleeve.

Heinrich looked at the woman again. Memories of Magda competed with the memories of breasts; and, of the two, the latter were the fresher. He allowed Sepp to pull him along and stood to the side while his friend talked to the woman. Heinrich craned his neck for another glimpse down her blouse. Yes, they were very fine. Not so fine as Magda's must be, but . . .

Sepp leaned his weight on his good leg. He reached out and touched her hair, running his fingers through it. The woman turned her head.

"Sepp, I don't think you should—"

"Ach, nonsense. She likes it. I can tell. Don't you, sweet one?"

The woman looked up, her face a blank. "I must," she said in passable German, and her voice was so dead of emotion that Heinrich recoiled.

Sepp wound a lock of hair around his finger. "Is there someplace we can go?"

She turned her head toward the shell of a building beside the rubble where they stood. "There," she said. "The shoemaker, he is dead, and his wife is disappeared. I have use their house now."

Sepp grinned at Heinrich. "You see? She likes it. She wants it. Bring my things. You can be second."

Heinrich thought about the breasts again and felt the longing. So why not? Magda was far away and would never know. It wasn't as if it were love or anything; it was more like a physical release; like eating to calm a hunger. And it would be a way of forgetting about the shells and the devil-bats and the Frenchman with the ragged moustache.

The woman put a hand on Sepp's chest. "Wait. How many you pay?"

"How many?" Sepp blinked, confused by her mangled German.

"Yes! Money? Food? What give you? I say if enough."

Heinrich snorted. "She likes it," he said. "She wants it. She'll sell it, but she won't give it."

Sepp gave him a funny look. "And why should she? What else has she to sell?"

They had reached the entrance to the shoemaker's house and, through the doorway, Heinrich could see a considerable cache of goods: food, a bedroll, cooking utensils, parts of uniforms gradually transforming into skirts. Business, it seemed, was doing very well. Considering how short a time the village had been occupied, the woman had been remarkably active.

Well, she was a survivor, too. Like Heinrich. Like Sepp. Like everyone else who had lived through the Battle of the Frontiers. Perhaps that was all his longing meant. That having dispensed death, he was now compelled to dispense life in a kind of symmetry. Thesis and antithesis, as the philosophers liked to say.

His thoughts were brought up short. One of the creatures had landed in the path. Heinrich heard his pulse in his ears. *Don't look at it!* The creature walked over to the woman. It was a curious, scuttling walk.

The devil-bat stretched itself up and placed its mouth on the woman's body. Heinrich felt the bile rise in his throat. He closed his eyes and looked away. *It's not there. It's not there.* After a moment, he heard a distant rustling sound. When he opened his eyes the beast was gone. *Thank God,* he thought.

"Heinrich!" hissed Sepp. He looked up and saw that the other two had already gone inside the ruin. Sepp was taking his uniform coat off. The woman had carried something over to her booty pile. Sepp's payment. Heinrich hoped that his friend hadn't given away anything that would cause him trouble with his lieutenant. The woman knelt before her hoard; her hand caressed it and a smile flickered at the corners of her mouth.

Na, we all get our pleasures, thought Heinrich, *in different ways.*

The woman pulled her dress up and over her head and she stood there, bare and bony. Heinrich felt himself stir. Magda must look like that, he thought, only fuller and more rounded. His eyes were drawn to her secret places. The woman went to Sepp and wrapped her arms around his neck. Heinrich leaned his rifle against the doorframe and sat back to await his turn. His tongue wet his lips. He hoped he would not embarrass himself when the time came.

Two of the creatures landed on the broken windowsill.

Heinrich closed his eyes and pretended they were not there. *The first one went back and invited a friend for dinner.* It was a mad thought; but something about the creatures' behavior reminded him of feeding.

He opened his eyes, unable to tolerate not seeing, and saw four bodies writhing on the dirty blanket. The woman looked stiff and bored; Sepp grunted and strained atop her. The two creatures kept their faces pressed tightly against Sepp and the woman; but from time to time, one or the other would raise its head and look around. This close to them, he could see that the devil-bats did not have true mouths. The darkness that covered the lower half of their faces was a membrane of some sort. It was darker than the rest of their skin and, from a distance, had given the impression of an ever-gaping maw.

Feeding, he thought. *They must be feeding.* He grabbed his rifle and bolted through the door. One of the creatures looked up at the movement.

"Heinrich!"

He turned at the sound of Sepp's voice. "What?"

"It's your turn."

Heinrich tried not to see the thing on his friend's back. The woman leaned on her elbows. She smiled at Heinrich and ran the fingers of her right hand up the inside of her thigh. He barely glanced at her. There was nothing the least bit erotic about the sight. The flesh was just flesh. The creature fixed like a leech to her body had made her unclean. He couldn't bring himself to touch her.

"No," he said. "I feel dizzy. My wound." He touched the side of his head. "I need the fresh air." The second creature stared at him with eyes that blazed like lamps. *It knows I see him*, came the unbidden thought, and he stumbled outside into the sunlight.

During the next few weeks, Heinrich caught occasional glimpses of the creatures. Now that he knew what to look for, he saw them in many places. The conviction grew on him that the creatures had always been there, invisible save to a maddened few. He wondered if, in the days before he could see them, they had ever ridden his back, or Magda's.

He often saw them engaged in their "feeding," mounted upon his fellow soldiers or upon natives. Frequently, however, they paid no mind to the humans around them. They perched in trees or flew in the air. Sometimes in groups and sometimes alone. Days would pass when he would see none; then, they would be about him in great flocks.

He learned to expect the things during battle.

And he learned that, if he watched them too long or thought about them too much, he would draw their attention to him. And that meant he must not look at what he saw, must not think about what it meant. Only in that way could he find a measure of calm.

The days fell into a routine. March, fight, rest. March, fight, rest. It was a job. One rested at night; rose and walked to work; did what was required by one's superiors. The young Frenchman he had killed in the Ardennes faded into the anonymity of the masses, became simply one among many. Too many to be seen as individuals. Devil-bats were a spray in the air, soaring, swooping, sucking whatever nourishment it was that they obtained from the men who fought. Perhaps for them it was only a job as well.

The French fell back day after day. They retreated; but, as Sepp had warned, they were not routed. They fell back in good order, taking their weapons. Orders came from the Crown Prince to slow the advance, lest the enemy retreat too fast and escape the encircling First Army, moving down from the north.

Heinrich and his comrades trudged kilometers of endless roads. They heard rumors that the English had landed and other rumors that the English had not entered the war at all. By 28 August they had passed Sedan and their company was pulled off the front for rest and refitting.

Heinrich lay in the shadow of a great elm tree, enjoying the late-summer breeze. His boots had been resoled; he had had a leisurely meal; and no one was shooting at him. What soldier could ask for more? He could pretend that the distant crump of artillery was only dry thunder.

He wondered how he would spend the remainder of his leave time. His unit would return to the front tomorrow. The invasion timetable had been carefully calculated, day by day, for each army. But the planner had never walked the route himself, had never had to march and fight and fight and march. The men were growing weary. Heinrich knew he could no longer cover the same distance in a day's march as he had at the beginning. And losses from casualties and garrisoning were narrowing the fronts, opening gaps between columns, so that they zigzagged their way across the countryside, closing first the left-hand gap, then the right.

"Heinrich!" He twisted his neck and saw Georg waving to him. Karl was with him, and some other men he did not know. They came to him, laughing and drinking. "We're going over to see the old battlefield. Do you want to come along?"

Heinrich shrugged. "Why not? Where is Fat Willi? Is he coming, too?"

Karl had a bottle of French wine. He gave it to Heinrich, and Heinrich swallowed from it gratefully. The liquid warmed his throat and belly. Karl jerked his thumb over his shoulder. "Willi is having his third serving of cabbage and potatoes. Do not sleep downwind from him tonight, the old pumpernickel."

Heinrich looked at Willi. One of the devil-bats sat on his shoulder and, while Willi fed, so did it. He looked away quickly. "Where is the battle-field?" He was anxious to be away. It was the first creature he had seen in several days, and he did not want to draw its attention.

The walk to the battlefield of Sedan was not a long one. The terrain had already been turned muddy by the number of boots that had tramped across it. Heinrich, Karl, and the others crowded around the monument. "What does it say?" asked Karl, and Georg translated it for them.

"Isn't that just like the French?" asked someone. "To raise a monument to a defeat?"

"They have few enough victories," said another.

Georg pointed. "Isn't that the hill where the Old Kaiser sat and watched the battle? Yes, and the French General Margueritte's charge came across this way, I think." He waved his arms about, pointing everywhere. The others listened carefully to his description of the long-ago battle; but Heinrich wandered away from them and sat on the hillside, where he could see the whole field.

He closed his eyes and tried to imagine what it had been like when the Old Kaiser had crushed Napoleon the Little. Long ago? Why, it was barely forty-four years! Yet, the armies of those days had gone to war in gorgeous plumage and bright colors. There were no machine guns or aeroplanes or barbed wire then. Only the cavalry charge, with cocked lances and helmets bright in the sun.

His father had been there, in the Bavarian Army, as young then as Heinrich was now. He felt a sudden rush of comradeship with the white-haired, old man, gruff, unemotional, who sat and stared for long hours into the fire. A bond of understanding that stretched between them despite the years, that his older brothers could not share. A world of experience that could be exchanged in a single, knowing look.

"Heinrich!" called Karl.

He looked where the others stood. "What?" He wondered if creatures had fed on the men in the older war. How far back did it go? As far as Old Napoleon? Prince Eugene? Tilly and Wallenstein? As far back as the legends of dæmons?

"We have it figured out! The Bavarians and the Saxons were over there and the Prussians were there." There had been no Reich in those days; just the confederated German armies. Karl pointed energetically to various points of the compass.

Heinrich crossed the field and rejoined them. "Then General Margueritte led his charge across here?" He had just walked in the path of heroes. Perhaps his father had fought on this very ground.

Georg spoke up. "That was when the Old Kaiser said, 'Oh, those brave men!' He said it in French, too. My grandfather told me that, and he was there."

"Brave," said Karl, "but stupid."

"Do you think this war will see anything so grand?" Heinrich asked.

"Heroism is for fools," Karl told him. "The important thing is to stay alive. What did Sedan ever gain the French?"

They began walking back toward their bivouac. "I heard that the people of Paris ate rats during the siege."

"That's true," said Karl. "I read it in a book. They ate rats, and cats, and shoe leather." He shook his head. "They should have surrendered right off."

Heinrich shrugged. "Maybe it was pride."

"Ah, pride. And envy, lust, and hate. The capital sins," said Karl broadly. "Each of us will be laid low by one of them." He grinned.

"What's that?" asked Heinrich.

"Pay attention, worm! The capital sins. Don't you remember your schooling? There are supposed to be seven, but I only remember four." He nudged Heinrich. "But they are the four most useful."

Georg poked him. "Don't you remember *your* schooling?"

"Greed!" said Heinrich suddenly recalling.

"I was wrong," Karl said. "That is useful, too!"

"And gluttony," added Georg.

"Like Willi," laughed Karl.

"That's still only six," protested Heinrich.

Karl drained his wine bottle and threw it so that it smashed against the Sedan monument. "Who cares? It is only a færie tale told by the priests."

Georg looked wistful. "I studied for the priesthood once."

"Ah, then you should know all about sin."

"Maybe. As much as any sinner." He brightened. "I remember there are three sources of sin!"

"Ahhh!" Karl waved his arm and quickened his pace, leaving Heinrich and Georg behind.

"You've offended him," Heinrich said.

Georg shook his head. "No, he just did not want to be reminded that sin and damnation are real."

"Are they? I think you should have stayed in the priesthood." There was a distant speck in the sky. It caught the sun and flashed. Perhaps it was a bird; or an aeroplane. Perhaps it was a nightmare. "What are they?" he whispered.

"What are what?"

He had not realized he had spoken aloud. "The three sources of sin," he said, casting the first random thought into his mouth.

"Oh." They walked a few paces farther. "The world is one," Georg said. "It provides opportunity. A pretty girl. An unwatched billfold. A careless enemy. Then, the flesh provides weakness. We call that Original Sin. It makes us prey to the temptations of the world. Then, finally: the Devil."

"And what does the Devil do?"

"Why, as we stand there weakening before temptation, the little pumpernickel creeps up behind us and gives us a push."

September followed August as the armies of the right wing marched across northern France. To Heinrich the advance became one weary kilometer after another. He began to wonder if the French would ever make a stand.

His boots were in tatters. The cobbler wagons could no longer keep up with the worn-out footgear. He staggered as he marched, and at night he threw himself to the ground and took a numb sleep by the side of the road.

His companions began to lighten their loads by discarding equipment as they marched. Shovels, belts, packs, even extra ammunition. Seeing the litter by the side of the road, Heinrich began to wonder which was the defeated army.

On one particularly long day the captain kept them marching long after sunset. They were behind schedule and keeping the schedule was the most important thing. Sometimes Heinrich wondered whether the war were being run by generals or by timekeepers.

Heinrich slumped down, leaning on his rifle. Sergeants were calling off the platoons, and men slipped wearily into the darkness. Heinrich lay back and looked into the night sky. The stars were very clear. There were no clouds. Heinrich tried to pick out the constellations, as he used to in his childhood, but he had forgotten too much and soon gave up.

Karl fell to the earth at his side. The distant rumble of artillery sounded like thunder. "Paris," he whispered. "Soon, Paris. Then all this will be over." He was asleep even as he said it.

Heinrich wanted nothing more than to lie there forever. He could not summon the energy to unbuckle his pack. His feet hurt unbearably. Soon he fell into an uneasy slumber.

His sleep was disturbed by dreams. He dreamed that devil-bats drifted through the night sky, their pale, leathery bodies glimmering in the dark. Their eyes were burning coals, watching, watching. He dreamed that they alighted on the men and pressed their horrid faces to their sleeping bodies. Feeding. Sucking the juices out of them, like vampires.

And he dreamed that one, at last, alighted on him.

With a cry, he sat upright. His heart hammered. He was covered with sweat. He took a slow, deep breath and let it gust out. The back of his neck tingled where the dream-beast had put its mouth. Absently, he scratched it. He turned around.

And the red smoky eyes were staring at him.

He cried again; but it was no more than a whimper that escaped his throat. The creature sat on its haunches no more than three feet from him. Its arms and wings were folded and its head was cocked a little to one side. Heinrich turned away quickly. "It wasn't a dream," he whispered.

It was not.

Heinrich's head jerked. Voices in his head. Was he going mad?

Not mad; not yet. It was a voice, yet not a voice, sounding sardonic, amused. He shook his head wildly. Is it so humorous to go mad? Is the mind's last rational act to laugh at its own fate?

The sound of dried leaves in his ears. Was the creature coming closer? Heinrich rolled away, bumping into Karl as he did so. Karl stirred but did not awaken.

Am I so repulsive, then? Amusement. *Consider how you appear to me. Swollen, lumbering, moist.*

Heinrich did not look back. His mind was out of gear. There was terror in it, locked away somewhere, spinning furiously but producing no motion. He felt as if he were watching himself from afar. "What are you?" he croaked.

What am I? Cobwebs tickled his brain. In a convulsive gesture, Heinrich ran his hand through his hair. *There are no words for what I am.*

"Not dæmon? Not monster?"

Laughter. *In my own eyes?*

Steeling himself, Heinrich turned. The creature's eyes burned and boiled like lava. They held him transfixed. They seemed to roil in constant motion.

"Are you speaking to me?"

If you choose to believe so.

"But ... how?" Heinrich held his hands to his ears, blotting out all sound; but the voice echoed clear and true.

How? Puzzlement. *It is as it is.*

There was silence in his mind, and Heinrich took his hands from his ears. "Do you truly exist? Are you real?" Can one ask a nightmare if it is real? How would the nightmare answer? Is the ultimate horror a lie—or the truth? *Yes, I am real?* Terrifying. Unbearable. *No, I am not?* Bearable; but only in the oblivion of madness. And yet the reply, when it came, was an unexpected one.

How is it you can see me when no others can?

Now Heinrich was puzzled. Could one debate a dream? "I was wounded in a battle. I saw you there." Images of fear-crazed soldier charging. The man he had impaled, gushing his life's blood onto Heinrich, legs kicking, sightless eyes staring at him. The cathedral of corpses sculpted by machine gun on massed bayonet charge. The convulsive jerk of the bodies as the captain fired into their temples. He covered his face with his hands. "I saw scores of you. Whatever you are."

Call us refugees.

"Refugees." Heinrich spoke the word aloud. Vision of uprooted peasants fleeing the plundering armies. "Refugees. From where? From what?"

There was a struggle. We lost. It was an eon ago, and even Time forgets. We are here; but once we were there.

Heinrich turned and saw that the creature had turned its lava eyes to the sky. A clawed hand thrust toward the star-filled heavens. Heinrich felt a shiver run through him. He followed the direction of the arm out into the blackness of the night. Stars twinkled coldly in the sky.

I do not know which one was ours. That, too, has been forgotten.

Heinrich sat silently. He craned his neck to watch the stars. The Milky Way was a slash through the velvet night. What a God-awful distance to fall.

"Thrown down from Heaven, were you? Then this must, indeed, be Hell." Hell? Perhaps. He had seen suffering enough for a dozen hells.

I had thought that one of your kind had become aware. A sense from time to time that someone was watching. A foreboding. A . . .

"A haunting?"

Yes. It frightened me.

Heinrich turned and stared at the devil-bat. "*You?* You were frightened?" He nearly giggled. In his mind, Heinrich saw the devil-bats: on the French soldier screaming his hate as he charged; riding the captain and the officers at the medal ceremony; squirming with Sepp and the woman in a travesty of love. Flocks of devil-bats swarming in the sky. "You were frightened?"

He swung his fist at the devil-bat and his arm passed through the image as if through smoke. The punch carried Heinrich to the ground, and he lay prone, with his face pressed into the dirt. "Oh, God. I'm mad. I'm going mad." He looked up at where the creature sat perched upon a rock. "You're a devil, come to destroy me. You are hungry so you stir up our passions and then you feed upon them!"

Would you have us starve to please your sensibilities?

The dæmon-filled battlefield skies . . . The rotting corpses . . . "Yes," he whispered. "Oh, yes."

Dæmon-filled? You see what you want to see. Do not charge this slaughter to us. You nurtured it. You suckled it. Who marched away to music and lovers' kisses? No, we reap where we did not sow.

Ah, and if not the Devil, who sowed Cædmon's teeth? Heinrich no longer knew if his mind gibbered to itself or if he sat in the night and conversed with a dæmon. It did not matter. Nothing mattered anymore.

The creature's ghastly countenance filled his vision. *Despair,* it seemed to say, *is most delicious.* And it applied its mouth to him.

The next day was the Battle of the Marne. And there were some among the Allied soldiers who, in those desperate hours, saw golden-eyed angels in flowing white robes hovering over the field.

ABOUT "THE FEEDERS"

Some people find the boundary between fantasy and science fiction difficult to draw and claim that the borderland is so fuzzy the two cannot be distinguished. However, the existence of dawn and dusk does not invalidate the distinction between night and day. And fantasy and science fiction are that different.

We may call the difference "left brain — right brain," "intellect — will," "artifice — nature," or even "male — female." None of them are satisfactory dichotomies. Men write fantasy; women, science fiction. "Right brain" intuition is important in science; "left brain" logic, in fantasy. Maybe "yin — yang," being more context-free in English, is a better description.

Being different does not mean that one is "better" than the other. Some fantasy enthusiasts put SF down as "boys and their toys." Some SF enthusiasts put fantasy down as "playing tennis without the net." In many cases it is true. Sturgeon's Law — 90 percent of anything is junk. But golf is not playing tennis without a net. It's simply a different kind of game, with different rules. And fantasy is a different game, too. The central metaphor is myth. The magic and the mythic creatures might sometimes be nothing more than stage props for an "elf opera," but the best fantasy illuminates our internal realities.

There is one critical difference between SF and fantasy, though. Outside the boundaries of your own skull, science delivers tangible results. Magic does not.

In my card file, "The Feeders" is Opus 2. It was the second story I submitted for publication, following the acceptance of "Slan Libh." It hadn't quite jelled at the time; so, following its rejection, I put it aside to age.

Earlier, I wrote that "The Common Goal of Nature" is my only story about aliens. I didn't lie. "The Feeders" can be read three ways:

1. The creatures are aliens (science fiction)
2. The creatures are fallen angels (fantasy)
3. It's all in Heinrich's head (magical realism)

Anyone who knows which is the "correct" interpretation knows more than I do. When the creature "speaks" near the end, Heinrich could interpret its tale in terms of aliens coming to Earth, à la Wells's 1898 *War of the Worlds;* in terms of angels cast down from heaven, per Revelation 12:7; or in terms of his own head injury. There are difficulties with any reading. Why would aliens feed on the Seven Cardinal Sins? If demons, why is their behavior so mundane? Perhaps Heinrich is only projecting his childhood catechism on the horrors he sees. Or projecting Wells. I tried to be ambiguous, though the story's original appearance in the hard science-fiction magazine, *Analog,* predisposed many to view it as pure science fiction.

Look, I told you the borderland was fuzzy. . . .

Melodies of the Heart

I have never been to visit in the gardens of my youth. They are dim and faded memories, brittle with time: A small river town stretched across stony bluffs and hills. Cliffside stairs switchbacking to a downtown of marvels and magical stores. A little frame house nestled in a spot of green, with marigolds tracing its bounds. Men wore hats. Cars gleamed with chrome and sported tail fins enough to take flight. Grown-ups were very tall and mysterious. Sometimes, if you were good, they gave you a nickel, which you could rush to the corner grocery and buy red-hot dollars and jaw-breakers and licorice whips.

I don't remember the music, though. I know I should; but I don't. I even know what the tunes must have been; I've heard them often enough on Classic Rock and Golden Oldy shows. But that is now; my memories are silent.

I don't go back; I have never gone back. The town would be all different—grimier and dirtier and twenty years more run-down. The house I grew up in was sold, and then sold again. Strangers live there now. The cliffside stairs have fallen into disrepair, and half the downtown stores are boarded-up and silent. The corner groceries are gone, and a nickel won't buy you squat. Grown-ups are not so tall.

They are still a mystery, though. Some things never change.

> *The melody's dumb, repeat and repeat;*
> *But if you can sing, it's got a good beat.*

I remember her as I always remember her: sitting against the wall in the garden sunshine, eyes closed, humming to herself.

The first time I saw Mae Holloway was my first day at Sunny Dale. On a tour of the grounds, before being shown to my office, the director pointed out a shrunken and bent old woman shrouded in a shapeless, pale-hued gown. "Our Oldest Resident." I smiled and acted as if I cared. What was she to me? Nothing, then.

The resident doctor program was new then. A conservative looking for a penny to pinch and a liberal looking for a middle-class professional to kick had gotten drunk together one night and come up with the notion that, if you misunderstood the tax code, your professional services could be extorted by the state. My sentence was to provide on-site medical care at the Home three days a week. Dr. Khan, who kept an office five miles away, remained the "primary care provider."

The Home had set aside a little room that I could use for a clinic. I had a metal desk, an old battered filing cabinet, a chair with a bad caster that caused the wheel to seize up—as if there were a rule that the furniture there be as old and as worn as the inhabitants. For supplies, I had the usual med-icines for aches and pains. Some digitalis. Ointments of one sort or another. Splints and bandages. Not much else. The residents were not ill, only old and tired. First aid and mortuaries covered most of their medical needs.

The second time I saw Mae Holloway was later that same first day. The knock on the door was so light and tentative that at first I was unsure I had heard it. I paused, glanced at the door, then bent again over my medical journal. A moment later, the knock came again. Loud! As if someone had attacked the door with a hammer. I turned the journal down open to the page I had been reading and called out an invitation.

The door opened and I waited patiently while she shuffled across the room. Hobble, hobble, hobble. You would think old folks would move faster. It wasn't as though they had a lot of time to waste.

When she had settled into the hard plastic seat opposite my desk, she leaned forward, cupping both her hands over the knob of an old blackthorn walking stick. Her face was as wrinkled as that East Tennessee hill coun-try she had once called home. "You know," she said—loudly, as the slightly deaf often do, "you oughtn't leave your door shut like that. Folks see it, they think you have someone in here, so they jes' mosey on."

That notion had been in the back of my mind, too. I had thought to use this time to keep up with my professional reading. "What may I do for you, Mrs. Holloway?" I said.

She looked away momentarily. "I think—" Her jaw worked. She took a breath. "I think I am going insane."

I stared at her for a moment. Just my luck. A nutcase right off the bat. Then I nodded. "I see. And why do you say that?"

"I hear music. In my head."

"Music?"

"Yes. You know. Like this." And she hummed a few bars of a nondescript tune.

"I see—"

"That was 'One O'Clock Jump!' " she said, nearly shouting now. "I used to listen to Benny Goodman's band on *Let's Dance*! Of course, I was younger then!"

"I'm sure you were."

"WHAT DID YOU SAY?"

"I SAID, 'I'M SURE YOU WERE'!" I shouted at her across the desk.

"Oh. Yes," she said in a slightly softer voice. "I'm sorry, but it's sometimes hard for me to hear over the music. It grows loud, then soft." The old woman puckered her face and her eyes drifted, becoming distanced. "Right now, it's 'King Porter.' A few minutes ago it was—"

"Yes, I'm sure," I said. Old folks are slow and rambling and forgetful; a trial to talk with. I rose, hooking my stethoscope into my ears, and circled the desk. Might as well get it over with. Mrs. Holloway, recognizing the routine, unfastened the top buttons of her gown.

Old folks have a certain smell to them, like babies; only not so pleasant. It is a sour, dusty smell, like an attic in the summer heat. Their skin is dry, spotted parchment, repulsive to the touch. When I placed the diaphragm against her chest, she smiled nervously. "I don't think you'll hear my music that way," she said.

"Of course not," I told her. "Did you think I would?"

She rapped the floor with her walking stick. Once, very sharp. "I'm no child, Dr. Wilkes! I have not been a child for a long, long time; so, don't treat me like one." She waved her hand up and down her body. "How many children do you know who look like me?"

"Just one," I snapped back. And instantly regretted the remark. There was no point in being rude; and it was none of her business anyway. "Tell me about your music," I said, unhooking my stethoscope and stepping away.

She worked her lips and glared at me for a while before she made up her mind to cooperate. Finally, she looked down at the floor. "It was one, two nights ago," she whispered. Her hands gripped her walking stick so tightly that the knuckles stood out large and white. She twisted it as if screwing it into the floor. "I dreamed I was dancing in the Roseland Ballroom, like I used to do years and years ago. Oh, I was once so light on my feet! I was dancing with Ben Wickham—he's dead now, of course; but he was one smooth apple and sure knew how to pitch woo. The band was a swing band—I was a swinger, did you know?—and they were playing Goodman tunes. 'Sing, Sing, Sing. Stardust.' But it was so loud, I woke up. I thought I was still dreaming for a while, because I could still hear the music. Then I got riled. I thought, who could be playing their radio so loud in the middle of the night? So I took myself down the hall, room by room, and listened at each door. But the music stayed the same, no matter where I went. That's when I knowed . . ." She paused, swallowed hard, looked into the corner. "That's when I knowed, knew, it was all in my head."

I opened the sphygmomanometer on my desk. Mae Holloway was over a hundred years old, according to the Home's director, well past her time to shuffle off. If her mind was playing tricks on her in her last years, well, that's what old minds did. Yet, I had read of similar cases of "head" music. "There are several possibilites, Mrs. Holloway," I said, speaking loudly and distinctly while I fastened the pressure cuff to her arm, "but the best bet is that the music really *is* all in your head."

I smiled at the *bon mot*, but all the wire went out of her and she sagged shapelessly in her chair. Her right hand went to her forehead and squeezed. Her eyes twisted tight shut. "Oh, no," she muttered. "Oh, dear God, no. It's finally happened."

Mossbacks have no sense of humor. "Please, Mrs. Holloway! I didn't mean 'in your head' like that. I meant the fillings in your teeth. A pun. Fillings sometimes act like crystal radios and pick up broadcast signals, vibrating the small bones of the middle ear. You are most likely picking up a local radio station. Perhaps a dentist could . . ."

She looked up at me and her eyes burned. "That was a wicked joke to pull, boy. It was cruel."

"I didn't mean it that way—"

"And I know all about fillings and radios and such," she snapped. "Will

Hickey had that problem here five years ago. But that can't be why I hear music." And she extruded a ghastly set of false teeth.

"Well, then—"

"And what sort of radio station could it be? Swing tunes all the time, and only those that I know? Over and over, all night long, with no interruptions. No commercials. No announcements of song titles or performers." She raised her free hand to block her ear, a futile gesture, because the music was on the other side.

On the other side of the ear . . . ? I recalled certain case studies from medical school. Odd cases. "There are other possibilities," I said. "Neurological problems . . ." I pumped the bulb and she winced as the cuff tightened. She lowered her hand slowly and looked at me.

"Neuro . . . ?" Her voice trembled.

"Fossil memories," I said.

She shook her head. "I ain't—I'm not rememberin'. I'm hearin'. I know the difference."

I let the air out of the cuff and unfastened it. "I will explain as simply as I can. Hearing occurs in the brain, not the ear. Sound waves vibrate certain bones in your middle ear. These vibrations are converted into neural impulses and conveyed to the auditory cortex by the eighth cranial nerve. It is the auditory cortex that creates 'sound.' If the nerve were connected to the brain's olfactory region, instead, you would 'smell' music."

She grunted. "Quite a bit of it smells, these days."

Hah, hah. "The point is that the sensory cortices can be stimulated without external input. Severe migraines, for example, often cause people to 'see' visions or 'hear' voices. And sometimes the stimulus reactivates so-called 'fossil' memories, which your mind interprets as contemporary. That may be what you are experiencing."

She looked a little to the side, not saying anything. I listened to her wheezy breath. Then she gave me a glance, quick, almost shy. "Then, you don't think I'm . . . You know . . . Crazy?" Have you ever heard hope and fear fused into a single question? I don't know. At her age, I think I might prefer a pleasant fantasy world over the dingy real one.

"It's unlikely," I told her. "Such people usually hear voices, not music. If you were going insane, you wouldn't hear Benny Goodman tunes; you would hear Benny Goodman—probably giving you important instructions."

A smile twitched her lips, and she seemed calmer, though still uneasy. "It's always been a bother to me," she said quietly, looking past me, "the notion that I might be—well, you know. All my life, it seems, as far back as I can remember."

Which was not that far, the director had told me that morning. "All your life. Why is that?"

She looked away and did not speak for a moment. When she did, she said, "I haven't had no, any, headaches, Doc. And I don't have any now. If that's what did it, how come I can still hear the music?"

If she did not want to talk about her fears, that was fine with me. I was no psychiatrist, anyway. "I can't be sure without further tests, but a trigger event—possibly even a mild stroke—could have initiated the process." I had been carefully observing her motor functions, but I could detect none of the slackness or slurring of the voice typical of severe hemiplegia. "Dr. Wing is the resident neurologist at the hospital," I said. "I'll consult with him."

She looked suddenly alarmed, and shook her head. "No hospitals," she said firmly. "Folks go to hospitals, they die."

At her age, that was largely true. I sighed. "Perhaps at Khan's clinic, then. There really are some tests we should run."

That seemed to calm her somewhat, for she closed her eyes and her lips moved slightly.

"Have you experienced any loss of appetite, or episodes of drowsiness?" I asked. "Have you become irritable, forgetful, less alert?" Useless questions. What geezer did not have those symptoms? I would have to inquire among the staff to find out if there had been a recent change in her behavior.

And she wasn't listening anymore. At least, not to me. "Thank you, Dr. Wilkes. I was so afraid . . . That music . . . But only a stroke, only a stroke. It's such a relief. Thank you. Such a relief."

A relief? Compared to madness, I suppose it was. She struggled to her feet, still babbling. When she left my office, hobbling once more over her walking stick, she was humming to herself again. I didn't know the tune.

> *Are you lonesome tonight? Do you miss me tonight?*
> *Are you sorry we drifted apart?*
> *Does your memory stray to a bright summer day*
> *When I kissed you and called you sweetheart?*

It was dark when I arrived home. As I turned into the driveway, I hit the dashboard remote, and the garage door rose up like a welcoming lover. I slid into the left-hand slot without slowing, easing the Lincoln to a halt just as the tennis ball, hanging by a string from the ceiling, touched the windshield. Brenda never understood that. Brenda always came to a complete stop in the driveway before raising the garage door.

I could see without looking that I had beaten her home again. And they said doctors kept long hours . . . When I stepped from the car, I turned my back on the empty slot.

I stood for some moments at the door to the kitchen, jiggling the car keys in my hand. Then, instead of entering the house, I turned and left the garage through the backyard door. I had seen the second-story light on as I came down the street. Deirdre's room. Tonight, for some reason, I couldn't face going inside just yet.

The backyard was a gloom of emerald and jade. The house blocked the glare of the streetlamps, conceding just enough light to tease shape from shadow. I walked slowly through the damp grass toward the back of the lot. Glowing clouds undulated in the water of the swimming pool, as if the ground had opened up and swallowed the night sky. Only a few stars poked through the overcast. Polaris? Sirius? I had no way of knowing. I doubted that half a dozen people in the township knew the stars by name, or perhaps even that they had names. We have become strangers to our skies.

At the back of the lot, the property met a patch of woodland—a bit of unofficial greenbelt, undeveloped because it was inaccessible from the road. Squirrels lived there, and blue jays and cardinals. And possum and skunk, too. I listened to the rustle of the night dwellers passing through the carpet of dead leaves. Through the trees I could make out the lights of the house opposite. Distant music and muffled voices. Henry and Barbara Carter were throwing a party.

That damned old woman . . . Damn all of them. Shambling, crackling, brittle, dried-out old husks, clinging fingernail-tight to what was left of life . . .

I jammed my hands in my pockets and stood there. For how long, I do not know. It might have been five minutes or half an hour. Finally the light on the second floor went out. Then I turned back to the house and reentered through the garage. The right-hand stall was still empty.

·　　·　　·

Consuela sat at the kitchen table near the French doors, cradling a ceramic mug shaped like an Olmec head. Half the live-in nurses in the country are Latin; and half of those are named Consuela. The odor of cocoa filled the room, and the steam from the cup wreathed her broad, flat face, lending it a sheen. More *Indio* than *Ladino,* her complexion contrasted starkly with her nurse's whites. Her jet black hair was pulled severely back, and was held in place with a plain, wooden pin.

"Good evening, Nurse," I said. "Is Dee-dee down for the night?"

"Yes, Doctor. She is."

I glanced up at the ceiling. "I usually tuck her in."

She gave me an odd look. "Yes, you do."

"Well. I was running a little late today. Did she miss me?"

Consuela looked through the French doors at the backyard. "She did."

"I'll make it up to her tomorrow."

She nodded. "I'm sure she would like that."

I shed my coat and carried it to the hall closet. A dim night-light glowed at the top of the stairwell. "Has Mrs. Wilkes called?"

"An hour ago." Consuela's voice drifted down the hallway from the kitchen. "She has a big case to prepare for tomorrow. She will be late."

I hung the coat on the closet rack and stood quietly still for a moment before closing the door. Another big case. I studied the stairs to the upper floor. Brenda had begun getting the big cases when Deirdre was eighteen months and alopecia had set in. Brenda never tucked Dee-dee into bed after that.

Consuela was washing her cup at the sink when I returned to the kitchen. She was short and dark and stocky. Not quite chubby, but with a roundness that scorned New York and Paris fashion. I rummaged in the freezer for a frozen dinner. Brenda had picked Consuela from among a dozen applicants. Brenda was tall and thin and blond.

I put the dinner in the microwave and started the radiation. "I met an interesting woman today," I said.

Consuela dried her cup and hung it on the rack. "All women are interesting," she said.

"This one hears music in her head." I saw how that piqued her interest.

"We all do," she said, half-turned to go.

I carried my microwaved meal and sat at the table. "Not like this. Not like hearing a radio at top volume."

She hesitated a moment longer; then she shrugged and sat across the table from me. "Tell me of this woman."

I moved the macaroni and cheese around on my plate. "I spoke with Dr. Wing over the car phone. He believes it may be a case of 'incontinent nostalgia,' or Jackson's Syndrome."

I explained how trauma to the temporal lobe sometimes caused spontaneous upwellings of memory, often accompanied by "dreamy states" and feelings of profound and poignant joy. Oliver Sacks had written about it in one of his best-sellers. "Shostakovitch had a splinter in his left temporal lobe," I said. "When he cocked his head, he heard melodies. And there have been other cases. Stephen Foster, perhaps." I took a bite of my meal. "Odd, isn't it, how often the memories are musical."

Consuela nodded. "Sometimes the music is enough."

"Other memories may follow, though."

"Sometimes the music is enough," she repeated enigmatically.

"It should make the old lady happy, at least."

Consuela gave me a curious look. "Why should it make her happy?" she asked.

"She has forgotten her early years completely. This condition may help her remember." An old lady reliving her childhood. Suddenly there was bitterness in my mouth. I dropped my fork into the serving tray.

Consuela shook her head. "Why should it make her happy?" she asked again.

I'm telling you, Jack, Great days are back.
Take the word of a bird with an ear.

The universe balances. For every Consuela Montejo there is a Noor Khan.

Dr. Noor Khan was a crane, all bones and joints. She was tall, almost as tall as I, but thin to the point of gauntness. She cocked her head habitually from side to side. That, the bulging eyes, and the hooked nose accentuated her birdlike appearance. A good run, a flapping of the arms, and she might take squawking flight—and perhaps appear more graceful.

"Mae Holloway. Oh, my, yes. She is a feisty one, is she not?" Khan rooted in her filing cabinet, her head bobbing as she talked. "Does she have a problem?"

"Incontinent nostalgia, it's sometimes called," I said. "She is experiencing spontaneous, musical recollections, possibly triggered by a mild stroke to the temporal lobes." I told her about the music and Wing's theories.

She bobbed her head. "Curious. Like *déjà vu*, only different." Then, more sternly. "If she has had a stroke, even a mild one, I must see her at once."

"I've told her that, but she's stubborn. I thought since you knew her better . . ."

Noor Khan sighed. "Yes. Well, the older we grow, the more set in our ways we become. Mae must be set in concrete."

It was a joke, and I gave it a thin smile. *The older we grow . . .*

The file she finally pulled was a thick one. I took the folder from her and carried it to her desk. I had nothing in particular in mind, just a review of Holloway's medical history. I began paging through the records. In addition to Dr. Khan's notes, there were copies of records from other doctors. I looked up at Khan. "Don't you have patients waiting?"

She raised an eyebrow. "My office hours start at ten, so I have no patients at the moment. You need not worry that I am neglecting them."

If it was a reproof, it was a mild one, and couched in face-saving Oriental terms. I hate it when people watch me read. I always feel as if they were reading over my shoulder. I wanted to tell Khan that I would call her if I needed her; but it was, after all, her office, and I was sitting at her desk, so I don't know what I expected her to do. "Sorry," I said. "I didn't mean to ruffle your feathers."

Holloway was in unusually good health for a woman her age. Her bones had grown brittle and her eyes nearsighted—but no glaucoma; and very little osteoporosis. She had gotten a hearing aid at an age when most people were already either stone deaf or stone dead. Clinical evidence showed that she had once given birth, and that an anciently broken leg had not healed entirely straight. What right had she to enjoy such good health?

Khan had been on the phone. "Mae has agreed to come in," she told me as she hung up. "I will send the van to pick her up on Tuesday. I wish I could do a CAT scan here. I would hate to force her into hospital."

"It's a waste, anyway," I muttered.

"What?"

I clamped my jaw shut. All that high technology, and for what? To add a few miserable months to lives already years too long? How many dollars per day of life was that? How much of it was producitvely returned? That governor, years ago. What was his name? Lamm? He said that the old had a duty to die and make room for the young. "Nothing," I said.

"What is wrong?" asked Khan.

"There's nothing wrong with me."

"That wasn't what I asked."

I turned my attention to the folder and squinted at the spidery, illegible handwriting on the oldest record: 1962, if the date was really what it looked like. Why did so many doctors have poor handwriting? Holloway's estimated age looked more like an 85 than a 65. I waved the sheet of stationery at her. "Look at the handwriting on this," I complained. "It's like reading Sanskrit."

Khan took the letter. "I can read Sanskrit, a little," she said with a smile. "It's Dr. Bench's memo, isn't it? Yes, I thought so. I found it when I assumed Dr. Rosenblum's practice a few years ago. Dr. Bench promised he would send Mrs. Holloway's older records, but he never did, so Howard had to start a medical history almost from scratch, with only this capsule summary."

I took the sheet back from her. "Why didn't Bench follow through?"

She shrugged. "Who knows? He put it off. Then one of those California brushfires destroyed his office. Medically, Mae is a blank before 1962."

Just like her mind, I thought. Just like her mind.

> "Why should a Sheik learn how to speak
> Latin and Greek badly?
> Give him a neat motto complete
> 'Say it with feet gladly.' "

The third time I saw Mae Holloway, she was waiting by the clinic door when I arrived to open it. Eyes closed, propped against the wall by her walking stick, she hummed an obscure melody. "Good morning, Mrs. Holloway," I said. "Feeling better today?"

She opened her eyes and squeezed her face into a ghastly pucker. "Consarn music kept me awake again last night."

I gave her a pleasant smile. "Too bad you don't hear Easy Listening." I stepped through the door ahead of her. I heard her cane tap-tap-tapping behind me and wondered if a practiced ear could identify an oldster by her distinctive cane tap. I could imagine Tonto, ear pressed to the ground. "Many geezer come this way, *kemo sabe*."

Snapping open my briefcase, I extracted my journals and stacked them on the desk. Mae lowered herself into the visitor's chair. "Jimmy Kovacs will be coming in to see you later today. He threw his back out again."

I opened the issue of the *Brain* that Dr. Wing had lent me. "Never throw anything out that you might need again later," I said, running my eye down the table of contents.

"You do study on those books, Doctor."

"I like to keep up on things."

I flipped the journal open to the article I had been seeking and began to read. After a few minutes, she spoke again. "If you spent half the time studying on people as you do studying on books, you'd be better at doctorin'."

I looked up scowling. Who was she to judge? A bent-up, shriveled old woman who had seen more years than she had a right to. "The body is an intricate machine," I told her. "The more thoroughly I understand its mechanisms, the better able I am to repair it."

"A machine," she repeated.

"Like an automobile."

"And you're jest an auto mechanic." She shook her head.

I smiled, but without humor. "Yes, I am. Maybe that's less glamorous than being a godlike healer, but I think it's closer to the truth." An auto mechanic. And some cars were old jalopies destined for the junk heap; so why put more work into them? I did not tell her that. And others were not built right to begin with. I did not tell her that, either. It was a cold vision, but in its way, comforting. Helplessness is greater solace than failure.

Mae grunted. "Mostly milk sours 'cause it's old."

I scowled again. More hillbilly philosophy? Or simply an addled mind unable to hold to a topic? "Does it," I said.

She studied me for a long while without speaking. Finally, she shook her head. "Most car accidents are caused by the driver."

"I'll pass that along to the National Transportation Safety Board."

"What I mean is, you might pay as much attention to the driver as to the automobile."

I sighed and laid the journal aside. "I take it that you want to tell me what is playing on your personal Top 40 today."

She snorted, but I could see that she really did. I leaned back in my chair and linked my hands behind my head. "So, tell me, Mrs. Holloway, what is 'shaking'?"

She made fish faces with her lips. Mentally, I had dubbed her Granny Guppy when she did that. It was as if she had to flex her lips first to ready them for the arduous task of flapping.

" 'Does Your Mother Know You're Out, Cecelia?' "

"What?" It took a moment. Then I realized that it must have been a song title. Some popular ditty now thankfully forgotten by everyone save this one old lady. "Was that a favorite song of yours?" I asked.

She shook her head. "Oh, mercy, no; but there was a year when you couldn't hardly avoid it."

"I see."

"And, let's see . . ." She stopped and cocked her head. The Listening Look, I called it. "Now it's 'The Red, Red Robin' —"

"Comes bob-bob-bobbing along?"

"Yes, that's the one. And already today I've heard 'Don't Bring Lulu' and 'Side by Side' and 'Kitten on the Keys' and 'Bye-bye Blackbird.' " She made a pout with her lips. "I do wish the songs would play out entirely."

"You told me they weren't your favorite songs."

"Some are, some aren't. They're just songs I once heard. Sometimes they remind me of things. Sometimes it seems as if they *almost* remind me of things. Things long forgotten, but waiting for me, just around a corner somewhere." She shook herself suddenly. "Tin Pan Alley wasn't my favorite, though," she went on. "I was a sheba. I went for the wild stuff. The Charleston; the Black Bottom. All those side kicks . . . I was a little old for that, but . . . Those were wild days, I tell you. Hip flasks and stockings rolled down and toss away the corset." She gave me a wink.

This . . . *prune* had gone for the wild stuff? Though, grant her, she had had her youth once. It didn't seem fair that she should have it twice. "Sheba?" I asked.

"A sheba," she said. "A flapper. The men were sheiks. Because of that . . . What was his name?" She tapped her cane staccato on the floor. "Valentino, that was it. Valentino. Oh, those eyes of his! All the younger girls dreamed about having him; and I wouldn't have minded one bit, myself. He had It."

"It?"

"It. Valentino drove the girls wild, he did. And a few boys, too. Clara Bow had It, too."

"Sex appeal?"

"Pshaw. Sex appeal is for snugglepups. A gal didn't have It unless both sexes felt something. Women, too. Women were coming out back then. We could smoke, pet, put a bun on if we wanted to—least, 'til the dries put on the kabosh. We had the vote. Why we even had a governor, back in Wyoming, where I once lived. Nellie Taylor Ross. I met her once, did I tell you? Why I remember—"

Her sudden silence piqued me. "You remember what?"

"Doc?" Her voice quavered and her eyes looked right past me, wide as tunnels.

"What is it?"

"Doc? I can see 'em. Plain as day."

"See whom, Mrs. Holloway?" Was the old biddy having a seizure right there in my office?

She looked to her left, then her right. "We're sitting in the gallery," she announced. "All of us wearing pants, too, 'stead o' dresses. And down there . . . Down there . . ." She aimed a shaking finger at a point somewhere below my desk. "That's Alice with the gavel. Law's sake! They're ghosts, Doc. They're ghosts all around me!"

"Mrs. Holloway," I said. "Mrs. Holloway, close your eyes."

She turned to me. "What?"

"Close your eyes."

She did. "I can still see 'em," she said, with a wonder that was close to terror. "I can still see 'em. Like my eyes were still open." She raised a shaking hand to her mouth. Her ragged breath slowly calmed and, more quietly, she repeated, "I can still see 'em." A heartbeat went by, then she sighed. "They're fading, now," she said. "Fading." Finally, she opened her eyes. She looked troubled. "Doc, what happened to me? Was it a hallucynation?"

I leaned back in my chair and folded my hands under my chin. "Not quite. Simply a nonmusical memory."

"But . . . It was so *real*, like I done traveled back in time."

"You were here the whole time," I assured her with a grin.

She struck the floor with her cane. "I know that. I could see you just as plain as I could see Alice and the others."

I sighed. Her sense of humor had dried out along with the rest of her. "Patients with your condition sometimes fall into 'dreamy states,' " I explained. They see or hear their present and their remembered surroundings simultaneously, like a film that has been double-exposed. Hughlings Jackson described the symptom in 1880. He called it a 'doubling of consciousness.' " I smiled and tapped the journal Wing had given me. "Comes from studying on books," I said.

But she wasn't paying me attention. "I remember it all so clearly now. I'd forgotten. Alice Robertson of Oklahoma was the first woman to preside over the House of Representatives. June 20, 1921, it was. Temporary Speaker. Oh, those were a fine fifteen minutes, I tell you." She sighed and shook her head. "I wonder," she said. "I wonder if I might remember my ma and pa and my little brother. Zach . . . ? Was that his name? It's always been a trouble to me that I've forgotten. It don't seem right to forget your own kin."

An inverse square law, I suppose. Memories dim and blur with age, their strength depending on distance and mass. Too many of Mae's memories were too distant. They had passed beyond the horizon of her mind, and had faded like an old photograph left too long in the sun. And yet sometimes, near the end, like ashes collapsing in a dying fire, the past can become brighter than the present.

"No," I said. "It don't seem right."

"And Mister . . . Haven't thought on that man in donkey's years," she said. "Green Holloway was my man. I always called him Mister. He called me his Lorena."

"Lorena?"

Mae shrugged. "I don't remember why. There was a song . . . He took the name from that. It was real popular, so I suppose I'll recollect it by and by. He was an older man, was Mister. I remember him striding up through Black's hell—gray and grizzled, but strong as splo. All brass and buckles in his state militia uniform. Company H, 5th Tennessee. Just that one scene has stayed with me all my life, like an old brown photograph. Dear Lord, but that man had arms like cooper's bands. I can close my eyes and feel them around me sometimes, even today." She shivered and looked down.

"Splo?" I prompted.

"Splo," she repeated in a distracted voice. Then, more strongly, as if shoving some memory aside, "Angel teat. We called it apple john back then. Mister kept a still out behind the joe. Whenever he run off a batch, he'd invite the spear-side over and we'd all get screwed."

I bet. Whatever she had said. "Apple john was moonshine?" *Hightail it, Luke. The revenooers are a-coming.* What kind of Barney Google life had she led up in those Tennessee hills? "So when you say you got screwed, you mean you got drunk, not, uh . . ."

Mae sucked in her lips and gnawed on them. "It was good whilst we were together," she said at last. "Right good." Her lips thinned. "But Mister, he lit a shuck on me, just like all the others." She gave me a look, half-angry, half-wary; and I could almost see the shutter come down behind her eyes. "Ain't no use getting close to nobody," she said. "They're always gone when you need them. Why, I ain't, haven't seen Little Zach nigh unto . . ." She looked momentarily confused. "Not for years and years. I loved that boy like he was more'n a brother; but he yondered off and never come back." She creaked to her feet. "So, I'll just twenty-three skidoo, Jack. You got things to do; so do I."

I watched her go, thinking she was right about one thing. Old milk does go sour.

> *Would you like to swing on a star?*
> *Carry moonbeams home in a jar?*
> *And be better off than you are?*
> *Or would you rather be a mule?*

Brenda's silver Beemer was parked in the garage when I got home. I pulled up beside it and contemplated its shiny perfection as I turned my engine off. Brenda was home. How long had it been, now? Three weeks? Four? It was hard to remember. Leave early; back late. That was our life. A quick peck in the morning and no-time-for-breakfast-dear. Tiptoes late at night; and the sheets rustle and the mattress sags; and it was hardly enough even to ruffle your sleep. Always on the run; always working late. One of us would have to slow down, or we might never meet at all.

My first thought was that I might give Consuela the night off. It had been so long since Brenda and I had been alone together. My second thought was that she had gotten in trouble at the office and had lost her job.

Doctors make good money. Lawyers make good money. Doctors married to lawyers make *very* good money. It was not enough.

"Brenda?" I called as I entered the kitchen from the garage. "I'm home!" There was no one in the kitchen, though something tangy with orange and sage was baking in the oven. "Brenda?" I called again as I reached the hall closet.

A squeal from upstairs. "Daddy's home!"

I hung up my overcoat. "Hello, Dee-dee. Is Mommy with you?" Unlikely, but possible. Stranger things have happened.

"No." Followed by a long silence. "Connie is telling me a story, about a mule and an ox."

Another silence; then footsteps on the stairs. Consuela looked at me over the banister as she descended.

"The mule and the ox?" I said.

"Nothing," she replied curtly. "An old Mayan folk tale."

"Where's Brenda?" I asked her. "I know she's home; her car is in the garage." Maybe she was in the backyard; by the pool or in the woods.

No, she didn't like the woods; she was afraid of deer ticks.

"Mrs. Wilkes came home early," Consuela said, "and packed a bag—"

Mentally, I froze. Not *this*. Not *now*. Without Brenda's income . . . "Packed a bag? Why?"

"She said she must go to Washington for a few days, to assist in an argument before the Supreme Court."

"Oh." Sudden relief coupled with sudden irritation. She could have phoned. At the Home. In my car. I showed Consuela my teeth. "The Supreme Court, you say. Well. That's quite a feather in her cap."

"Were she an Indio, a feather in the cap might mean something."

"Consuela. A joke? Did Brenda say when she would be back?"

Consuela hesitated, then shook her head. "She came home; packed her bag; gave me instructions. When the car arrived, she left."

And never said good-bye to Dee-dee. Maybe a wave from the doorway, a crueler good-bye than none at all. "What sort of instructions?" That wasn't the question I wanted to ask. I wanted to ask whose car had picked her up. Whom she was assisting in Washington? Walther Crowe, the steel-eyed senior partner with the smooth, European mannerisms? FitzPatrick, the young comer who figured so often on the society pages? But Consuela would not know; or, if she did, she would not say. There were some places where an outsider did not deliberately set herself.

"The sort of instructions," she replied, "that are unnecessary to give a professional. But they were only to let me know that I was her employee."

"You're angry." I received no answer. Then I asked, "Have you and Deedee eaten yet?"

"No." A short answer, not quite a retort.

"I didn't pull rank on you. Brenda did."

She shrugged and looked up at me with her head cocked to the side. "You are a doctor; I am a nurse. We have a professional relationship. Mrs. Wilkes is only an employer."

She was in a bad mood. I had never seen her angry before. I wondered what patronizing tone Brenda had used with her. I always made the effort to treat Consuela as an equal; but Brenda seldom did. Sometimes I thought Brenda was half-afraid of our Deirdre's nurse; though for what reason, I could not say. I glanced at the overcoat in the closet. "Would you and Deedee like to go out to eat?"

She gave me a thoughtful look; then shook her head. "She will not leave the house."

I glanced at the stairs. "No, she'll not budge, will she?" It was an old argument, never won. "She can play outside. She can go to school with the other children. There is no medical reason to stay in her—"

"There is something wrong with her heart."

"No, it's too soon for—"

"There is something wrong with her heart," she repeated.

"Oh." I looked away. "But . . . We'll eat in the dining room today. The three of us. Whatever that is you have in the oven. I'll set the table with the good dinnerware."

"A special occasion?"

I shook my head. "No. Only maybe we each have a reason to be unhappy just now." I wondered if Brenda had left a message in the bedroom. Some hint as to when she'd return. I headed toward the dining room.

"The ox was weary of plowing," Consuela said.

"Eh?" I turned and looked back at her. "What was that?"

"The ox was weary of plowing. All day, up the field and down, while the farmer cracked the whip behind him. Each night in the barn, when the ox complained, the mule would laugh. 'If you detest the plowing so much, why do it?' 'It is my job, señor mule,' the ox would reply. 'Then do it and don't complain. Otherwise, refuse. Go on strike.' The ox thought about this and, several days later, when the farmer came to him with the harness, the ox would not budge. 'What is wrong, señor ox?' the farmer asked him. 'I am on strike,' the ox replied. 'All day I plow with no rest. I deserve a rest.' The farmer nodded. 'There is justice in what you say. You have worked hard. Yet the fields must be plowed before the rains come.' And so he hitched the mule to the plow and cracked the whip over him and worked him for many weeks until the plowing was done."

Consuela stopped and, with a slight gesture of the head, turned for the kitchen.

Although entitled to two evenings a week off, Consuela seldom took them, preferring the solitude of her own room. She lived there quietly, usually with the hall door closed, always with the connecting door to Dee-dee's room open. Once a month, she sent a check to Guatemala. She read books. Sometimes she played softly on a sort of flute: weird, serpentine melodies that she had brought with her from the jungle. More than once, the strange notes had caused Brenda to stop whatever she was doing, whether mending or reading law or even making love, and listen with her head cocked until the music stopped. Then she would shiver slightly, and resume whatever she had been doing as though nothing had happened.

Consuela had furnished her room with Meso-American bric-a-brac. Colorful, twisty things. Statuettes, wall hangings, a window treatment. Squat little figurines with secretive, knowing smiles. A garland of fabric flowers. An obsidian carving that suggested a panther in mid-leap. Brenda found it all vaguely disturbing, as if she expected chittering monkeys swinging from the bookshelves and curtains, as if Consuela had brought a part of the jungle with her into Brenda's clear, ordered, rational world. It wasn't proper, at all. It was somehow out of control.

"Did you like having dinner downstairs today?" I asked Dee-dee as I studied Consuela's room through the connecting door. The flute lay silent on Consuela's dresser top. It was the kind you blew straight into, with two rows of holes, one for each hand.

"It was okay, I guess." A weak voice, steady but faint.

I turned around. "Only okay?" There was an odd contrast here, a paradox. Although it was evening and Deirdre's room was shrouded in darkness, Consuela's room had seemed bright with rioting colors.

"Did I leave any toys downstairs?" A worried voice in the darkness. Anxious.

"No, I checked." I resolved to check again, just in case we had overlooked something that had rolled under the sofa. Brenda detested disorder. She did not like finding things out of place.

"Mommy won't mind, will she? That I ate downstairs."

I turned. "Not if we don't tell her. Mommy will be at the Supreme Court for a few days."

Dee-dee made a sound in her throat. No sorrow, no joy. Just acknowledgment. Mommy might never come home at all for all the difference it made in Dee-dee's life. "Ready to be tucked in?"

Dee-dee grinned a delicious smile and snuggled deeper into the sheets. It was a heartbreaking smile. I gave her back the best one I could muster, and took a long, slow step toward her bed. She shrieked and ducked under the covers. I waited until she peeked out and took another step. It was a game we played, every move as encrusted with ritual as a Roman Mass.

Hutchinson-Gilford Syndrome. Dee-dee's smile was snaggle-toothed. Her hair, sparse; her skin, thin and yellow.

Manifestations: Alopecia, onset at birth to eighteen months, with degeneration of hair follicles. Thin skin. Hypoplasia of the nails . . . I had read the entry in *Smith's* over and over, looking for the one item I had missed, the loophole I had overlooked. It was committed to memory now; like a mantra. *Periarticular fibrosis; stiff or partially flexed prominent joints. Skeletal hypoplasia, dysphasia and degeneration.*

Dee-dee had weighed 2.7 kilos at birth. Her fontanel had ossified late, but the slowness of her growth had not become apparent until seven months. She lagged the normal growth charts by one-third. When she lost hair, it did not grow back. Her skin had brownish yellow "liver" spots.

Natural history: Deficit of growth becomes severe after one year. The tendency to fatigue easily may limit participation in childhood activities. Intelligence and brain development are unimpaired.

Deirdre Wilkes was an alert, active mind trapped in a body aging far too quickly. A shrunken little gnome of a ten-year-old. *Etiology: Unknown.* I hugged her and kissed her on the cheek. Then I tucked the sheets tightly under the mattress.

Prognosis: The life span is shortened by relentless arterial atheromatosis. Death usually occurs at puberty.

There were no papers delivered on Hutchinson-Gilford that I had not crawled through word after word, searching for the slightest whisper of a breakthrough. Some sign along the horizon of research. But there were no hints. There were no loopholes.

Prognosis: death.

There were no exceptions.

Deirdre could smile because she was only a child and could not comprehend what was happening to her body. She knew she would have to "go away" someday, but she didn't know what that really meant.

Smiling was the hardest part of the game.

> *Come along, Josephine, In my flying machine.*
> *We'll go up in the air . . .*

How can I explain the feelings of dread and depression that enveloped me every time I entered Sunny Dale? I was surrounded by ancients. Bent, gray, hobbling creatures forever muttering over events long forgotten or families never seen. And always repeating their statements, always repeating their statements, as if it were I who were hard of hearing and not they. The Home was a waiting room for Death. Waiting and waiting, until they had done with waiting. Here is where the yellowed skin and the liver spots belonged. Here! Not on the frame of a ten-year-old.

The fourth time I saw Mae Holloway, she crept up behind me as I opened the door to the clinic. "Morning, Doc," I heard her say.

"Good morning, Mrs. H.," I replied without turning around. I opened the door and stepped through. Inevitably, she followed, humming. I wondered if this was going to become a daily ritual. She planted herself in the visitor's chair. Somehow, it had become her own. "The show just ended," she announced. "Oh, it was a peach." She waved a hand at my desk. "Go on, set down. Make yourself pleasant."

It was my own fault, really. I had shown an interest in her tiresome recollections, and now she felt she had to share everything with me, as if I were one of her batty old cronies. No good deed goes unpunished. Perhaps I was the only one who put up with her.

But I did have a notion that could wring a little use out of my sentence. I could write a book about Mae Holloway and her musical memories. People were fascinated with how the mind worked; or, rather, with how it failed to work. Sacks had described similar cases of incontinent nostalgia in one of his books; and if he could make the best-seller lists with a collection of neurological case studies, why not I? With fame, came money, and the things money could buy.

But my book would have to be something new, something different, not just a retelling of the same neurological tales. The teleology, perhaps. Sacks had failed to discover any meaning to the music his patients had heard, any reason *why* this tune or that was rememb-heard. If I kept a record, I might discover enough of a pattern to form the basis of a book. I rummaged in my desk drawer and took out a set of file cards that I had bought to make notes on my patients. Might as well get started. I poised my pen over a card. "What show was that?" I asked.

"*Girl of the Golden West.* David Belasco's new stage play." She shook her head. "I first seen it, oh, years and years ago, in Pittsburgh; before they made it a highfalutin opera. That final scene, where Dick Johnson is hiding in the attic, and his blood drips through the ceiling onto the sheriff . . . That was taken from real life, you know."

"Was it." I wrote *Girl of the Golden West* and *doubling episode* and made a note to look it up. Then I poised my pen over a fresh card. "I'd like to ask you a few questions about your music, Mrs. Holloway. That is, if you don't mind."

She gave me a surprised glance and looked secretly pleased. She fussed with her gown and settled herself into her seat. "You may fire when ready, Gridley."

"You *are* still hearing the music, aren't you, Mrs. Holloway?"

"Well, the songs aren't so loud as they were. They don't keep me awake anymore; but if I concentrate, I can hear 'em."

I made a note. "You've learned to filter them out, that's all."

" 'If You Talk in Your Sleep, Don't Mention My Name.' "

"What?"

" 'If You Talk in Your Sleep, Don't Mention My Name.' That was one of 'em. The tunes I been hearing. Go on, write that down. Songs were getting real speedy in those days. There was 'Mary Took the Calves to the Dairy Show' and 'This is No Place for a Minister's Son.' Heh-heh. The blues was all in a lather over 'em. That, and actor-folks actually kissing each other in the moving picture shows. They tried to get that banned. And the animal dances, too."

"Animal dances?"

"Oh, there were a passel of 'em," she said. "There was the kangaroo dip, the crab step, the fox trot, the fish walk, the bunny hug, the lame duck . . . I don't remember them all."

"The fox trot," I offered. "I think people still dance that."

Mae snorted. "All the fire's out of it. You should have read what the preachers and the newspapers had to say about it back then. They sure were peeved; but the kids thought it was flossy. It was a way to get their parents' goat. 'Bug them,' I guess you say now."

"Kids? Isn't the fox trot a ballroom dance for, well, you know—mature people?"

She made her sour-lemon face. "Sure. Now. But today's old folks were yesterday's kids. And they still like the music they liked when they were young. Heh-heh. When you're ninety or a hundred, sonny, you'll be a-listening to that acid rock stuff and telling your grandkids what hell-raisers you used to be. And they won't believe you, either. We tote the same bags with us all our lives, Doc. The same interests; the same likes and dislikes. Those older'n us and those younger'n us, why, they have their own bags." A sudden scowl, halfway between fright and puzzlement, passed across her face like the shadow of a cloud. Then she hunched her shoulders. "Me, I've got too many bags."

She'd get no argument from me on that. "Have you heard any other songs?" I asked.

She folded her hands over the knob of her walking stick and rested her chin on them. "Let's see . . . Yesterday, I heared, heard 'Waiting for the Robert E. Lee' and 'A Perfect Day.' Those were real popular, once. And lots of Cohan songs. 'Oh, it was Mary, Mary, long before the fashion changed . . .' And 'Rosie O'Grady.' Then there was 'Memphis Blues.' Young folks thought it was 'hep.' Even better than ragtime."

She shook her head. "I never cottoned too well to those kids, though," she said. "They remind me of the kids nowadays. A little too . . . What do they say now? 'Close to the edge.' Ran wild when they were young 'uns, they did. Hung around barbershops. Hawked papers as newsies. Worked the growler for their old man."

I looked up from my notes. "Worked the growler?"

"Took the beer bucket to the saloon to get it filled. Imagine sending a child—even girls!—into a saloon! No wonder Carrie and the others wanted to close 'em up. Maybe folks my age were a little too stuck on ourselves, like the younger folks said; but at least we had principles. With us, it wasn't all just to have a good time. We fought for things worth fighting for. Suffrage. Prohibition. Birth control. Oh, those were times, I tell you. Maggie, making those speeches about birth control and standing up there on the stage that one time with the tape over her mouth, because they wouldn't let her talk. I helped her open that clinic of hers over in Brooklyn, though I never did care for her attitude about Jews and coloreds. Controlling 'undesirables' wasn't the real reason for birth control, anyway."

"Mrs. Holloway!"

She looked at me and laughed. "Now, don't tell me your generation is shocked at such talk!"

"It's not that. It's . . ."

"That old folks wrangled over it, too? Well, folks aren't born old. We were young, too; and as full of piss and vinegar as anyone else. I read *Moral Physiology* when it first come out; though Mister did try mightily to discourage me. And, later, there was *The Unwelcomed Child*. Doc, if men had babies, birth control would never have been a crime."

Folks aren't born old . . . I squared off my deck of index cards. "I suppose not." My generation had been as strong as any for civil rights and feminism. Certainly stronger than the hard-edged, cynics coming up behind us. It sounded as if Mae had had a similar generational experience. Though, that would put her in the generation *before* the hell-raising Lost Generation. What was it called? The Missionary Generation? Maybe she was older than she looked; though that hardly seemed possible. "Let's get back to the songs—" I suggested.

"Yes, the songs," she said. "The songs. Why, I recollect a man had a right good voice . . . Now what was his name . . . ? A wonderful dancer, too."

"Ben Wickham?" I suggested.

"No. No, Ben was later. This was out Pittsburgh way. Joe Paxton. That was it." She tilted her head back. "He was a barnstormer, Joe was. He knew 'em all. Calbraith Rodgers, Glenn Curtiss, Pancho Barnes, even Wilbur Wright. Took me up once, through the Alleghenies. Oh, my, that was something, let me tell you. The wind in your face and the ground drifting by beneath you, and the golden sun peeking between the shoulders of the hills . . . And you felt you were dancing with the clouds." She sighed, and the light in her eyes slowly faded. "But he was like all the rest." Her face closed up, became hard. "I come on him one day packing his valise, and when I asked him why he was cutting out, all he would say was, 'How old is Ann?'"

"What?"

She blinked and focused moistened eyes on me. Slowly, before they could even fall, her tears vanished into the sand of her soul. "Oh, that's what everyone said back then. 'How old is Ann?' It meant 'Who knows?' Came from one of those brain teasers that ran in the *New York Press*. You know. 'If Mary is twice as old as Ann was when Mary . . .' And it goes through all sorts of contortions and ends up 'How old is Ann?' Most folks hadn't the foggiest notion and didn't care, so they started saying 'How old is Ann?' when they didn't know the answer to something." She pushed down on her walking stick and started to rise.

"Wait. I still have a few questions."

"Well, I don't have any more answers. Joe . . . Well, he turned out worthless in the end; but we had some high times together." Then she sighed and looked off into the distance. "And he did take me flying, once, when flying was more than just a ride."

As I was walking down the street, down the street, down the street,
A handsome gal I chanced to meet. Oh, she was fair to view.
Lovely Fan', won't you come out tonight, come out tonight, come out tonight?
Lovely Fan', won't you come out tonight, and dance by the light of the moon?

It was late in the evening—midnight, perhaps—and, dressed in house-coat and slippers, I was frowning over a legal pad and a few dozen index cards, a cup of cold coffee beside me on the kitchen table. I was surrounded by small, sourceless sounds. If you have been in a sleeping building at night, you know what I mean. Creaks and rustlings and the sighs of . . . What? Spirits? Air-circulation vents? The soft groan of settling timbers. The breath of the wind against the windows. The staccato scritching of tiny night creatures dancing across the roof shingles. The distant rumble of a red-eye flight making its descent into the metropolitan area. Among such confused, muttering sounds, who can distinguish the pad of bare feet on the floor?

A gasp, and I turned.

I had never seen Consuela when she was not wearing nurse's whites. Perhaps once or twice, bundled in a coat as she sought one of her rare nights out; but never in a red-and-yellow flowing flowered robe. Never with her black hair unfastened and sweeping around her like a raven-feather cape. She stood in the kitchen doorway, clenching the collar in her fist.

"Consuela," I said.

"I—saw the light on. I thought you had already gone to sleep. So I—" Consuela flustered was a new sight, too. She turned to go. "I did not mean to disturb you."

"No, no. Stay a while." I laid my pen down and stretched. "I couldn't get to sleep, so I came down here to work a while." When she hesitated, I stood and pulled a chair out for her. She gave me a sidelong look, then bobbed her head once and took a seat. I wondered if she thought I might "try something." Late at night; wife away; both of us in pajamas, thoughts of bed in our minds. Hell, *I* wondered if I might try something. Brenda had grown more distant each year since Deirdre's birth.

But Consuela was not my type. She was too short, too wide, too dark. I studied her covertly while I handled her chair. Well, perhaps not "too." And she did have a liquid grace to her, like a panther striding through the jungle. Brenda's grace was of a different sort. Brenda was fireworks arcing and bursting across the night sky. You might get burned, but never bitten.

"Would you like something to drink?" I asked when she had gotten settled. "Apple juice, orange juice." Too late for coffee; and a liqueur would have been inappropriate.

"Orange juice would be fine, thank you," she said.

I went to the refrigerator and removed the carafe. Like everyone else, we buy our OJ in wax-coated paperboard containers; but Brenda transferred the milk, the juices, and half a dozen other articles into carafes and canisters and other more appropriate receptacles. Most people shelved their groceries. We repackaged ours.

"Do you remember the old woman I told you about last week?"

"The one who hears music? Yes."

I brought the glasses to the table. "She's starting to remember other things, now." I told her about Mae's recollections, her consciousness doubling. "I've started to keep track of what she sees and hears," I said, indicating the papers on the table. "And I've sent to the military archives to see if they could locate Green Holloway's service records. Later this week, I plan to go into the city to check the census records at the National Archives."

Consuela picked up the legal pad and glanced at it. "Why are you doing this thing?"

"For verifiction. I'm thinking I might write a book."

She looked at me. "About Mrs. Holloway?"

"Yes. And I think I may have found an angle, too." I pointed to the pad she held. "That is a list of the songs and events Holloway has remembheard."

After a moment's hesitation, Consuela read through the list. She shook her head. "You are looking for meaning in this?" Her voice held a twist of skepticism in it. For a moment, I saw how my activities might look from her perspective. Searching for meaning in the remembered songs of a half-senile old woman. What should that be called, senemancy? Melodimancy? What sort of auguries did High Priest Wilkes find, eviscerating this morning's ditties?

"Not meaning," I said. "Pattern. Explanation. Some way to make sense of what she is going through."

Consuela gave me that blank look she liked to affect. "It may not make sense."

"But it almost does." I riffed the stack of index cards. Each card held information about a song Mae had heard. The composer, songwriter, performer; the date, the topic, the genre. Whether Mae had liked it or not. "The first time she came to me," I said, "she was 'remembhearing' swing tunes from the 1930s. A few days later, it was music of the 'Roaring Twenties.' Then the jazz gave way to George M. Cohan and the 'animal dance' music of the Mauve Decade. Do you see? The songs keep coming from earlier in her life."

"Memphis Blues," 1912. "A Perfect Day," 1910. "Mary Took the Calves to the Dairy Show," 1909. "Rosie O'Grady," 1906. Songs my grandparents heard as children. "East side, west side, All around the town . . ." I remembered how Granny used to sit my brother and me on her lap, one on each knee, and rock us back and forth while she sang that. I paused and cocked my head, listening into the silence of the night.

But I could hear nothing. I could remember *that* she sang it, but I could not remember the singing.

"It is a voyage," I said, loudly, to cover the silence. "A voyage of discovery up the stream of time."

Consuela shook her head. "Rivers have rapids," she said, "and falls."

> *Hello, my baby, hello, my honey, hello, my ragtime gal . . .*
> *Send me a kiss by wire,*
> *Baby, my heart's on fire.*

Mae's morning visits fell into a routine. She settled herself into her chair with an air of proprietorship and croaked out snatches of tunes while I wrote down what I could, recording the rest on a cheap pocket tape recorder I had purchased. She hummed "The Maple Leaf Rag" and "Grace and Beauty" and the "St. Louis Tickle." I suffered through her renditions of "My Gal Sal" and "The Rosary." ("A big hit," she assured me, "for over twenty-five years.") She rememb-heard the bawdy "Hot Time in the Old Town Tonight" (sounding grotesque on her ancient lips), the raggy "You've Been a Good Old Wagon, But You've Done Broke Down," and the poignant "Good-bye, Dolly Gray."

She frowned for a moment. "Or was that 'Nellie Gray'?" Then she shrugged. "Those were happy songs, mostly," she said. "Oh, they were such good songs back then. Not like today, all angry and shouting. Even the sad songs were sweet. Like 'Tell Them That You Saw Me' or 'She's Only a Bird in a Gilded Cage.' And Mister taught me 'Lorena,' once. I wish I could recollect that 'un. And 'Barbry Ellen.' I learned me that 'un when I was knee-high to a grasshopper. Pa told me it was the president's favorite song. The old president, from when his pappy fought in the War. I haven't heard those yet. Or—" She cocked her head to the side. "Well, dad-blast it!"

"What's wrong, Mrs. Holloway?"

"I'm starting to hear coon songs."

"Coon songs!"

She shook her head. "Coon songs. They was—were—all the rage. 'Coon, Coon, Coon' and 'All Coons Look Alike to Me' and 'If the Man in the Moon Were a Coon.' Some of them songs were writ by coloreds themselves, because they had to write what was popular if they wanted to make any money."

"Mrs. Holloway . . . !"

"Never said I liked 'em," she snapped back. "I met plenty of coloreds in my time, and there's some good and some bad, just like any other folks. Will Biddle, he farmed two hollers over from my pa when I was a sprout, and he worked as hard as any man-jack in the hills, and carried water for no man. My pa said—My pa . . ." She paused, frowned, and shook her head.

"Pa?"

"What is it?"

"Oh."

"Mrs. Holloway?"

She spoke in a whisper, not looking at me, not looking at anything I could see. "I remember when my pa died. Him a-laying on the bed, all wore out by life. Gray and wrinkled and toothless. And, dear Lord, how that ached me. I remember thinking how he'd been such a strong man. Such a strong man." She sighed. "It's an old apartment, and the wallpaper is peeling off'n the walls. There's a big, dark water stain on one wall and the steam radiator is hissing like a cat."

"You don't remember where you were . . . are?" I asked, jotting a few quick notes.

She shook her head. "No. I'm humming 'In the Good Old Summertime.' Or maybe the tune is just running through my head. Pa, he . . ." A tear formed in the corner of her eye. "He wants me to sing him the song."

"The song? What song is that?"

"An old, old song he used to love. 'Sing it to me one last time,' he says. And I can't sing at all because my throat's clenched up so tight. But he asks me again, and . . . Those eyes of his! How I loved that old man." Mae's own eyes had glazed over as she lived the scene again in her mind. She reached out as if clasping another pair of hands in her own and croaked haltingly:

> *"I gaze on the moon as I tread the drear wild,*
> *And feel that my mother now thinks of her child . . .*
> *Be it ever so humble . . ."*

She could not finish. For a time, she sobbed softly. Then she brushed her eye with her sleeve and looked past me. "I never knew, Doc. I never knew at all what a blessing it was to forget."

> *Come and sit by my side if you love me.*
> *Do not hasten to bid me adieu,*
> *But remember the bright Mohawk Valley*
> *And the girl that has loved you so true.*

Later that day, as I was leaving the Home, I noticed Mae sitting in the common room and paused a moment to eavesdrop. There were a handful of other residents moldering in chairs and rockers; but Mae sat singing quietly to herself and I thought what the hell, and pulled out my pocket tape recorder and stepped up quietly beside her.

It was a patriotic hymn. "America, the Beautiful." I'm sure you've heard it. Even I know the words to that one. Enough to know that Mae had them all wrong. *Oh beautiful for halcyon skies? Above the enameled plain?* And the choruses . . . The way Mae sang it, "God shed his grace for thee" sounded more like a plea than a statement.

> *America! America! God shed his grace for thee*
> *Till selfish gain no longer stain The banner of the free!*

The faulty recollection disturbed me. If Mae's memories were unreliable, then what of my book? What if my whole rationale turned out wrong?

Her croakings died away, and she opened her eyes and spotted me. "Heading home, Doc?"

"It's been a long day," I said. There was no sign on her face of her earlier melancholy, except that maybe her cheeks sagged a little lower than before, her eyes gazed a little more sadly. She seemed older, somehow, if such a thing were possible.

She patted the chair next to her. "Hotfoot it on over," she said. "You're just in time for the slapstick."

She was obviously having another doubling episode, and, in some odd way, I was being asked to participate. I looked at my watch, but decided that since our morning session had been cut short, I might as well make the time up now. My next visit was not until Friday. If I waited until then, these memories could be lost.

"Slapstick?" I asked, taking the seat she had offered.

"You never been to the Shows?" She tsk-ed and shook her head. "Well, Jee-whiskers. They been the place to go ever since Tony Pastor got rid of the cootchee-cootchee and cleaned up his acts. A young man can take his steady there now and make goo-goo eyes." She nudged me with her elbow. "A fellow can be gay with his fairy up in the balcony."

I pulled away from her. "I beg your pardon?"

"Don't you want to be gay?" she asked.

"I should hope not! I have a wife, a dau . . ."

Mae laughed suddenly and capped a gnarled hand over her mouth. So help me, she blushed. "Oh, my goodness, me! I didn't mean were you a *cake-eater*. I got all mixed up. I was sitting down front at the burly-Q and I was sitting here in the TV room with you. When we said, 'be gay,' we meant let your hair down and relax. And a 'fairy' was your girlfriend, what they used to call a chicken when I was younger. All the boys wanted to be gay blades, with their starched collars and straw hats and spats. And their moustaches! You never saw such moustaches! Waxed and curled and barbered." She chuckled to herself. "I was a regular daisy, myself." She closed her eyes and leaned back.

"A regular daisy?"

"A daisy," she repeated. "Like in the song. Gals was going out to work in them days. So they made a song about it. Now, let me see . . ." She pouted and stared closed-eyed at the sky. "How did that go?" She began to sing in a cracked, quavery voice.

> "My daughter's as fine a young girl as you'll meet
> In your travels day in and day out;
> But she's getting high-toned and she's putting on airs
> Since she has been working about . . .
> When she comes home at night from her office,
> She walks in with a swag like a fighter;

And she says to her ma, 'Look at elegant me!'
Since my daughter plays on the typewriter.

"She says she's a 'regular daisy,'
Uses slang 'til my poor heart is sore;
She now warbles snatches from operas
Where she used to sing 'Peggy O Moore.'
Now the red on her nails looks ignited;
She's bleached her hair 'til it's lighter.
Now perhaps I should always be mad at the man
That taught her to play the typewriter.

"She cries in her sleep, 'Your letter's to hand.'
She calls her old father, 'esquire';
And the neighbors they shout
When my daughter turns out,
'There goes Bridget Typewriter Maguire.' "

When Mae was done, she laughed again and wiped tears from her eyes. "Law's sake," she said. "Girls a-working in the offices. I remember what a stir-up that was. Folks said secretarial was man's work, and women couldn't be good typewriters, no how. There was another song, 'Everybody Works but Father,' about how if women was to go to work, all the men would be out of jobs. Heh-heh. I swan! It weren't long afore one gal in four had herself a 'position,' like they used to say; and folks my age complained how the youngsters were 'going to pot.' " She shook her head and chuckled.

"I always did find those kids more to my taste," she went on. "There was something about 'em; some spark that I liked. They knew how to have fun without that ragged edge that the next batch had. And they had, I don't know, call it a dream. They were out to change the world. They sure weren't wishy-washy like the other folks my age. 'Middle-aged,' that's what the kids back then called us. We were 'Professor Tweetzers' and 'Miss Nancys' and 'goo-goos.' And to tell you the truth, Doc, I thought they pegged it right. People my age grew up trying to imitate their parents; until they saw how much more fun the kids were having. Then they tried to be just like their kids. Heh-heh."

I grunted something noncommittal. Middle-aged crazy, just like my uncle Larry. "I suppose there were a lot of 'mid-life crises' back then, too," I ventured. Uncle Larry had gone heavy into love beads and incense, radical politics. He grew a moustache and wore bell-bottoms. The whole hippie scene. Walked out on his wife for a young "chick" and thought it was all "groovy." I remember how pathetic those thirtysomething wannabes seemed to us in college.

Dad, now, he never had an "identity crisis." He always knew exactly who he was. He had gone off to Europe and saved the world and then came back home and rebuilt it. Uncle Larry was too young to save the world in the forties, and too old to save it in the sixties. He was part of that bewildered, silent generation sandwiched between the heroes and the prophets.

"Neurasthenia," Mae said. "We called it neurasthenia back then. Seems everyone I knew was getting divorced or having an attack of 'the nerves.' Even the president was down in the mullygrubs when he was younger. Nervous breakdown. That's what you call it nowadays, isn't it? Now, T.R. There was a man with sand in him. Him and that 'strenuous life' he always preached about. Why, he'd fight a circle saw. Saw him that time in Milwaukee. Shot in the chest, and he still gave a stem-winder of a speech before he let them take him off. Did you know he got me in trouble one time?"

"Who, Teddy Roosevelt? How?"

"T.R., he was a-hunting and come on a bear cub; but he wouldn't shoot the poor thing because it wasn't the manly thing to do. So, some sharper started making stuffed animal dolls and called 'em Teddy's Bear. I given one to my neighbor child as a present." Mae slapped her knee. "Well, her ma had herself a conniption fit, 'cause the experts all said how animal dolls would give young 'uns the nightmares. And the other president who had the neurasthenia." Mae scowled and waved a hand in front of her face. "Oh, I know who it was," she said in an irritated voice. "That college professor. What was his name?"

"Wilson," I suggested, "Woodrow Wilson."

"That's the one. I think he was always jealous of T.R. He wouldn't let him take the Rough Riders into the Great War."

I started to make some comment, but Mae's mouth dropped open. "The war . . . ?" she whispered. "The war! Oh, Mister . . ." Her face crumpled. "Oh, Mister! You're too old!" She covered her face and began to weep.

She felt in her sleeves for a handkerchief, then wiped her eyes and looked at me. "I forgot," she said. "I forgot. It was the war. Mister went away to the war. That's why he never come back. He never run out on me, at all. He would have come back after it was over, if he'd still been alive. He would have."

"I'm sure he would have," I said awkwardly.

"I told him he was too old for that sort of thing; but he just laughed and said it was a good cause and they needed men like him to spunk up the young 'uns. So he marched away one day and someone he never met before shot him dead and I don't even know when and where it happened."

"I'm sorry," I said, at a loss for anything else to say. A good cause? The War to End All Wars, nearly forgotten now; its players, comic-opera Ruritanians on herky-jerky black-and-white newsreels. The last war begun in innocence.

Her hands had twisted the handkerchief into a knot. She fussed with it, straightened it out on her lap, smoothed it with her hand. In a quiet voice, she said, "Tell me, Doc. Tell me. Why do they have wars?"

I shook my head. Was there ever a good reason? To make the world safe for democracy? To stop the death camps? To free the slaves? Maybe. Those were better reasons than cheap oil. But up close, no matter what the reason, it was husbands and sons and brothers who never came home.

> *Oh, them golden slippers, Oh, them golden slippers,*
> *Golden slippers I'm gonna wear, Because they look so neat;*
> *Oh, them golden slippers, Oh, them golden slippers,*
> *Golden slippers I'm gonna wear To walk them golden streets.*

Ever since our late-evening encounter, Consuela had begun wearing blouses, skirts, and robes around the house instead of her nurse's whites. The colors were bright, even garish; the patterns, blocky and intricate. The costumes made the woman more open, less mysterious. It was as if, having once seen her deshabille, a barrier had come down. She had begun teaching Dee-dee to play the cane flute. Sometimes I heard them in the evening, the notes drifting down from above stairs, lingering in the air. Was it a signal, I wondered? I sensed that the relationship between Consuela and me had changed; but in what direction, I did not know.

Dee-dee should have been in school. She should have been in fifth grade; and she should have come home on the school bus, full of laughter and bursting to tell us what she had learned that day. Brenda and I should have helped her with her homework, nursed her bruises, and hugged her when she cried. That was the natural order of things.

But Dee-dee lived in her room, played in the dark. She studied at home, tutored by Consuela or me or by private instructors we sometimes hired. School and other children were far away. She was a prisoner, half of her mother's strained disapproval, half of her own withdrawal. Save for Consuela and myself and a few, brief contacts with Brenda, she had no other person in her short, bounded life. Who could dream what scenarios her dolls performed in the silence of her room?

I found the two of them at the kitchen table, Consuela with her inevitable cocoa, Dee-dee with a glass of milk and a stack of graham crackers. There were cracker crumbs scattered across the Formica and a ring of white across Dee-dee's lip.

I beamed at her. "The princess has come down from her tower once more!"

She tucked her head in a little. "It's all right, isn't it?"

I kissed her on the forehead. How sparse her hair had grown! "Of course, it is!"

I settled myself across the table from Consuela. She was wearing an ivory blouse with a square-cut neck bordered by red stitching in the shape of flowers. "Thank you, nurse," I said. "She should be downstairs more often."

"Yes, I know."

Was there a hint of disapproval there? A slight drawing together of the lips? I wanted to make excuses for Brenda. It was not that Brenda made Dee-dee stay in her room, but that she never made her leave. It was Deirdre who stayed always by herself. "So, what did you do today, Dee-dee?"

"Oh, nothing. I read my schoolbooks. Watched TV. I helped Connie bake a cake."

"Did you? Sounds like a pretty busy day to me."

She and Consuela shared a grin with each other. "We played ball, a little, until I got tired. And then we played word games. I see something . . . blue! What is it?"

"The sky?"

"I can't see the sky from here. It's long and thin."

"Hmm. Long, thin and blue. Spaghetti with blueberry sauce?"

Dee-dee laughed. "No, silly. It has a knot in it."

"Hmm. I can't imagine what it could be." I straightened my tie and Dee-dee laughed again. I looked down at the tie and gave a mock start. "Wait! Long, thin, blue, and a knot . . . It's my belt!"

"No! It's your tie!"

"My tie? Why . . ." I gave her a look of total amazement. "Why, you're absolutely, positively right. Now, why didn't I see that. It was right under my nose. Imagine missing something right under your nose!"

We played a few more rounds of "I see something" and then Dee-dee wandered back to the family room and settled on the floor in front of the TV. I watched her for a while as she stared at the pictures flickering there. I thought of how little time was left before cartoons would play unwatched.

Consuela placed a cup of coffee in front of me. I sipped from it absently while I sorted through the day's mail stacked on the table. "Brenda will be coming home on Monday," I said. Consuela already knew that, and I knew that she knew, so I don't know why I said it.

But why Monday? Why not Friday? Why spend another weekend in Washington with Walther Crowe? I could think of any number of reasons, I could.

"Deirdre will be happy to have her mother back," Consuela said in flat tones. I was looking at the envelopes, so I did not see her face. I knew what she meant, though. No more flute lessons; no more games downstairs. I reached across the table and placed my hand atop one of hers. It was warm, probably from holding the cocoa mug.

"Deirdre's mother never left," I said.

Consuela looked away. "I am only her nurse."

"You take care of her. That's more . . ." I caught myself. I had started to say that that was more than Brenda did; but there were some things that husbands did not say about their wives to other women. I noticed, however, that Consuela had not pulled her hand away from mine.

I released her hand. "Say, here's a letter from the National Archives." I said with forced heartiness, dancing away from the sudden abyss that had yawned open before me. Too many lives had been ruined by reading invitations where none were written.

Consuela stood and turned away, taking her cup to the sink. I slit the envelope open with my index finger and pulled out the yellow flimsy. *Veteran: Holloway, Green. Branch of Service: Infantry (Co. H, 5th Tennessee). Years of Service: 1918 or 1919.* It was the order form I had sent to the Military Service Records department after Mae's earlier recollection of her husband. As I unfolded it, Consuela came and stood beside me, reading over my shoulder. Somehow, it was not uncomfortable.

✓ *We were unable to complete your request as written.*

✓ *We found additional pension and military service files of the same name (or similar variations).*

✓ *The enclosed records are those which best match the information provided. Please resubmit, if these are not the desired files.*

I grunted and paged through the sheets. Company muster rolls. A Memorandum of Prisoner of War Records: *Paroled and exchanged at Cumberland Gap, Sept. 5/62.*

The last page was a white photocopy of a form printed in an old-fashioned typeface. **Casualty Sheet**. The blanks were penned in by an elegant Spencerian hand. Name, *Green Holloway*. Rank, *Private*. Company "*H*", Regiment 5". Division, 3". Corps, 23". Arm, *Inf*. State, *Tenn*.

Nature of casualty, *Bullet wound of chest (fatal)*.

Place of casualty, *Resaca, Ga*.

Date of casualty, *May 14, 1864, the regiment being in action that date*.

Jno. T. Henry, Clerk.

I tossed the sheets to the kitchen table. "These can't be right," I said.

Consuela picked them up. "What is wrong?"

"Right name, wrong war. These are for a Green Holloway who died in the Civil War."

Consuela raised an eyebrow. "And who served in the same company as your patient's husband?"

"State militia regiments were raised locally, and the same families served in them, generation after generation. Green here was probably 'Mister's' grandfather. Back then children were often given their parents' or grandparents' names." I took the photocopies from Consuela and stuffed them back in the envelope. "Well, there was a waste of ten dollars." I dropped the envelope on the table.

Dee-dee called from the family room. "What's this big book you brought home?"

"*The Encyclopedia of Song*," I said over my shoulder. "It's to help me with a patient I have."

"The old lady who hears music?"

I turned in my chair. "Yes. Did Connie tell you about her."

Dee-dee nodded her head. "I wish I could hear music like that. You wouldn't need headphones or a Walkman, would you?"

I remembered that Mae had had two very unhappy recollections in one day. "No," I said, "but you don't get to pick the station, either."

Later that evening, after Dee-dee had been tucked away, I spread my index cards and sheets of paper over the kitchen table and arranged the tape recorder on my left where I could replay it as needed. The song encyclopedia lay in front of me, open to its index. A pot of coffee stood ready on my right.

Consuela no longer retreated to her own room after dinner. When I looked up from my work I could see her, relaxed on the sofa in the family room, quietly reading a book. Her shoes off, her legs tucked up underneath her, the way some women sit curled up. I watched her silently for a while. So serene, like a jaguar indolent upon a tree limb. She appeared unaware of my regard, and I bent again over my work before she looked up.

I soon verified that Mae's latest recollections were from the Gay Nineties. The earliest one, "Ta-Ra-Ra Boom-der-ay," had been written in 1890, and the others dated from the same era. "Good-bye, Dolly Gray," had been a favorite of the soldiers going off to fight in the Philippine "insurrection," while "Hot Time in the Old Town" had been the Rough Riders' "theme song." Mae's version of "America the Beautiful," I discovered, was the original 1895 lyrics. Apparently, Katherine Lee Bates had written the song as much for protest as for patriotism.

When I had finished the cataloguing, I closed the songbook, leaned back in my chair, and stretched my arms over my head. Consuela looked up at the motion and I smiled at her and she smiled back. I checked my watch. "Almost bedtime," I said. Consuela said nothing, but nodded slightly.

Middle-aged?

The thought struck me like a discordant note and I turned back to my work. I ran the tape back and forth until I found what I was looking for. Yes. Mae had said that the "young folks" at the turn of the century had called her age-mates "middle-aged." So Mae must have already been mature by then. How was that possible? At most, she might have been a teenager, one of the "young folks," herself.

Unless she had looked old for her age.

God! I stabbed the shut-off button with my forefinger.

After a moment, I ran the tape through again, listening for Mae's descriptions of her peers and her younger contemporaries. "Wishy-washy." Folks her age had been wishy-washy. Yet, in an earlier session, she had described her age-mates as moralistic. I flipped through my written notes until I found it.

Yes, just as I remembered. But, psychologically, that made no sense. Irresolute twentysomethings do not mature into fortysomething moralists. The irresolute become the two-sides-to-every-question types: the mediators, the compromisers, the peace-makers. The ones both sides despise—and miss desperately when they are gone. The moralists are no-compromise world-savers. They preach "prohibition," not "temperance."

The wild youth Mae remembered from the Ragtime Era and the Mauve Decade—the hard-edged "newsies"—those were the young Hemingways, Bogies, and Mae Wests; the "Blood-and-Guts" Pattons and the "Give-'em-Hell" Harrys. The Lost Generation, they had been called. The idealistic, young teeners and twentysomethings of the Gay Nineties that Mae found so simpatico were the young FDR, W.E.B. DuBois, and Jane Addams. The generation of "missionaries" out to save the world. They had all been "the kids" to her. But that would put Mae into the even older, Progressive Generation, a contemporary of T.R. and Edison and Booker T. Washington.

I drummed my pencil against the tabletop. That would make her 120 years old, or thereabout. That wasn't possible, was it? I pushed myself from the table and went to the bookcase in the family room.

The *Guinness Book of Records* sat next to the dictionary, the thesaurus, the atlas, and the almanac, all neatly racked together. Sometimes, Brenda's obsessive organizing paid off. I noticed that Dee-dee had left one of her own books, *The Boxcar Children*, on the shelf and made a mental note to return it to her room later.

According to Guinness, the oldest human being whose birth could be authenticated was Shigechiyo Izumi of Japan, who had died in 1986 at the ripe age of 120 years and 237 days. So, a few wheezing, stumbling geezers did manage to hang around that long. But not many. Actuarial tables suggested one life in two billion. So, with nearly six billion of us snorting and breathing and poking each other with our elbows, two or three such ancients were possible. Maybe, just maybe, Mae could match Izumi's record. The last surviving Progressive.

The oldest human being.

The oldest human being remembers.

The oldest human being remembers pop music of the last hundred years.

A *Hundred-and-Twentysomething*. Great book title. It had "best-seller" written all over it.

> *'Neath the chestnut tree, where the wild flow'rs grow,*
> *And the stream ripples forth through the vale,*
> *Where the birds shall warble their songs in spring,*
> *There lay poor Lilly Dale.*

On my next visit, Mae was not waiting by the office door for me to unlock it. So, after I had set my desk in order, I hung the "Back in a Minute" sign on the doorknob and went to look for her. Not that I was concerned. It was just that I had grown used to her garrulous presence.

I found Jimmy Kovacs in the common room watching one of those inane morning "news" shows. "Good morning, Jimmy. How's your back?"

He grinned at me. "Oh, I can't complain." He waited a beat. "They won't let me."

I smiled briefly. "Glad to hear it. Have you seen—"

"First hurt my back, oh, it must have been '66, '67. Lifting forms."

"I know. You told me already. I'm looking for—"

"Not forms like paperwork. Though nowadays you could strain your back lifting them, too." He cackled at his feeble joke. It hadn't been funny the first two times, either. "No, I'm talking about those six-hundred pound forms we used to use on the old flatbed perfectors. Hot type. Blocks of lead quoined into big iron frames. Those days, printing magazines was a *job*, I tell you. You could smell the ink; you could feel the presses pounding through the floor and the heat from the molten lead in the linotypes." He shook his head. "I saw the old place once a few years back. A couple of prissy kids going ticky-ticky on those computer keyboards . . ." He made typing motions with his two index fingers.

I interrupted before he could give me another disquisition on the decadence of the printing industry. I could just imagine the noise, the lead vapors, the heavy weight lifting. Some people have odd notions about the Good Old Days. "Have you seen Mae this morning, Jimmy?"

"Who? Mae? Sure, I saw the old gal. She was headed for the gardens."
He pointed vaguely.

Old gal? I chuckled at the pot calling the kettle black. But then I realized with a sudden shock that there were more years between Mae and
Jimmy than there were between Jimmy and me. There was old, and then
there was *old*. Perhaps we should distinguish more carefully among them
. . . say "fogies," "mossbacks," and "geezers."

Mae was sitting in the garden sunshine, against the redbrick back wall,
upon a stone settee. I watched her for a few moments from behind the large
plate-glass window. The sun was from her right, illuminating the red and
yellow blossoms around her and sparkling the morning dew like diamonds
strewn across the grass. The dewdrops were matched by those on her
cheeks. She wore a green print dress with flowers, so that the dress, the grass,
and the flower beds; the tears and the dew, all blended together, like old
ladies' garden camouflage.

She did not see me coming. Her eyes were closed tight, looking upon
another, different world. I stood beside her, unsure whether to rouse her.
Were those tears of joy or tears of sorrow? Would it be right to interrupt either? I compromised by placing my hand on her shoulder. Her dry, birdlike claw reached up and pressed itself against mine.

"Is that you, Dr. Wilkes?" I don't know how she knew that. Perhaps her
eyes had not been entirely closed. She opened them and looked at me, and
I could see that her regurgitated memories had been sorrowful ones. That
is the problem with Jackson's syndrome. You remember. You can't help
remembering. "Oh, Dr. Wilkes. My mama. My sweet, sweet mama. She's
dead."

The announcement did not astonish me. Had either of Mae Holloway's
parents been alive, I would have been astonished. I started to tell her that,
but my words came out surprisingly gentle. "It happened a long time ago,"
I told her. "It's a hurt long over."

She shook her head. "No. It happened this morning. I saw Pa leaning
over my bed. Oh, such a strong, young man he was! But he'd been crying.
His eyes were red and his beard and hair weren't combed. He told me that
my mama was dead at last and she weren't a-hurtin' no more."

Mae Holloway pulled me down to sit beside her on the hard, cold bench, and she curled against me for all the world like a little girl. I hesitated and almost pulled away; but I am not without pity, even for an old woman who half thought she was a child.

"He told me it was my fault."

"What?" Her voice had been muffled against my jacket.

"He told me it was my fault."

"Who? Your father told you that? That was . . . cruel."

She spoke in a high-pitched, childish voice. "He tol' me that Mama never gotten well since I was borned. There was something about my birthin' that hurt her inside. I was six and I never seen my mama when she weren't abed . . ."

She couldn't finish. Awkwardly, I put an arm around her shoulder. A husband who lost his wife to childbirth would blame the child, whether consciously or not. Especially a husband in the full flush of youth. Worse still, if it was a lingering death. If for years the juices of life had drained away, leaving a gasping, joyless husk behind.

If for years the juices of life had drained away, leaving a gasping, joyless husk behind.

"I have to get back to my office," I said, standing abruptly. "There may be a patient waiting. Is there anything I can get you? A sedative?"

She shook her head slowly back and forth several times. When she spoke, she sounded more like the adult Mae. "No. No, thank you. I ain't— haven't had these memories for so long that I got to feel them now, even when it pains me. There'll be worse coming back to me, by and by. And better, too. The Good Man'll help me bear it."

It wasn't until I was back behind my desk and had made some notes about her recollection for my projected book that I was struck with an annoying inconsistency. If Mae's mother had died from complications of childbirth, where did her "little brother Zach" come from?

Stepbrother, probably. A young man like her father would have sought a new bride before too long. Eventually, we put tragedy behind us and get on with life. But if I was going to analyze the progress of Mae's condition, I would need to confirm her recollections. After all, memories are tricky things. The memories of the old, trickier than most.

> *Peaches in the summertime,*
> *Apples in the fall;*

> *If I can't have the girl I love,*
> *I won't have none at all.*

There was music in the air when I returned home, and I followed the thread of it through the garage and into the backyard, where I found Consuela sitting on a blanket of red, orange, and brown, swathed in a flowing, pale green muumuu, and Deirdre beside her playing on the cane flute. Dee-dee's thin, knobby fingers moved haltingly, and the notes were flat, but I actually recognized the tune. Something about a spider and a waterspout.

"Hello, Dee-dee. Hello, Consuela."

Deirdre turned. "Daddy!" she said. She pulled herself erect on Consuela's gown and hobbled across the grass to me. I crouched down and hugged her. "Dee-dee, you're outside playing."

"Connie said it was all right."

"Of course it's all right. I wish you would come out more often."

A cloud passed across the sunshine. "Connie said no one can see me in the yard." A hesitation. "And Mommy's not home."

No one to tell her how awful she looked. No cruel, taunting children. No thoughtlessly sympathetic adults offering useless condolences. Nothing but Connie, and me, and the afternoon sun. I looked over Dee-dee's shoulder. "Thank you, nur—Thank you, Connie."

She blinked at my use of her familiar name, but made no comment. "The sunshine is good for her."

"She *is* my sunshine. Aren't you, Dee-dee?" *You are my sunshine, my only sunshine.* A fragment of tune. Only, how did the rest of it go?

"Oh, Daddy . . ."

"So, has Connie been teaching you to play the flute?"

"Yes. And she showed me lots of things. Did you know there are zillions of different bugs in our grass?"

"Are there?" *You make me happy when skies are gray.*

"Yeah. There's ants and centipedes and . . . and mites? And honeybees. Honeybees like these little white flowers." And she showed me a ball of clover she had tucked behind her ear.

"You better watch that," I said, "or the bees will come after you, too."

"Oh, Daddy . . ."

"Because you're so sweet." *You'll never know, dear, how much I love you.*

"Daa_addyy^y. I saw some spiders, too."

"Going up the waterspout?"

She giggled. "There are different kinds of spiders, too. They're like eensy-weensy tigers, Connie says. They eat flies and other bugs. Yuck! I wouldn't want to be a spider, would you?"

"No."

"But you are!" Secret triumph in her voice. She had just tricked me, somehow. "There was this spider that was nothing but a little brown ball with legs *this* long!" She held her arms far enough apart to cause horror movie buffs to blanch. "They named it after you," she added with another giggle. "They call it a Daddy-long-legs. You're a daddy and you have long legs, so you must be a spider, too."

"Then . . . I've got you in my web!" I grabbed her and she squealed. "And now I'm going to gobble you up!" I started kissing her on the cheeks. She giggled and made a pretense of escape. I held her all the tighter. *Please don't take my sunshine away.*

We sat for a while on the blanket, just the three of us. Consuela told us stories from Guatemala. How a rabbit had gotten deeply into debt and then tricked his creditors into eating one another. How a disobedient child was turned into a monkey. Dee-dee giggled at that and said she would *like* to be a monkey. I told them about Mae Holloway.

"She didn't give me any new songs today," I said, "but she finally remembered something from her childhood." I explained how her mother had died, and her father had blamed her for it.

"Poor girl!" Consuela said, looking past me. "It's not right for a little girl to grow up without a mother."

"Deirdre Wilkes! What on *earth* are you doing out*side* in the *dirt?*"

Dee-dee stiffened in my arms. I turned and saw Brenda in the open garage door, straight as a rod. A navy blue business suit with white ruffled blouse. Matching overcoat, hanging open. A suitbag slung from one shoulder; a briefcase clenched in the other hand. "Brenda," I said, standing up with Dee-dee in my arm. "We didn't expect you until Monday."

She looked at each of us. "Evidently not."

"Dee-dee was just getting a little sunshine."

Brenda stepped close and whispered. "The neighbors might see."

I wanted to say, So what? But I held my peace. You learn there are times when it is best to say nothing at all. You learn.

"Nurse." She spoke to Consuela. "Aren't you dressed a bit casually?"

"Yes, señora. It is after five." When she had to, Consuela could remember what was in her contract.

"A professional does not watch the clock. And a professional dresses appropriately for her practice. How do you think it would look if I went to the office in blouse and skirt instead of a suit? Take Deirdre inside. Don't you know there are all sorts of bugs and dirt out here? What if she were stung by a bee? Or bitten by a deer tick?"

"Brenda," I said, "I don't think—"

She turned to me. "Yes, exactly. You didn't think. How could you have allowed this, Paul? Look, in her hand. That's Nurse's whistle, or whatever it is. Has Deirdre been playing it? Putting it in her mouth. How unsanitary! And there are weeds in her hair. For God's sake, Paul, you're a doctor. You should have said something."

Sometimes I thought Brenda had been raised in a sterile bubble. The least little thing out of place, the least little thing done wrong, was enough to set her off. Dust was a hanging offense. She hadn't always been that way. At school, she'd been reasonably tidy, but not obsessed. It had only been in the last few years that cleanliness and order had begun to consume her life. Each year, I could see the watchspring wound tighter and tighter.

Consuela bundled up flute, blanket, and Dee-dee and took them inside, leaving me alone with Brenda. I tried to give her a hug, and she endured it briefly. "Welcome home."

"Christ, Paul. I go away for two weeks and everything is falling apart."

"No, Nurse was right to bring her outside. Deirdre should have as much normal activity as possible. There is nothing wrong with her mind. It's just her body aging too fast." That wasn't strictly true. Hutchinson-Gilford was sometimes called *progeria*, but it differed in some of its particulars from normal senile aging.

Brenda swatted at a swarm of midges. "There are too many bugs out here," she said. "Let's go inside. Carry my suitbag for me."

I took it from her and followed her inside the house. She dropped her briefcase on the sofa in the living room and continued to the hall closet, where she shed her overcoat. "You're home early," I said again.

"That's right. Surprised?" She draped her overcoat carefully across a hanger.

"Well . . ." *Yes, I was.* "Did Crowe drop you off?"

She shoved the other coats aside with a hard swipe. "Yes." Then she turned and started up the stairs. I closed the closet door for her.

"How was Washington?" I asked. "Did you impress the Supremes?"

She didn't answer, and I followed her up the stairs. I found her in our bedroom, shedding her travel clothes. I hung the suit bag on the closet door. "Did you hear me? I asked how—"

"I heard you." She dropped her skirt to the floor and sent it in the direction of the hamper with a flick of her foot. "Walther offered me a partnership."

"Did he?" I retrieved her skirt and put it in the hamper. "That's great news!" It was. Partners made a bundle. They took a cut of the fees the associates charged. "It opens up all sorts of opportunities."

Brenda gave me a funny look. "Yes," she said. "It does." If I hadn't known better, I would have said she looked distressed. It was hard to imagine Brenda being unsure.

"What's wrong?" I said.

"Nothing. It's just that there are conditions attached."

"What conditions? A probationary period? You've been an associate there for seven years. They should know your work by now."

"It isn't that."

"Then, what . . ."

Deirdre interrupted us. She stood in the doorway of our bedroom, one foot crossed pigeon-toed over the other, a gnarled finger tucked in one shrunken cheek. "Mommy?"

Brenda looked at a point on the doorjamb a quarter inch above Deedee's head. "What is it, honey."

"I should tell you 'welcome home' and 'I missed you.' "

I could almost hear *Connie said . . .* in front of that statement, and I wondered if Brenda could hear it, too.

"I missed you, too, honey," Brenda told the doorknob.

"I've got to take my bath, now."

"Good. Be sure to get all that dirt washed off."

"Okay, Mommy." A brief catch, and then, "I love you, Mommy."

Brenda nodded. "Yes."

Dee-dee waited a moment longer, then turned and bolted for the bathroom. I could hear Connie already running the water. I waited until the bathroom door closed before I turned to Brenda. "You could have told her that you loved her, too."

"I do," she said, pulling on a pair of slacks. "She knows I do."

"Not unless you tell her once in a while."

She flashed me an irritated look, but made no reply. She took a blouse from her closet and held it in front of her while she stood before the mirror. "Let's go out to eat tonight."

"Go out? Well, you know that Dee-dee doesn't like to leave the house, but . . ."

"Take Deirdre with us? Whatever are you thinking of, Paul? She would be horribly embarrassed. Think of the stares she'd get! No, Consuela can feed her that Mexican goulash she's cooking."

"Guatemalan."

"What?"

"It's Guatemalan, whatever it is."

"Do you have to argue with everything I say?"

"I thought, with you being just back and all, that the three of us"—*the four of us*—"could eat dinner together, for a change."

"I won't expose Deirdre to the rudeness of strangers."

"No, not when she can get it at home." I don't know why I said that. It just came out.

Brenda stiffened. "What does that crack mean?"

I turned away. "Nothing."

"No, tell me!"

I turned back and faced her. "All right. You treat Dee-dee like a nonperson. She's sick, Brenda, and it's not contagious and it's not her fault."

"Then whose fault is it?"

"That's lawyer talk. It's no one's fault. It just happens. We've been over that and over that. There is no treatment for progeria."

"And, oh, how it gnaws at you! *You can't cure her!*"

"No one can!"

"But especially you."

No one could cure Dee-dee. I knew that. It was helplessness, not failure. I had accepted that long ago. "And *you're* angry and bitter," I replied, "because there's nobody you can sue!"

She flung her blouse aside and it landed in a wad in the corner. "Maybe," she said through clenched teeth, "Maybe I'll take that partnership offer, after all."

It was not until much later that evening, as I lay awake in bed, Brenda a thousand miles away on the other side, that I remembered Consuela's remark. *It's not right for a little girl to grow up without a mother.* I wondered. Had she been making a comment, or making an offer?

> *I don't want to play in your yard.*
> *I don't like you anymore.*
> *You'll be sorry when you see me*
> *Sliding down our cellar door.*

The next time I saw Mae Holloway, we quarreled.

Perhaps it was her own constant sourness coming to the fore; or perhaps it was her fear of insanity returning. But it may have been a bad humor that I carried with me from Brenda's homecoming. We had smoothed things out, Brenda and I, but it was a fragile repair, the cracks plastered over with I-was-tired and I-didn't-mean-it, and we both feared to press too hard, lest it buckle on us. At dinner, she had told me about the case she had helped argue, and I told her about Mae Holloway, and we both pretended to care. But it was all monologue. Listening holds fewer risks than response; and an attentive smile, less peril than engagement.

Mae wouldn't look at me when I greeted her. She stared resolutely at the floor, at the medicine cabinet, out the window. Sometimes, she stared into another world. I noticed how she gnawed on her lips.

"We have a couple of days to catch up on, Mrs. Holloway," I said. "I hope you've been making notes, like I asked."

She shook her head slowly, but in a distracted way. She was not responding to my statement, but to some inner reality. "I just keep remembering and remembering, Doc. There's music all the time, and that double vision—"

"Consciousness doubling."

"It's like I'm in two places at once. Sometimes, I forget which is which, and I try to step around things only I cain't, because they're only ghosts, only ghosts. And sometimes, I recollect things that couldn't have . . ."

The "dreamy states" of Jackson patients often grow deeper and more frequent. In one woman, they had occupied nearly her entire day; and, in the end, they had crowded out her normal consciousness entirely. "I could prescribe something, if you like," I said. "These spells of yours are similar to epileptic seizures. So, there are drugs that . . ."

She shook her head again. "No. I won't take drugs." She looked directly at me at last. "Don't you understand? I've got to know. It's always been bits and pieces. Just flashes. A jimble-jamble that never made sense. Now . . ." She paused and took a deep breath. "Now, at least, I'll know."

"Know what, Mrs. Holloway."

"About . . . Everything." She looked away again. Talking with her today was like pulling teeth.

"What about the songs, Mae? We didn't get anything useful on Wednesday, and I wasn't here Tuesday or yesterday, so that's three days we have to catch up on."

Mae turned and studied me with lips as thin as broth. "You don't care about any of this, do you? It's all professional; not like you and I are friends. You don't care if'n I live or die; and I don't care if'n you do."

"Mrs. Holloway, I . . ."

"Good." She gave a sharp nod of her head. "That's jake with me. Because I don't like having friends," she said. "I decided a long time ago if'n I don't have 'em, I won't miss 'em when they cut out. So let's just keep this doc and old lady." Her stare was half admonition, half challenge, as if she dared me to leap the barriers she had set down around her.

I shrugged. Keep things professional. That was fine with me, too. A crabby old lady like her, it was no wonder they all ran out on her.

She handed over a crumpled, yellow sheet of lined paper, which I flattened out on my desk. She had written in a soft pencil, so I smeared some of the writing and smudged my palm. I set a stack of fresh index cards by and began to copy the song titles for later research. "Where Did You Get That Hat?" "Comrades." "The Fountain in the Park." "Love's Old Sweet Song." While I worked, I could hear Mae humming to herself. I knew without looking that she had her eyes closed, that she was living more and more in another world, gradually leaving this one behind. "White Wings." "Walking for That Cake." "My Grandfather's Clock." "In the Gloaming." "Silver Threads among the Gold." "The Mulligan Guard." Mae was her own Hit Parade. Though if the music did play continually, as she said, this list could only be a sample of what she had heard over the last three days. "The Man on the Flying Trapeze." "Sweet Genevieve." "Champagne Charlie." "You Naughty, Naughty Men." "When You and I Were Young, Maggie." "Beautiful Dreamer." Three days' worth of unclaimed memories.

I noticed that she had recorded no doubling episodes, this time. Because she had not had any? It seemed doubtful, considering. But one entry had been crossed out; rubbed over with the pencil until there was nothing but a black smear and a small hole in the paper where the pencil point had worn through. I held it up to the light, but could make out nothing.

I heard Mae draw in her breath and looked up in time to see a mien on her face almost of ecstasy. "What is it?"

"I'm standing out in a meadow. There's a sparkling stream meandering through it, and great, gray, rocky mountains rearing all around. Yellow flowers shivering in the breeze and I think how awful purty and peaceful it is." She sighed. "Oh, Doc, sometimes, just for a second, we can be so happy."

Jackson had often described his patients' "dreamy states" as being accompanied by intense feelings of euphoria; sudden bursts of childlike joy. No doubt some endorphin released in the brain.

"There's a fellow coming up toward me from the ranch," she continued, trepidation edging into her voice. "My age, maybe a little older. Might be Mister's younger brother, because he favors him some. He's a-weeping something awful. I reach out to him and he puts his head on my shoulder and says . . ." Mae stopped and winced in pain. She sucked in her breath and held it. Then she let it out slowly. "And he says how Sweet Annie is dead and the baby, too; and there was nothing the sawbones could do. Nothing at all. And I think, *Thank you, Goodman Lord. Thank you, that she won't suffer the way that Ma did.* And then a mockingbird takes wing from the aspen tree right in front of me, and I think how awful peaceful the meadow is now that the screaming has stopped."

She wiped at her nose with her sleeve. "Listen to it. Can you hear it, Doc? There ain't a sound but for the breeze and that old mockingbird." The look on her face changed somehow, changed subtly. "Listen to the mockingbird," she croaked. "Listen to the mockingbird. Oh, the mockingbird still singing o'er her grave . . ."

Then she looked about in sudden surprise. "Land's sake! Now, how did I get here? Why, everybody's so happy; singing the mockingbird song and dancing all over the lawn and a-hugging each other." A smile slowly came over her face. She had apparently tripped from one doubling episode directly into another, because of some association with the song, and the imprinted emotions were playing back with it, overwriting the melancholy of the first episode. Or else she had seized on the remembered joy herself, and had wrapped herself in it against the cold.

"I'm a-wearing my Sanitary Commission uniform," she went on, preening her shabby, faded gown. She shot her cuffs, straightened something at her throat that wasn't there. "I was a nurse, you know; and when the news come that the war was finally over we all hied over to the White House and had ourselves a party on the lawn, the whole kit 'n' boodle of us. Then the president his-self come out and joined us." She turned in her seat and pointed toward the medicine cabinet. "Here he comes now!"

And in that instant, her joy became absolute terror. "Him?" Her smile stretched to a ghastly rictus and she cowered into her chair, covering her eyes with her hand. But you can't close your eyes to memory. You can't. "No! I kin still see him!" she said.

What was so terrifying about seeing President Wilson close up? "What's wrong, Mrs. Holloway?"

"They shot him."

"What, on the White House lawn? No president has been shot there . . ." And certainly not Wilson.

She took her hands away from her eyes, glanced warily left, then right. Slowly, she relaxed, though her hands continued to tremble. Then, she looked at me. "No, the shooting happened later," she snapped, anger blossoming from her fear. Then she closed up and her eyes took on a haunted look. "I'm taking up too much of your time, Doc," she said, creaking to her feet.

"No, you're not. Really," I told her.

"Then you're taking up too much of mine." I thought her blackthorn stick would punch holes in the floor tiles as she left.

After a moment's hesitation, I followed. She had recalled her father's death. She had remembered that her birth had killed her mother and that her father had blamed her for it. She had remembered her husband going off to war, never to return. Sad memories, sorrowful memories; but there was something about this new recollection that terrified her.

She thought she was going crazy.

It was easy to track her through the garden. Deep holes punched into the sod marked her trail among the flower beds. When I caught up with her, she was leaning over a plot of gold and crimson marigolds. "You know, I remember exactly where I was when President Kennedy was shot," I said by way of easing her into conversation.

Mae Holloway scowled and bent over the flower bed. "Don't make no difference nohow," she said. "He's dead either way, ain't he?" She turned her back on me.

"No particular reason." I had figured it out. She had seen McKinley, not Wilson; and her husband had fought in the Spanish-American War, not World War I.

She turned her dried-out old face to me. "Think I'm getting senile, Doc? Why aren't you back in your office reading on your books? You might have a patient to ignore."

"They'll find me if they need me."

"I tol' you the songs I been remembering. Why did you follow me out here, anyway?"

I had better things to do than have a bitter old woman berate me. "If you feel in a friendlier mood later," I said, "you know where to find me."

Back in my office, I began checking the latest tunes against the song encyclopedia. The mindless transcription kept me busy, so that I did not dwell on Mae's intransigence. Let her stew in her own sour juices.

But I soon noticed a disturbing trend in the data. "Champagne Charlie" was written in 1868. "You Naughty, Naughty Men" ("When married how you treat us and of each fond hope defeat us, and there's some will even beat us . . .") had created a scandal at Niblo's Gardens in 1866. And "Beautiful Dreamer" dated from 1864. Mae could not have heard those songs when they were new. Born in the early seventies at best, tucked away back in the hills of Tennessee—"So far back in the hollers," she had said one time, "that they had to pipe in the daylight."—She must have heard them later.

And if a little bit later, why not a whole lot later?

And there went the whole rationale for my book.

The problem with assigning dates to Mae's neurological hootenanny was that she could have heard the songs at any time. A melody written in the twenties, like "The Red, Red Robin, is heard and sung by millions of children today. Scott Joplin created his piano rags at the turn of the century;

yet most people knew them from *The Sting,* a movie made in the seventies and set in the thirties, an era when ragtime had been long out of fashion.

(The telescoping effect of distance. From this far down the river of years, who can distinguish the Mauve Decade from the thirties? Henry James and Upton Sinclair and Ernest Hemingway came of age in very different worlds; but they seem alike to us because they are just dead people in funny clothing, singing quaint, antique songs. "Old-fashioned" is enough to blur them together.)

Face it. Many of those old songs were still being sung and recorded when *I* was young. Lawrence Welk. Mitch Miller. Preservation Hall. Leon Redbone had warbled "Champagne Charlie" on *The Tonight Show* in front of God and everybody. Wasn't it far more likely that Mae had heard it then, than that she had heard it in 1868?

A Hundred and Twentysomething. I had deduced a remarkable age for Mae from the dates of the songs she remembered. If that was a will-o'-the-wisp, what was the point? There was no teleology to interest the professionals, no hook to grab the public. How many people would care about an old woman's recollections? Not enough to make a best-seller.

And what right had that old bat, what right had anyone, to live so long when *children* were dying? What use were a few extra years remembering the past when there were others who would never have a future?

Damn! I saw that I had torn the index card. I rummaged in the drawer for tape, found none, and wondered if it made any sense to bother re-copying the information. The whole effort was a waste of time. I picked up the deck of index cards and threw them. I missed the wastebasket and they fluttered like dead leaves across the room.

> *Oh, how old is she, Billy Boy, Billy Boy?*
> *Oh, how old is she, charming Billy?*
> *She's twice six and she's twice seven,*
> *Forty-eight and eleven.*
> *She's a young thing that cannot leave her mother.*

I could have gone home, instead, and gotten an early start on the weekend.

I had planned to visit the National Archives today, but to continue the book project now seemed pointless. The whole rationale had collapsed; and Mae had withdrawn into that fearful isolation in which I had found her. There was no reason not to go home. Brenda had taken the day off to recuperate from her trip. She was probably waiting for me. So, I closed the clinic at noon and took the Transit to Newark's Penn Station, where I transferred to the PATH train into the World Trade Center. From there a cab dropped me at Varick and Houston in lower Manhattan.

If we did not meet, we could not quarrel.

The young woman behind the information desk was a pixie: short, with serious bangs and serious, round glasses. Her name tag read SARA. "Green?" she said when I had explained my mission. "What an odd name. It might be a nickname. You know, like 'Red.' One of my grandfathers was called 'Blackie' because his family name was White." She took out a sheet of scratch paper and made some notes on it. "I'd suggest you start with the 1910 Census and look for Green Holloway in the Soundex."

"Soundex?" I said. "What is that?"

"It's like an index, but it's based on sounds, not spelling. Which is good, since the enumerators didn't always spell the names right. Holloway might have been recorded as, oh, H-a-l-i-w-a-y, for example, or even H-a-l-l-w-a-y; but the Soundex code would be the same."

"I see. Clever."

She took out a brochure and jotted another note on the scratch pad. "Holloway would be . . . H. Then L is a 4, and the W and Y don't count. That's H400. There will be a lot of other names listed under H400, like Holly and Hall, but that should narrow your search." She filled out a request voucher for me. "Even with the Soundex," she said as she wrote, "there are no guarantees. There are all sorts of omissions, duplicates, wrong names, wrong ages. Dad missed his great-grandmother in the 1900 Census, because she was living with her son-in-law and the enumerator had listed her with the son-in-law's family name. One of my great-great-grandfathers 'aged' fourteen years between the 1870 and 1880 Censuses; and his wife-to-be was listed twice in 1860. People weren't always home; so, the enumerator would try to get the information from a neighbor, who didn't always know. So you should always cross-check your information."

She directed me to an empty carrel, and, shortly after, an older man delivered the 1910 Soundex for Blount County, Tennessee. I threaded the microfilm spool into the viewer and spun forward, looking for H400. Each frame was an index card with the head of household on top and everyone else listed below with their ages and relationships.

I slowed when I started to see first names starting with G: Gary . . . George . . . Gerhard . . . Glenn . . . Granville . . . Gretchen . . . Gus . . . No Green. I backed up and checked each of the G's, one by one, thinking Green might be out of sequence.

Still, no luck. And I couldn't think of any other way "Green" might be spelled. Unless it was a nickname, in which case, forget it. I scrolled ahead to the M's. If the census taker had interviewed Mae, Green might be listed as "Mister."

But . . . No "Mister." Then I checked the M's again, this time searching for "Mae" or "May," because if Mister had died in the Spanish-American War rather than World War I, Mae herself would have been listed as head-of-household in 1910.

Still nothing. It was a fool's errand, anyway. For all I knew, Mae was really Anna-Mae or Lulu-Mae or some other such Appalachianism, which would make finding her close to impossible.

I tried the 1900 Soundex next. But I came up dry on that, too. No Green, no Mister, no Mae. Eventually, I gave up.

I leaned back in the chair and stretched my arms over my head. Now what? *We lived so far back in the hollers they had to pipe in the daylight.* It could be that the census takers had flat out missed her. Or she had already left the hills by 1900. In which case, I did not know where to search. She had gone to Cincinnati, I remembered. And to California. At one time or another, she had mentioned San Francisco, and Chicago, and Wyoming, and even New York City. The old bag had a lot of travel stickers on her.

I took a walk to stretch my legs. If I left now, and the trains were on time, and the traffic was light, I could still be home in time to tuck Dee-dee in. But a check of the sidewalk outside the building showed the crowds running thick. The Financial District was getting an early start on the weekend. Not a good time to be leaving the city. Not a good time at all. Traffic heading for the tunnels sat at a standstill. Tightly packed herds of humans trampled the sidewalks. I would have likened them to sheep, but for the in-your-face single-mindedness with which they marched toward their parking lots and subway entrances.

The trains would be SRO, packed in with tired, sweaty office workers chattering about Fashion Statements or Sunday's Big Game; or (the occasional Type A personality) hunched over their laptops, working feverishly on their next deal or their next angina, whichever came first.

Was there ever a time when the New York crowds thinned out? Perhaps there was a continual stream of drones flowing through the streets of Manhattan twenty-four hours a day. Or maybe they were simply walking around and around this one block just to fool me. A Potemkin Crowd.

I returned to the information desk. "I guess as long as I'm stuck here I'll check 1890." That would be before the Spanish-American War, so Green might be alive and listed.

"I'm sorry," Sara told me. "The 1890 Census was destroyed in a fire in 1921, and only a few fragments survived."

I sighed. "Dead end, I guess. I'm sorry I took up so much of your time."

"That's what I'm here for. You could try 1880, though, and look for the parents. There's a partial Soundex for households with children aged ten and under. If the woman was born in the 1870s like you think . . ."

I shook my head. "No. I know she was born a Murray, but I don't know her father's name." Checking each and every M600 for a young child named Mae was not an appealing task. I might only be killing time; but I had no intention of bludgeoning it to death. I'd have a better chance hunting Holloways, because Green's name was so out of the ordinary. But I'd have to go frame by frame there, too, since I didn't know his parents' names, either. That sort of painstaking research was the reason why God invented professionals.

Sara pointed to a row of shelves near the carrels. "There is one other option. There are printed indices of Heads of Households for 1870 and earlier."

I shook my head. "The grandparents? I don't know their names, either."

"Did she have a brother?"

"Zach," I said. "Just the two of them, as far as I know. At least, she's never mentioned any other siblings."

"Children sometimes were given their grandparents' names. Maybe her father's parents were Zach and Mae Murray. It's a shot in the dark, but what do you have to lose? If you don't look, you'll never find anything."

"Okay, thanks." I wandered over to the row of index volumes and studied them. I was blowing off the time now and I knew it. Still, I could always strike it lucky.

The indices for Tennessee ran from 1820 through 1860. Thick, bound volumes on heavy paper. No Soundex here. I'd have to remember to check alternate spellings. I pulled out the volume for 1860 and flipped through the pages until I found Murray. Murrays were "thick as ticks on a hound dog's hide," but none of them were named Zach. However, when I checked *H*, I did find a "Green Holloway" in District 2, Greenback, Tennessee. Mister's grandfather? How many Green Holloways could there be? I copied the information and put in a request for the spool; then, just for luck, I checked 1850, as well.

The 1850 Census listed a "Greenberry Hollaway," also in District 2, Greenback P.O. I chuckled. Greenberry? Imagine sending a kid to school with a name like Greenberry!

Green appeared in the 1840 and 1830 indexes, too. And 1830 listed a "Josh Murry" in the same census district as Green. Mae's great-grandfather? Worth a look, anyway.

The trail ended there. The Blount County returns for 1820 were lost, and all the earlier censuses had all been destroyed when the British burned Washington in 1814.

I put the volumes back on the shelf. There was a thick atlas on a reading stand next to the indices and, out of curiosity, I turned it open to Tennessee. It took me a while to find Greenback. When I finally did, I saw that it lay in Loudon County, not Blount.

"That doesn't make any sense," I muttered.

"What doesn't?" A shriveled, dried-up old man with wire-frame glasses was standing by my elbow waiting to use the atlas.

"The indices all say Blount County, but the town is in Loudon." I didn't bother to explain. It wasn't any of his business. There could be any number of reasons for the discrepancy. The Greenback post office could have serviced parts of Blount County.

The man adjusted his glasses and peered at the map. I stepped aside. "It's all yours," I said.

"Now, hold on, sonny." He opened his satchel, something halfway between a purse and a briefcase, and pulled out a dog-eared, soft-bound red book. He licked his forefinger and rubbed pages aside. He hummed and nodded as he read. "Here's your answer," he said, jabbing a finger at a table. "Loudon County was erected in 1870 from parts of Blount and neighboring counties. Greenback was in the part that became Loudon

County. See?" He closed the book one-handed with a snap. "It's simple."

I guess if hanging around musty old records is your whole life, it's easy to sound like an expert. He looked like something the Archives would have in storage anyway. "Thanks," I said.

The whole afternoon had been a waste of time. I had been searching in the wrong county. Blast the forgetfulness of age! Mae had said she had been born in Blount County, so I had looked in Blount County. And all the while, the records were tucked safely away under Loudon.

I checked the clock on the wall. Four-thirty? Too late to start over. Time to pack it in and catch the train.

When I returned to my carrel, however, I found the spool for 1860 Blount County had already been delivered. I considered sending it back, but decided to give it a fast read before leaving. I mounted the spool and spun the fast forward, slowing when I reached District 2. About a third of the way through, I stopped.

NAMES	AGE	SEX	COLOR	OCCUPATION, ETC.	VALUE OF REAL ESTATE	VALUE OF PERSONAL PROPERTY	BIRTHPLACE
Holloway, Green	56	M	W	Farmer	$800	$100	Tenn
" Mabel	37	F	"				"
" Zachary	22	M	"				"

Hah! There it was. Success — of sorts — at last! This Green Holloway must have been the same one whose Civil War records I had gotten. Green and Mabel Holloway begat Zach Holloway, who must have begat Green "Mister" Holloway. Jesus. If those ages were correct, Mabel was only fifteen when she did her begatting. Who said babies having babies was a modern thing? But, kids grew up faster back then. They took on a lot of adult responsibilities at fifteen or sixteen. Today, they behave like juveniles into their late twenties.

Now that I knew what I was looking for and where it was, it didn't take me very long to check the 1850 Census, as well.

NAMES	AGE	SEX	COLOR	OCCUPATION, ETC.	VALUE OF REAL ESTATE	BIRTHPLACE
Holloway, Greenberry	45	M	W	Farmer	$250	Tenn
" Mae	32	F	"			"
" Zach^y	12	M	"			"

Those names . . . The eerie coincidence gave me a queer feeling. And Mabel should have been twenty-seven, not thirty-two. (Or else she should have been forty-two in 1860.) But then I remembered Sara's cautions. How easy it was for enumerators to get names and ages wrong; and how the same names were used generation after generation.

Just one more spool, I promised myself. Then I head home.

Uncle Sugar had been less nosy in 1840. The Census listed only heads of households. Everyone else was tallied by age bracket.

NAMES OF HEADS OF FAMILIES	FREE WHITE PERSONS, INCLUDING HEADS OF FAMILIES																							
	MALES												FEMALES											
	To 5	5-10	10-15	15-20	20-30	30-40	40-50	50-60	60-70	70-80	80-90	90-100	To 5	5-10	10-15	15-20	20-30	30-40	40-50	50-60	60-70	70-80	80-90	90-100
Green^y Holloway	1					1											1							

The "white female" was surely Mabel, and she was in her twenties. So her age in 1860 had been wrong. She must have been forty-two, not thirty-seven. Twenty-two, thirty-two, forty-two. That made sense. I folded the sheet with the information and stuffed it in my briefcase. Sara had been right about cross checking the documentation. The census takers had not always gotten the straight skinny. Mabel had probably looked younger than her years in 1860 and a neighbor, asked for the data, had guessed low.

"She looks younger than her years." The phrase wriggled through my mind and I thought fleetingly of Dee-dee looking older than her years. For every yin there is a yang, and if the universe did balance . . . If for some reason Mabel herself never spoke to the enumerator and a neighbor in the next holler guessed her age instead, the guess would be low. So, twenty-seven, thirty-two, thirty-seven made a weird kind of sense, too. And it actually agreed better with the written documents!

And what if she kept it up? I laughed to myself. Now there was a crazy thought! Aging five years to the decade, by 1870 she would have seemed . . . mmm, forty-two. And today? Add another sixty-odd years, and Mabel would appear to be . . . A hundred and five or thereabouts. About as old as Mae seemed to be.

I paused with one arm in my jacket.

About as old as Mae seemed to be? I stared at the spool boxes stacked in the carrel, ready for pickup.

Greenberry and Mabel. Green and Mae? No, it was absurd. A wild coincidence of names. *The census records are not that reliable. And it's only that Dee-dee is aging too fast that you even* thought *about someone aging too slow.* I took a few steps toward the door.

And the 1830 Census? I hadn't bothered checking it. What if it listed a Green Holloway aged 20–29 and a "white female" *still* aged 20–29?

I turned and looked back at the reading room and my heart began to pound in my ears, and all of a sudden I knew why Dr. Bench had figured Mae for eighty-five three decades ago, and why Mae had feared for her sanity all her life.

> So early in the month of May,
> As the green buds were a-swelling.
> A young man on his death-bed lay,
> For the love of Barbry Ellen.

It was pitch-black out when I finally arrived home. There was a light on in the kitchen, none abovestairs. I parked in the driveway and got out and walked around the end of the garage through the gate into the backyard. The crickets were chirruping like a swing with a squeaky hinge. Lightning bugs drifted lazily through the air. I walked all the way to the back of the yard, to the edge of the woods, and leaned against a bent gum tree. The ground around me was littered with last year's prickly balls. I listened to the night sounds.

I had checked 1830 and found . . . I didn't know what I had found. Nothing. Everything. A few tantalizing hints. Greenberry, Mabel, and Zachary. Mister, Mae and . . . Zach? Not a younger brother, but a son? And another entry: Wm. Biddle, Jr., *a free man of color.* Mae had spoken of "Will Biddle who farmed two hollers over from us when I was a child . . ." But in 1830? In 1830?

There was a logical part of my mind that rejected those hints. Each had an alternative explanation. Coincidence of names. Clerical errors. Senile memory.

Sometimes we remember things only because we have been told them so often. I remember that I stepped in a birthday cake when I was two years old. It had been placed on the floor in the back of the family car and I had climbed over the seat and . . . But do I *remember* it? Or do I remember my parents telling me the story—and showing me the snapshot—so many times over the years that it has become real to me. Mae could be remembering family tales she had heard, scrambled and made *hers* by a slowly short-circuiting brain.

But there was another part of me that embraced those hints, that wanted to believe that Mae had known Margaret Sanger, had voted for Teddy Roosevelt, had danced on the White House lawn in a Sanitary Commission uniform, because if they were true . . .

I stepped away from the tree and a rabbit shot suddenly left to right in front of me. I watched it bound away . . . And spied figures moving about in the Carters' backyard. Henry and Barbara. I watched them for a while, wondering idly what they were up to. Then I recalled Henry's nickname for his wife—and a song that Mae had known.

I took the same route the rabbit had taken. Last year's dead leaves crackled and dry twigs snapped beneath my feet. I saw one of the Carters— Henry, I thought—come suddenly erect and look my way. I hoped he wouldn't call the police. Then I thought, Christ, they're newlyweds. What sort of backyard shenanigans was I about to walk in on?

I stopped and waved a hand. "That you, Henry? Barbara? It's Paul Wilkes."

A second shadow stood erect by the first. "What's wrong?" It was Barbara's voice.

"I—I saw you moving around back there and thought it might be prowlers. Is everything all right?"

"Sure," said Henry. "Come on out. You'll get tick-bitten if you stay in there."

"Why don't you have your yard light on?" I asked as I stepped from the woods. Stupid question. I could think of a couple of reasons. Brenda and I had once gone skinny-dipping in our pool at three in the morning. *Stifled laughter and urgent play, and the water glistening like pearls on her skin.* That had been years ago, of course; but sometimes it was good to remember that there had once been times like that.

"It would spoil the viewing," Henry said.

Now that I was close enough, I saw that they had a telescope set up on a tripod. It was a big one. "Oh. Are you an astronomer?"

Henry shook his head. "I'm a genetic engineer, or I will be when I finish my dissertation. Barbry's going to be a biochemist. Astronomy is our hobby."

"I see." I felt uncomfortable, an intruder; but I had come there with a purpose. I made as if to turn away and then turned back. "Say, as long as I'm here, there is a question you might be able to answer for me."

"Sure." They were an obliging couple. The moon was half-full, the air was spring evening cool, they did not really want me there interrupting whatever it was that the sky-gazing would have led to.

"I've heard Henry call you Barbry," I said to Barbara. "And . . . Do you know a song called 'Barbry Ellen'?"

She laughed. "You mean 'Barbara Allen.' Sure. That's where Henry came up with the nickname. He's into folksinging. 'Barbry Ellen' is an older version."

"Well, someone told me it was the 'old president's favorite song,' and I wondered if you knew—"

"Which old president? That's easy. George Washington. You see, he had this secret crush on his best friend's wife, and . . ."

"George Washington? Are you sure?"

"Well, there might have been other presidents who liked it. But Washington's partiality is on the record, and the song has been out of vogue a long, long time."

"Was that all you wanted to know?" asked Henry. There was something in his voice that sounded a lot like "good-bye." He wasn't happy, I could tell. I had spoiled the mood for him.

"Yes, certainly," I said. "I thought you might have been prowlers." I backed away into the woods, then turned and walked quickly home.

I learned me that 'un when I was knee-high to a grasshopper. Pa told me it was the president's favorite song. The old president, from when his pappy fought in the War.

The old president, from when his pappy fought in the War.

> *Lost my partner, what'll I do?*
> *Lost my partner, what'll I do?*
> *Lost my partner, what'll I do?*
> *Skip to my love, my darling.*

Brenda drank tea. She always allowed the bag to steep for a precise five minutes (read the package) and always squeezed it dry with her teaspoon. She always disposed of the bag in the trash before drinking from the cup. When she drank, she held the saucer in her left hand and the cup in her right and hugged her elbows close to her body. She stood near the French doors in the family room, gazing out toward the backyard and the woods beyond. I had no idea if she had heard me.

"I said, I think I'll go over to Sunny Dale today and look in on Mrs. Holloway."

Brenda held herself so still she was nearly rigid. Not because she was reacting to what I had said. She always stood that way. She spent her life at attention.

"You didn't have any plans, did you?"

A small, precise shake of the head. "No. No plans. We never have any plans." A sip of tea that might have been measured in minims. "Maybe I'll go into the office, too. There are always cases to work on."

I hesitated a moment longer before leaving. When I reached the front door, I heard her call.

"Paul?"

"Yes?" Down the length of the hall I could see her framed by the glass doors at the far end. She had turned around and was facing me. "What?"

"Why do you have to go in today? It's Saturday."

"It's . . . nothing I can talk about yet. A wild notion. It might be nothing more than a senile woman's ravings, but it might be the most important discovery of the century. Brenda, if I'm right, it could change our lives."

Even from where I stood I could see the faint smile that trembled on her lips. "Yes, it could, at that." She turned around and faced the glass again. "You do what you have to do, Paul. So will I."

It was odd, but I suddenly remembered how much we had once done together. Silly things, simple things. Football games, Scrabble, Broadway shows. Moments public and private. The party had asked Brenda to run for the state legislature one time, and I had urged her to accept, but the baby had been due and . . . Somehow, now we stood at opposite ends of the house. I thought for a moment of asking her to come with me to the Home, but thought better of it. Brenda would find those old, gray creatures more distressing than I did. "Look," I said, "this should only take a couple hours. I'll call you and we'll do something together this afternoon. Take in a movie, maybe."

She nodded in her distracted way. I saw that she had spilled tea into her saucer.

Once at the Home, I sought out Mae in her garden retreat, hoping that she was in a better mood than yesterday. I had a thousand questions to ask her. A dozen puzzles and one hope. But when she saw me coming, her face retreated into a set of tight lines: Eyes, narrowed; mouth and lips, thin and disapproving.

"Go away," said Mae Holloway.

"I only wanted to ask a few—"

"I said, go away! Why are you always pestering me?"

"Don't mind her," said a voice by my elbow. "She's been that way since yesterday." I turned and saw Jimmy Kovacs, the retired printer. "Headache. Maybe you should give her something."

"You don't need a doctor to take aspirin."

He shook his head. "Aspirin didn't work. She needs something stronger. Might be a migraine. I had an allergy once. To hot dog meat. Every time I had a frank, my head felt like fireworks going off inside. So, my doc, he tells me—"

"I'll see what I can do," I said. Old folks chatter about little else than their ailments. They compare them the way young boys compare . . . Well, you know what I mean. "Mine is bigger than yours." They have contests, oldsters do, to see who has the biggest illness. The winner gets to die.

I sat on the stone bench beside Mae. "Jimmy tells me you have a headache," I said.

"Jimmy should mind his own affairs."

"Where does it hurt?"

"In my haid, jackass. That's what makes it a headache."

"No, I mean is it all over or in one spot? Is it a dull ache or sharp points. Is it continual, or does it come in bursts? Do you see or hear anything along with the headache?"

She gave me a look. "How do you make a headache into such a contraption?"

I shrugged. "There are many things that can cause a headache. When did it start?" If I could relieve her pain, she might be willing to answer the questions I had about her family history.

She squinted at the ground, her face tight as a drum. I heard her suck in her breath. Bees danced among the flowers to our right; the fragrances hung in the air. "Yesterday afternoon," she said. "Yesterday afternoon, after you left. It was like the sun come up inside my head. I was lying down for a nap when everything turned blind white for a few seconds and I heard a chorus a-singing hymns. I thought I'd surely died and gone to heaven." She took a deep breath and massaged her left temple with her fingers. "Somedays I'ud as lief I were dead. All these here aches and pains . . . And I cain't do the things I used to. I used to dance. I used to love to dance, but I can't do that no more. And everybody who ever mattered to me is a long time gone."

Her parents. Little Zach. Green Holloway. Gone a very long time, if I was right. Joe Paxton. Ben Wickham. There must have been plenty of others, besides. Folks in Cincinnati, in California, in Wyoming. She left a trail of alienation behind her every place she had ever been. It was a cold trail, in more ways than one.

"When the white light faded out, I saw it weren't an angel choir, after all. It were Christy's Minstrels that time when they come to Knoxville, and Mister and me and . . ." She frowned and shook her head. "Mister and me, we tarryhooted over to hear 'em. Doc, it was the clearest spell I ever had. I was a-settin' in the audience right down in front. I clean forgot I was a-bedded down here in Sunny Dale."

Sometimes migraines triggered visions. Some of the saints had suffered migraines and seen the Kingdom of God. "Yes?" I prompted.

"Well, Mister was a-settin' on my left holding my hand; and someone's man-child, maybe fifteen year, was press't up agin me on my right—oh, we was packed in almighty tight, I tell you—but, whilst I could see and hear as clear as I can see and hear you, I couldn't feel any of them touching me. When I thunk on it, I could feel that I was lying abed with the sheets over me."

I nodded. "You weren't getting any tactile memories, then. I think your—"

She didn't hear me. "The troupe was setting on benches, with each row higher than the one in front—Tiers, that be what they call 'em. They all stood to sing the medley, 'cept 'Mr. Interlocutor,' who sat in a chair front and center. Heh. That was the out-doin'est chair I ever did see. Like a king's throne, it was. They sang 'Jim Along Josie' and 'Ring, Ring the Banjo.' I h'ain't heared them tunes since who flung the chuck. The interlocutor was sided by the soloists on his right and the glee singers—what they later called barbershop singers—on the left." She gestured, moving both hands out from the center. "Then the banjo player and the dancer. Then there was four end men, two t' either side. Those days, only the end men were in the Ethiopian business."

"The Ethiopian business?"

"You know. Done up in blackface."

Images of Jolson singing "Mammy." Exaggerated lips; big, white, buggy eyes. An obscene caricature. "Blackface!"

My disapproval must have shown in my voice, for Mae grew defensive. "Well, that was the only way us reg'lar folks ever got to hear nigra music back then," she said, rubbing her temple. "The swells could hear 'em anytime; but the onlyest nigras I ever saw 'fore I left the hills was Will Biddle and his kin, and they didn't do a whole lot of singing and dancing."

"Nigras?" That was worse than blackface. I tried to remind myself that Mae had grown up in a very different world.

Mae seemed to refocus. Her eyes lost the dreamy look. "What did I say? Nigra? Tarnation, that isn't right, anymore, is it? They say 'coloreds' now."

"African-American. Or black."

She shook her head, then winced and rubbed her temple again. "They weren't mocking the col—the black folks. The ministrels weren't. Not

then. It was fine music. Toe-tapping. And the banjo . . . Why, white folks
took that up from the coloreds. But we'uns couldn't go to dark-town shows,
and they couldn't come to us—not in them days. So, sometimes white folks
dressed up to play black music. Daddy Rice, he was supposed to be the
best, though I never did see him strut 'Jim Crow'; but James Bland that
wrote a lot of the tunes was a black man his own self. I heared he went off
to France later 'cause of the way the white folks was always greenin' him."

"I see. Has your headache subsided since then?" *Minstrel shows*, I
thought.

"It's all so mixed up. These memories I keep getting. It's like a kalidey-
scope I had as a young 'un. All those pretty beads and mirrors . . ."

"Your headache, Mrs. Holloway. I asked if it was still the same." Try to
keep old folks on the track. Go ahead, try it.

She grimaced. "Why, it comes and goes, like ocean waves. I seen the
ocean onct. Out in Californey. Now, that was a trek, let me tell you. Folks
was poor on account of the depression, so I took shank's mare a long part
of the way, just like Sweet Betsy." She sighed. "That was always a favorite
of mine. Every time I heared it, it was like I could see it all in my mind.
The singing around the campfire; the cold nights on the prairie. The In-
juns a-whooping and a-charging . . ." She began to sing.

> *"The Injuns come down in a great yelling horde.*
> *And Betsy got skeered they would scalp her adored.*
> *So behind the front wagon wheel Betsy did crawl.*
> *And she fought off the Injuns with powder and ball."*

Mae tried to smile, but it was a weak and pained one. "I went back to
Californey years later. I taken the *Denver Zephyr*, oh, my, in the 1920s I
think it was. Packed into one of them old coach cars, cheek by jowl, the
air so thick with cigar smoke. And when you opened the window, why you
got coal ash in your face from the locomotive."

"Look, why don't you come to the clinic with me, and I'll see if I have
anything for that headache of yours."

She nodded and rose from her bench, leaning on her stick. She took
one step and looked puzzled. Then she staggered a little. "Dizzy," she muttered. Then she toppled forward over her stick and fell to the ground. I leapt
to my feet and grabbed her by the shoulders, breaking her fall.

"Hey!" I said. "Careful! You'll break something."

Her eyes rolled back up into her head and her limbs began to jerk uncontrollably. I looked over my shoulder and saw Jimmy Kovacs hurrying up the garden path. "Quick," I said. "Call an ambulance! Call Dr. Khan! Tell her to meet us at the hospital."

Jimmy hesitated. He looked at Mae, then at me. "What's wrong?" he said.

"Hurry! I think she's having another stroke."

Jimmy rushed off and I turned back to Mae. Checkout time, I thought. But why now? Why now?

I have always loved hospitals. They are factories of health, mass producers of treatments. The broken and defective bodies come in, skilled craftsmen go to work—specialists from many departments, gathered together in one location—and healthy and restored bodies emerge. Usually. No process is one hundred percent efficient. Some breakdowns cannot be repaired. But it is more efficient to have the patients come to the doctor than to have the doctor waste time traveling from house to house. Only when health is mass produced can it be afforded by the masses.

Yet, I can see how some people would dislike them. The line is a thin one between the efficient and the impersonal.

Khan and I found Mae installed in the critical care unit. The ward was shaped like a cul-de-sac, with the rooms arranged in a circle around the nurses' station. White sheets, antiseptic smell. Tubes inserted wherever they might prove useful. Professionally compassionate nurses. Bill Wing was waiting for us there. With clipboard in hand and stethoscope dangling from his neck, he looked like an archetype for The Doctor. We shook hands and I introduced him to Khan. Wing led us out into the corridor, away from the patient. Mae was in a coma, but it was bad form to discuss her case in front of her, as if she were not there.

"It was not a stroke," he told us, "but a tumor. An astrocytoma encroaching on the left temporal lobe. It is malignant and deeply invasive." Wing spoke with an odd Chinese-British accent. He was from Guandong by way of Hong Kong.

I heard Khan suck in her breath. "Can it be removed?" she asked.

Wing shook his head. "On a young and healthy patient, maybe; though I would hesitate to perform the operation even then. On a woman this old and weak . . ." He shook his head again. "I have performed a decompression to relieve some of the pressure, but the tumor itself is not removable."

Khan sighed. "So sad. But she has had a long life."

"How much longer does she have?" I asked.

Wing pursed his lips and looked inscrutable. "That is hard to say. Aside from the tumor, she is in good health . . . for a woman her age, of course. It could be tomorrow; it could be six months. She has a time bomb in her head, and no one knows how long the fuse is. We only know that the fuse . . ."

"Has been lit," finished Khan. Wing looked unhappy, but nodded.

"As the tumor progresses," he continued, "her seizures will become more frequent. I suspect there will be pain as the swelling increases." He paused and lowered his head slightly, an Oriental gesture.

"There must be something you can do," I said. Khan looked at me.

"Sometimes," she said, "there is nothing that can be done."

I shook my head. "I can't accept that." Holloway could not die. Not yet. Not now. I thought of all those secrets now sealed in her head. They might be fantasies, wild conclusions that I had read into partial data; but I had to know. I had to know.

"There is an end to everything." Noor Khan gazed toward the double doors that led to the medical CCU. "Though it is always hard to see the lights go out."

I drew my coat on. "I'm going to go to the university library for a while."

Khan gave me a peculiar look. "The library?" She shrugged. "I will stay by her side. You know how she feels about hospitals. She will be frightened when she recovers consciousness. Best if someone she knows is with her."

I nodded. "She may not regain consciousness for some time," I reminded her. "What about your patients?"

"Dr. Mendelson will handle my appointments tomorrow. I called him before I came over."

All right, let her play the martyr! I tugged my cap onto my head. Khan didn't expect thanks, did she? I could just picture the old crone's ravings. The hysteria. She would blame Khan, not thank her, for bringing her here.

As I reached the door, I heard Khan gasp. "She's singing!"

I turned. "What?"

Khan was hovering over the bed. She flapped an arm. "Come. Listen to this."

As if I had not listened to enough of her ditties. I walked to the bedside and leaned over. The words came soft and slurred, with pauses in between as she sucked in breath: "There was an old woman . . . at the foot of the hill . . . If she ain't moved away . . . she's living there still . . . Hey-diddle . . . day-diddle . . . de-dum . . ." Her voice died away into silence. Khan looked at me.

"What was that all about?"

I shook my head. "Another random memory," I said. "The tumor is busy, even if she is not."

It was not until midafternoon, buried deep in the stacks at the university library, that I remembered my promise to call Brenda. But when I phoned from the lobby, Consuela told me that she had gone out and that I was not to wait up for her.

> *But the summer faded, and a chilly blast.*
> *O'er that happy cottage swept at last;*
> *When the autumn song birds woke the dewy morn,*
> *Our little "Prairie Flow'r" was gone.*

In the year before Deirdre was born, Brenda and I took a vacation trip to Boston and Brenda laid out an hour-by-hour itinerary, listing each and every site we planned to visit. Along the way, she kept detailed logs of gas, mileage, arrival and departure times at each attraction, expenses, even tips to bellboys. It did not stop her from enjoying Boston. She did not insist that we march in lockstep to the schedule. "It's a guide, not a straitjacket," she had said. Yet, she spent an hour before bed each night updating and revising the next day's itinerary. Like an itch demanding a scratch, like a sweet tooth longing for chocolate, satisfying the urge to organize gave her some deep, almost sensual pleasure.

Now, of course, everything was planned and scheduled, even small trips. Sometimes the plan meant more than the journey.

Brenda frowned as I pulled into the secluded lot and parked in front of an old, yellow, wood-frame building. A thick row of fir trees screened the office building from the busy street and reduced the sound of rushing traffic to a whisper.

"Paul, why are we stopping? What is this place?"

"A lab," I told her. "That phone call just before we left the house . . . Some work I gave them is ready."

"Can't you pick it up tomorrow when you're on duty?" she said. "We'll be late."

"We won't be late. The Sawyers never start on time, and there'll be three other couples to keep them busy."

"I hope that boy of theirs isn't there. He gives me the creeps, the way he stares at people . . ."

"Maybe they changed his medication," I said. "Do you want to come in, or will you wait out here?"

"Is there a waiting area?"

"I don't know. I've never been here before."

Brenda gave a small sound, halfway between a cough and a sigh. Then she made a great show of unbuckling her seat belt.

"You don't have to come in if you don't want to," I said.

"Can't you just get this over with?"

Inside the front door was a small lobby floored with dark brown tiles. The directory on the wall listed three tenants in white, plastic, pushpin letters: a management consulting firm, a marriage counselor, and the genetics lab.

When Brenda learned that S/P Microbiology, was situated on the third floor, she rolled her eyes and decided to wait in the lobby. "Don't be long," she said, her voice halfway between an order, a warning, and a plaintive plea to keep the schedule.

The receptionist at S/P was a young redhead wearing a headset and throat mike. He showed me to a chair in a small waiting room, gave me a not-too-old magazine to read, and spoke a few words into his mouthpiece. When the telephone rang, he touched his earpiece once and answered the phone while on his way back to his station. Clever, I thought, to have a receptionist not tied to a desk.

I was alone only for a moment before Charles Randolph Singer himself came out. He was a short, slightly rumpled-looking man a great deal younger than his reputation had led me to expect. His white lab coat hung open, revealing a pocket jammed full of pens and other instruments. "Charlie Singer," he said. "You're Dr. Wilkes?"

"Yes."

He shook my hand. "You sure did hand us one larruping good problem." Then he cocked his head sideways and looked at me. "Where'd you get the samples?"

"I'd . . . rather not say yet."

"Hunh. Doctor-patient crap, right? Well, you're paying my rent with this job, so I won't push it. Come on in back. I'll let Jessie explain things."

I followed Singer into a larger room lined with lab benches and machines. A dessicator and a centrifuge, a mass spec, a lot of other equipment I didn't recognize. A large aquarium filled with brackish water, fish and trash occupied one corner. The plastic beverage can rings and soda bottles were dissolving into a floating, liquid scum, which the fish calmly ignored.

"Jessie!" Singer said. "Wilkes is here."

A round-faced woman peered around the side of the mass spectrometer. "Oh," she said. "You." She was wearing a headset similar to the receptionist's.

"Jessica Burton-Peeler," said Singer introducing us, "is the second-best geneticist on the face of the planet."

Peeler smiled sweetly. "That was last year, Charlie." She spoke with a slight British accent.

Singer laughed and pulled a stick of gum from the pocket of his lab coat. He unwrapped it and rolled it into a ball between his fingers. "Tell Doctor Wilkes here what we found." He popped the wad of gum into his mouth.

"Would you like some tea or coffee, Doctor? I can have Eamonn bring you a cup."

"No, thanks. My wife is waiting downstairs. We were on our way to a dinner party, but I couldn't wait until tomorrow to find out."

Peeler said, "I'll have Eamonn take her something, too."

Singer gave me a speculative look. "Find out what?"

"What you found out."

After a moment, Singer grunted and shrugged. "All right. We cultured all three cell samples," he said. "The 'B' sample was normal in all respects. The cells went through fifty-three divisions."

"Which is about average," Peeler added. "As for the other two . . . One of them divided only a dozen times—"

"The 'A' sample," I interjected.

"Yes," she said after a momentary pause. "The 'A' sample. But the 'C' sample . . . That one divided 123 times."

I swallowed. "And that is . . . abnormal?"

"Abnormal?" Singer laughed. "Doc, that measurement is so far above the Gaussian curve that you can't even see abnormal from there."

"The 'A' sample wasn't normal, either," said Peeler quietly.

I looked at her and she looked at me calmly and without expression. "Well," I said and coughed. "Well."

"So, what's next?" Singer demanded. "You didn't send us those tissue samples just to find out they were different. You already knew that—or you suspected it—when you sent them in. We've confirmed it. Now what?"

"I'd like you to compare them and find out how their DNA differs."

Singer nodded after a thoughtful pause. "Sure. If the reason is genetic. We can look for factors common to several 'normal' samples but different for your 'A' and 'C' samples. Run polymerase chain reactions. Tedious, but elementary."

"And then . . ." I clenched and unclenched my fists. "I've heard you work on molecular modifiers."

"Nanomachines," said Singer. "I have a hunch it'll be a big field some-day, and I'm planning to get in on the ground floor." He jerked a thumb over his shoulder at the aquarium. "Right now I'm working on a bacterium that eats plastic waste."

"Dear Lord," said Burton-Peeler in sudden wonder. "You want us to modify the DNA, don't you?"

Singer looked from me to his wife. "Modify the DNA?"

"Yes," I started to say.

Burton-Peeler pursed her lips. "Modify the 'A' sample, of course. What-ever factor we find in the 'C' sample that sustains the cell division . . . You want us to splice that into the short-lived sample."

I nodded, unable to speak. "I thought it might be possible to bring it up to normal."

Singer rubbed his jaw. "I don't know. Splicing bacterial DNA is one thing. Human DNA is another. A universe more of complexity. Of course, there is that business with the cystic fibrosis aerosol. They used a modified rhinovirus to carry the mucus-producing genes into the lungs. If the fac-tor is gene specific, we could do something similar. Infect the cells with a retrovirus and . . ."

"Then you can do it?"

"Now hold on. I said no such thing. I said *maybe* it was possible, *if* the chips fall right. But there'll be some basic research needed. It will cost. A lot."

"I'll . . . find the money. Somehow."

Singer shook his head slowly. "I don't think you can find that much. You're talking about maybe three to five years research here."

"Three to—" I felt the pit of my stomach drop away. "I don't have three to five years." Dee-dee would be dead by then. And Mae, too, taking the secret in her genes with her.

"We'll do it at cost," said Burton-Peeler. Singer turned and looked at his wife.

"What?"

"We'll do it at cost, Charlie. I'll tell you why later." She looked back to me. "Understand, we still cannot promise fast results. When you set off into the unknown, you cannot predict your arrival time."

Go for broke. Damn the torpedoes. "Just try is all I ask."

Burton-Peeler saw me out. On the landing to the stairwell she stopped. "You're the father of the young girl with progeria," she said. "I saw it in the paper a few years ago. The 'A' sample was hers, wasn't it?"

I nodded. "Yes, and the second sample was my own. For comparison." I turned to go.

Peeler stopped me with an arm on my sleeve. She looked into my eyes. "Whose was the third sample?" she asked.

I smiled briefly and sadly. "My faith, that the universe balances."

In the lobby, Brenda was just handing a teacup and saucer back to Singer's red-haired receptionist when she saw me coming. With a few brisk motions she collected her things and was already breezing out the door as I caught up with her.

"I'll drive," she said. "We're way behind schedule now, thanks to you."

I said nothing, and she continued in what was supposed to be an idly curious tone. "Who was that woman with you? The one on the landing."

"Woman? Oh, that was Jessica Burton-Peeler. Singer's wife."

Brenda arched an eyebrow and made a little moue with her lips. "She's a little on the plump side," she said. "Do you find plump women attractive?"

I didn't have the time to deal with Brenda's insecurities. "Start the car," I told her. "We'll be late for dinner."

> They say we are aged and gray, Maggie
> As spray by the white breakers flung;
> But to me you're as fair as you were, Maggie,
> When you and I were young.

Mae Holloway lay between white sheets, coupled to tubes and wires. She lay with her eyes closed, and her arms limp by her sides atop the sheets. Her mouth hung half-open. She seemed gray and shrunken; drawn, like a wire through a die. Her meager white hair was nearly translucent.

She looked like a woman half her age.

Noor Khan was sitting near the wall reading a magazine. She looked up as I entered the room. "They told you?"

"That Mae has recovered consciousness? Yes. I'm surprised to see you still here."

Khan looked at the bed. "I have made arrangements. She has no family to keep watch."

"No," I agreed. "They are long gone." Longer than Khan could suppose. "Is she sleeping?"

She hesitated a moment, then spoke in a whisper. "Not really. I think that as long as she keeps her eyes closed she can pretend she is not in hospital. Those memories of hers . . . The consciousness-doubling, you called it. I think they play continually, now. The pressure from the tumor on the temporal lobe."

I nodded. Suppress all external stimuli and Mae could—in a biological kind of virtual reality—live again in the past. If we spoke too loudly, it would bring her back to a time and place she did not want. "Why don't you take a break," I said. "I'll sit with her for a while."

Khan cocked her head to the side and looked at me. "You will."

"Yes. Is that so surprising?"

She started to say something and then changed her mind. "I will be in the cafeteria." And then she fluttered out.

When she was gone, I pulled the chair up to the bedside and sat in it. "Mae? It's Dr. Wilkes." I touched her gently on the arm, and she seemed to flinch from the contact. "Mae?"

"I hear yuh," she said. Her voice was low and weak and lacked her usual snap. I had to lean close to hear her. "It'ud pleasure me if you'd company for a mite. It's been mighty lonely up hyar."

"Has it? But Dr. Khan—"

"I kilt the b'ar," she whispered, "but it stove up Pa something awful. He cain't hardly git around no more, so I got to be doin' for him." She paused as if listening. "I'm not so little as that, mister; I jest got me a puny bone-box. I ain't no yokum. I been over the creek. And I got me a Tennessee toothpick, too, in case you have thoughts about a little girl with a crippled-up pa. What's yore handle, mister?"

"Mrs. Holloway," I said gently. "Don't you know me?"

Mae giggled. "Right pleased to meet you, Mister Holloway. Green-berry's a funny name, so I'll just call you Mister. If you'll set a spell, I'll whup you up a bait to eat. H'ain't much, only squirrel; but I aim to go hunting tomorry and find a deer that'll meat us for a spell."

I pulled back and sat up straight in my chair. She was reliving her first meeting with Green Holloway. Was she too far gone into the quicksand of nostalgia to respond to me? "Mae," I said more loudly, shaking her shoulder. "It's Dr. Wilkes. Can you hear me?"

Mae gasped and her eyes flew open. "Whut . . . ? Where . . . ?" The eyes lighted on me and went narrow. "You."

"Me," I agreed. "How are you feeling, Mrs. Holloway?"

"I'm a-gonna die. How do you want me to feel?"

Relieved? Wasn't there a poem about weary rivers winding safe to the sea? But, no matter how long and weary the journey, can anyone face the sea at the end of it? "Mrs. Holloway, do you remember the time you were on the White House lawn and the president came out?"

Her face immediately became wary and she looked away from me. "What of it?"

"That president. It was Lincoln, wasn't it?"

She shook her head, a leaf shivering in the breeze.

I took a deep breath. "The Sanitary Commission was the Union Army's civilian medical corps. If you were wearing that uniform, you were re-membering the 1860s. That business on the lawn. It happened. I looked it up. The dancing. 'Listen to the Mockinbird.' Lincoln coming outside to join the celebration. The whole thing. You know it, but you won't admit it because it sounds impossible."

"Sounds impossible?" She turned her head and looked at me at last. "How could I remember Lincoln? I'm not *that* old!"

"Yes, you are, Mae. You are that old. It's just that those early memories have gone all blurry. It's become hard for you to tell the decades apart. Your oldest memories had faded entirely, until your stroke revived them."

"You're talking crazy."

"I think it must be a defense mechanism," I went on as if she had not spoken. "The blurring and forgetting. It keeps the mental desktop cleared of clutter by shoving the old stuff aside."

"Doc . . ."

"But, every now and then, one of those old, faded memories would pop up, wouldn't it? Some impossible recollection. And you would think . . ."

"That I was going crazy." In a whisper, half to herself, she said, "I was always afraid of that, as long back as I can remember."

No wonder. Sporadic recollections of events generations past . . . Could a sane mind remember meeting Lincoln? "Mae. I found your name in the 1850 census."

She shook her head again. Disbelief. But behind it . . . Hope? Relief that those impossible memories might be real? "Doc, how can it be possible?"

I spread my hands. "I don't know. Something in your genes. I have some people working on it, but . . . I think you have been aging slow. I don't know how that is possible. Maybe it has never happened before. Maybe you're the only one. Or maybe there were others and no one ever noticed. Maybe they were killed in accidents; or they really did go mad; or they thought they were recalling past lives. It doesn't matter. Mae, I've spent the last week in libraries and archives. You were born around 1800."

"No!"

"Yes. Your father was a member of Captain James Scott's settlement company. The Murrays, the Hammontrees, the Holloways, the Blacks, and others. The overmountain men, they were called. They bought land near Six Mile Creek from the Overhill Cherokees."

I paused. Mae said nothing, but she continued to look at me, slowly shaking her head. "Believe me," I said. "Your father's name was Josh, wasn't it?"

"Josiah. Folks called him Josh. I . . . I had forgotten my folks for such a long time; and now that I can remember, it pains me awful."

"Yes. I overheard. A bear mauled him."

"Doc, he was such a fine figure of a man. Right portly—I mean, handsome. He cut a swath wherever he walked. To see him laid up like that . . . Well, it sorrowed me something fierce. And him always saying I shouldn't wool over him."

"He died sometime between 1830 and 1840, after you married Green Holloway."

She looked into the distance. "Mister, he was a long hunter. He come on our homestead one day and saw how things stood and stayed to help out. Said it wasn't fittin' for a young gal to live alone like that with no man to side her. 'Specially a button like I was. There was outlaws and renegades all up and down the Trace who wouldn't think twice about bothering a young girl. When Pa finally said 'twas fittin', we jumped the broom 'til the preacher-man come through." She stopped. "Doc?"

"Yes?"

"Doc, you must have it right. Because . . . Because, how long has it been since folks lived in log cabins, and long hunters dressed up in buckskins?"

"A long time," I said. "A very long time."

"Seems like just a little while ago to me, but I know it can't be. The Natchez Trace? I just never gave it much thought."

Have you ever seen a neglected field overgrown with weeds? That was Mae's memory. Acres of thistle and briar. All perspective lost, all sense of elapsed time. "Your memories were telescoped," I said. "Remember when you sang 'Sweet Betsy from Pike' for me, and you said how real it all seemed to you? Well, after the Civil War, sometime during the Great Depression of the 1870s, you went out West, probably on one of the last wagon trains, after they finished the railroad. After that, I lost track."

She stayed quiet for a long time, and I began to think she had dozed off. Then she spoke again.

"Sometimes I remember the Tennessee hills," she said in a faraway voice, "all blue and purple and cozy with family." She sighed. "I loved them mountains," she said. "We had us a hardscrabble, side-hill farm. The hills was tilted so steep we could plow both sides of an acre. And the cows had their legs longer on the one side than the other so's they could stand straight up." She chuckled at the hillbilly humor. "Oh, it was a hard life.

You kids today don't know. But in the springtime, when the piney roses and starflowers and golden bells was in bloom, and the laurel hells was all purpled up; why, Doc, you couldn't ask God for a purtier sight." She sighed. "And other times . . . Other times, I remember a ranch in high-up, snowcapped mountains with long-horned cattle and vistas where God goes when He wants to feel small. There was a speakeasy in Chicago, where the jazz was hot; and a bawdy house in Frisco, where I was." She let her breath out slowly and closed her eyes again. "I remember wearing bustles and bloomers, and linen and lace, and homespun and broadcloth. I've been so many people, I don't know who I am."

She opened her eyes and looked at me. "But I was always alone, except in them early years. With Mister. And with Daddy and my brother Zach." A tear dripped down the side of her face. I pulled a tissue from the box and blotted it up for her. "There weren't nobody left for me. Nobody."

I hesitated for a moment. Then I said, "Mae, you never had a brother."

"Now what are you talking about? I remember him clear as day."

"I've checked the records. Your mother died, and your father never re-married."

Mae started to speak, then frowned. "Pa did tell me once that he'd never hitch ag'in, because he loved the dust of Ma's feet and the sweat of her body more than he loved any other woman. But Zach—"

"Was your own child."

She sucked in her breath between clenched teeth. "No, he weren't! He was near my own age."

"You remember Zach from 1861 when he followed your husband into the army. He was twenty-two then, and you . . . Well, you seemed to be thirty-seven to those around you. So, in your memory he seems like a brother. By the time you rejoined him on his ranch in Wyoming, he was even a bit older than your apparent age. Remember how you thought he resembled Mister? Well, that was because he was Mister's son. I think . . . I think that was when you started forgetting how the years passed for you. Mae, no one ever ran out on you. You just outlived them. They grew old and they died and you didn't. And after a while you just wouldn't dare get close to anyone."

Tears squeezed from behind her eyes. "Stop it! Every time you say something, you make me remember."

"In all this time, Mae, you've never mentioned your child. You did have one; the clinical evidence is there. If Zach wasn't your boy, who was? Who was the boy sitting next to you at the minstrel show in Knoxville?"

She looked suddenly confused, and there was more to her confusion than the distance of time. "I don't know." Her eyes glazed and she looked to her right. I knew she was reseeing the event. "Zach?" she said. "Is that you, boy? Zach? Oh, it is. It is." She refocused on me. "He cain't hear me," she said plaintively. "He hugged me, but I couldn't feel his arms."

"I know. It's only a memory."

"I want to feel his arms around me. They grow up so fast, you know. The young 'uns. One day, they're a baby, cute as a button; the next, all growed up and gone for a soldier. All growed up. I could see it happening. All of 'em, getting older and older. I thought there was something wrong with me. That I'd been a bad girl, because I kilt my ma; and the Good Man was punishing me by holding me back from the pearly gates. If'n I never grew old, I'd never die. And if I never died, I'd never see any of my kinfolk again. Doc, you can't know what it's like, knowing your child will grow old and wither like October corn and die right before your eyes."

For a moment, I could not breathe. "Oh, I know," I whispered. "I know."

"Zach . . . I lived to see him turn to dust in the ground. He died in my own arms, a feeble, old man, and he asked me to sing 'Home, Sweet Home,' like I used to when he was a young 'un. Oh, little Zach!" And she began to cry in earnest. She couldn't move her arms to wipe the tears away, so I pulled another tissue from the box on the tray and dabbed at her cheeks.

She reached out a scrawny hand and clutched my arm. "Thank you, Doc. Thank you. You helped me find my child again. You helped me find my boy."

And then I did an odd thing. I stood and bent low over the bed and I kissed Mae Holloway on her withered cheek.

I'm going there to see my mother.
She said she'd meet me when I come.
I'm only going over Jordan,
I'm only going over home.

My days at the Home passed by in an anonymous sameness, dispensing medicines, treating aches and pains. Only a handful of people came to see me; and those with only trivial complaints. Otherwise, I sat unmolested in my office, the visitor's chair empty. I found it difficult even to concentrate on my journals. Finally, almost in desperation, I began making rounds, dropping in on Rosie and Jimmy and the others, chatting with them, enduring their pointless, rambling stories; sometimes suggesting dietary or exercise regimens that might improve their well-being. Anything to feel useful. I changed a prescription on Old Man Morton, now the Home's Oldest Resident, and was gratified to see him grow more alert. Sometimes you have to try different medications to find a treatment that works best for a particular individual.

Yet, somehow those days seemed empty. The astonishing thing to me was how little missed Mae Holloway was by the other residents. Oh, some of them asked after her politely. Jimmy did. But otherwise it was as if the woman had evaporated, leaving not even a void behind. Partly, I suspect, it was because they were unwilling to face up to this reminder of their own mortality. But partly, too, it must have been a sense of relief that her aloof and abrasive presence was gone. If she never had any friends, Mae had told me, she wouldn't miss them when they were gone. But neither did they miss her.

I usually stopped at the hospital on my way home, sometimes to obtain a further tissue sample for Singer's experiments, sometimes just to sit with her. Often, she was sedated to relieve the pain of the tumor. More usually, she was dreaming; adrift on the river of years, connected to our world and time by only the slenderest of threads.

When she was conscious, she would spin her reminiscences for me and sing. "Rosalie, the Prairie Flower." "Cape Ann." "Woodsman, Spare That Tree." "Ching a Ring Chaw." "The Hunters of Kentucky." "Wait for the Wagon." We agreed, Mae and I, that a wagon was just as suitable as a Chevrolet for courting pretty girls, and Phyllis and her wagon was the ancestor of Daisy and her bicycle, Lucille and her Oldsmobile, and Josephine and her flying machine. And someday, I suppose, Susie and her space shuttle.

It was odd to see Mae so at peace with her memories. She no longer feared them, no longer suppressed them. She no longer fled from them. Rather, she embraced them and passed them on to me. When she sang, "Roisin the Beau," she remarked casually how James Polk had used its melody for a campaign song. She recollected without flinching that she had stumped for Zachary Taylor. "Old Rough and Ready," she said. "There was a man for you. 'Minds me some'at of that T.R. Too bad they pizened him, but he was out to break the slave power." It gave her no pause to recall how at New Orleans, *"There stood John Bull in martial pomp/ And there stood Old Kentucky."* It must have been an awful relief to acknowledge those memories, to relax in their embrace.

There were fond memories of her "bean," Green the Long Hunter. Of days spent farming or hunting or spinning woolen or cooking 'shine. Of nights spent "setting" by the fire, smoking their pipes, reading to each other from the Bible. Quiet hours from a time before an insatiable demand for novelty—for something always to be *happening*—had consumed us. Green had even taken her down to Knoxville to see the touring company of *The Gladiator*, a stage play about Spartacus. Tales of slave revolts did not play well elsewhere in the South, but the mountaineers had no love for the wealthy flatland aristocrats.

She recalled meeting Walt Whitman, a fellow nurse in the Sanitary Commission. "A rugged fellow and all full of himself," she recalled, "but as kind and gentle with the men as any of the womenfolk."

She still confused her son sometimes with a brother, with her father, with Green. He was younger, he was older, he was of her own age. But there were childhood memories, too, of the sort most parents have. How he had "spunked up with his gal," "spooned with his chicken," or "lollygagged with his peach," depending on the slang of the decade. How they had "crossed the wide prairie" together after the war and set up a ranch in Wyoming Territory. How he met and wed Sweet Annie, a real "piece of calico."

Not all the memories were pleasant—Sweet Annie had died screaming—but Mae relished them just the same. It was her life she was reclaiming, and a life consists of differents parts, good and bad. The parts make up a whole. I continued to record her tales and tunes, as much because I did not know what else to do as because of any book plans, and I noticed that, while her doubling episodes often hopscotched through her life—triggered by associations and chance remarks—the music that played in her mind continued its slow and inexorable backward progression, spanning the 1840s and creeping gradually into the mid-thirties.

Slowly, a weird conviction settled on me. When the dates of her rememb-heard tunes finally reached 1800, she would die.

Time was running short. Most brain tumor patients did not survive a year from the time of first diagnosis; and Mae was so fragile to begin with that I doubted a whole year would be hers. Reports from Singer alternated between encouragement and frustration. Apparent progress would evaporate with a routine, follow-up test. Happenstance observation would open up a whole new line of inquiry. Singer submitted requests for additional cell samples almost daily. Blood, skin, liver. It seemed almost as if Mae might be used up entirely before Singer could pry loose the secret of her genes and splice that secret into my Deirdre.

I began to feel as if I were in a race with time. A weird sort of race in which time was speeding off in both directions. A young girl dying too old. An old woman dying too young.

One day, Wing was waiting for me when I entered the hospital. Seeing the flat look of concern on his face, my heart faltered. *Not yet,* I thought; *not yet!* My heart screeched, but I kept my own face composed. He took me aside into a small consultation room. Plaster walls with macro designs painted in happy, soothing colors. Comfortable chairs; green plants. An appallingly cheerful venue in which to receive bad news.

But it was not bad news. It was good news, of an odd and unexpected sort.

"Herpes?" I said when he had told me. "Herpes is a cure for brain tumors?" I couldn't help it. I giggled.

Wing frowned. "Not precisely. Culver-Blaese is a new treatment and outside my field of specialty, but let me explain it as Maurice explained it to me." Maurice LeFevre was the resident in genetic engineering, one of the first such residencies in the United States. "Several years ago," said Wing, "Culver and Blaese successfully extracted the gene for the growth enzyme, thymidine kinase, from the herpes virus, and installed it into brain tumor cells using a harmless retrovirus."

"I would think," I said dryly, "that an enzyme that facilitates reproduction is the last thing a brain tumor needs spliced into its code."

Wing blinked rapidly several times. "Oh, I'm sorry. You see, it's the ganciclovir. I didn't make that clear?"

"Ganciclovir is—?"

"The chemical used to fight herpes. It reacts with thymidine kinase, and the reaction products interfere with cell reproduction. So if tumor cells start producing thymidine, injecting ganciclovir a few days later will gum up the tumor's reproduction and kill it. There have been promising results on mice and in an initial trial with twenty human patients."

"What is 'promising'?"

"Complete remission in seventy-five percent of the cases, and appreciable shrinkage in all of them."

I sucked in my breath. I could hardly credit what Wing was telling me. Here was a treatment, a *deus ex machina*. Give Singer another year of live-tissue experiments and he would surely find the breakthrough we sought. "What's the catch?" I asked. There had to be a catch. There was always a catch.

There were two.

"First," said Wing, "the treatment is experimental, so the insurance will not cover it. Second . . . Well, Mrs. Holloway has refused."

"Eh? Refused? Why is that?"

Wing shook his head. "I don't know. She wouldn't tell me. I thought if I caught you before you went to see her . . ."

"That I could talk her into it?"

"Yes. The two of you are very close. I can see that."

Close? Mae and I? If Wing could see that, those thick eyeglasses of his were more powerful than the Hubble telescope. Mae had not been close to anyone since her son died. *Since her child died in her arms, an old, old man.* Inwardly, I shuddered. No wonder she had never gotten close to anyone since. No wonder she had lost an entire era of her life.

"I'll give it a try," I said.

When I entered her room, Mae was lying quietly in her bed, humming softly. Awake, I knew, but not quite present. Her face was curled into a smile, the creases all twisted around in unwonted directions. There was an air about her, something halfway between sleep and joy, a *calm* that had inverted all those years of sourness, stood everything on its head, and changed all her minus signs to plus.

"Setting" on her cabin porch, I imagined, gazing down the hillside at the laurel hells, and at a distant, pristine stream meandering through the holler below. At peace. At last.

I pulled the visitor's chair close by the bedside and laid a hand lightly on her arm. She didn't stir. "Mae, it's me. I've come to set a spell with you."

"Howdy there, Doc," she whispered. "Oh, it's such a lovely sunset. All heshed. I been telling Li'l Zach about the time his grandpap and Ol' Hickory went off t' fi't the Creeks. I was already fourteen when Pa went off, so I minded the cabin while he was away."

I leaned closer to her. "Mae, has Dr. Wing spoken to you about the new treatment?"

She took in a long, slow breath, and let it out as slowly. "Yes."

"He told me you refused."

"I surely did that."

"Why?"

"Why?" She opened her eyes and looked at me, looked sadly around the room. "I been hanging on too long. It's time to go home."

"But—"

"And what would it git me, anyways. Another year? Six months? Doc, even if I am nigh on to two hunnert year, like you say, and my bone-box only thinks it's a hunnert, *that's still older'n most folks git.* Even if that Dr. LeFevre can do what he says and rid me of this hyar tumor, there'll be a stroke afore long or my ticker'll give out, or something. Doc, *there ain't no point to it.* When I was young, when I was watching everyone I knew grow old and die, I wanted to go with them. I wanted to be with them. Why should I want to tarry now? If the Lord'll have me, I'm ready." She closed her eyes again and turned a little to the side.

"But, Mae . . ."

"And who'll miss me, beside," she muttered.

"I will."

She rolled out flat again and looked at me. "You?"

"Yes. A little, I guess."

She snorted. "You mean you'll miss whatever you want that you're wooling me over. Always jabbing me with needles, like I was a pincushion. There's something gnawing away at you, Doc. I kin see it in your eyes when you think no one is looking. Kind of sad and angry and awful far away. I don't know what it is, but I know I got something to do with it."

I drew back under her speech. Her words were like slaps.

"And suppose'n they do it and they do git that thang outen my brain. Doc, what'll happen to my music? What'll happen to my memories?"

"I—"

"You done told me they come from that tumor a-pressing against the brain. What happens if it's not pressin' any longer?"

"The memories might stay, now that they've been started, even with the original stimulus removed. It might have been a 'little stroke' that started it, just like we thought originally."

"But you can't guarantee it, can you?" She fixed me with a stare until I looked away.

"No. No guarantees."

"Then I don't want it." I turned back in time to see her face tighten momentarily into a wince.

"It will relieve the pain," I assured her.

"Nothing will relieve the pain. Nothing. Because it ain't that sort of pain. There's my pa, my ma, Green, Little Zach and his Sweet Annie. Ben and Joe and all the others I would never let cozy up to me. They're all waiting for me over in Gloryland. I don't know why the Good Man has kept me here so long. H'isn't punishment for killing Ma. I know that now. There must be a reason for it; but I'm a-weary of the waiting. If'n I have this operation like you want, what difference will it make? A few months? Doc, I won't live those months in silence."

> *My Chloe has dimples and smiles, I must own;*
> *But, though she could smile, yet in truth she could frown.*
> *But tell me, ye lovers of liquor divine,*
> *Did you e'er see a frown in a bumper of wine?*

There is something about the ice-cold shock of a perfect martini. The pine tree scent of the gin. The smooth liquid sliding down the throat. Then, a half second later, wham! It hits you. And in that half second, there is an hour of insight; though, sometimes, that hour comes very late at night. You can see with the same icy clarity of the drink. You can see the trail of choices behind you. Paths that led up rocky pitches; paths beside still waters. You can see where the paths forked, where, had you turned that way instead of this, you'd not be here today. You can even, sometimes, see where, when the paths forked, people took different trails.

"Paul!"

And you can wonder whether you can ever find that fork again.

I turned to see Brenda drop her briefcase on the sofa. "Paul! I *never* see you drinking."

Subtext: Do you drink a lot in secret when I can't see you? Sub-subtext:

Are you an alcoholic? Holding a conversation with Brenda was a challenge. Her words were multilayered; and you never knew on which layer to answer.

I placed my martini glass, still half-full, carefully down upon the sideboard, beside the others. It spilled a little as I did, defying the laws of gravity. I faced her squarely. "I'm running out of time," I said.

She looked at me for a moment. Then she said, "That's right. I'd wondered if you knew."

"I'm running out of time," I repeated. "She'll die before I know."

"*She* . . ." Brenda pulled her elbows in tight against her sides. "I don't want to hear this."

"That old woman. To live so long, only to die just now."

"The old woman from the Home? *She* has you upset? For God's sake, Paul." And she turned away from me.

"You don't understand. She could save Dee-dee."

Brenda's head jerked a little to the left. Then she retrieved her briefcase and shook herself all over, as if preparing to leave. "How can a dying old woman save a dying old girl?"

"She's yin to Dee-dee's yang. The universe is neutral. There's a plus sign for every minus. But she wants to go over Jordan and I . . . can't stop her. And I don't understand why I can't."

"You're not making any sense, Paul. How many of those have you had?"

"She's two centuries old, Brenda. Two centuries old. She was a swinger and a sheba and a daisy and a pippin. She hears songs, in her head; but sometimes they're wrong, except they're right. The words are different. Older. 'Old Zip Coon,' instead of 'Turkey in the Straw.' 'Lovely Fan',' instead of 'Buffalo Gals.' 'Bright Mohawk Valley,' instead of 'Red River Valley.' She read *Moral Physiology*, when it first came out. Mae did. Do you know the book? *Moral Physiology*, by Robert Dale Owen? No, of course not. It was all about birth control and it sold twenty-five thousand copies even though newspapers and magazines refused to carry the ads *and it was published in 18-god-damned-30.* She campaigned for Zachary Taylor, and her Pa fought in the Creek War, and her husband died at Resaca, and she saw Abraham-fucking-Lincoln—"

"Paul, can you hear yourself? You're talking crazy."

"Did you know *The Gladiator* debuted in New York in 1831? 'Ho! slaves, arise! Freedom . . . Freedom and revenge!' " I struck a pose, one fist raised.

"I can't stand to watch you like this, Paul. You're sopping drunk."

"And you're out late every night." Which was totally irrelevant to our discussion, but the tongue has a life of its own.

Through teeth clenched tight, she answered: "I have a job to keep."

I took a step away from the sideboard, and there must have been something wrong with the floorboards. Perhaps the support beams had begun to sag, because the floor suddenly tilted. I grabbed for the back of the armchair. The lamp beside it wobbled, and I grabbed it with my other hand to keep it still.

Awkwardly twisted, half-bent-over, I looked at Brenda and spoke distinctly. "Mae Holloway is two centuries old. There is something in her genes. We think. Singer and Peeler and I. We think that with enough time. With enough time. Singer and Peeler can crack the secret. They can tailor a . . . Tailor a . . ." I hunted for the right word, found it scuttling about on the floor, and snatched it. "Nanomachine." Triumph. "Tailor a nanomachine that can repair Dee-dee's cells. But Mae is dying. She has a brain tumor, and it's killing her. There's a treatment. An experimental treatment. It looks very good. But Mae won't take it. She doesn't want it. She wants to sleep."

I don't know what I expected. I expected hope, or disbelief. I expected a demand for proof, or for more details. I expected her to say, "do anything to save my daughter!" I expected anything but indifference.

Brenda brushed imaginary dust from her briefcase and turned away. "Do what you always do, Paul. Just ignore what she wants."

I was in the clinic at the Home the next day when I received the call from the hospital. My head felt as if nails had been driven into it. I was queasy from the hangover. When the phone rang and I picked it up, a tinny voice on the other end spoke crisply and urgently and asked that I come over right away. I don't remember what I said, or even that I said anything; and I don't suppose my caller expected a coherent answer. My numb fingers fumbled the phone several times before it sat right in its cradle. *Heart attack*, I thought. And as quickly as that, the time runs out.

But they hadn't said she was dead. They hadn't said she was dead.

I hope that there was no traffic on the road when I raced to the hospital, for I remember nothing of the journey. Three times along the way I picked up the car phone to call the hospital for more information; and three times I replaced it. It was better not to know. Half an hour, with the lights right and the speed law ignored. That was thirty minutes in which hope was thinkable.

Smythe, the cardiovascular man, met me in the corridor outside her room. He grabbed me by both my arms and steadied me. I could not understand why he was grinning. What possible reason could there be?

"She'll live, mon," he said. "It was a near thing, but she'll live."

I stared at Smythe without comprehension. He shook me by the arm, hard. My head felt like shattered glass.

"She'll live," he said again. His teeth were impossibly white.

I brushed him off and stepped into the room. *She'll live?* Then there was still time. Everything else was detail. My body felt suddenly weak, as if a stopcock had been pulled and all my sand had drained away. I staggered as far as the bedside, where I sank into a steel-and-vinyl chair. Smythe waited by the door, in the corridor, giving me the time alone.

Dee-dee lay asleep upon the bed, breathing slowly and softly through a tube set up her nose. An intravenous tube entered her left arm. Remote sensor implants on her skull and chest broadcast her heartbeat and breathing and brain waves to stations throughout the hospital. Smythe was never more than a terminal away from knowing her condition. I reached out and took her right hand in mine and gently stroked the back of it. "Hello, Dee-dee, I came as fast as I could. Why didn't . . ." I swallowed hard. "Why didn't you wait for me to tuck you in."

Dee-dee was still unconscious from the anesthetic. She couldn't hear me; but a quiet sob, quickly stifled, drew my attention to the accordion-pleated expandable wall, drawn halfway out on the opposite side of the bed. When I walked around it, I saw Consuela sitting in a chair on the other side. Her features were tightly leashed, but the tracks of tears had darkened both her cheeks. Her hands were pale where they gripped the arms of the chair.

"Connie!"

"Oh, Paul, we almost lost her. We almost lost her."

It slammed against my chest with the force of a hammer, a harder stroke for having missed. *Someday we will.* I took Connie's hand and brushed the back side of it as I had brushed Dee-dee's. "It's all right now," I said.

"She is such a sweet child. She never complains."

Prognosis: The life span is shortened by relentless arterial atheromatosis. Death usually occurs at puberty.

"She's all right now."

"For a little while. But it will become worse, and worse; until . . ." She leaned her head against me and I cradled her; I rubbed her neck and shoulders, smoothed her hair. With my left hand, I caressed her cheek. *It is not the end; but it is the beginning of the end.*

"We knew it would happen." The emotions are a very odd thing. When all was dark, when I believed myself helpless, I could endure that knowledge. It was my comfort. But now that there was a ray of light, I found it overwhelming me, crushing me so that I could hardly breathe. A sliver of sunshine makes a darkened room seem blacker still. I could live with Fate, but not with Hope. I found that there was a new factor in the equation now. I found that I could fail.

"Where is Brenda?" I asked.

Connie pulled herself from my arms, turned, and pulled aside the curtain that separated her from Deirdre. "She didn't come."

"What?"

"She didn't come."

Something went out of me then, like a light switch turned off. I didn't say anything for the longest time. I drifted away from Connie over toward the window. A thick stand of trees filled the block across the street from the hospital. Leaves fresh and green with spring. Forsythia bursting yellow. A flock of birds banked in unison over the treetops and shied off from the high-tension lines behind. I thought of the time when Brenda and I first met on campus, both of us young and full of the future. I remembered how we had talked about making a difference in the world.

I found Brenda at home. I found her in the family room, late at night after I had finally left the hospital. She was still clad in her business suit, as if she just come from the office. She was standing rigidly by the bookcase, with her eyes dry and red and puffy, with Dee-dee's book, *The Boxcar Children*, in her hands. I had the impression that she had stood that way for hours.

"I tried to come, Paul," she said before I could get any words out. "I tried to come, but I couldn't. I was paralyzed; I couldn't move."

"It doesn't matter," I said. "Connie was there. She'll stay until I get changed and return." I rubbed a hand across my face. "God, I'm tired."

"She's taken my place, hasn't she? She feeds Deirdre, she nurses her, she tutors her. Tell me, Paul, has she taken over *all* my duties?"

"I don't know what you mean."

"I didn't think there was room in your life for anyone beside your daughter. You've shut everyone else out."

"I never pushed you away. You ran."

"It needs more than that. It needs more than not pushing. You could have caught me, if you'd reached. There was an awful row at the office today. Crowe and FitzPatrick argued. They're dissolving the partnership. I was taking too long to say yes to the partnership offer; so Sèan became curious and . . . He found out Walther had wanted a 'yes' on a lot more, so we filed for harrass . . . Oh, hell. It doesn't matter anymore; none of it."

She was talking about events on another planet. I stepped to her side and took hold of the book. It was frozen to her fingers. I tugged, and pried it from her grasp. Slowly, her hands clenched into balls, but she did not lower her arms. I turned to place the book on the shelf and Brenda said in a small voice, "It doesn't go there, Paul."

"Damn it, Brenda!"

"I'm afraid," she said. "Oh, God, I'm afraid. Someday I will open up the tableware drawer and find her baby spoon; or I'll look under the sofa and find a ball that had rolled there forgotten. Or I'll find one of her dresses bundled up in the wash. And I won't be able to take it. Do you understand? Do you know what it's like? Do you have any feelings at all? How can you look at that shelf and remember that *her* book had once lain there? Look at that kitchen table and remember her high chair and how we played airplane with her food? Look into a room full of toys, with no child anymore to play with them? Everywhere I look I see an aching void."

With a sudden rush of tenderness, I pulled her to me, but she remained stiff and unyielding in my arms. Yet, we all mourn in our own ways. "She did not die, Brenda. She'll be okay."

"This time. But, Paul, I can't look forward to a lifetime looking back. At the little girl who grew up and grew old and went away before I ever got to know her. Paul, it isn't right. It isn't right, Paul. It isn't right for a child to die before the parent."

"So, you'll close her out of your mind? Is that the answer? Create the void now? You'll push all those memories into one room and then close the door? You can't do that. If we forget her, it will be as if she had never lived."

She softened at last and her arms went around me. "What can I do? I've lost her, and I've lost you, and I've lost . . . everything."

We stood there locked together. I could feel her small, tightly controlled sobs trembling against me. Sometimes the reins have been held so close for so long that you can never drop them, never even know if they have been dropped. The damp of her tears seeped through my shirt. Past her, I could see the shelf with *The Boxcar Children* lying flat upon it, and I tried to imagine how, in future years, I could ever look on that shelf again without grief.

> *"Tell me the tales that to me were so dear*
> *Long, long ago; long, long ago.*
> *Sing me the songs I delighted to hear*
> *Long, long ago, long ago."*

Dee-dee was wired. There was a tube up her nose and another in her arm. A bag of glucose hung on a pole rack by her bed, steadily dripping into an accumulator and thence through the tube. A catheter took her wastes away. A pad on her finger and a cuff around her arm were plugged into a CRT monitor. I smiled when I saw she was awake.

"Hi, Daddy . . ." Her voice was weak and hoarse, a by-product of the anesthesia.

"Hi, Dee-dee. How do you feel?"

"Yucky . . ."

"Me, too. You're a TV star." I pointed to the monitor, where red and yellow and white lines hopped and skipped across the screen. Heart rate, blood pressure. Every time she breathed, the white line crested and dropped. She didn't say anything, and I listened for a moment to the sucking sound that the nose tube made. A kid trying for the last bit of soda in the can. The liquid it carried off was brown, which meant that there was still a little blood. "Connie is here." I nodded to the other side of the bed.

Dee-dee turned her eyes, but not her head. "Hello, Connie. I can't see you."

Consuela moved a little into her field of vision. "Good morning, Little One. You have a splendid view from your window."

"Nurse Jeannie told me that . . . Wish I could see . . ."

"Then, I will tell you what it looks like. You can see the north end of town—all those lovely, old houses—and far off past them, on the edge of the world, the blue-ridge mountain wall and, in the very center of it, the Gap; and through the Gap, you can see the mountains beyond."

"It sounds beautiful . . ."

"Oh, it is. I wish I could be here instead of you, just so I could have the view."

I looked up at Connie when she said that and, for a moment, we locked gazes with one another. I could see the truth of her words in her eyes.

And then I saw surprise. Surprise and something else beside. I looked over my shoulder—and Brenda was standing there in the doorway, smartly dressed, on wobbly legs, with her purse clutched tightly in her hands before her.

"The nurses," she said. "The nurses said she could only have two visitors at a time." Visiting was allowed every three hours, but only for an hour and only two visitors at a time. I was a doctor and Connie was a nurse and the staff cut us a little slack, but the rules were there for a reason. Consuela stood.

"I will leave."

Brenda looked at her and caught her lower lip between her teeth. She laid her purse with military precision on a small table beside the bed. "I would like to spend some time with Deirdre, Paul. If you don't mind."

I nodded. As I stood up I gave Dee-dee a smile and a little squeeze on her arm. "Mommy's here," I told her.

Connie and I left them alone together (a curious expression, that—"alone together") and waited in the outer nursing area. I didn't eavesdrop, though I did overhear Brenda whisper at one point, "No, darling, it was never anything that *you* did wrong." Maybe it wasn't much, not when weighted against those years of inattention. It wasn't much; but it wasn't nothing. I knew—maybe for the first time—how much it cost Brenda to take on these memories, to take on the risks of remembering; because she was right. If in laters years you remembered nothing, you would feel no pain.

And yet, I had seen two centuries of pain come washing back, bringing with it joy.

Children recover remarkably well. Drop them, and they bounce. Maybe not so high as before, but they do rebound. Dee-dee bore a solemn air about her for a day or two, sensing, without being told, that she had almost "gone away." But to a child, a day is a lifetime, and a week is forever; and she was soon in the recovery ward, playing with the other children. Rheumatic children with heart murmurs; shaven-headed children staring leukemia in the face; broken children with scars and cigarette burns . . . They played with an impossible cheerfulness, living, as most children did, in the moment. But then, the Now was all most of them would ever have.

There came a day when Dee-dee was not in her room when I arrived. Connie sat framed in a bright square of sunlight, reading a book. She looked up when I walked in. "Deirdre has gone to visit a new friend," she said.

"Oh." A strange clash of emotions: Happy she was up and about again, even if confined to a wheelchair; disappointed that she was not there to greet me.

"She will return soon, I think."

"Well," I said, "we had wanted her to become more active."

Consuela closed her book and laid it on the small table beside her. "I suppose you will no longer need my services," she said. She did not look at me when she said it, but out the window at the newborn summer.

"Not need you? Don't be foolish."

"She has her mother back, now."

Every morning before work; every evening after. Pressing lost years into a few hours. "She still needs you."

"The hospital staff cares for her now."

I shook my head. "It's not that she *needs* you, but that she needs *you*. You are not only her nurse."

"If I take on new clients," she went on as if I had not spoken, "I can do things properly. I can visit at the appointed times, perform my duties, and leave; and not allow them such a place in my heart when they are gone."

"If people don't leave a hole in your life when they are gone, Consuela, they were never in your life at all."

She turned away from the window and looked at me. "Or two holes."

I dropped my gaze, looked instead at the rumpled bed.

"In many ways," I heard her say, "you are a cold man, Doctor. Uncaring and thoughtless. But it was the fruit of bitterness and despair. I thought you deserved better than you had. And you love her as deeply as I. If death could be forestalled by clinging tight, Deirdre would never leave us."

I had no answer for her, but I allowed my eyes to seek out hers.

"I thought," she said, "sometimes, at night, when I played my flute, that because we shared that love . . . That we could share another."

"It must be lonely for you here, in a strange country, with a strange language and customs. No family and fewer friends. I must be a wretched man for never having asked."

She shook her head. "You had your own worry. A large one that consumed you."

"Consuela Montejo, if you leave, you would leave as great a hole in my life as in Dee-dee's."

"And in Mrs. Wilkes's." She smiled a little bit. "It is a very odd thing, but I believe that if I stayed, I might even grow to like her."

"She was frightened. She thought she could cauterize the wound before she received it. It was only when she nearly lost Dee-dee that she suddenly realized that she had never had her."

Consuela stood and walked to the bed. She touched the sheet and smoothed it out, pulling the wrinkles flat. She shook her head. "It will hurt if I go; it will hurt if I stay. But Mrs. Wilkes deserves this one chance."

I reached out and took her hand and she reached out and took mine. Had Brenda walked in then, I do not know what she would have made of our embrace. I do not know what I made of it. I think I would have pulled Brenda in with us, the three of us arm in arm in arm.

The really strange thing was how inevitable it all was in hindsight.

When I left Consuela, I went to visit Mae. It had been nearly two weeks since I last saw her, and it occurred to me that the old bat might be lonely, too. And what the hell, she could put up with me and I could put up with her.

I found my Dee-dee in Mae Holloway's room. The two of them had their heads bent close together, giggling over something. Deirdre was strapped to her electric wheelchair, and Mae lay flat upon her bed; but I was struck by how alike they looked. Two gnarled and bent figures with pale, spotted skin stretched tight over their bones, lit from within by a pure, childlike joy. Two old women; two young girls. Deirdre looked up and saw me.

"Daddy! Granny Mae has been teaching me the most wonderful songs."

Mae Holloway lifted her head a little. "Yours?" she said in a hoarse whisper. "This woman-child is yours?"

"Yes," I said, bending to kiss Dee-dee's cheek. "All mine." No. Not *all* mine. There were others who shared her.

"Listen to the song Granny Mae taught me! It goes like this."

I looked over Dee-dee's head at the old woman. "She didn't tell you?"

"Noor brought her in, but didn't say aye, yea, or no. Just that she thought we should meet."

Dee-dee began singing in her high, piping voice.

> *"The days go slowly by, Lorena.*
> *The snow is on the grass again.*
> *The years go slowly by Lorena . . ."*

"Her days are going by too fast, ain't they?" Mae said. I nodded and saw how her eyes lingered on my little girl. "Growing old in the blink of an eye," she said softly. "Oh, I know how that feels."

"Granny Mae tells such interesting stories," Dee-dee insisted. "Did you know she saw Abraham Lincoln one time?" I rubbed her thinning hair. Too young to know how impossible that was. Too young to doubt.

Mae's hand sought out Dee-dee's and clenched hold of it. "Doc, I'll have me that operation."

"What?"

"I'll have me that operation. The one that's supposed to make this tumor of mine go away. I'll have it, even if my music and my memories go with it."

"You will. Why?"

"Because I know why you been poking me and taking my blood. And I know why the Good Lord has kept me here for all this long time."

Noor Khan was waiting in the hallway when I stepped out of the room.

"Ah, Doctor," I said. "How are things at Sunny Dale."

"Quiet," she said. "Though the residents are all asking when you will be back."

I shrugged. "Old people dislike upsets to their routine. They grew used to having me around."

Khan said, "I never knew about your little girl. I heard it from Smythe. Why did you never tell me?"

I shrugged again. "I never thought it was anyone's business."

Khan accepted the statement. "After you told Wing and me of Mae's remarkable longevity . . . I knew you were taking blood samples to that genetic engineering firm—"

"Singer and Peeler."

"Yes. I thought you had . . . other reasons."

"What, that I would find the secret of the Tree of Life?" I shook my head. "I never thought to ask for so much. Mae has lived most her life as an old woman. I would not count that a blessing. But to live a normal life? To set right what had come out wrong? Yes, and I won't apologize. Neither would you, if it were your daughter."

"Is Singer close? To a solution?"

"I don't know. Neither do they. We won't know how close we are until we stumble right into it. But we've bought a little time now, thanks to you. Is that why you did it? Because you knew that meeting my daughter would convince Mae to accept the Culver-Blaese gene therapy?"

Khan shook her head. "No. I never even thought of that."

"Then, why?"

"Sometimes," said Khan, looking back into the room where the young girl and the old girl taught each other songs. "Sometimes, there are other medicines, for other kinds of hurts."

> *I seek no more the fine and gay,*
> *For each does but remind me*
> *How swift the hours did pass away*
> *With the girl I left behind me.*

They are all gone now. All gone. Mae, Dee-dee, all of them. Consuela was first. Brenda's partnership arrangement with FitzPatrick—telecommuting, they called it—left no place for her at the house. She came to visit Dee-dee, and she and Brenda often met for coffee—what they talked about I do not know—but she stopped coming after Dee-dee died, and I have not seen her in years.

Brenda, too. She lives in LA, now. I visit her when I'm on the Coast and we go out together, and catch dinner or a show. But she can't look at me without thinking of *her*; and neither can I, and sometimes, that becomes too much.

There was no bitterness in the divorce. There was no bitterness left in either of us. But Dee-dee's illness had been a fault line splitting the earth. A chasm had run through our lives, and we jumped out of its way, but Brenda to one side and I, to the other. When Dee-dee was gone, there was no bridge across it, and we found that we shared nothing between us but a void.

The operation bought Mae six months. Six months of silence in her mind before the stroke took her. She complained a little, now and then, about her quickly evaporating memories; but sometimes I read to her from my notes, or played the tape recorder, and that made her feel a little better. When she heard about seeing Lincoln on the White House lawn, she just shook her head and said, "Isn't that a wonder?" The last time I saw Mae Holloway, she was fumbling after some elusive memory of her Mister that kept slipping like water through the fingers of her mind, when she suddenly brightened, looked at me, and smiled. "They're all a-waiting," she whispered, and then all the lights went out.

And Dee-dee.

Dee-dee.

Still, after all these years, I cannot talk about my little girl.

They call it the Deirdre-Holloway treatment. I insisted on that. It came too late for her, but maybe there are a few thousand fewer children who die now each year because of it. Sometimes I think it was worth it. Sometimes I wonder selfishly why it could not have come earlier. I wonder if there wasn't something I could have done differently that would have brought us home sooner.

Singer found the key; or Peeler did, or they found it together. Three years later, thank God. Had the breakthrough followed too soon on Deirdre's death, I could not have borne it. The income from the book funded it, and it took every penny, but I feel no poorer for it.

It's a mutation, Peeler told me, located on the supposedly inactive Barr body. It codes for an enzyme that retards catabolism. There's a sudden acceleration of fetal development in the last months of pregnancy that almost always kills the mother, and often the child, as well. Sweet Annie's dear, dead child would have been programmed for the same future had she lived. After birth, aging slows quickly until it nearly stops at puberty. It only resumes after menopause. In males, the gene's expression is suppressed by testosterone. Generations of gene-spliced lab mice lived and died to establish that.

Is the line extinct now? Or does the gene linger out there, carried safely by males waiting unwittingly to kill their mates with daughters?

I don't know. I never found another like Mae, despite my years of practice in geriatrics.

When I retired from the Home, the residents gave me a party, though none of them were of that original group. Jimmy, Rosie, Leo, Old Man Morton . . . By then I had seen them all through their final passage. When the residents began approaching my own age, I knew it was time to take down my shingle.

I find myself thinking more and more about the past these days. About Mae and the Home; and Khan—I heard from my neighbor's boy that she is still in practice, in pediatrics now. Sometimes, I think of my own parents and the old river town where I grew up. The old cliffside stairs. Hiking down along the creek. Hasbrouk's grocery down on the corner.

The memories are dim and faded, brittle with time.

And I don't remember the music, at all. My memories are silent, like an old Chaplin film. I've had my house wired, and tapes play continually, but it isn't the same. The melodies do not come from within; they do not come from the heart.

They tell me I have a tumor in my left temporal lobe, and it's growing. It may be operable. It may not be. Wing wants to try Culver-Blaese, but I won't let him. I keep hoping.

I want to remember. I want to remember Mae. Yes, and Consuela and Brenda, too. And Dee-dee most of all. I want to remember them all. I want to hear them singing.

One of the most important qualities of fantastic literature is its realism.

That may sound like a contradiction, but the stories I have found most difficult to read are those that don't know how to embed the fantastic element in the mundane. Take immortals, for example . . .

Oliver Sacks describes "incontinent nostalgia" in *The Man Who Mistook His Wife for a Hat*, a book I have mentioned already. Patients, some of whom had entirely forgotten their childhood, reheard snatches of tunes and resaw early scenes and refelt emotions of poignancy and joy. I wondered how this might be treated as an SF theme.

I imagined an old woman telling her doctor about the music she hears. With each session, the music comes from earlier times. Eventually, from times too early to be possible, unless the woman is a lot older than she seems. An immortal? This is where my sense of realism kicked in.

Not immortal; just long-lived. (Besides, after Poul Anderson's *The Boat of a Million Years*, who can write another immortals story?) I checked the *Book of Records*: oldest authenticated human age was just shy of 121 years. So the woman, let's say she's two hundred years old. Something that, maybe, it could happen. Some mutation is pressing her "hold" button. But she doesn't know it, because what she has not forgotten has become blurred by the mental distance.

Okay, so what was the story? "Doctor listens to old woman hum tunes" is not a story. Even "doctor discovers old woman's age" is not a story. Who is the doctor? Who is the woman? Why would it matter, to either one of them, how old she is?

Mae Holloway became real first. I knew from the start she was from the East Tennessee hills—remote enough in that era that she could grow old slowly among mind-yer-own-business neighbors, the nearest one a hoot and a holler away. My wife's Hammontree ancestors came from there, so I had already done some research. (Her greatgrandmother was Nancy Holloway.) "Green Holloway's" Civil War records are essentially those of Margie's greatgrandfather, who was wounded at Resaca. And up in Kentucky, another of her ancestors was a neighbor of Tom Lincoln and his boy, Abe: Greenberry (and no, I'm not fooling) Harris.

The most painful thing about living a long, long time is that everyone you love does not. And so Mae became cynical and aloof, refusing to form close relationships.

Still no story, but a hint that the story must end with Mae forming a close relationship.

Mae is now dying. Conflict. The doctor wants to keep her from dying. Why? Because it's his job? Naah. I didn't want to write about "right to die" and why would she have to be two hundred years old for that? Realizing how long-lived she is, the doctor keeps her alive despite the pain to discover her "secret"? Naah. Too much mad-scientist melodrama. Fiction works best when both protagonist and antagonist have believable motives over which they can agonize.

When I thought of the progeria angle, everything fell into place. Paul Wilkes became real. I understood his motives, his unkind feelings toward the elderly, his relations with his wife and Consuela. Brenda was harder, but I finally understood her, too. Sometimes what you have to do is just start writing and let the characters interact. At some point comes the "aha!" and you can go back and start for real.

"Doctor discovers old woman's age" is not a story. But "Paul Wilkes, tormented by his daughter's progeria, discovers that bitter, old Mae Holloway is two centuries old . . ." now, that had possibilities.

Enough possibilities to put the story on the Hugo ballot, and to put it in Gardner Dozois's annual *Year's Best* collection, making this story the perfect companion bookend to "The Forest of Time."